Hurrish: A Study

Emily Lawless

BIBLIOLIFE

HURRISH

A STUDY

BY

THE HON. EMILY LAWLESS

AUTHOR OF 'A CHELSEA HOUSEHOLDER,'
'A MILLIONAIRE'S COUSIN'

A NEW EDITION

WILLIAM BLACKWOOD AND SONS
EDINBURGH AND LONDON
MDCCCLXXXVI

TO

MRS OLIPHANT,

WITH A GREAT DEAL OF ADMIRATION

AND MORE AFFECTION,

THIS STORY IS DEDICATED BY

ITS AUTHOR.

CONTENTS.

HURRISH: A STUDY.

CHAPTER I.

AN IRON LAND.

WILDER regions there are few to be found, even in the wildest west of Ireland, than that portion of north Clare known to its inhabitants as "The Burren." Seen from the Atlantic, which washes its western base, it presents to the eye a succession of low hills, singularly grey in tone,—deepening often, towards evening, into violet or dull reddish plum colour—sometimes, after sunset, to a pale ghostly iridescence. They are quite low these hills — not above a thousand feet at their highest point, and for the most part considerably less. Hills of this height, whatever their other merits, seldom attain to the distinction of being spoken of as "grand." Their character is essentially "mutton-suggesting." You picture them dotted over with flocks of sheep, which nibble the short sweet grass, and frisk in their idle youth over the little declivities. If here and there

A

a rib or so of rock protrudes, they merely seem to be
foils to the general smoothness.   But these Burren
hills are literally not clothed at all.   They are startlingly, I may say scandalously, naked.   From their
base up to the battered turret of rock which serves
as a summit, not a patch, not a streak, not an indica-
tion even, of green is often to be found in the whole
extent.   On others a thin sprinkling of grass struggles
upward for a few hundred feet, and in valleys and
hollows, where the washings of the rocks have accumulated, a grass grows, famous all over cattle-
feeding Ireland for its powers of fattening.   So, too,
in the long vertical rifts or fissures which everywhere
cross and recross its surface, maiden-hair ferns and
small tender-petalled flowers unfurl, out of reach of
the cruel blasts.   These do not, however, affect the
general impression, which is that of nakedness per-
sonified—not comparative, but absolute.   The rocks
are not scattered over the surface, as in other stony
tracts, but the whole surface is rock.   They are not
hills, in fact, but skeletons—rain-worn, time-worn,
wind-worn,—starvation made visible, and embodied
in a landscape.

   And these strange little hills have had an equally
strange history.   They were the last home and the
last standing-ground of a race whose very names
have become a matter of more or less ingenious guess-
work.   Formorians ?   Firbolgs ?   Tuatha da Danaans ?
Who were they, and what were they ?   We know
nothing, and apparently are not destined to know
anything.   They came—we know not whence, and
they vanished—to all appearance into the Atlantic ;
pushed westward, like the Norwegian lemming, until,

like that most unaccountable of little animals, they, too, sprang into the waves and were lost. Little change has taken place in the aspect of the region since those unknown races passed away. Their great stone-duns are even still in many places the largest buildings to be seen,—the little oratories and churches which succeeded them having become in their turn, with hardly an exception, ruins like themselves, their very sites forgotten, melted into the surrounding stoniness. The Burren is not—in all probability never will be—a tourist-haunt, but for the few who know it, it has a place apart, a distinct personality—strange, remote, indescribable. Everything that the eye rests on tells us that we are on one of the last standpoints of an old world, worn out with its own profusion, and reduced here to the barest elements. Mother Earth, once young, buxom, frolicsome, is here a wrinkled woman, sitting alone in the evening of her days, and looking with melancholy eyes at the sunset.

The valley of Gortnacoppin is a sort of embodiment of the Burren. Standing in it you might fairly believe yourself in the heart of some alpine region, high above the haunts of men, where only the eagle or the marmot make their homes. All the suggestions are alpine, some of them almost arctic. The white stream cutting its way through the heaped-up drift; the water churning and frothing hither and thither in its impatience, and leaving a white deposit upon all the reeds and stones; the pallid greyish-green vegetation, with here and there a bit of dazzling red or orange; the chips and flakes of rock which lie strewn about; the larger stones and boulders

toppled down from the cliff above, and lying heaped
one over the other in the bed of the stream,—many
of the latter, you may perceive, have not long fallen,
for their edges are still unweathered.   Here and
there over the top and sides of the drift a little thin
grass has spread itself, through which trenches have
been torn, showing the earth and stones below.   Truly
a grim scene !—suggestive of nothing so much as one
of those ugly little early German prints, where every
stick and stone seems to be grimacing with unpleasant intention.   Only look hard enough at any of the
rocks, and you will assuredly see a gnome appear !

Towards the bottom, where it approaches the sea,
this valley, however, expands, and becomes an irregular lake-like circle, mapped out into · small fields,
separated from one another by tottering lace-work
walls.   After following the downward course of the
upper valley, you would have been surprised at the
. sudden fertility of this little space, the greenness of
the grass, the promising look of the small crops of
bottle-green potatoes.   If something of a geologist, ·
however, you would have suspected that the mass
of detritus, borne down from the hills, and spread
abroad here at their feet, had something to say to
that satisfactory result.

Between five and six years ago the greater part of
this little fertile oasis was rented by Horatio, or, as
he was less classically called by his neighbours, Hurrish O'Brien, one of the countless O'Briens of Clare.
His cabin—a rather large one, built of stone and
thatched—stood upon the summit of a little ridge,
conspicuous, like a small fly upon a large window-
pane, in the absence of any other building ; rendered

still more so by a good-sized ash-tree, which stood upon the ridge beside it—a noticeable distinction in so leafless a district.

It was a warm morning late in May, and even the stony Burren had begun to feel a touch of spring, its ferns and little delicate-petalled blossoms to reach out inquiring heads over their stony prisons. Hurrish had just returned to breakfast. He had been down early to the sea, to set some fishing-lines—for, like most of the inhabitants of that amphibious part of the island, he was part farmer and part fisherman,—perhaps it would be more accurate in his case to say three-parts farmer to one-part fisherman, the latter vocation being, in fact, rather a matter of " intertainment " than profit.

The door of the cabin was open, and the window unshuttered (the latter for an excellent reason, there were no shutters), yet the cabin itself was lit by its fire. The light, spreading from the blazing turf, broke in red flakes upon the bare rafters of the roof, upon the roughly plastered walls, upon a quantity of highly coloured pious prints upon the walls, upon others of a less pious character pinned beside them, upon a rough white terrier, two solemn black pigs, and three children scattered over the mud floor, upon an *omnium gatherum* of tags and rags, stray fragments of furniture, tools, clothing, straw, bedding, sacks, heaps of potatoes,—an indescribable and incalculable collection of long accumulated rubbish, huddled, in more or less picturesque confusion, one on top of another—the sort of picturesqueness which fastidious people prefer in its painted rather than in its actual form !

Hurrish sat upon a low " creepy " stool, with a

huge mug of stirabout (known to the ignorant as por-
ridge) upon his knees, which he was shovelling down
his throat by the aid of a large iron spoon. A broad-
shouldered, loose-limbed, genial-faced giant was Hurrish, such as these western Irish counties occasionally
breed. Irish in every feature, look, and gesture, there
was yet a smack of something foreign about him, to
be accounted for possibly by that oft-quoted admix-
ture of Spanish blood, the result of bygone centuries
of more or less continuous intercourse. His hair was
black as a cormorant's wing, and curly under the old
felt hat, half of whose brim had vanished in some distant engagement ; his beard was curly too, and black,
yet his eyes were grey, his skin evidently originally
fair, and his expression open, good-humoured, irreso-
lute, with a spice of native fun and jollity about it.
Despite the jollity which was its prevailing expression, he did not seem to be altogether a contented
giant. There were lines of perplexity and disturbance
here and there discernible. Yet Hurrish O'Brien was
a well-to-do man. He had a good stock of cows and
calves ; he held his farm on a moderate rental ; his
wife had brought him fifty gold sovereigns tied up in
a pocket-handkerchief ; his children were strong and
healthy ; and he was regarded by his neighbours generally as one of the " warmest " men between Blackhead and the mouth of the Shannon.

Opposite, upon another low creepy-stool, sat his
mother, Bridget O'Brien, engaged in stirring a steam-
ing black pot—an employment which would have
given a sensitive looker-on a delightful thrill, so
appropriate was the operation to the operator. In
Bridget O'Brien the Southern type was also strongly

visible. Women like her—as gaunt, as wrinkled, as
black-browed, as witch-like—may be seen seated upon
thousands of doorsteps all over the Spanish peninsula.
It is not a very comfortable type, one would think,
for everyday domestic use; too suggestive of an
elderly bird of prey—a vulture, old, yet with claws
ever upon the watch to tear, and a beak which yearns
to plunge itself into the still palpitating flesh. Her
eyes were black—a wicked black—and bright still
amid the multiplicity of wrinkles which surrounded
them, as cracks a half-dried pool. Her hair, too,
was dark, and hung in heavy hanks about her forehead, reaching nearly to the grizzled eyebrows, projecting like unclipped eaves over her eyes.

Bridget O'Brien was an ardent patriot! The latest
tide of revolutionary sentiment had begun to spread
its waves even to the heart of remotest Burren, and
she was the chief recipient of it in the O'Brien
household. It was she who knew when, where,
how, and why the latest agrarian outrage had been
committed, and was the first to raise the war-cry of
triumph and exultation upon these joyful occasions.
Not that the rest of the family were backward in
their degree. Hurrish had called himself a Fenian
almost ever since he could remember, and nothing
but his distance from the seat of war had prevented
him from striking a blow when that ill-starred apology
for a rebellion came to its final and melancholy close.
Animosity against England was a creed with him, a
sort of shibboleth—something like the middle-class
English hatred of France some three-quarters of
a century ago. His belief in its wickedness and
atrocities was a belief that knew absolutely no mis-

givings. Had he been assured that, like Herod of
old, an order had just been issued by its Government
for all infants under two years of age to be slaughtered,
I doubt if it would have struck him as at all incredible, or even out of character with what he supposed
to be the normal nature of its proceedings.

Hurrish's patriotic potations, however, were mild
and diluted compared with those quaffed to the very
dregs by his mother. He was not a man easily
roused to bitterness, and would hardly, I think, have
cared to kill even an Englishman, unless some very
good purpose could have been served by so doing.
When Bridget brought back tales of vengeance,
executed upon the latest enemies of their country,
he listened, but rarely found himself warmed to the
point of emulation ; the details of those gallant
achievements being apt, in fact, to have rather a
chilling and discouraging effect upon his imagination. What he enjoyed was what may be called the
frivolous side of patriotism,—the mere noise, the
crowd, the excitement, the waving flags, the new
tin-pikes, the thrilling, delightful, inexhaustible
oratory of his chosen leaders. All this was meat,
drink, and clothing to him, and he would have
walked thirty miles any day of his life to enjoy it.
On the other hand, the detailed projects of vengeance were apt to pass over his head. He admitted
their necessity, but blinked the details. When Ned
Clancy, for instance, with his wife and four small
children, were turned out of their cabin in the dead
of a January night, because Clancy had taken Lynch's
farm, contrary to well-known if unwritten local laws,
Hurrish had been disposed to feel sorry for the more

juvenile of the criminals. Not so his mother. " What ailed he to be pityin' of thim ? wasn't it known they wouldn't have been sarved so if they hadn't been desarvin' ? " that thorough-going woman asked fiercely. Hideous prints, of still more hideous significance, disfigured a considerable portion of the cabin walls. There was one cheerful design in particular, repre- senting the roasting alive of men in swallow-tail coats, tall hats, and white neck-cloths, presumably landlords and their myrmidons. The intention was allegorical, probably, but to Bridget it was literal enough, and it was upon such pabulum she feasted her eyes with all the relish of a petticoated vampire.

Poor little Alley Sheehan, Hurrish's niece by marriage, could not so much as bear to look at the side of the wall where these prints hung, and averted her eyes whenever she happened to approach them. They made her feel cold and sick. She was too much afraid of old Bridget, however, to show this repugnance openly, for Bridget was a domestic despot, and not by any means one of the benevo- lent variety. There was no blood tie between them, either, to soften the yoke. When Alley's mother died, Hurrish and his wife had taken her to live with them out of sheer charity and kindness of heart. When poor Mary O'Brien in her turn died, old Bridget would willingly have turned Alley out upon the cold highroad to beg. There were points, however, where Hurrish, yielding as he was, could hold his own, and this was one of them. He had a very tender spot in his heart for little Alley, whose great grey eyes it was hard to meet without

softening. They were wonderful eyes, such as are
only to be seen in their perfection west of the
Shannon,—violet grey, with lashes which fell in a
straight black drift upon the cheek below,—eyes
with a rippling light and shade in the irises, such
as streams show when flowing clear over a pebbly
bottom. The face, too, which went with them,
suited the eyes, which is by no means invariably
the case, more especially in Ireland.

For all her eyes, Alley counted for very little in
the estimation of her contemporaries. The average
young Irish male is not perhaps a particularly dis-
criminating animal, and the finer points are apt to
be undiscernible by him. Hers was the sort of
beauty which needs indeed some eye-culture to appreciate, a beauty which clings with peculiar tenacity
to the inward vision after the outward presentment
has faded, which no rags, no dirt, no circumstances,
however repellent, avail to spoil—nay, which seem
to bloom the brighter for such accessories, as the
peculiar blue of a speedwell shines best on that
discarded heap of refuse where we grudge yet delight to see it. There was a touch of ascetic
dreaminess about her which suited her stony environment, and remotely suggested the cloister—a sort of
nun-like fragility and separateness. Yet Alley was
not really delicate. She could carry her creel of
turf or her can of butter-milk as long and as lightly
as any girl in the Burren. Her small shapely brown
feet could tramp unwearily a long summer's day over
the stones. Those beautiful pathetic eyes of hers
had never known the shelter of a hat or a bonnet in
all their days. Strange flower of humanity, a very

young girl's beauty! Springing, we hardly know whence ; dropped often where it seems least to tell ; with something pathetic about it always, and most of all where so few years seem bound, as in a case like this, to bring it to an end.

The party in the cabin had been silent while the work of breakfast went steadily on. A ray of sunshine—the pallid ineffectual sunshine of the far, far west—was making its way across the floor, and disputing the ground with the paling light from the turf. Through the open doorway they could see the little hollow below, looking like a green saucer upon a grey floor. The drills of potatoes were appearing in dark-green jagged rows between the boulders, and over the grey shoulder of the next ridge the long heave of the Atlantic could be heard rising and falling in a slow harmonious cadence.

Alley, with an iron spoon in her hand, was feeding the youngest child, a rosy creature of three, who sat plump upon the ground, its fat bare feet and legs outstretched, and its round red mouth agape, like a young hedge-sparrow, for the mouthful of stirabout. The other two children had finished their breakfast, and were rolling about the floor trying to induce Lep, —short for Leprehaun,—Hurrish's yellow-and-white terrier, to join them—who, however, sat stiff and erect, his eyes intently fixed upon his master, his ugly, honest, mongrel face irradiated with patient adoration. It is rather rare to see any strong symptoms of mutual regard between an Irish peasant and his dog—such as, for instance, links the Scotch shepherd to his collie. The dogs have to take their chance with the pigs, children, and poultry. They

have not the financial value, and therefore dignity,
of the first-named, nor the natural claims of the
second; neither, again, has kindly nature endowed
them with the same convenient capacity for escaping
sticks, heels, and other weapons of offence that it has
bestowed upon the last. They receive food when
there is plenty going; when times are short they
are kicked out to seek or steal their dinners as they
can. Hurrish, however, was an exception, and his
ragged Lep loved him with as deep and adoring
a love as ever tender-hearted cur lavished upon indifferent man.

The stillness outside was wonderful, such stillness
as could only exist in so depopulated a region—a
region where there were no fields to plough, few seeds
to be sown, no carriages to drive, and hardly any
roads to drive them on; nothing but sea, sky, rocks,
cloud,—a stillness that was like death, broken only
by the larks, which wheeled and circled overhead,
pouring out their heavenly notes over those grey
unfriendly rocks in a melodious and interminable
cataract.

All at once this death-like silence was violently
broken. A shrill cry—the cry of a woman—rang
out across the stony stillness, and with one accord
every one, even the dog and the children, sprang up
and ran to the door. Up the stony slope, at a pace
only possible to one accustomed from childhood to
that rugged fragment of earth's surface, came a girl.
After her in full pursuit followed a man—unwieldy,
red-faced, heavy-jawed, brutal — a sort of human
orang-outang or Caliban, whose lumbering action and
coarse gesture had something grotesque and even

repulsive about them, as it were a parody or perversion of humanity.

Hurrish ran hastily down the slope and met the girl, who clutched frantically at his arm, turning round as she did so to look back at her pursuer, who on his side stopped short upon the platform of rock which he had reached, and remained there bellowing forth indistinct curses and half inarticulate threats of vengeance. Then, like some baffled beast of prey, he turned, and strode sulkily back over the narrow rifts of rocks, his brutish figure—reflected in all its uncouthness upon the wet surfaces as upon a sheet of dulled ice—disappearing a minute later over the next perpendicular descent.

The other two returned to the cabin, where the rest of the party had remained in an excited group around the door. Entering, the girl—a handsome florid creature of twenty or thereabouts—flung herself down with an air of exhaustion upon a stool. It was evident, however, in spite of her first words, that she was not quite so much frightened as she pretended to be.

" 'Tis scared I am half to death !" she declared, pantingly. "Alley, darlint, you're whiter nor the driven snow ! Bad luck to that baste for scarin' yis. 'Twas drunk he was—mad drunk an' quarrelsome. I was comin' round the corner of Gortnacoppin, thinkin' of nothink 'tall, when all at onst he lep at me from behind of th' ould chapel place, an' swore roight or wrong to kiss me—the ondacent bliggard ! I lit out one screech an' run, and he afther me over the racks.. Trath, I thought onst I was cotched, but he was too drunk to go stiddy, thanks be to God, and

I heard him stumblin' about like a sale behint ov
me. 'Tis a moighty quare way to be coortin' a gurl
—scarin' her out ov her raison !" she added, meditatively. "I'll thank ye kindly, Mrs O'Brien, for
a sup ov cow's milk. 'Tis parched I am wid the
drought."

Sal Connor was the beauty of Tubbamina, and its
heiress too. Her father was not long dead, and she,
singular to relate, had been his only child. To her
belonged the cabin in which she and her mother then
lived. Hers were the two fine cows tethered beside
it ; hers the goats and sheep which fed on the short
sweet grass sprouting between the rocks. Needless
to say she had had her choice of suitors, the unattractive Caliban who had just been pursuing her being
one of them, and the most persevering of the band.
By a piece of contrariety, Sal Connor, however, had
fixed her heart upon Hurrish O'Brien, who upon his
side cared not at all for her. Though a widower,
and therefore at a disadvantage, he was the biggest,
the strongest, the best-looking, and the best-tempered
man in the whole neighbourhood of Tubbamina, and
ever since poor Mary O'Brien's death, nearly three
years before, Sal had made up her mind to fill that
vacant place—a resolve which she by no means confined to her own maidenly bosom. She was a good-
hearted girl, and if she married Hurrish, had every
intention of making him the best of wives—as wife-
hood is understood in the west of Ireland. She
would certainly not have felt it incumbent upon her
to mend his clothes, or keep his cabin in order ;
neither would she have desired that the children
should learn the use of soap, or go to school, with

the exception, that is, of the elder girls, for whom she would have scraped together money enough to send them to a convent, where they might learn to play the pianoforte, make lead-pencil drawings of surpassing shininess, perhaps even acquire the French language, as spoken at Buttevant or Ahascragh,—generally, in short, pick up such accomplishments as were likely to be of most service to them in the sphere of life they were destined to occupy.

Meantime that more advanced stage of the seven ages of womanhood had not yet arrived, and Sal Connor was in the earlier, provocative, coquettish stage of the young hen-pheasant or curassow, who is courted by half-a-dozen aspiring males, only that whereas those ignorant birds go arrayed for the most part in sober greys and browns, leaving the more gorgeous hues for their admirers, Sal delighted all Tubbamina, and Gortnacoppin too, by the splendours of her shawls and petticoats—on Sunday outshining even the painted images in the chapel. Old Bridget favoured Sall, and would willingly have seen her married to Hurrish. The money was the main consideration, of course; but besides this, her own influence with him, she was aware, had been rather waning of late, and a daughter-in-law, whom she could easily, she flattered herself, win over to her way of thinking, would be a prime auxiliary in stirring up that sluggish spirit to greater activity.

" An' what ailed that baste to run after ye to-day, 'cushla?" she inquired curiously. " Was it anythink new, or just th' ould divilmint?"

"Och, I dunno; 'tis jalous, I think, he is. He can't 'bide for me comin' this way 'tall, whativer

the raison is!" with a coy glance under her eyelashes
at Hurrish, who was mixing a pot of tar with a bit
of stick, and therefore unfortunately unconscious of
the tender provocation.

"Bad ind to his soul,—he's the curse ov the
counthry!" the old woman growled savagely. "An'
if he doesn't be mendin' his manners, he'll be makin'
it too hot for him, too, so he will—the bletherin'
baste!"

"He's rich, they say," Sal said, in a tone of ex-
tenuation. It is never well to run down an admirer
overmuch, even if you have no immediate intention
of accepting him.

"Rich! Och, bedad, if riches was all, 'tis rich he
is an' to spare! Why, the whisky alone he drinks
wud float a ship, so 't wud—a ship of war! Ould
Mrs Connor—that's Darby Connor's widy—telled me
she seen a man comin' up the car-thrack beyant his
house wid an ass, an' a barrel on the top ov it
wuldn't barely cum in at the door. An' he outs
hisself and helps to rowl it in; an' never a dhrop
to n'er a one, but sittin', an' swillin', an' a-makin'
a baste ov hisself, all *to* hisself—iless maybe that
bruther of his does be helpin' him"—with a glance
out of her black eyes to where Alley was sitting a
little apart, with the youngest child on her lap.

This roused Hurrish.

"Morry never dhrinks a drop, mother—ye know
that as well as meself," he said, quietly.

"Trath, I know nothing 'bout it," she answered,
angrily.

"Thin I do, an' I tell ye 'tis so. The two is no
more 'like nor a garden flower an' my old blackthorn

there. 'Tis the hoight ov wonders to ivery sowl in
the warld how they comes to be bruthers 'tall."

"Och, yer allays moighty sot upon yer Morry!
Wait till the bruther does be a cuttin' of yer throat,
an' him helpin' him for to do it! Maybe ye won't
think so moighty much ov him *thin!*"

To this rhetorical thrust Hurrish made no reply,
and a silence ensued of several minutes' duration.

"So the poor Maloneys is out 't last!" Sal Connor
observed, by way perhaps of giving a new and more
agreeable turn to the conversation. "Poor Mrs Maloney! dacent woman! 'Tis a power of trouble she's
had first and last. An' who'll be takin' the farm?
'Twud be a hundred ov pities for that gran' ground to
go waste. 'Tis the iligantest grazin', they say, in the
Burren. 'Twud be moighty convanient for yourself,
Mr O'Brien, wudn't it, now?" she added, turning to
Hurrish. "So handy to your own; an' you an' the
Meejor so frindly, more be token."

This brought Bridget out once more on to the war-
path.

"Divil a one will take that farm, not if it was the
last bit ov grazin' in all Oirland, an' ivery baste in the
warld dyin' for the want ov a bite!" she announced,
bringing her closed fist down upon the dresser with
a thump that made the crockery jingle. "Whoiver
goes in at Mick Maloney's door comes out ov't on his
back, and roightly sarved too, an' I'd say the same if
it was twinty sons ov me own was attimptin' to do
such a thing!"

She looked round the cabin as if to challenge con-
tradiction, but no one responded. Hurrish continued
to mix his pot as if nothing in the least affecting him

B

had been said. Like many mild men blessed with a
turbulent womankind, he had long learned to regard
these outbursts as part of the everyday order of things,
like the roaring of the wind or the crumbling of the
turf, and to pay as little attention. He had no more
idea of taking the farm from which the Maloneys had
just been evicted than he had of taking Dublin Castle,
and this his mother knew quite as well as he did
himself. If she liked, therefore, to utter blood-curd-
ling predictions as to what she could, would, or might
do in the inconceivable event of his doing anything
of the sort, why, he was not the man to grudge her so
innocent an amusement.

"Well, I must be goin'," Sal Connor said at last,
rising and complacently shaking out her skirts as she
spoke. Although she had only come, as had been
seen, for a mere morning call, her petticoat was a
new purple rep, edged with broad magenta braid, and
trimmed with three rows of canary-coloured lace, over
which she wore a new green calico bodice.

" 'Tis 'feared I am to be going back 'lone," she
added, coquettishly. "Maybe that baste is waitin' for
me still, an' the drink not out ov him yit ! Alley,
darlint, you'll cum wid me, won't you ? Ach, *doee*,
lovey," with a glance at some one who was not by
any means Alley.

Poor Alley turned quite pale.

"Usha, don't ask me, Sall, I durstn't," she said,
clasping her hands appealingly. "He run out at me
once, an' I thought I'd die—I did indade !"

"Gorra, did he want to be a-kissin' ov *you* too ?"
the other inquired, not without a touch of disdain.

Alley turned a delicate rose-colour.

" I dunno what he wanted, but he frighted me sore. He's a wicked, bad man. He'd dishtroy th' whole ov us out an' out, av he had the chance, just for spite ov Hurrish. 'Tis a fearful thing to have him 'bout the country. I'd leaver meet a mad dog nor a bull any day."

" Trath an' he won't be 'bout it *long*, I tell yis all that !" Bridget said emphatically. " There's buoys that, for the wink ov an eyelid, wud put him out of that,—yis, an' glad, an' proud to do it too; if there is *sum* so mane-spirited they'd take tratement wud insinse a babby—an' unwaned babby—an' only say ' Thank ye !' " with a glance of fiery disdain at her son.

Hurrish laughed.

" 'Tis an iligant Christsheen yer makin' me out, mother, anyhow," he said, good-humouredly.

" Christsheen !" Bridget threw all the power of her scorn into the second syllable. " Christ*sheen*, indade ! Give me a little spurit ! To be growed a man—shtrong, an' tall, an' shtraight—the biggest man out an' out in the counthry—able to dishtroy th' whole ov thim iv he'd a moind, an' niver to lift a hand,—no, nor th' half ov a hand ! Shtrike me dead this minite iv I wudn't rayther have a son like Sheeny O'Callaghan, wid niver a leg to put undher him 'tall —so I wud ! Shtrike me dead ilse !"

CHAPTER II.

HURRISH SUSPECTS THE UNSEEN POWERS.

In the end old Bridget herself escorted Sal Connor
back to her cottage, which was upon the outskirts of
Tubbamina, the village just over the ridge of the hill,
Hurrish excusing himself on the score of having to
see to his boat, which he had left on the sands, and
which would certainly be washed away if he delayed
much longer. His fishing, as already hinted, was
rather an excuse. Now and then, when he got a
good haul, he would make a little money by sending
a donkey-load to Lisdoonvarna, the water-cure place
six or eight miles away, but for the most part it was
more pleasure than profit. He had a hankering for
the sea, and was not sorry to find an excuse for escaping his mother's tongue and the humdrum monotony
of the farm, and for both these purposes the boat was
a good excuse.

He did not start, however, for some minutes after
his mother and Sal Connor had gone down the slow
incline, and were lost to sight over the next grey ridge.
Though he had taken the former's threats lightly, they
had rather startled him. He had heard them fre-
quently before, it is true, but never expressed quite so
definitely. Mat Brady was his enemy, declared and
deadly ; still, enemy as he was, and brutal, dangerous
bully and savage as he was, Hurrish had no particular
desire to have him murdered, still less to have his
own mother mixed up in that informal transaction.

Murder as a recognised social institution had never somehow quite commended itself either to his intelligence or his humanity ! Though he had openly and enthusiastically joined himself to every association which had even nominally the emancipation of Ireland for its aim, he had never allied or desired to ally himself to any of those less avowed societies with which Clare, like every other part of Ireland, is honeycombed, and which subsist upon murder, and upon murder only. He had been elected to one of them, it is true, in his absence, and had weakly refrained from insisting upon his name being struck off again. Through his mother, too, he was better acquainted with the underground doings of the neighbourhood than he by any means ought to have been ; but it was reluctantly, and he struggled stoutly to shake himself free from the participation, and to defend, whenever it was possible, the victims of it.

But if he disapproved, why not have given notice to the police, and have had the perpetrators brought to justice ? the innocent reader will perhaps inquire. The reader who asks that question must indeed be very innocent, or very slightly acquainted with those unseen springs which make up by far the more important of our inner machinery. The position of the informer in Ireland, to begin with, is the position of an outcast, cursed and abhorred of all men, to be disposed of, so soon as safe opportunity presents itself. It was not fear, however, so much as other hindrances that hampered Hurrish. Claims of all sorts—of honour, of good fellowship, of pity—plucked at him, now on this side and now on that, as the demons in Holbein's print plucked at Sintram as he

rode through the dark valley.   Hurrish was no
Sintram, yet there was something tragic, as well as
decidedly ridiculous, in the acuteness of his dilemma.
His very good-nature and sociability were all against
him.   For what, it may be asked, *is* a good-natured
and a naturally gregarious man to do, when all
the sociability of his neighbourhood is concentrated
around a single focus, and that focus a criminal one ?

His own impulses were all of the old-fashioned,
easy-going, jovial. kind.   He hated fighting—except,
of course, the open and fisticuff variety ; he hated
dark deeds and dark secrets, and everything that
savoured of unpleasantness and treachery.   He would
have liked from year's end to year's end to go on in
the same genial friendly fashion, the same happy-go-
lucky indifference to the future.   Pity such natures
when their lot has been cast into the bitter yeast of
a social revolution !   They are the clay pots amongst
the iron ones, and the fate of the clay pot is theirs.

He got up after a while, pushed away a chicken
which had perched itself meditatively upon his foot,
whistled to Lep, and started towards the sea, leaving
Alley Sheehan to look after the house and mind the
children.

His way led across about half a mile of gradually
descending ground, over a succession of slabs of
rock, many of them as much as a dozen or more feet
in diameter.   In all directions these slabs were
divided and subdivided by an endless multiplicity
of narrow fissures or crevasses, varying from a few
inches to a foot across, but reaching down apparently
to immeasurable depths.   There was something about
it that might have reminded a climber of a moder-

ately level glacier—the Mer-de-Glace above Cha-
mounix, for instance,—and like a glacier, the edges
or lips of these fissures were worn, channelled, and
smoothed away, presenting a curiously molten effect,
the result in this case of the action of rain and running water upon the soluble particles of limestone.
Instead of naked ice, these crevasses, however, were
crammed to the very brim with a green tide of vegetation—ferns and mosses, hairbells, saxifrages, silver
silenes, and white mountain dryas, red - petalled
daisies, lifting sweet impertinent faces out of their
hollow prisons, trailing sprays of clematis and honey-
suckle flinging their scent-laden treasures broadcast
across the scentless rocks—as if earth, defrauded
of her natural growths, had crowded all possible
accumulations into these receptacles which had
been torn so capriciously out of her sides for their
reception.

Hurrish strode on, stepping over the narrow
fissures, whose edges gave out a responsive click to
the contact of his boots—small fragments of stone,
detached from the edges, falling with a metallic ring
into the nearest cleft. He was in a hurry, for he
had really left his boat too close to the edge of the
water, having expected to return much sooner. At
last he reached the top of the cliff, and could see
down into the little horseshoe - shaped bay which
served him for a boat-house. All right, the boat was
there! and he was able, therefore, to pause for a
moment to look around him before beginning the
descent.

Picturesqueness *as* picturesqueness counted probably little enough with Hurrish, yet in another

way he was more sensitive to outward impressions
than many a cultured gentleman with a brain well
stocked with quotations. The roar of the sea, the
wet-surfaced rocks, the streaks of sunshine dashed
with rain, the wild west wind which had travelled
over so many miles of liquid ridge and furrow,—
all this was a sort of natural fuel to his imagination,
stirring it unconsciously to sudden feats of activity.
His was the genuine Celtic temperament — poetic,
excitable, emotionable, unreasoning. Of the more
brutal and cruel elements, which too often, alas!
streak and disfigure that strain, he had hardly a
trace. He was kindly to softness, and tender-hearted
almost to womanliness. Those schemes of personal
vengeance—dark, bloody, tiger-like—which, century
after century, have nourished the sense of injury,
while they soothed the immediate lot of many a
half-starved Celt, were almost as foreign to him as
that ox-like indifference which enables men of other
races to submit to the dreariest of daily drudgeries,
without a thought or a dream of escape. Hurrish had
a vein of poetic excitability which craved nourish-
ment. Temperaments which, under happier circumstances, might very well have been the homes of a
genuine fount of poetry, will often, for lack of better
aliment, feed upon the veriest garbage, and accept
the most worthless of sawdust-cakes for bread. The
magnificent promises, the fiery denunciations, the
windy turbid patriotism of his favourite newspapers
— by preference the contraband ones — were such
sawdust-cakes to him ; he could stand and hear
them read aloud by the hour, without even requiring
the additional stimulus of whisky. He was not quite

without other imaginative provision, however.   Like
many a letterless Irish peasant, his mind was stored
with an endless stock of old songs and ballads, the
sonorous lilt of which has charms even for those
least in sympathy with them.   To-day, for instance,
as he turned from the cliff-edge and hurried down
the narrow break-neck path, Lep at his heels, the
rapid movement, the wind, the sudden vivifying
touch of spring—all excited him without his knowing how or why, and he broke into a strain, half-
singing, half-shouting,—

> " Think av ould Brian,
> War's moighty lion,
> 'Neath that banner 'twas that he shmote the Dane !
> The Northman an' Saxon,
> Aft turned their backs on
> Those who——"

The strain stopped abruptly !   A huge piece of rock
came thundering down the side of the cliff, only
missing the singer by about half a foot, plunging
over the brim of the next ridge, and falling with a
tremendous splash, splash, splash into the sea below !
A second followed, and then a third.   Then a train
of smaller ones, each as big as a child's head.

Lep gave a wild bound of dismay, and fled down
the path, his tail tucked tight between his legs.
Hurrish sprang nimbly aside ; then, when the falling avalanche had ceased, he turned, and, keeping as
close as he could to the edge of the cliff-wall, clambered hastily up the track, his teeth set, and his soul
on fire for vengeance.   Woe betide the man, whoever he was, who had set those stones rolling !   Like
many a mild man, Hurrish, with the hero of his song,

could be a lion when he was roused, and his blood
was thoroughly up now.

When he got to the top not a soul, however, was
to be seen! not a trace or a symptom of any human
being. The bare cliff edge stood bathed in light;
the little wind-beaten camomile flowers turned up
innocent dog-eared faces to him; the wild stony
country on the one side, the untravelled wastes of
sea on the other, seemed equally void of humanity.
He scratched his head, and looked round and round,
furious, yet without an object to vent his wrath upon.
A trying predicament truly for an infuriated giant!
. Where the rocks came from was at any rate easily
seen. Along a considerable distance of one part of
the top of the cliff ran a sort of natural rampart,
known to geologists as a " block beach,"—proof of
the stupendous power of the waves which had deposited them there during a long succession of howl-
ing winters. Many of these blocks were of enormous
size, larger even than those which had so nearly anni-
hilated Hurrish; and beyond this natural barrier, a
little way from the edge, stood a small rath or dun,
two-thirds of which had been demolished.

Finding no clue to the phenomenon, he at last
slowly retraced his steps, looking back from time to
time in hopes of espying an antagonist, his soul hot
within him and longing for revenge. At the very
bottom of his anger there was, however, an under-
lying touch of mystery,—a suspicion of something
not altogether natural. The old demon-worship dies
hard in remote regions like the stony-hearted Burren;
it forms so large and so strong an element in the
traditional inheritance of the Celt, that it seems almost

impossible that it can ever be entirely extirpated.
Hurrish was not more superstitious than his neighbours, yet he by no means felt sure that what had
just befallen him had not been the work of some
malevolent spirit or spirits. What more likely than
that an unseen something had toppled those rocks
down the cliff for the amusement of seeing a man
hop like a hailstone in a shower, or, if he was in a
specially malignant mood, to crush him flat under
them like a beetle under a warming-pan ? It was not
such an uncommon occurrence ! At Ailleenahaseragh,
only a few miles down the coast, there was a hole in
a rock that was known to be permanently occupied by
an evil spirit. Fishermen had heard him picking
loose pieces off the rock at night, and throwing them
into the sea. Nay, an old woman, who was passing
the place late one evening on her way home from a fair,
had actually *seen* something sitting upon the top, with
its legs crossed, a pipe in its mouth, and a hump on
its back. She would have taken it, she admitted, for
a pedlar wearing a pack, but that, fortunately, just as
she was getting near she saw that there was a large
hole—big enough, she declared, to put a couple of
chickens through—in the middle of its back. Now no
respectable pedlar, it will be admitted, has ever a hole
of that kind through the middle of *his* back ! It was
one of the disadvantages of that part of Clare, that it
was rather a favourite haunt of beings of this kind.
There was a lake only three miles away which was
haunted by the *Each-Uisge*, or water-horse, a supernatural animal of particularly unpleasant manners.
A full account of its appearance and behaviour was
written down from the report of an eyewitness, and

is still preserved for reference.   It is described as
having " a black shining skin," a " switch tail without hair," and " a mule's head, with fins like a had-
dock."   Its habit is to wait till some one passes close
to its lair, then to spout out an enormous quantity of
water from its mouth, and before he has recovered the
shock, it darts upon him, and draws him into the lake,
where it rarely happens that even his bones are recovered again.   Hurrish's own father had had an adven-
ture with a monster almost more terrible.   He was
fishing off the island of Ard-oilen, which has always
borne a bad reputation ever since it gave the holy
Saint Gormgal such an amount of trouble.   For during
the time that the saint was building his " hermitical
retirement " there, he was perpetually tormented by
devils in the shape of black choughs, with red legs
and bills—two very diabolical traits !—which choughs
or devils, so soon as he planted anything, pulled them
out again with their bills—a fact to verify which any
one who doubts need only visit the island, which will
be found to be void of all cultivation unto this day.
Hurrish's father, I was about to remark, was pulling
up his lines, for it was getting dark, when suddenly
they were almost pulled out of his hands by a tremendous weight.   He thought that it must be a
dozen fish on at least, but when it got near the surface, he saw a blue mist or jelly, with eyes all over
it, and in the middle of this jelly a pea-green face,
covered with huge warty knobs, and shiny yellow
arms and legs, which waved about in all directions,
and—what was naturally still more startling—a large
whisky-bottle sticking out of a loose flap of skin about
the middle of its body.   He had given himself up for

lost, but that, happily, he had had an uncle who was
learned in such matters, so that he knew at once
from his descriptions that this could be no other than
Gougalidimus, king of oysters, who was known to
frequent these rocks.   Accordingly, quick as thought,
he dropped a burning spark into the water out of his
pipe, which he was fortunately smoking at the time,
whereupon the creature melted away immediately and
vanished ; for fire is the one thing such supernatural
beings cannot endure, as all but the most ignorant are,
indeed, well aware.

With these occurrences fresh in his mind, it is not
to be wondered at that Hurrish felt doubtful as to the
real nature of the accident which had befallen him,
and that, in any case, he felt that it was just as well
to pocket the insult and descend before worse happened.   He descended the cliff accordingly, this time
without any unpleasant accompaniments, and gained
the little strip of land, on the very edge of which,
half-surrounded by water, his boat was lying.   It was
one of the ordinary curaghs or coracles of the country,
consisting of a heavy framework of wood, covered
with the tarred canvas which has replaced the tra-
ditioual ox-hide.   The canvas was worn in several
places—a serious matter in a boat in which the
smallest hole is sufficient to send you without warning to the bottom.   Hurrish had brought down his
pot of tar, also a bundle of fine twigs tied together,
which served as a brush, and accordingly he now set
to work at once to patch up the places.

His excitement had by this time passed away, and
had taken his anger with it.   Man or goblin, whatever it was that had thrown those stones, they had

missed him, and therefore, with the help of the saints, might miss him again. By-and-by, as he warmed to his work, he broke out into a new tune—this time a loftier and more heroic strain :—

" 'Lord Clare,' he said, 'y' have your wish, there are yer Saxon foes ; '
The marshal almost smiled to see how furiously he goes.
How fierce a look thim ixiles wear, were wont to be so gay ;
The trisured wrongs of tharty years were in their haa-arts to-day ;
Their priesthood hunted down like wolves, their counthry over-thrown ;
Each felt as if rivinge for all——"

There was another pause. The coracle required turning. It was a job that generally needed two men, for though light, these boats were cumbersome to lift. Hurrish, however, required no aid. Stooping, he embraced the huge black thing—so like some ugly, uncouth animal—in his arms, reared it on end by main force, and propped it against a low rock, in which position he could more readily see what was amiss with the bottom. This done, he finished his strain,—

" was shtaked in him alone.
On Fontenoy ! on Fontenoy ! H-aaa-rk to the wild hurrah !
Rivinge ! Rimimber Limerick ! Wh-oooo-p ! Down wid the Sase-nagh ! "

CHAPTER III.

THE UNSEEN POWERS STAND REVEALED.

What Fontenoy was beyond a fight of some sort Hurrish had not a notion. He had not, therefore, the satisfaction of knowing that it really had been a recognised battle—a genuinely respectable European victory,—and a victory, too, due in great part to the prowess of his home-exiled compatriots. It might have been fought in Tierra del Fuego or Nova Scotia, for anything he knew to the contrary. That the Lord Clare who figured in it had fought against England, that much, indeed, was clear to him, and that probably was all he cared to know.

Hurrish possessed an idiosyncrasy which was a very serious scandal to his more thorough-going friends and relatives. This was a sort of sneaking regard, an acknowledged kindliness with which in his heart of hearts he regarded the " ould stock,"— the time-out-of-mind landlords, men as much part of the country they lived in as its rocks, rivers, magpies, or buttercups. For the new-comer, the man of yesterday, of the Encumbered Estates Court—every one who could, rightly or wrongly, be ticketed by the detested word " land-grabber "—his scorn was unmeasured, and his conscience void of reproach. But for the " ould stock,"—the aboriginal landlord, so to speak, — the Fitzgeralds, the O'Kellys, the Macmahons, his own O'Briens of Clare—over these and such as these his heart secretly yearned as a

brother over erring brothers. This general sentiment was strengthened by a personal one, for there
was a member of this degenerate race for whom
Hurrish cherished a strong feeling of personal regard, nay, affection, and that one—crowning shame
and scandal to relate—was no other than his own
landlord !

When Hurrish had been a lad of sixteen, but as
stout on his legs and as broad-chested nearly in his
ragged corduroy jacket as he was to-day, Mr O'Brien
—the " Captin " he was then called—used from
time to time to be at home on leave from his regi-
ment, and on these occasions used often to send for
his namesake—finding him strong and reasonably
intelligent—to carry his game or his fishing-basket,
as the case might be. The " Captin " and his father
were not always upon the best of terms, and the
regular gamekeeper, if such a functionary existed,
was rarely available. Hurrish was the stanchest of
henchmen, and the most admiring. Did a salmon
stick—as salmon will stick—amongst `the roots and
snarls at the bottom of the stream, — Hurrish's
clothes were off in a minute, and he would be in
the water, no matter how cold the weather or how
swift the current. Was a wild duck lost in the
bushes,—Hurrish would stay out all night, but he
would find it in the end. He possessed a strong
native fount of admiration, which craved something
to expend itself upon, and in those days the " Captin "
supplied that need. He was the idol and ideal of
his henchman's youthful admiration, and his feats of
fishing and shooting a source of as deep a pride as
though achieved by himself — rather considerably

more so. All this, of course, was changed now; nevertheless, an unacknowledged remnant of his former devotion for the " Captin " still lingered in Hurrish's frieze-covered breast. His was a nature that did not readily drop any habit of kindness it had once formed. Perhaps, too, unconsciously to himself, there was some clannish feeling mingling with this regard, though it may be doubted whether he had ever heard the word. Sentiments revert as well as features, and his forebears had followed the " Captin's " forebears quite often enough and long enough to have cut the sentiment deep into their descendant's consciousness. His mother certainly was guiltless of fostering any such slavish or syco-phantic notion ! In that thorough-going woman's eyes, the best landlord and the worst were exactly equal—as to the inquisitors of old, petty distinctions like virtue or vice counted nothing one way or other in the case of a declared heretic. Contrary to the practice of most Irish landlords, Mr O'Brien had never employed an agent, and his dealings with his tenants were, in consequence, all direct and personal. This in Hurrish's case had kept up the kindly feel-ing, though where no such kindly feeling existed, the dislike, which otherwise might have been diluted by division, had become concentrated and embittered. A man who could get another to do an unpleasant office, and yet persists in doing it himself, must take the con-sequences, which are not likely to be agreeable !

Meanwhile the beautiful morning was clouding over, as is apt to be the case where every bit of rising ground acts as a cloud detainer. It had begun to rain, though as yet slightly. The sea was

C

·moaning, and the tide ran farther and farther up into
the narrow cove, threatening to leave no standing-
room. A sudden scud of wind blowing inshore was
cutting off the tops of the waves, and sending the
froth flying in ragged clots through the air ; a couple
of fishing-boats were making all haste to win the
little harbour before the gale overtook them ; the
very puffins and cormorants were coming shorewards
with wild discordant cries, winged by the fury of the
squall. Suddenly the rain descended in a perfect
deluge, washing over the face of the rocks in a
white-edged torrent, and rushing down to meet the
incoming waves in a hundred mimic rivulets.

Hurrish, however, went doggedly on with his work.
He had never had rheumatism, and cared not a
jot for the wet. If one left off what one had in
hand for rain in Clare, one would rarely do anything
there at all.

Lep was less philosophic. With a yelp full of
discomfort he ran up to his master, rubbing his white
shaggy head against his knee, as if to entreat him to
take shelter. Finding that his appeal was disre-
garded, he, too, submitted to the inevitable, declining
to take refuge by himself among the rocks as he
might have done, and sitting shivering on the soak-
ing sand, his white coat gradually turning to a collection of ragged wisps of wool, as the drenching water
soaked it through and through; his brown eyes,
ordinarily hidden under their overhanging thatch,
becoming large and glittering, like some sort of gela-
tinous sea organisms which the retreating sea-weeds
have left dry.

At length the tarring of the curagh was finished,

and Hurrish stood back a little way to contemplate it.
It looked more like some strange antediluvian animal
than ever—a seal or walrus perhaps, of archaic type,
left behind in the march of improvement! The
shower was beginning to wear away. There were
already clear bits in the middle of the clouds, and
away towards Ballyvaughan a ray of sunshine broke
in a pallid wistful gleam upon the wet rocks.

Hurrish shook himself. Heavy as it had been,
the rain had not penetrated his thick frieze clothes,
and if the sun came out again he should be dry in a
trice. He put the coracle right end up, threw away
his twig brush, picked up the pot of tar, and prepared
to retrace his steps.

Lep, delighted at the thought of getting home, ran
on ahead, his mind already filled with the cabin
hearth and its heavenly glow, so much better in his
experience than any delusive sunlight. His master
delayed a few minutes longer in order to secure the
boat with a rope passed round the corner of one of
the big rocks, already worn smooth by that service.
He was about to mount the path when a sudden
howl of anguish, followed by yelp upon yelp of pain
and terror, reached him from above. With a bound
he was at the cliff and beginning to mount. He had
not gone many yards before he paused, riveted to the
spot by what he saw. On a sort of outlier of rock,
a little to the left of where he was standing, stood
his enemy, Mat Brady, with an evil grin on his
hideous brutalised face, and alas! alas! in his throt-
tling grasp poor faithful white-coated Lep, his master's inseparable companion ever since five years ago
he had saved him from drowning as a pup.

The dog's fate was evident. The other brute was going to throw him over the cliff, only delaying, in fact, in order to enhance the agony, and his own consequent enjoyment of it. Hurrish started forward. Lep caught sight of his master, and again and again howled for help. Hurrish redoubled his efforts, but the distance was still considerable. Before he could reach the spot the deed would have been done, and the doer of it safe from pursuit.

Once, twice, Mat Brady had swung the dog over the yawning height. The third time he was about to launch him upon his fatal journey, when—not his arms, but—his legs were suddenly pinioned fast from behind.

A wild tatterdemalion figure, with white vacant face, starting eyes, and long lank hair streaming in the wind, had sprung up, it was not easy to say from where, and had delayed the execution.

"Hould him tight thin, Thady, more power to ye ! Thunder and turf, hould him till I git t' him !" Hurrish shouted from below.

His astonishment over, Mat Brady's native brutality returned in all its force. With a howl of fury he turned and clutched the new-comer by the throat, necessarily dropping Lep, who thereupon took to his heels, never resting until he was once more safe under his master's shield. It seemed at first as if one victim was simply going to be substituted for another. Mat Brady's clutch was upon the new-comer's throat, and he was dragging him nearer and nearer to the brink. Now one foot was over it ; now the other ; now he was all but gone. Happily Hurrish was by this time close at hand, and with a hideous execration, and a kick which stretched his victim full length upon the very verge, Mat Brady broke away, betaking himself once more to the rocks, and scrambling over the rifts with that odd shambling gait of his, more like the ungainly movement of a sloth or some such plantigrade animal than anything more distinctively human.

Hurrish did not attempt to follow. He stood still and watched him, an expression of dark animosity settling down upon his good-looking placable face.

"Rin! trath ye'd bether rin!" he muttered. "Maybe y' havn't forgot th' batin I gave ye last Michelmas was a twilvemonth! But what's the good of a batin to the loikes of you? All the batin in life wudn't bate dacency into ye, so't wudn't. 'Tis *shootin'* ye want, ye baste of the world, an' I'd shoot ye as riddy as an ould scauld-crow any day in the week if it wasn't for Morry. Poor Morry! God help ye for a misfortunate gossoon! 'Tis an iligant brother ye have, achorra, sure an' sartin; an' 'tisn't the ind of him we've seen neither, more's the pity!"

CHAPTER IV.

INTRODUCES THE READER TO A FOOL AND A PHILOSOPHER.

Thady Connor, or Thady-na-Taggart, was the idiot or "natural" of Tubbamina. Village idiots, once common institutions in England, are now scarce—

increasing civilisation, or possibly increasing dislike
to people who give trouble, having tended to cause
their disappearance, or their concentration in the
parish workhouse. In Ireland, civilisation has not
yet reached this point, and the village idiot is still
a recognised member of the community—nay, an
appreciated one. The " natural " only does rather
better what every one else does more or less—namely,
as little as possible. As a mere standard of comparison, too, and as a pleasant stimulus to compla-
cency, he can never be other than a somewhat popular
institution.

Out of all the neighbourhood of Tubbamina there
was no fire to which Thady-na-Taggart gravitated
with so unhesitating a readiness as to Hurrish
O'Brien's, or so profound a certainty of a hearty
welcome. Poor Thady had a dumb passionate affec-
tionateness that is to be found in hardly any perfectly sane citizens, and only in a few exceptionally
natured dogs. For those he loved he would cheer-
fully have walked into the fire or into the sea had
they requested him to do so. When Hurrish went
for a day's fishing, Thady would wade out waist-
deep to meet him upon his return, to help to pull in
the boat, and to caper round him with fond gesture
of affection and exuberance, like some uncouth but
tender-hearted cow or colt.

Thady was no respecter of persons. Even before
the recent socialistic illumination, the difference
between frieze-coat and broadcloth was practically
non-existent for him. He would sit on his heels,
with a laugh of derision on his face, when Sir Thomas
MacDoual, who owned half Tubbamina, rode by.

Even when his lordship, the lord Bishop of Killa-
gobbet, came to open the new parish church, Thady,
to the scandal of all his relatives—the female ones
especially—declined to get up or pay any respect to
that august prelate, so that they were obliged to stand
in a cluster before him, with petticoats extended,
curtseying down to the ground in order to avert the
curse of heaven from his contumacious head.

The thoughts of an idiot are mysteries!   Like
dreams, or the visions of a man under chloroform,
they need an exponent.   That Thady did think was
evident, for his lips would work rapidly, and his forehead knit, and he would mutter half-expressed words,
which sounded like arguments or expostulations addressed to some unseen auditor.   There was no one,
however, to interpret these arguments, — certainly
no one at Tubbamina ; so that, like other veiled sayings of greater celebrity, their secret remained for
ever locked up in their utterer's own breast.

When Hurrish O'Brien reached the scene of the
late conflict, he found poor Thady sitting up and rubbing his head, the back of which had sustained several
severe contusions against the pointed stones at the
top of the cliff.   Even although your head may not
be worth very much when it is whole, a hurt to the
back of it is probably quite as uncomfortable as
though it were the honoured brain-box of a Solon or
a Solomon.   Poor Thady's innocent face was puckered
up like a baby's, preparatory to a cry.   It was evident
that he was in considerable pain.

Hurrish supplied probably the best immediately
available remedy by rushing up, grasping him warmly
by the hand, and thanking him again and again for

his timely support, Lep playing a good second by
wagging his tail and licking his defender's hand—
an act of politeness which he had never before condescended to perform to this poor shred and outcast
of humanity.

If he did not understand all that they intended to
convey, Thady at least took in the general meaning,
his poor vacant white face growing suddenly rosy
with delight. He did not say anything, but he
opened and shut his mouth a great many times in
succession, each time emitting an odd jerking noise,
something like the click of a lock, or the startled
note of the bald-coot. It was poor Thady-na-Taggart's way of laughing.

When he had a little recovered, Hurrish helped
him to his feet, and took him back with him, sup-
porting his steps carefully over the rocks. Lep,
much subdued by his late experience, followed close
" at heel," glancing nervously to right and left for
fear of a fresh surprise. Once, when they were passing a suspicious-looking shieling, whose roofless walls
rose grey and forlorn over the stony platform, he
might have been observed to wriggle round to the
far-side of his master, so as to interpose that substantial barrier between himself and it. Another
time when a fieldfare rose suddenly out of a ferny
fissure where, for lack of better retreat, it had built
its nest, Lep trembled violently from head to foot, and
was some minutes before he recovered his equanimity.
His nerves, it was evident, were seriously upset !

Some time before they reached the cabin, its blunt
gable-ends could be seen rising over the grey encompassing brows of rock. It stood so completely

detached from everything else, that it seemed to be considerably larger than it actually was. The solid stone walls had happily never been whitewashed, so that years, instead of degrading them to a ducketty grey with inky streaks, had endowed them with a delightfully diffusive crop of yellow lichens, which produced in sunlight a golden and gleaming effect. Another advantage was, that the enormous size of the material and stoniness of the surroundings lent a certain air of stern and arid purity to the immediate neighbourhood of the house. There was no repulsive muck-heap before the door, and no puddled mud. Instead, there were enormous paving-flags—natural, not artificial—which it took four of Hurrish's longest strides to traverse, and upon which the house seemed to stand as if just set down upon them out of a box. Everything, save the actual building itself, was upon the same Brobdingnagian scale. A low wall, ·that encircled three sides of the cabin, was built of gigantic oblong pieces of stone, amongst which might be seen the dismembered trunk of a cross,—not in its present condition recognised as such. There was no porch, but on one side of the door had been erected a side-screen, of the kind known as a *lascaur*—an obvious necessity, where the wind often drives with a force that would blow a stray child or loose piece of furniture straight up the chimney. And this *lascaur* consisted mainly of a single block of stone, which might have come in usefully in building the great Pyramid, and which looked like a legacy left from the days of King Goll MacMorna and his eight hundred giants.

Old Bridget was sitting as usual over the fire, stir-

ring the pot for the mid-day meal. At sight of her
son, however, she at once sprang up, and came forward with gleaming eyes to meet him.

"Hurrish, avick, whar have ye been? Have ye
heard what happened this day? glory be to God and
the saints for the same! Buggle—the little black
villin that was servin' writs, ye know—he's *dead*.
The boys dun for him on yesternight at the Killi-
maney cross-roads! An' my blessin' an' the blessin'
of heaven be upon thim for the same, Amen! Arrah,
where were ye, not to be lendin' a hand? That I
should have a son—a growd man—the strongest and
biggest man in the countbry,—and him never strikin'
a blow wid the rist!"

Hurrish made no immediate reply. Somehow this
excellent piece of news did not seem particularly to
raise his spirits. This was not the sort of warfare
that had warmed his heart, and filled his head, as he
painted his boat in the Tullymaney saleen.

"Sure I hard the crature was lame, mither," he
said, in a tone of expostulation. "'Tisn't much
killin' he'd take, God help him!"

"Lame!" Bridget's eyes blazed, and she set her
teeth like a tigress. "An' is't *his* part ye're takin',
now? Faith it wanted but that! *His* part!—the
dirty spalpeen,—the black Pratestant whilp! Lame?"
she went on, raising ˙her voice louder and louder,—
"I warrant ye, he's lame enough now, anyhow!
Limpin' down the road to hell, that's what he is
doin' this minute, the little thievin' Shingann! Och,
an' I'd give me two eyes to see it, so I would! I'd
laugh,—I'd laugh till the tears rin down me cheeks,
only to see him goin'!"

" Whist, mither, whist! My God! is it a woman
ye are, at all, at all? Ye make me 'shamed, ye
do. D'ye think the crature hadn't a mither, too—
one that's cryin' her heart out for him most like
this minute, God hilp her! I'm not sayin' that he
oughtn't to hav been shtopt," Hurrish continued,
rather shocked apparently at his own heretical
humanity. " But to be baten to death!—an' him
all by hisself—by a hape of big men! Och, mither
'cushla, 'taint that way ould Oireland's to be freed
anyhow. 'Tis thim sort o' doin's that makes the
Cause be 'bused, so it do! A dozen big men settin'
on one poor trimblin' little bodagh, and batin' the
life out on him wid shticks at night! 'Tis cold
my blood is this very minute, to think ov it."

" 'Twasn't sticks at all, so that shows how much
ye know. 'Twas *shtones* they dun it with," Bridget
said sullenly.

" Will, 'sn't that wurst, if anythink? If he was
to be kilt, sure shootin' ud be the marcifulest."

" Och, wud ye be takin' powder and shot to the
loikes of that?" she retorted with fine scorn.
" 'Twould be like takin' the fire-shovel to kill a flea,
so 'twud—no better."

Hurrish said no more. The relative advisability
of shooting a process-server or stoning him to death
did not, perhaps, seem to him to be worth a domestic
argument. Still he felt disturbed. It was not the
mode of warfare which he would have preferred.

Thady-na-Taggart was meanwhile sitting huddled
up on the stool which had been set for him,—the
two boys, who had just come in from school, making
furtive faces at him whenever their father's back was

turned. He was dimly aware when people were
talking around him, but what they were talking
about he had not a notion. As for taking part in
any conversation himself, he had never done such a
thing in his life! He was as nearly dumb, in fact,
as any creature born with the complete use of his
tongue and his palate could be. What conversation
he had was either with himself, or with the magpies
and saddle-crows, whom he was sometimes set to
scare. At present he was employed in counting his
fingers, and seemed to find the calculation inconveniently abstruse.

Old Bridget—of whom he was desperately afraid,
and was secretly watching under his eyelashes—
stalked about the cabin, swinging her skinny arms,
and making a clean sweep of any one who ventured
to approach her. Lep, who was peeping innocently
into a pot, on the chance of finding something edible
in it, received a kick which sent him yelping back
to his master. She was certainly not an agreeable
old woman this! Looking at her at such moments,
you would have been irresistibly reminded of those
historic beldames who, from time to time, have
revelled in perfect carnivals of horrors. In times
of revolution she would have been certain to have
come conspicuously to the front. Her wrinkled face
would have been a sort of inevitable accompaniment
to the gibbet or the guillotine, and in more irregular
executions she would probably have developed into
a perfect demon of ingenuity,—one of those horrible,
but unfortunately not impossible, incarnations of
cruelty that make hideous the last moments of
murdered men.

There was not a redeeming point, not a touch of softness or tenderness, anywhere in her whole composition, with the exception, perhaps, of the inevitable she-wolf's love for the offspring she herself has borne. No tenderness, no weakness, no submission disarmed her. Alley Sheehan's fragile girlish beauty, for instance, had never moved her to anything but hatred. She could have turned her out a dozen times to starve, if Hurrish would only have let her. In vain the poor child tried to conciliate her with untiring submissiveness; her very sweetness and gentleness seemed only an additional incentive to the other's rage, as is by no means unfrequently the case. The poor girl used to wake at night in an agony of terror, thinking that Bridget was standing over her, or that she was shouting some order which she had failed to obey. The very sound of her voice made her tremble painfully; indeed it was not unfrequently followed by the discharge of some handy missile, such as a bottle or a broken seat of a chair, sometimes—more terribly still—by personal chastisement, administered by her own hard and merciless hands. Alley never complained to Hurrish of these persecutions. She used to run away whenever she could, and hide herself amongst the rocks; and when evening came she would cry herself to sleep, night after night, in the little black corner of the inner room which she shared with Katty, the baby of the O'Brien brood. She had a longing, amounting often to absolute agony, for a mother's care, or for some womanly tenderness;—it was the strongest yearning by far of her nature. She was too much of a child still herself to take the children to her heart, other-

wise than as playfellows, often as fellow-victims
and to have revealed her own innermost feelings to
any man, even Hurrish, would have been utterly
wounding to her feelings of delicacy.

Poor little Alley Sheehan! Hers was certainly
the tiniest atom of a mind that could readily be conceived, comparing unfavourably probably in several
important particulars with that of many a well-in-
structed cat or dog. What there was of it, however,
was pure as crystal—pure as one of those rock-girt
pools amongst the crests of the mountains she could
see across the bay,—pools into which nothing looked
but the floating clouds, the cold white moon, the
great encompassing galaxies of stars. There was a
sort of petal-like delicacy of texture about her moral
and spiritual nature, an alpine-flower bloom and fra-
grance, which is rare, as all fine things are rare, but
not rarer, I conceive, in her class than in any other ;
a sensitiveness, too, which made all unkindness cut
like a lash, and which lent a terrible strength to her
gaunt old tyrant's ferocity. Hurrish was well aware
of all this, and though, with a mixture of indolence
and traditional reverence, he never directly reproved
his mother, he was often on the watch to intervene,
generally jocosely and as if accidentally, between her
and her victim. Alley, in her turn, knew this, and
her gratitude flew out to him for it in a perpetual
benediction. She loved Hurrish as she loved God!
There was no idea of irreverence in the juxtaposition
of the two ideas. Her mind, in fact, was too simple,
too inherently limited, to admit of any large or complicated variety of emotions. It was an instrument of
but few strings, but those few were exquisitely strung.

A shadow came to the cabin-door. Hurrish turned, and his face lit up with pleasure, while Bridget's grew if anything rather darker. An old man stood there, a very small and wrinkled old man, neatly dressed in an old tail-coat with brass buttons, corduroy knee-breeches, blue stockings, and a high black beaver hat, considerably bent but well brushed, who came forward with a polite salutation and the old-fashioned greeting, " God save all here ! "

Hurrish went to meet him with hands outstretched. " Phil Rooney, is that yerself ! Come in, man; yer welcome kindly. Clancy, go git a chair out of the bedroom for Mr Rooney—d'ye hear me, ye clip, be shmart ! Maybe ye'll stip down to the little bit of pasture, though," he added, rather hastily. " There's a baste I bought last Tuam was a twelvemonth, I'd take it kindly if y'd throw yer oye over him. 'Tis wakely the creature seems, whatever ails it."

Phil Rooney was a man of a type and generation fast passing away. He and an old maiden sister lived quite alone in a small cabin upon the main road to Ennis, and save when appealed to on some farriery question, upon which he was an acknowledged expert, he rarely stirred off his own little bit of land. After his rent was paid he was worth perhaps at most ten pounds a-year, and without the smallest accusation of exaggeration he might be called a finished gentleman, if self-respect and the most perfect breeding in the world are the essentials of that disputed term. Whatever admirable qualities the new proletariat may attain to, when the present frothy effervescence subsides, that particular type, it is to be feared, it never can resuscitate. It

is doomed, like the elk or the old Irish wolf-hound,
—productions which, once extinct in a country, are
extinct in it for ever and ever.

The young fellows of Tubbamina thought very
little of old Phil Rooney. He was but a poor patriot to begin with. The great lights of America
had been flashed in his eyes, but they had been
flashed in vain. He was too old-fashioned properly
to appreciate the merits of the great dynamite pro-
paganda, and even the simpler home-grown methods
of carrying on the warfare were often quite beyond
him. When that fine young fellow, Hyacinth Rutty,
for instance, was retailing before a sympathetic audience the part he had himself taken in the execution
of Mr Dempster of Rath's bailiff, who had been set
upon one night by twenty armed men, killed, and
hastily buried in a bog, old Rooney got up, before
that exciting tale was even completed, knocked the
ashes out of his pipe, pocketed it, and walked slowly
out of the cabin, though it was raining a perfect
deluge as it happened at the moment.

The only one of the younger generation who really
appreciated him and enjoyed his conversation was
Hurrish O'Brien ; but then Hurrish himself, as we
have seen, was considered a very second-rate sort of
patriot by the more out-and-out spirits of the neighbourhood.

The two men went down the little hill together ;
—an odd contrast, one so big, broad, and stalwart, in
his loose ill-fitting clothes ; the other so small, neat,
precise, like a model of an Irishman upon a bog-oak
inkstand. In his anxiety about the cow, and still
more perhaps to avoid a quarrel, Hurrish had forgot-

ten all about poor Thady. No sooner, however, had
the idiot perceived that his protector had departed,
than he too sprang from his stool, and fled out of the
cabin and after them in full pursuit down the hill.
He would just as soon have remained shut up with
an unchained lioness—if he had ever heard of so
dangerous an animal—as with old Bridget in her
present humour! When he reached the little field,
Hurrish and Phil Rooney were already standing
beside the cow, the former explaining the symptoms,
the latter—a pair of big horn spectacles perched
upon his nose—feeling the patient's pulse, and forming a diagnosis with all the dignity and importance
of a Court physician. Poor Thady—idiot though he
was—was as sensitive as any high-flown lover as to
the sentiments of those he cared for. Seeing, therefore, after a few minutes' patient waiting, that he was
not wanted, and that his presence had not even been
perceived, he stole silently away, getting slowly and
laboriously over the rough ground, his white lack-
lustre face and queer bleached tatterdemalion garments constituting as perfect a resemblance to his
stony surroundings as ever the coat or feathers of
arctic bird or beast to its eternal snow-fields.

The absorbing interest of the cow's illness over,
and its future treatment decided upon, the conversation of the other two lapsed, as a matter of course,
to the day's tragedy, which both agreed in regretting,
though both held the unfortunate Buggle to be pri-
marily responsible for his own fate,—a process-server,
as every reasonable person knows, having no more
human rights than a stoat, and being liable, like that
vermin, to be killed whenever met with.

D

"I wud wunder a dacent man wud do it, yis indeed," Old Rooney said in his cracked treble. (English was a foreign language to him, and at home he
never spoke anything but his native tongue, whereas
Hurrish, like most of the younger generation, preferred
the former,—despite its name, by the way, which will
doubtless be changed for the better when the new
Irish Republic finds time to look about it.)

"I'm not sayin' he oughtn't to ha' been shtopped,"
he observed, in response to his friend's remark. "Don't
mistake me, Phil. But shtones !—they're nasty cruel
things shtones is ! The blood rins cowld through my
body when I think of that cratur all by hisself—
rinnin' for the bare life, an' beggin' an' prayin' ov
thim to let him off, and they throwin' the stones at
him an' laughin' ! Lord ! I can see it 's if I'd been
there ! an' the moon gallivantin' along the sky the
way it does, an' not carin' th' half of a ratten pittatee
what goes on underneath ! An' niver a one nigh
him—'less God, maybe," Hurrish added, with a considerable doubt in his mind as to whether God would
have anything to say to a process-server. " 'Twas
only yesterday one of the bhoys telled me some wan
ax'd him if he wasn't 'feared to be goin' about the
counthry servin' writs an' suchlike, an' that he ups
an' says no, for he knew they'd niver touch a hair ov
his head, 'case of his bein' a cripple an' not able for to
defind hisself ! Och, Phil ! man alive, 'taint that way
the counthry's to be righted, howsomedever ! What,
killin' a man here and killin' a man there, and frightenin' a lot of poor foolish colleens, wid rushin' in to
the houses in the dead of the night, cuttin' off their
hair, an' makin' them sware—the divil a bit they

know what! Dishtroying dumb bastes, too, that
never did no one any harm. Sure, that's not *fightin'*!
D'ye think the *Inglish*—me curses on thim—care
how many of wan anither we dishtroy? Isn't that
what they're *wantin'*, the bliggards? I'm not spakin',
mind ye, agin the Laigue—God defind it—only I
wish they'd make thim shtop this potterin' sort of
work intoirely, an' pass the word for the risin'. 'Tis
fightin' we want, and fightin' *men*, not cows and
colleens!"

Phil Rooney took out his snuff-box—a brass one
with a medallion of the Liberator on the top. He
was a philosopher, and opined that a great deal of
fuss was made by young men who had not had *his*
experience. *He* could remember the pre-famine days
and the rising of '48, and Macmanus, and O'Doherty,
and Meagher of the Sword, and most of the heroes of a
generation ago, and it was his opinion that the time had
now come when what the country wanted was peace
and quietness. Of the modern race of agitators he
did not hesitate to profess the profoundest contempt.

"There's bad times and there's good times," he
said sententiously in Irish, "and I don't see that
there's so very much amiss with these. If you young
fellows had seen the times *I* have, you might talk!
Why, I remember in Ballysadare, when there were
forty-three corpses lying dead at one time! Forty-
three! yes, indeed, and they didn't need to be buried
either to be skeletons most of them! The changes
too! Why, I can remember when it was all the
masters the bailiffs was after! Did I ever tell you
of the time a bailiff came down to Lugnaskeagh, all
the way from London it was, with a writ for the

master ?   A terrible wild man he was, Sir Malachy
O'Donel, God rest his soul ! but there wasn't a boy on
the place wouldn't have died and gone to jail for him,
so there wasn't.   Well, the bailiff man brought the
writ all the way over the sea—a fine upstanding
young fellow, with a blue waistcoat, and a gold watch,
and a necktie right up to his chin.   And he wanted,
right or wrong, to get up to the house to serve it on
the master.   But if he did, the boys caught him just
as he was reaching the great door, and nothing would
do them but he must eat it ; and eat it he did, sure
enough,—paper, and ink, and seals, and all, and the
sputtering and the fighting !—oh, wirrastrue, wirrastrue ! that *was* a sight.   And his honour, Sir Malachy,
peeping out behind the window-curtains all the while,
and laughing fit to split.   And when the last bit of
paper was eaten, and the young man had gone away,
spitting, and swearing to have the law on them, he
came out and gave them a glass of whisky all round,
and they hurrahed—I was only a slip of a gossoon
myself at the time—they hurrahed, so you'd have
heard them at Gort !   Seems odd to remember now,
when it's nothing but killing the landlords will do
them," Phil added, with another philosophic sniff out
of the brass snuff-box.

Hurrish laughed loud and long at this story,
though, as will easily be imagined, he had heard it a
few times before.   He loved old Phil Rooney's yarns,
and often felt a secret regret that he had not himself
belonged to an earlier generation.   The faction-fights,
scrimmages, and " diversions " generally of a generation or two ago, seemed to him to be of a much
more delectable type than anything which came in

a man's way nowadays. Not that there was any lack of fighting or head-breaking either, thank God, but it all seemed to have grown duller somehow. There was too much earnest about it all. Men killed one another for *reasons*, not from pure love and friendliness. You took measures to rid yourself of any one, as you might take measures to rid your house of rats; there was no risk or " intertainmint " about it at all. Now Hurrish was sportsman enough to think a game decidedly the better for a spice of danger !

CHAPTER V.

AN ENLIGHTENED VARIETY OF PATRIOTISM.

While this conversation was going on, the two men had left the small green oases, and were making their way up the stony sides of Gortnacoppin, above the rapid stream which ran white as milk over its boulder-strewn bed. Hurrish rented one-half of this valley from Mr O'Brien of Donore, and kept sheep upon it—goat-like creatures, which appeared to feed upon the stones, there was so little else to be seen. What grass there was, however, was sweet and good, like all the Burren pasture ; nor was their hunger to be balked even by the deep stony rifts which seemed set there for the express purpose of breaking their legs, but into which they complacently poked their noses as into so many recognised food-troughs.

A little higher up, the stream they had been following suddenly disappeared, as the way of streams
is in these thirsty limestone regions.   The valley
thereupon changed its character.   From a roughly
sawn trench, broken in every direction with loose
boulders, and presenting all the appearance of a
half-emptied stone quarry, it suddenly became a sym-
metrical bowl, rising in an architectural - looking
crescent, the lines of stratification following directly
one above the other, like the seats of an amphitheatre.
All over the Burren this oddly architectural effect
presents itself.   You are brought face to face with
a frowning fortress, outworks, glacis, ramparts, all
complete ; or you drop suddenly into a stony amphitheatre, with orderly ranges of seats one above
the other, which appear to be only waiting for some
dilatory audience.   In this instance the human part
of the scene was represented by two sets of habitations, ruins both of them, but ruins of widely different
dates.   One a group of cabins — deserted perhaps
twenty years back — roofless, blear - eyed, smoke-
blackened,—repellent even in their very piteousness ;
the other a group of those far-famed " clochauns " or
beehive oratories, which rejoice the soul of the anti-
quary in these Celtic solitudes.   Mysterious-looking,
wigwam-like abodes, built of undressed stones, put
together without the aid of mortar, larger stones
projecting here and there, like sticks out of a bird's
nest.   A doorway at one side—the doorway of a
dog-kennel—averaging perhaps three feet and a half
in height, and over this doorway a window, five,
or in unusually boldly proportioned specimens six
inches across, while over this window again five white

quartz pebbles set perpendicularly and three horizon-
tally combine to make a little cross, looking at a distance as if splashed in in whitewash.   Three of these
Liliputian cells—all that remained of a once popu-
lous monastery—dotted the grey floor of the amphitheatre.   Fancy pictured the wild head of an Irish
monk—say about the year 850—protruded through
his doorway of a morning, like his cousin the her-
mit-crab's through the mouth of its shell, while its
owner—crouched necessarily upon all-fours—looked
round the valley and considered the prospects of
breakfast !

Our two friends paused a moment and looked up
this stony valley, which was threaded by a tiny path
trodden by the feet of passers-by, and leading to the
high-road which lay upon the other side of the next
ridge.   Some one was descending this path—a tall
young man, dressed, not like Hurrish and his old
companion in rough home-spun frieze, but in one of
those suits of ready-made tweed which are rapidly
taking the place of the older costume all over the
country.   A well-built, well-looking young fellow,
showing a pale, rather sun-deepened complexion, close-
cropped hair, large reddish moustache, and a chin
betokening firmness, not to say obstinacy.   A pleasant face and an intelligent one, yet a face, none the
less, which seemed meant to warn you not to quarrel, if you could conveniently avoid it, with its owner.

Hurrish's own genial face lit up with pleasure at
sight of the new-comer.

" Maurice Brady himself ! " he shouted, long before
they were within speaking distance.   " The top of
the mornin' and the best of good luck to you, Morry,

me boy; an' where have ye hid yerself this month ov
Sundays? 'Tis sick for the sight of you I've been,
an' some wan else too, that ye'd maybe think more
ov,' he added meaningly, as the young man drew
nearer.

Maurice Brady's mother and Hurrish had been
first-cousins, had spent their childhood next door to
one another, and had made mud-pies beside the same
puddles. It had been a bad day for the poor woman
when she was tormented by her relations into marrying old Michael Brady, the widower, and going to
live in his dirty cabin on the top of the ridge which
divided Gortnacoppin from Ballynadugal. The father
was no sooner dead than the brutal son had turned
upon the unfortunate woman, and had literally harried
her out of existence,—the first quarrel between him
and Hurrish arising out of the latter's interference on
her behalf. After his stepmother's death, some com-
punction seemed to have come over the savage, or
natural feelings may have asserted themselves, for his
treatment of his brother, though bad enough, was,
comparatively speaking, humane. The boy had been
considered to show a turn for learning, and it had
even been at one time proposed that he should be
sent to Maynooth. This, however, as the time drew
nearer, he had himself strongly resisted—the limita-
tions of a priest's life, however balanced by other
advantages, having absolutely no charms for him.

Like every Irishman of the reigning generation,
Maurice Brady cherished dreams of ambition, —
dreams, too, by no means destitute, as it seemed to
him, of solid foundations. If every recruit of the
Grand Army carried a marshal's baton in his knap-

sack, surely every Nationalist recruit, that can read,
write, and spell, carries an appointment in the coming
Irish Republic somewhere or other about his personal
possessions.   Why not ?   Was there not young Egan
Shaughnessy, who had been foreman only the other
day in the same little haberdashery shop at Miltown-
Malbay in which Maurice Brady himself served, and
what was he now ?   Member for Polladoo, and likely
to rise to any dizzy height so soon as the Nationalists
began really to warm to their work !   Maurice had
taught himself shorthand in his leisure moments, and
had already done a certain amount of newspaper
work.   It was only for the ' Killogenesawee Shille-
lagh and Flag of Ballyduff,' it is true, at present, but
then everything in life, we know, depends upon a
beginning.

He had other tastes, however, besides his ambition
—besides, that is to say, what he called his patriotism.   He was a young man of remarkably good taste,
in fact, considering his opportunities ; and Alley
Sheehan's great grey eyes—wasted as they were upon
most of her contemporaries—had had their full effect
upon him.   From his boyhood Hurrish's cabin had
been far more of a home to him than the one he had
lived in.   Small, dark, and uninviting as it would
have seemed to most people, with its hermetically
sealed windows and immovable atmosphere of peat-
smoke, it was a palace in comparison with the foul
hovel in which he and his brother had herded together ;—a palace, too, lit by kind voices and friendly
looks—for even the termagant Bridget had in those
days had a good word for the handsome, quick-
witted lad, who seemed born to reflect credit upon his

belongings.   As for Hurrish, his pride and delight in
young Brady were simply limitless.   His own literary
attainments were strictly confined to being able to
spell out the contents of the dirty little newspaper
which went the rounds of the hamlet, and was often
a week old, and nearly in pieces, before it reached his
hands.   Like every member of his class, he had a
profound reverence, however, for education in the
abstract,—" Larnin's a load aisy carried," being one
of the commonest sayings to be heard upon an Irish
peasant's lips.   Maurice Brady's learning was not,
perhaps, a very formidable burden at present, still he
was a promising youngster unquestionably, and so
regarded by most people, Hurrish foremost.   " Bedad
an' 'tis a gran' man he'll be yit, niver *you* fear !" was
his invariable reply to those cavilling remarks which
even the most conspicuous merit in so invidious a
world is unfortunately always liable to.

When Maurice first announced his wish to marry
Alley, Hurrish had given a ready consent, and it was
settled that the marriage was to take place as soon as
Maurice could venture to support a wife.   Since then,
matters however had changed.   Fresh feuds had
broken out between the two houses, and it seemed
but too likely that in Tubbamina to-day, as in
Verona of old, the hopes of the lovers were to be
the sacrifice.

After a while, old Phil Rooney, between whom
and the new-comer there seemed to be no very warm
sympathy, took his departure, betaking himself·to the
narrow thread-like path leading to the top of the
ridge, his small bent figure in its grey antique dress
seeming to merge into the rocks as it vanished slowly

in the distance. As soon as he was safely out of
hearing, Maurice Brady stopped short, and pointed
towards the opposite side of the valley,—

" Hurrish, I'm afeared Mat means to have Maloney's farm," he said abruptly.

" Ye don't mane it, Morry! Sure 'tis more nor
his life's worth. The boys'll kill him sure as they
would a jack-snipe ! "

" He won't stop for that ! " the other answered, not
without a touch of pride. " If Mat's mind is made
up to have it, have it he will, if every soldier out of
Dublin is brought to guard it." He looked across
the valley at this so-called farm—a wild miz-maze of
rocks with small " fat " hollows at intervals,—the
sort of " farm " to make a Norfolk or Leicestershire
farmer's eyes start out of his head. Yet it was one
which in ordinary times commanded a good rent, and
—stranger still—was worth it too.

" What I'm most afraid of," he went on, after a
minute, " is about him and you. I don't know what's
come to him lately, but he's like a man distraught.
I was up at Slievefoore on my way here, and had to
wait, as he was out ; and when he came in he was
cursing—I never heard him so bad—raving and
swearing he'd have yer blood, — and not drunk
either," the brother added meditatively.

Hurrish's good-humoured brow grew dark.

" He was nigh upon killing poor Lep this
mornin'," he said, frowning at the recollection. " Begorra, if 't hadn't been for thinkin' of you, Morry,
I'd ha' throttled the life out of him thin and there.
Be my sowl, yis ! "

Young Brady made no answer, but he, too, frowned.

Mat's doings had long been beyond defence; still he
was his brother, and he had too deep-rooted a self-
respect not to consider that this fact imparted to
him an importance not his own. It offended him
that Hurrish should make such a speech in *his*
hearing.

" Is Alley 't home ? " he inquired rather haughtily,
after they had walked on some way in silence. It
was not often he allowed himself to slip into such
colloquialisms, for, like most aspirants to distinction,
he kept an anxious guard over his tongue. With
old acquaintances, however, old habits are apt to
break out.

" She is, Morry avick — but sure, I'm fear'd ye'd
betther not come in," Hurrish said apologetically.
" What wid these goin's on of Mat's, an' wan thing
an' another, *herself's* jist fit to be tied. Sure ye
know yerself how 'twas last toime ? "

Maurice did know unpleasantly well. Old Bridget
had set upon him with broom and mop, and had
fairly driven him away, threatening to upset the
boiling potato-pot over him if he came again.

" I never see Alley now at all," he answered
irritably. " It's an uncommonly queer way of being
engaged to a girl, never setting eyes upon her from
month's end to month's end, and I'm not going to
stand it much longer either, what's more," he added,
fiercely.

" 'Tis indade, Morry. Thrue for ye, me poor
bhoy," Hurrish said, deprecatingly. " 'Taint no doin'
of mine, anyhow. I'll tell ye what, now," he added,
brightening up under a sudden inspiration ; " come ov
Wi'nsday. *Herself* ull be at Tullalogue wid the spring

chickens, an' you'll find the coast clane an' clear, an'
n'er a one in it 't all, only just little Alley herself
and the childer."

Maurice Brady made no answer. The picture was
inspiriting certainly, still he did not choose to relax
too soon in his offended deportment. He knew very
well that, in point of fact, it was not Hurrish's fault,
—beyond the weakness, that is, of yielding for peace'
sake to old Bridget's furious animosities. He was
out of humour, however, and not inclined, therefore,
to make the admission. Besides, it was never necessary to stand upon ceremony with Hurrish.

" All right—I'll come on Wednesday," he said, at
last. " Mind you tell Alley so. I'll not go on now,
as it seems there's no use," he added, stopping short.
" I promised Phil Donellan to look him up some
time before he sailed, and I mightn't get another
chance."

He nodded to Hurrish, and turned abruptly away
and along a narrow " bohereen," between two loose
lacework walls leading in the direction of Tubbamina.
The other man stood still for several minutes, wistfully watching the tall active figure striding rapidly
along, until it had turned the next corner and was
lost to sight. Maurice, however, never looked back.
He knew that Hurrish was fonder of him than of
any other creature in the world—his own children
and Alley barely excepted,—and perhaps this knowledge gave him a sense of power over the older,
stronger, more tender-natured man. It is not, we
all know, an unfrequent source of superiority.

It would be difficult to imagine two men, born
under almost identical circumstances, more unlike

than those two who had just parted upon the ridge
of Gortnacoppin. To Hurrish, life in general—past,
present, and future—was all part of an abounding
mystery, which might be understood perhaps by
Father Denahy, or other competent authorities, but
into which he himself never dreamt of probing. He
was a devout Catholic, and had a tolerably clear con-
ception of a penal region in which unconverted Pro-
testants and other enemies of Ireland would form the
principal portion of the population. As for those
more cheerful realms to which he would wish to be
himself translated, they were to a great extent confused and mixed up with traditions of the O'Brasil,
Tir-nan-oge, and other paradises of departed Celtic
heroes, which he constantly scanned the Atlantic in
hopes of catching a glimpse of, and in whose reality
he believed very nearly as emphatically.

Maurice Brady professed Catholicism, of course,
and duly attended mass, but he certainly never
troubled his head about any future, orthodox or un-
orthodox. Life was far too clear and sharply defined
for him to need to expand his horizon in such unprofitable directions. His intellectual fabric, if not
very wide-reaching, was, at least, remarkably compact and coherent. He had not to lay it to his
conscience that he had ever wasted his opportunities,
or allowed foolishly sentimental considerations to
stand in his way. Clever young men, born under
peasants' roofs, often waste half their time in escaping from their early ties. The chrysalis is set fast
in its native soil, and its earliest efforts are all spent
in breaking free from that unyielding matrix. They
are tied to their hide-bound belongings by knots

which they find it hard to unloose, and which unites
their hearts to a state of things from which the intellectual side of them is in perpetual revolt. This
had never been Maurice Brady's case. With the
exception of his affection for Alley—a very gracious
and condescending sort of affection—he had no tender threads to break. His brother it would have
been difficult to feel very warmly towards; and as
regards Hurrish, his early boyish admiration for that
redoubtable son of Anak had long become modified
by a very clear-sighted appreciation of his intellectual capacity. Hurrish's primitive patriotism, for
instance, was a source of immeasurable amusement
to his more clear-sighted friend,—it was so incon-
ceivably old-fashioned and infantine. His besotted
affection for that wretched stony soil upon which he
happened to have been born, was another trait which
naturally moved his pity. Far from wasting any
affection upon it himself, he would have been only
too delighted to have been assured that he was never
to set eyes on it again. *His* likes and dislikes were
all rational ones, in fact, founded upon reason, not
merely instinctive and animal-like. Even his hatred
of England was a purely conventional hatred. It
was the " correct thing " to hate it, and therefore he
did so. He had a considerable gift of words, and
could at any moment have risen to any required
height of foaming sound and fury had he been called
upon to do so ; but it would have been a purely
oratorical and dramatic fury. There was not an
atom of uncomfortable heat or bitterness about it.
It was a profession, and, as times went, not a bad
profession either, but that was all.

All over Ireland this marked severance is growing
up between the younger, educated or half-educated
peasant or peasant's son, whose aspirations are all
Americanised, progressive, modern, and the earlier,
ruder type of peasant-farmer, whose union with the
actual piece of soil he cultivates—or does not culti-
vate—amounts to a partnership; a vital union, like
that of the grass and potatoes.   Hurrish belonged to
this elementary and elemental type.   If you had
offered him twice the acreage of the best grass lands
in Meath or Kildare, in exchange for his naked rock,
I doubt if he would have been even tempted to close
with it.   He was a sentimentalist—though he had
never heard the word; and the ground which he
had been born on—that hard, thankless, rock-bound
ground—was the object of his sentimental worship.

    As he walked home now along the rocky zigzag
track which led to his cabin, he was thinking very
anxiously over Maurice's piece of information about
the Gortnacoppin farm.   It was a very serious matter.   Mat Brady was quite bad enough and troublesome enough where he was—witness to-day, when
he had so nearly succeeded in wreaking his spite
upon poor Lep, not to speak of those tumbling rocks,
which Hurrish began now to suspect of having had
some human agency behind them.   How would it
be when he held land which actually " marched "
with Hurrish's own ?—when at all hours of the day
and night he would be in a position to wreak his
spite and malice upon his unfortunate neighbours ?
Even this was not the end of the trouble he foresaw.
Strong daring man as he was, there were points on
which Hurrish, it must be confessed, was an unmiti-

gated coward—a moral one. He had an awe, not
unmixed with secret dislike, for that unwritten law
under which he, like every one else in the neighbourhood, lay bound and fettered; he had also a long-
standing awe of his mother, and the two points
showed a good deal of electrical affinity. If Brady
was allowed to take this farm, he had a prevision
that the results would be decidedly serious. From
all that had taken place lately, and from the excited
state of feeling in the neighbourhood, he felt sure
that he would not be allowed to do so peaceably.
He was detested, and was just the sort of man to be
made an example of, since no foolish qualms of pity
were likely, in his case, to arise to mar the absolute
righteousness of the deed.

Now Hurrish, as already explained, had a dislike
to murder in the abstract. He had a feeling, too,
that if Mat Brady *was* made away with, the crime,
or the suspicion of it, would certainly be laid at the
door of his own cabin—nay, might be laid there not
entirely without reason. His mother would assuredly
know all about it, and would stir him up by every
means in her power to assist — indirectly if not
directly. Nay, he knew by bitter experience that
it was not by any means impossible that he might
be harassed into something like a passive participation in it,—a result which he honestly deprecated
beforehand. Was there no way of stopping Brady
from taking the farm ?—that was the problem which
he turned over and over all the way home. It was
a very difficult one to solve, — the man's brutal
courage, no less than his brutal pigheadedness, making it almost impossible to hit upon any hopeful

E

means of coercing him.   At last an idea struck him.
It was not very promising, perhaps ; still, under the
circumstances, it seemed worth trying.   He resolved
to put it to the test the very next day.

CHAPTER VI.

MR O'BRIEN OF DONORE.

If the cliffs of Clare are stern and terrible, its lakes
are seductive and bewitching beyond words—gems
whose beauty steals into the heart like love or sun-
beams.   Elsewhere the trees, wherever they once
grew, have been swept away bodily from the face of
the earth, a few stunted hollies, an occasional blighted
thorn, the only exception.   Around the lakes, on the
other hand, and along the streams which feed them,
there still springs up year by year a goodly growth,—
oak and birch, holly and mountain-ash,—fighting a desperate, but upon the whole a successful, battle against
the ever-marauding sheep and goats which prey upon
them, and tempt the sympathetic looker-on to sigh
for the fine old gristly Irish wolf, which—historically
speaking till the other day—kept those woolly ma-
rauders at home by the terrors of his fang.

Donore Lough is long and narrow, brown and clear ;
with its tributary streams it helps to form the bound-
ary of two very distinct districts.   Northward extends
the barren mountain limestone district of Burren, the
horizontal rocks of which come up to the very edge

of the lake. Southward the grass-covered sandstones
and coal-measures of Southern Clare begin, sweeping
away in a succession of irregular undulations, now
higher, now lower, until their farther course is cut
short by the waters of the Shannon. The geology of
a district matters, generally speaking, very little, save
to the geologist. Eye and foot alike pass from one
to the other without a suspicion of any change. Here,
however, it is not so. The two formations stand face
to face,—foes met in battle array, whose hostility
may be read in every ridge, and knoll, and scarped
hillside, the very wayside flower of the one disappearing often, as if by enchantment, when we pass to the
other.

All the country visible from the shores of Donore
Lough, limestones, sandstones, and coal-measures alike,
belongs to Major or—to drop the now generally disused military title—Mr O'Brien. It has never been
a very profitable property, and of late years it has produced hardly any margin at all. Not enough to keep
up that big ugly house you may see rising with an air
of ungainly pretension out of the trees to the south of
the lake ; hardly enough to pay for yonder posse of
workmen, shouldering their spades and shovels, and
marching off to their homes with the comfortable
consciousness of having done about as little work in
return for a day's wage as any conscientiously pains-
taking body of men in the three kingdoms.

Mr O'Brien was standing at the lake edge and
looking about him as he had done every evening of his
life for the last sixteen years. The dark-blue rippling
water was washing the stones to whiteness at his feet ;
the young trees—nearly in full leaf—feathered down

almost on to its surface.   Upon the other side of the
lake lay a long stretch of blue-grey road, along which
a small donkey-cart was coming towards him at the
rate of perhaps a quarter of a mile an hour.   Facing
it upon the same road he could see a party of constabulary just breasting the brow of the hill, the reddish rays of the setting sun catching upon the barrels
of their guns and the hilts of their side-arms.   Fine
soldierly fellows they were too, pleasant to see in their
smart dark uniforms, stepping well together, tall, erect,
well disciplined.   Handy, well-disposed fellows moreover, as Mr O'Brien knew, for they were part of his
own bodyguard, coming down from the newly-erected
iron barracks on the top of the Gortnacoppin ridge.
Their merits were not apparently what chiefly engaged
his attention at that moment.   His brow contracted,
his whole face changed, and he turned away from the
sight with a groan of unmitigated disgust.

Poor Major Pierce !   Sixteen years had passed
since he had returned to the home of his fathers,
with a heart full and brains primed for its regenera-
tion.   They were not bad brains either, if not perhaps precisely the sort best suited for the work that
they had undertaken.   Clare, with its wild neglected
hillsides ; its lakes set like bright blue eyes in old
and wrinkled faces ; its tracts of naked rocks ; its
sweet rich snatches of pasture ; its kindly, ragged,
shiftless people ; its tales of the fighting O'Briens ;
its vast cliffs and matchless breadths of sea and sky —
that home air which a man never breathes save at
one spot in this whole wide world, — all this had
been very dear to him, and, in spite of all that had
come and gone, it was dear to him in a sense still.

And yet what a failure! What a failure! Here
he was, after those sixteen years had passed and
gone, about the best hated man between Blackhead
and the mouth of the Shannon. A man, the news
of whose death would, as he himself well knew,
awaken rejoicing bonfires from one end of his own
property to the other! A man who was strictly forbidden to sit beside an open window, or to go abroad
upon his own fields without a tame turnkey at his
heels! Poor Pierce O'Brien! No wonder the streaks
of grey lay so thickly around his forehead; no wonder his wife and daughter preferred Brighton or
Bournemouth to Clare; no wonder that every post
brought volumes of entreaties that he would leave
that horrible, wicked, treacherous country, and come
where he could live in peace and safety. Still less
wonder, perhaps—being the sort of man he was—
that he should set his teeth doggedly, and swear
that, come what might, they should neither drive
nor cajole him out of the country. Castle Donore
of Clare was the proper place for an O'Brien of
Castle Donore, and they might rob him there, or
shoot him there at once and have done with it, but
they should never have it to say that they had made
him run away of his own accord.

His beard—two or three shades greyer than his
hair—had grown longer and rather dishevelled since
his womenkind had departed and had taken the con-
ventionalities of life with them. Yet, in spite of
this, and of a slight stoop which he had lately
acquired, he looked a soldier still every inch. A
close-cropped head, rather hollow above the temples,
and rather high at the top, where the hair still grew

thickly ; good, well-opened blue eyes, not large but
kindly ; a face which spoke of geniality and obstinacy, of amiability and irascibility—a very Irish face,
too, though it was rather difficult to say wherein the
distinctive Hibernianism consisted.   The geniality
and amiability, alas ! were fast losing ground.   Cares,
worries, loneliness, were doing their work, the friendly
blue eyes were fast becoming a mere nucleus of con-
centric wrinkles, and the hospitable genial mouth ac-
quiring a confirmed droop at the corners.

Poor Major Pierce !   Poor tenants !   Shall we—
ought we not perhaps in fairness—add poor " Government " that had to interpose between the two ?
What a hopeless dead-lock it all was !   What a dismal concatenation of blunders, misrepresentations, prejudices—prejudices from above, and prejudices from
below—prejudices which would have been laughable
but that they were so deplorably tragic !   In the
eyes of the people about Donore—all, that is, but a
few personal retainers—this poor, good-natured, well-
meaning, utterly puzzled and half heartbroken man
appeared in the light of an ogre—a sort of blood-suck-
ing, land-grabbing, body-and-soul-destroying monster
—who devoured widows' substances, and snatched the
bread from the starving lips of orphans !   One would
laugh, but that one is really more than half tempted
to cry—if crying, that is to say, would do any good.
Major Pierce used to laugh himself, but latterly he
had left off doing so.   There comes a point in even
the most ridiculous misfortunes, where the humour
ceases to be entertaining—at any rate to the victim.

He walked on along the edge, under a wistful rose-
tinted sky.   The wind was going down with the sun,

and the stillness spreading. There was a low stone
parapet at this part, with a few rotting stakes at intervals, to one of which an old black punt was attached.
A little farther on a stream fell over some rocks,
and the scent of the mosses and water-weeds rose
penetratingly.

How still it all was ! how serene ! how filled with
breathing from the very inmost soul of peace ! Everything that was grim in the day-time, was mellowed
now to peace and beauty. The grey terraced hills of
the Burren shone with a pale spectral glow, which
lingered upon their chiselled sides, as upon the bastions
of half-dismantled fortresses. The same glow floated
over the lake, which was golden in one part, and
transparent black in another; the rushes and little
upstanding water-weeds springing up, each in separate
beauty, against this agate setting. Hardly a sound.
Only a little lisp of water, only a distant leisurely
rumbling, only a far-off cry of hurrying sea-birds.
The ascetic dreamy beauty seemed endowed with a
voice that was simply itself made audible.

The poor owner of these serene possessions was
hardly as atuned as he should have been to their
enjoyment ! There was nothing, you see, dreamily
peaceful in the outlook which lay before him ! Only
worries and more worries—only the bitterness of a
mind which sees that everything it has set itself upon
is going contrariwise ; only a growing dogged determination to fight a losing battle, but to fight it out to
the bitter end.

He turned away from the lake and the peace and
the glow, and entered a narrow walk between tall,
rather neglected-looking trees, which led past the gate

of a disused churchyard, beyond which stood a ruined
church, deep on every side with nettles, and beyond
which, again, could be seen the tangled opening of the
wood.

It was quite dusk here, and the shadows under the
trees were almost black. It was a little startling,
therefore, as he approached the middle of the walk,
to see a figure — tall, broad - shouldered, evidently
frieze-coated—waiting for him in one of the larger of
those patches of shadow, and close to the gate of the
disused churchyard.

A bolder man than Pierce O'Brien, I may say,
never breathed or fought. He utterly detested this
protection forced upon him by a paternal Government, and expended a good deal of rather misplaced
ingenuity in evading it whenever circumstances rendered such evasion possible. Again and again had
he obliged those unfortunate myrmidons of the law,
the " polis," to waste breath in an excited scurry
over hill and dale before they could come up to their
charge and take him under their bayoneted protection
again. He did not even, for his own part, believe
profoundly in this so-much-talked-of peril. If people
wanted to shoot him, he had given them no lack of
opportunities, and so far they had not availed themselves of them. Still, when you have been told for
months past that your life is hardly worth an hour's
purchase ; that dozens of people are thirsting to pour
your life's blood out upon your own threshold ; when
you have not only been assured that your execution
has been formally decided upon, but even the gentleman who has undertaken that delicate office has
again and again been confidentially named to you,—

it stands to reason that a suspicious stranger skulking
about your avenue awakens livelier emotions than
where you expect no more thrilling visitor than the
milkman or the post-boy !

He did not turn back, however,—merely put his
hand in his pocket, and produced an ugly sausage-
shaped parcel which presently gave forth a significant
click.

" Who is there ? " he inquired.

" 'Tis me, your anner—Hurrish O'Brien," came
from the depths of the ominous shadow.

Mr O'Brien gave a laugh—rather an angry one—
and put his parcel back into his pocket again.

" And what the devil, Hurrish O'Brien, do you
mean by hiding in the trees like that ? " he inquired,
irritably.

" I was waitin' to have a private word with yer
anner, Meejar,"—and slowly, like some unusually
substantial ghost, Hurrish emerged from the deep
blackness into the comparative illumination of the
tangled pathway.

" Private word ? What do you want a private
word about, eh ? "

" I'll tell yer anner that when we're to our two
selves," was the cautious reply.

Mr O'Brien groaned. " More worries, I suppose !
Hang me, if one is left in peace two days consecu-
tively, it is a wonder ! Well, come in here. We
shall be quiet enough, Lord knows, there ! "

He turned, and led the way into the churchyard,
through a rickety iron gate, which gave out a discordant croak as if in protestation. A big horse-
chestnut tree, one mass of flower to the very summit,

was lifting its crimson-tipped spikes above a pair of
stunted yews, spreading thick black arms over the
nettles.   Skulls and cross-bones—cheerful and apparently inevitable embellishments of an Irish churchyard — lay about in corners, so greened over and
harmonised, however, by mosses and lichens, that it
would have taken a somewhat anatomical eye to have
recognised them for what they were.

"Now, then, Hurrish, what is it you want ?   Be
quick, man ; I've no time to lose."

The tone was irritable, yet Major Pierce was not
ill-tempered, nor even, as a rule, wanting in courtesy
to those about him.   Some allowance must be made
for him.   When everything that a man sees and
hears is about as pleasant as a handful of sand upon
a newly-made wound, it is scarcely to be wondered at
if his tone grows querulous, and his style of conversation unconciliatory.

Hurrish was not to be hurried.   There was a sense
of solemnity to him in his mission.

"Furst an' foremoust, I want to pay yer anner the
bit of rint,"—and he mysteriously produced a large
canvas bag, which emitted a chinky sound.

Mr O'Brien glanced at it suspiciously.

"No reduction,—you understand that, Hurrish ? "
he said, sharply.   "Reduction ! God bless my soul ! "
the poor man burst out, stung by the mere mention
of that familiar grievance—" do you know that it is
forty-five years since a single rent upon the property
has been raised ?   Do you know how often I've been
advised to put another twenty-five per cent upon
every man jack of you all round, and have always
refused ?—upon principle, mind you—upon principle.

Do you know that I am asked now to take thirty per
cent reduction, the same that that fellow Maclellan
who bought the Tullaloe property only four years
ago, and whose rents have been raised twice since, has
given ?   Do you know that, I ask you, Hurrish ? "

" I do, yer anner."

" Very well, then I hope *you* won't begin talking
about a reduction, because I won't listen to it, so
there's an end of it."

For all answer, Hurrish poured out the contents of
the bag upon a flat tombstone, and began sorting the
coins into little heaps.

" Yer anner can count.   'Tis the same as iver," he
said, in a tone of expostulation.

Mr O'Brien felt a touch of vexation, perhaps even
of self-reproach.   He was a generous man by nature,
much more addicted to giving than to taking, if circumstances had only admitted of the possibility of
such a luxury.   It was the principle he fought for,
not the dirty pounds and shillings.   He liked Hurrish, and under ordinary circumstances would have
scorned to drive a bargain with him.   It was the
word " reduction " that stunk in his nostrils, and
fired his pride.   It was the shibboleth for the moment of the whole battlefield.

" Oh, if you say so, no doubt it's all right, Hurrish," he said, as he gathered the money up, and
shovelled it loosely into his pocket.   " I can count
it presently, and give you a receipt.   But why do
you want to pay me now, instead of waiting until
the 20th ? "

Hurrish, in lieu of reply, stuck his fingers into a
small hole in the wall near which they were standing,

and dislodged a loose stone, which fell with a dull
thud amongst the nettles. " I thought I'd as lief pay
yer anner to-day," he said stolidly.

" Mr O'Brien asked no more. He knew better
than to push the matter further. To do so would
have been to tempt the door of that inexhaustible
cavern of lies which is supposed to yawn around
every Irish proprietor. Hurrish had a good reputation in this particular, it is true, but no man should
be tempted beyond what he is able to bear.

" Thar's another matter I was wantin' to spake to
yer anner 'bout." Hurrish paused. and looked suspiciously round the churchyard, as if expecting to
detect some unseen eavesdropper, his eye resting
finally upon the skulls—safe and silent witnesses of
humanity. " For God's sake, don't let Mat Brady
have Maloney's farm!" he whispered, when he had
apparently satisfied himself on this point.

" Why not ? " Mr O'Brien inquired sharply.

" Becase, yer anner—becase—there'll be bad wark
—the divil's *own* bad wark—so sure as iver he does,"
was the emphatic reply.

Mr O'Brien uttered an angry expostulation, and
walked the length of the short path leading to the
gate, then turned back.

" How the deuce am I to help it, I should like to
know ? " he inquired, testily. If any one else makes
me an offer for the farm, I'm perfectly willing—if
he is a solvent man, that is—to give him the preference. No one can have a worse opinion of that
Brady fellow than I have myself—ill-conditioned
sot ! Still he has money—he is not likely to be
short at rent-day ; and I tell you plainly, Hurrish,

I can't afford to be out of pocket another farm.
Why, God bless my soul, man! I might just as well
have let the Maloneys remain in it if I am not to
get another tenant."

" An' that's true, yer anner."

Mr O'Brien did not seem particularly pleased with
this ready assent. He turned away with an angry
" Pish," and walked back to the gate.

" Make me an offer for it yourself, if it comes to that,
Hurrish," he said, when he had returned. " You're
a decent, sober man, and it would throw the two
farms into one, and make a good thing of it. Come,
is that what you have been driving at? If so,
speak up."

But Hurrish shook his head.

" Thank yer anner, I wasn't thinkin' ov meself,"
he answered, slowly. " I cudn't take the farm, not
if 't was iver so. I've 'nough land as 't is."

" That means you're afraid," the other retorted, hotly.
" You've got your orders, and daren't disobey. Eh ? "

Hurrish made no answer.

" It is inconceivable to me how respectable, well-
disposed men like yourself can let themselves be
made the cat's-paw of such a pack of scheming,
good-for-nothing rascals!" Mr O'Brien went on
with increased irritation—" fellows without a penny
to lose, who would throw you over like an old shoe
the instant you had served their turn! Come, pluck
up a little spirit, man, and defy them! You usen't
to be a coward. Look at me! They've been threatening death and destruction to me for the last two
years, and I don't see that I'm particularly the worse
for it."

Hurrish fixed his eyes where he was bidden, not without a discernible touch of pity, then shook his head again.

"Now, Meejar, sorr, sure don't ye know there's things a man can do, an' there's things he can't," he said, oracularly.

The Major this time was silent. He knew it well enough. His position and Hurrish's were not so utterly unlike but what a certain amount of fellow-feeling was inevitable. The reflection did not tend to make him any better contented.

"Very well, Brady has the farm," he said, curtly. "I shall let him know to-morrow."

Hurrish's face was by this time invisible, but his attitude was expressive. He stood still in the darkness, a formidable figure—big, black, and silently expostulatory.

Mr O'Brien experienced that uneasy sensation which we all know, even on less weighty occasions, when we reject some piece of advice, backed by shadowy, but none the less ominous, threats.

"It's a new thing for you to be so anxious upon Mat Brady's account," he said, irritably, as he turned and left the churchyard, Hurrish accompanying him a few yards behind. "How long have you and he been such friends, I should like to know?"

"I don't care a thawneen, no nor th' half ov a thawneen, what comes t' him," Hurrish answered, gloomily. "'Taint that I'm unaisy 'bout, anyway."

They were back on the walk now, and passing under the trees, through which a few white threads of light stole casually. When they reached the more open portion, Hurrish halted.

"I'll be wishin' yer anner good night, I'm thinkin'," he said, in his deep mellifluous brogue, rendered deeper than usual by his desire not to be overheard.

"Good night to you, Hurrish. Sorry I couldn't oblige you. You'll see me up at your house before very long."

"Thank yer anner. Good night, an' God save yer anner!"

When he went back to the house, Mr O'Brien was met by his old man-servant, who told him that the sub-inspector of police from Doocaher had called, and was waiting in the dining-room to speak to him.

Sub-inspector Higgins was a good-looking young gentleman of twenty-six or seven, whose dearest wish and dream of ambition had been to go into the army. This his father, a well-to-do London tradesman, had declined to allow of, but, as a compromise, had permitted his son to try for a commission in the Irish Constabulary, shrewdly suspecting that very little practical experience would suffice to cure him of any desire to continue wearing *that* uniform, while for any other it would by that time be too late. He was not, perhaps, what by very stern critics would be called quite a gentleman. Still, he was a harmless, well-meaning young fellow enough, and, under ordinary circumstances, Mr O'Brien would have been perfectly willing to show him every possible civility. Unfortunately, in one of their first interviews the young man had exhibited some of the importance of the newly-made jack-in-office, which the elder one had not unnaturally been

unable to stomach. As a magistrate, the police and
the police-officers were theoretically under his own
and his brother magistrate's orders. Practically,
however, it was not so. The head-inspector and
stipendiary magistrate, being the two officials directly
responsible to Government, were the two in whom
all real power was vested, the others being both
actually and visibly ciphers—not one of the least
vexatious of the many minor vexations of the
times.

"Good evening, Mr Higgins," he said, as he
entered the room and shook hands with his guest.
"A fine evening. You wanted to see me about
something, the servant said. Sit down. Take this
arm-chair."

"Yes, Mr O'Brien. I—ar—" the young man had
a very distinguished halt in his delivery—"I—ar—
called to speak to you about—ar—yourself."

"About myself!" Mr O'Brien's forehead and
eyebrows contracted suddenly. "Indeed! I am
sorry that you should be troubled about so unim-
portant a subject. What is it?"

"Well, the fact is, Sergeant Flynn has been complaining to me—complaining rather seriously, Mr
O'Brien. He tells me that he finds it absolutely
impossible to be answerable for your safety if you
persist in declining the escort which has been provided for you by the—ar—Government. Now I
put it to you, sir, as a—ar—former officer, is it fair
to subject those unfortunate men to the certainty of
a reprimand, and the—ar—probability of dismissal,
for a negligence which can scarcely, under the circumstances, be considered their—ar—fault?"

Mr Higgins had rehearsed this little address, and was not ill pleased with its effect. Upon Mr O'Brien the effect was exactly that of an application of mustard to a very sore spot. Three things especially offended him. First, the outrageous fact of a mere tenth-rate Government whipper - snapper like this young Higgins being in a position to lecture him— Pierce O'Brien of Donore—upon any subject whatsoever. Secondly, the undeniable fact that he *had* to some extent laid himself open to such an expostulation by his persistent evasion of his paternally provided protectors. Thirdly, the tone, air, and general delivery of the young man himself, which rendered that intolerable which under no circumstances would have been particularly palatable. If Mr Higgins had been an underbred and somewhat consequential young Irishman, the offence, though quite bad enough, would have been infinitely less; but being, unfortunately, a consequential and somewhat underbred young Englishman, the tone and accent with which the reproof was conveyed became part of the offence, and doubled its enormity. He endeavoured, however, to reply without visibly at least losing his temper.

"I am sorry to have to disagree with you, Mr Higgins; at the same time, I think you will admit that I am at least as good a judge of what is or is not necessary as you, with your very limited experience, can pretend to be," he said, quietly. "As you are probably aware, a considerable time has elapsed since any agrarian crime has been committed in this neighbourhood, and that being the case, if I —a native of the district—consider that the time

F

has also come when the inconvenience of a police
escort may be dispensed with, I really think that is all
that need concern any one, and so I shall make it
my business to inform the Government."

Mr Higgins in his turn was not a little nettled by
this reply. There was a touch of *hauteur*, particularly in the conclusion of it, which seemed to relegate
him from the position of the full-blown official to that
of the mere irresponsible under-strapper—naturally
offensive to a young man whose native self-im-
portance has latterly been fed with the sense of
authority.

" My acquaintance with Ireland is, as you say,
rather—ar—limited," he said, with a somewhat un-
successful air of indifference. " Under present circumstances I should hardly be likely to select it as
a place to come to for *pla-asure*, I must say. How
much worse it is capable of being I don't pretend
therefore to—ar—know ; all I can say is, that it
appears to me at present to be in a perfectly awful
condition. 'Pon my word and honour, perfectly
awful."

He really did *not* say " hawful," but the Cockney
inflexion was none the less perceptible.

Major Pierce O'Brien's temper, already pretty well
tried by the events of the evening, fairly boiled over.

" Then all *I* can say, Mr Higgins, is, that I wonder
you ever thought of coming to such an awful country." The " awful " was again a perceptible Cockney
awful. " As a native of that country, I am bound of
course to express my gratitude. At the same time,
I think you have really carried condescension far
enough, and might now, without loss of dignity, de-

vote your evidently brilliant talents to some more
congenial sphere of action. As regards my poor
safety, allow me to suggest, with all due deference
to your superior judgment, that that is a matter
which entirely and exclusively concerns *myself.* If
I prefer to run such risks as I may be exposed to in
this *hawful* country "—there was no disguise or
hesitation about the *h* now,—" rather than have the
annoyance which seems to be inseparable from the
present system of police protection, I have yet to
learn that I am not at liberty to do so. I am exceedingly sorry that you should have had the trouble
of coming here this evening upon so wholly unneces-
sary an errand. Mat, show Mr Higgins ' out.' "

Mr Higgins was shown out, and retreated with as
much dignity as was compatible with the somewhat
hasty nature of his exit. As he strode up the carriage road under the interlocking branches of laurel,
his mind was very nearly worked up to the point of
sending in his resignation. To have to live in an
odious climate, to put up with the most villanously
uncomfortable quarters, and to be called upon at any
moment to perform the most unpleasant offices,—all
this was surely bad enough. To be snubbed and
insulted into the bargain, merely because you dis-
charged an evident duty, was more than self-respect-
ing flesh and blood could be expected to bear !

His host meanwhile remained behind, boiling
over with unabated wrath. Oddly enough, it was
the slight to the country which chiefly infuriated
him ! " D——d Cockney whipper-snapper ! coming
and ventilating his twopenny-halfpenny insolence in
that fashion ! " he ejaculated. Yet this poor much-

abused Mr Higgins had said nothing surely half or
quarter as bad as he, Pierce O'Brien, had said a hundred thousand times over ?   True ; but then he was
a stranger, and that, it must be owned, made all the
difference.

The sense of country is a very odd possession, and
in no part of the world is it odder than in Ireland.
Soldier, landlord, Protestant, very Tory of Tories as
he was, Pierce O'Brien was at heart as out-and-out
an Irishman—nay, in a literal sense of the word, a
Nationalist—as any frieze-coated Hurrish of them all.
He was furious with himself that he had not, while
he was about it, given poor Mr Sub-inspector Higgins
even a yet more emphatic piece of his mind. " D——d
Cockney puppy !   But I'll make him smart for his insolence !   I'll report him, sure as my name is Pierce
O'Brien !   To come here and—and—and——"   So
he fumed to himself, there being no one else, unfortunately, to fume to.

His wrath, however, did not last long.   It evapor-
ated almost as quickly as it had arisen, and settled
down into a sort of moody discontent, the normal
condition of his mind of late.   After a while he began
even to reproach himself, not for having lost his temper, but for having done so under his own roof ; letting the other leave Donore in a fashion and under
circumstances which could hardly be called hospitable,
—Donore ! the very symbol formerly in Clare for hospitality !   He went back to the empty dining-room,
which he had left in the first exuberance of his anger,
lit a candle, and walked round the gloomy desolate
walls, looking at one thing after another, he hardly
knew why.   Then—setting the candle down upon

the mantelpiece—he stood with his back to the empty
fireplace, gazing in front of him, his forehead puckered
up into a fretwork of weary wrinkles. The old man-
servant, who had been to the hall-door, returned, and
started violently when he saw his master standing
thus, with a candle behind him and the windows
unshuttered, inviting—positively inviting—a chance
shot. Mr O'Brien stood still and watched, with a
mixture of vexation and pity, as the old fellow went
tremblingly round the windows, carefully shuttering
and barring each in succession, until darkness, pure
and unrelieved, had replaced the warm, widely diffused
summer twilight. It struck him that it was pretty
much what was happening to his own life !

"Poor old beggar ! evidently he too considers that
I require protection as long as I remain in this 'hawful' country," he said to himself grimly, as he took
up the candle again and went to wash his hands,
preparatory to sitting down to a solitary dinner.

CHAPTER VII.

MAURICE IS HURT BY ALLEY'S INGRATITUDE.

The appointed Wednesday came, and Maurice Brady
duly appeared at Hurrish O'Brien's cabin,—" herself "
(as the mistress of a house is always called in Ireland) being safe away at Donologue, where she had
gone in the ass-cart with the spring chickens. Those
poor spring chickens ! How they clucked, and cackled,

and fluttered their hapless wings before being deposited
at the bottom of that cart! It was a long way for
Maurice Brady to come, even with a lift part of the
way on the mail-car : he was in love, however—more
in love, perhaps, than he was himself aware—and the
obstacles recently set in the path of his passion had
tended to make him more consciously determined to
persevere with it than he had felt previously,—a
sensation experienced by other lovers before him.

Alley's beauty was certainly enough to tempt any
young man to obstinacy, especially one with ideas
above the standard of his contemporaries, and not
therefore to be affected by any want of appreciation
upon their part. It was odd how little the girl
seemed to realise it herself. It was as if the very
beginnings of vanity had never been born in her.
She was too humble-minded, dreamy, and nun-like,
for that sort of eager self-admiration which flows
spontaneously through so many young girls' veins,
and of which love itself, when it comes, is often only
the completion. It had been little fed by admiration either. From the bold admiring looks of passing
strangers she shrank with the instinctive modesty
both of her race and her own instincts ; and of the
little world around her, there were only two—Hurrish and Maurice Brady—who had ever even hinted
to her that she was handsome. There are no doubt
born nuns, just as there are born actors, or born viol-
inists, and the type is more often to be met with
amongst the pious peasant girls of the south and west
of Ireland, than perhaps in any other class or country
in the world. Alley had an elder sister who was a
nun in Galway, and until Maurice had asked her to

marry him, she had often thought that she would
like to join her, and to be one too.   Even as it was,
she sometimes thought with a wistful lingering regret
of the life.   It was so safe !   Poor Alley's being one
of those timorously sensitive natures to which the
horizon of fear will always be far, far wider than
that of hope.

She was simple-minded and ignorant beyond the
dreams of even the most simple-minded and the most
ignorant in more sophisticated regions.   She could
read, but except her national school lesson-books and
a few penny lives of the saints, she had hardly read,
or wished to read, a line ; as to newspapers, she would
not have glanced at one for the world.   She was exceedingly devout, and one of the bitterest trials of
her life was the impediments which old Bridget, with
specially vindictive malice, was fond of putting in the
way of her getting to mass upon a Sunday morning.
Food and the shelter of a home she had from Hurrish, but not a single possession that she could call
her own in the world.   The ordinary incitement,
therefore, to vanity of fine, or even what an English
or Scotch peasant would call decent clothes, she had
never had ; and except that her red flannel petticoat
was never ragged, and the coarse cotton bodices worn
with it scrupulously washed by herself, no beggar-girl
upon the high-road could have been more miserably
ill-clad.   This, however, she cared little about.   She
was inured to hardship.   That native asceticism, too,
which, under other circumstances, would have lent
itself easily to the imposed severities of any religious
order, helped her perhaps to bear the hardships of
her present lot.   She did not think about it, of course,

in that light, but it went towards making them seem
not only inevitable, but natural—a very different
thing.

When Maurice arrived, she was busily cleaning the
cabin, driving the dust before her through the open
door, to the surprise and evident indignation of an
elderly hen—the anxious mother of a large family—
who, tired with strolling over the rocks into the crevices of which her brood were inconveniently given to
dropping, had returned to the seclusion of the fireside,
only to find it in this state of revolution.

Alley, as it happened, had a turn for cleanliness,
though it was not often that she got a chance of in-
dulging her tastes in that direction, her poor little
attempts at orderliness being promptly nipped in the
bud by old Bridget, who—pronounced democrat as
she was in other respects—was a very conservative
of conservatives as regards household arrangements,
denouncing all variation from the traditional methods
as " thrash " and " thricks," not to be countenanced
for a moment by people who respected themselves or
the ways of their forefathers.

Young Brady found himself a three-legged stool,
and, placing it in the doorway, sat down, his legs clad
in well-fitting tweed trousers, stretched out with an
air of condescension across the threshold.   Little
Katty, the only child at home, had been bribed to
keep quiet during the sweeping by the temporary
loan of Alley's rosary—the one portable piece of property which the poor girl possessed—and was sitting
perched upon the low wall which surrounded the
little enclosure, running the red and white beads
through her fat baby fingers with all the self-

importance and apparent unction of some stout lady
abbess.

Everything in and about the house—even the
chickens and the weeds upon the roof—seemed rejoicing in the absence of the reigning tyrant.   There
was a sense of peace and comfort, even a vague touch
of beauty, about the little homestead to-day, which
was more due perhaps to the lovely cloud-dotted sky
and warm comforting glance of the sun than to anything more directly inherent to itself.   Over the fields
of rock around, the larks were singing jubilantly, one
now and then dropping with a sudden hush into some
gaping fissure, where, for lack of better lodgment, it
had made its nest, and was rearing a brood of callow
choristers.   A warm but boisterous and self-important
little breeze whisked round the house, astonished apparently to find anything standing against it.   It sent
the dust that Alley had swept outside whirling about
in little fantastic curves and spirals, finally settling
into a thick grey drift in one of the corners.   The old
hen had by this time returned, and was establishing
herself and family, with much chuckling volubility, in
the bottom of a broken chair, which had been half
filled with straw for their especial convenience.

Marvellous the amount of rubbish of one sort and
another accumulated within the compass of that one
small room!   Odds and ends of all sorts, domestic, agricultural, piscatorial ;—a broken harrow, past its work,
reared against the wall ; odd boots of Hurrish's, still
coated thickly with mud ; fishing tackle, and bits of
oars ; pans of milk which had been " set " for butter,
but out of which the cats and children were perpetually taking surreptitious sips.   Everything that any

member of the family had ever used in their whole
lives was probably to be found represented in some
corner or other. No one, however, except Alley, ever
thought that any of these things would be better put
away into receptacles of their own. Even Maurice
Brady—fastidious young man as he was in some
respects—regarded it all as perfectly natural, and was
not in the least offended or disconcerted by the utterly
inconceivable squalor of the whole arrangement.

This indifference to squalor—rather the admission
of it—is not certainly the pleasantest bit of duty
which falls to the lot of the modest chronicler of
peasant Ireland. Since it now and then has to be
faced, however, it is as well perhaps to do so steadily
and unshrinkingly, as we confront any of the other
hundred thousand not particularly pleasant facts of
life. Cleanliness and purity are words which admit,
too, of more than one meaning, it must be remembered, and some of those meanings are not necessarily
compatible with well - scoured floors and furniture
gleaming with hand-polish,—meanings which might
even not a little surprise those uncivilised ones to
whom the floor seems a far handier receptacle for
rubbish than a dust-bin, and who have no squeamish
prejudices against the indoor society of ducks, or a
cheerful, if vociferous, nursery of young pigs. When
all is said, however, we must leave the ill to work its
own cure. National idiosyncrasies are hard things to
mend, and exceedingly awkward ones to meddle with.
They yield, if they yield at all, very slowly—often
almost imperceptibly. " We cannot measure worlds
by rule, or put a continent to school," sings a poet of
to-day ; and perhaps even one small island may fairly,

therefore, decline to be lessoned save by the great
head-schoolmaster—Time.

Maurice Brady was certainly not thinking of national failings at that moment, nor was he even
thinking of his own budding ambition,—of the days
when he, too, would stand amongst his fellows in the
halls of Westminster, and fling the scornful defiance
of an Irish patriot in the very teeth of the foreign
tyrant.   He was thinking of a much prettier subject,
—namely, of Ally Sheehan's arms.   She had given
up her sweeping upon his appearance, and had taken
up a half-knitted blue stocking, destined for Hurrish,
the needles of which she was deftly moving to and
fro in her small slight hands.   They were unusually
delicately shaped hands, though as brown almost as if
dipped in walnut juice.   Higher up, however, where
her faded cotton sleeve had been pushed for the convenience of sweeping, a space of arm immediately
below the elbow—a space not usually exposed to the
sun and wind—was left visible, and no white rose-
bud petal could well have boasted a prettier colour.
The young man fixed his eyes upon it with an air of
approval.

" Some of these days see if I don't bring you a
dress, a real silk one, Alley," he said, in a tone of
lordly decision,—" a light green, perhaps, or maybe
one of those fashionable reds.   Dress you as you
should be dressed, and you'd take the shine out of
half the ladies that come to Miltown-Malbay, or Kilkee
either, that you would ! "

Alley blushed a little and held her head down,
pleased, but shy.   Though he was her lover, Maurice
was not usually prodigal of compliments.

"An' what ud I do 't all in a silk dress, Morry,
dear," she said in her gentle sing-song western tones,
so infinitely pleasanter to listen to than the hideous
gutturals of the opposite side of the island.

"Do?" Maurice grew quite excited at the thought.
"Begad, and there's plenty of things you'd do! Look
like a lady, born and bred,—as I mean. *my* wife to
look, I can tell you ; wear shoes and stockings every
day of your life,—the best to be had,—and gloves
too, and a hat or bonnet, with a veil, of course, when
you went out in the sun. And you'd have a satin
parasol,—a white one with a proper lining, and lace
that deep "—Maurice's haberdashery experience lent,
it will be observed, a certain amount of practical
detail to his imagination—" and your dress down to
the ground, and humped up so "—with a little necessary dramatic explanation—" for every lady, and
plenty that's not ladies at all, has it so ; and you'd
walk along beside of me, picking your steps carefully and pointing your toes *so*, and when the fellars
looked at you admiring like—as dozens would—
you'd just look over their heads, or to one side, so—
as much as to say that you wasn't aware they were
in it at all ! "

Alley burst into a peal of laughter — pretty,
silvery, ringing laughter—which rang through the
stony surroundings of the cabin, and made little
Katty look up at her playfellow with an air of
momentary astonishment on her rosy, dusty little
face.

"Arrah, Morry, dear, 'tisn't me 't all 't all, 'tw'd
be thin," she said ; " 'tis some gran' lady ye've seen
at Miltown yer thinkin' ov ! Sure how ud *I* know

how to wear a veil, or to put me toes *so?* 'Tis
laughin' at me y'ar!"

"Not at all, Alley." Maurice's expression showed
that he was in fact perfectly serious. "You don't
understand me, that's all!" (He had perceived that
in the enthusiasm of his last speech he had allowed
his rhetoric to run into somewhat native variations,
and was therefore additionally watchful now.) "Of
course you couldn't be expected to learn all these
things *at once,*" he went on condescendingly, "but *I*
should be there and able to train you, for I've
watched how ladies behave often and often, and
thought to myself,—'Alley Sheehan could give you
all a start, and beat you easy if she had her rights!'
Isn't that why I'm so *fond* of you?" he continued,
in an explanatory tone. "Sure, if 'twas money, or
that sort of thing I was thinking of, 'twouldn't be
yourself I'd look at, when you haven't a ha'porth—I
mean a pennyworth—good or bad in the world, as
you know very right well yourself."

This time Alley did not laugh. She sighed instead,
and let the stocking slide down upon her lap.

"But you've looks, and that's better," her lover
went on convincingly. "I'd rather have ye as you
are, than I'd have a common-looking girl with her
pockets full of gold—and 'tisn't many young fellars
in the country would say that!" he added, with not
unjustifiable self-exultation. "I'll be earning me
two pounds a-week before very long, and more than
that, too, in another way,—I'd tell you how, only
that you wouldn't understand me,—and then I'll
come or send for you, Alley, and marry you right
off; and we'll live in Limerick, or Dublin itself may-

be, and never come nigh these stupid old racks again,
or be bothered with any of the people, for 'tis sick
and tired to death of the sight of them I am!"

But Alley was not at all prepared for so heroic a
measure of transplantation.   On the contrary, a pang
of dismay, for which she could hardly herself account,
shot through her at the bare suggestion.

"Is it lave entoirely ?   Is it not see Hurrish 't all
't all ?   Och, Morry, sure I cudn't !   'Tud break me
heart out an' out !" she exclaimed, with sudden
panic.

Maurice Brady's brow clouded immediately.   His
expression, which had hitherto been all that was
complacently kind and protective, grew suddenly
hard and stern.

"That's a nice hearing for me, I must say !" he
exclaimed, angrily.   "To be told you're that set upon
Hurrish, that you wouldn't go away from where you're
so badly treated—not when it's to go along with *me* !
'Tis only what I might have expected, though.
Women are all like that.   No gratitude or feeling
in them at all at all,"—with the air of one deeply
versed in the ways of that perfidious sex.   "And *I*
that have been thinking of nothing but how soon I
could marry you, and get you away from it all, and
give you good clothes and mate—meat I mean—
every day, and every thing you could possibly want
or wish—and all at once to be told that you like
your rags and tatters and bits of potato-skin and
skilligolee—skim-milk—best !   If you hadn't told
me so yourself, I never would have *believed* it of you,
Alley—never !" he added, in a tone of high moral
reprobation.

Poor Alley was all penitence in a moment. Dis-
approbation from those she cared for was' like the
withdrawal of sunlight to a daisy,—it caused her to
curl up her petals and collapse immediately.

"Sure, Morry, I didn't mane to offind you," she
said, in a tone of deprecation, the tears beginning to
collect in her violet eyes and to fall upon the stocking in her hands. "I'd go anywhere 't all wid you,
—an' why not, iv course? But you see I'm only
a poor ignorant colleen, an' I get aisily dashed, not
bein' usted to shtrange people, or understandin' their
ways or gran' talk the way you do. Me heart seems
jist tied to the things I know—most of them, laste-
ways," with a recollection of old Bridget, to whom
even her gentle heart was not perhaps very warmly
tied. "I don't seem able to *think* even of goin'
away—not altogether. I'm like thim little yellar
shtrokes ye may see round the idges of the say-pools,
that go jumpin', an' hoppin', an' dancin', an' pullin'
away, as if they was wantin' to be flyin' aff all over
the country; an' all the while they niver gits raaly
away from the whater, an' I don't suppose they're
wantin' to, nayther."

"That's because you have no imagination, Alley,"
the young man answered promptly. "I'm not *blam-
ing* you for it, mind. If it isn't born in you, you
couldn't have it—not if you paid a hundred teachers
to learn you. Now I'm so different. Ever since
I was a little bit of a fellar I was always planning
and thinking and saying to myself, 'I'll do this, an'
I'll do that, when I'm growed a man.' And I'd lay
awake at night planning it all out—how I'd get all
the larnin'—learning, I mean—I could, and not mind

the botheration of it, becase it would all be wanted,
and more too, and I'd make friends with all the
shmart young fellars I met, and not be sticking to
the old ways—such as Hurrish and the rest of them
here 'bout does—but have an eye open to see what
was for me own good ; for there's a grand time coming entirely for shmart fellars in Ireland, Alley, I
tell you that—though 'tis little you understand, nor
would, I s'pose, if I was to talk from now till
to-morrow."

Poor Alley sighed, and was silent. The gulf of
inferiority which separated her from her brilliant
lover did indeed seem to her so wide as to be almost
impassable.   It frightened her, and made her wonder
whether he could really wish to marry her.   Surely
she would be nothing but an encumbrance to him.
He ought to marry one of those grand ladies whom
he had been describing, who came to Miltown-Malbay
or Kilkee for the bathing season, and who knew by
nature how to point their toes and all the rest of
those accomplishments which she could never, never,
she feared, acquire.   She had felt the same thing
often before, though seldom, perhaps, quite so acutely.
If at that moment he had told her that he had made
up his mind to throw her over, I almost suspect that
her first feeling would have been one of unconscious
relief.

Maurice, too, was silent—lost, perhaps, in a bea-
tific vision of future dignities to be attained to by
himself ; and in the stillness steps were heard coming
towards them—a pair of iron-bound boots striking
against the crisp edges of the rocks—and a minute
after Hurrish's big frame and broad genial face were

seen over the low wall encircling three sides of the cabin.

Katty—who had been getting desperately bored with her plaything—threw down the rosary disdainfully into the dust, and started off in a short scrambling run to meet him, clutching him tightly round the knees before he could get inside the enclosure, and throwing her whole baby weight against his legs.

Like all big mild men, Hurrish adored his children, and Miss Katty especially ruled over him like a despot.

"Well, Kitteen, ye tormint, an' what d'ye want wid yer da?" he asked admiringly, stooping down and picking her up in his arms. "Will I toss ye away an' be quit ov ye wance an' for all?"—pretending to throw her up on to the roof of the cabin, where a house-leek—emblem of good luck—reigned over a green forest of wild oats and nodding grass. "Luk where ye've thrown poor Alley's bades to, ye bad gurl," he added, stooping and picking them up. "For shame ov yer, Kitteen! 'Tis a big shtick ye want yer dada to cut for ye,—that's what yer after. Well, Morry, me bhoy, how's yerself?"

Young Brady responded with friendly warmth to Hurrish's greeting, and they talked together for a while. He did not care to stay much longer, however, now that the party was increased, so got up before long, saying that he must be off, as he had a long walk before him.

Hurrish thereupon went into the cabin, and returned with a bottle and a tumbler, which he proceeded to half-fill with unchristened—*i.e.*, unwatered

G

—poteen, explaining, as he did so, that he had got
it from Aranmore, where a barrel had lately been
landed by a friend of his under the very nose of the
Custom - house officers.   It was one of Hurrish's
idiosyncrasies—the most unaccountable of them to his
neighbours—that he rarely drank, and had never, it
was said, been known to be drunk in his life; though
this statement is so large a demand upon credulity,
that I rather hesitate to lay it before the reader.   Be
this as it may, to allow a guest to leave your roof
without offering him a glass of anything would have
been a high indecorum, not to speak of being the
worst luck possible—a consideration which he was
the last man in Ireland to disregard.

CHAPTER VIII.

THE BREATH OF CELTIC ELOQUENCE.

The poteen was excellent, and Maurice Brady
sipped it with slow enjoyment.   He was no more of
a drunkard than Hurrish, but he had a native liking
for anything that was good of its kind, and—decent
wines being unattainable—was necessarily a con-
noisseur in whisky.   He refused another glass, however, and got up, saying that he must be off.

Hurrish proposed to accompany him as far as the
turn to Miltown-Malbay, having something to see to,
he said, at Tubbamina.

The parting between the lovers was rather cold,

though Hurrish discreetly retired to put away the bottle, and remained inside long enough to have emptied three or four had he been so minded. Maurice was loftily offended, while Alley was in a state of trembling alarm and apprehension, fearing to offend, and yet not knowing how to avoid doing so.

When at last Hurrish came back there was no further delay, and the two men walked off together in the direction of the sea. They did not, however, cross the rocks at the narrowest point, but kept away for some distance to the south, until they came out again upon the edge at another point where the cliffs were higher, and almost vertical. Here, by mutual consent, they paused, and stood for a few minutes looking down at what lay below them.

It was worth looking at! Not that these were by any means the finest cliffs in Clare,—not to be compared, for instance, to the cliffs of Moher a few miles farther down, which lift their seven hundred and fifty feet of rock perpendicularly above the waves. For all that, it was such a cliff and such a scene as in any other part of the kingdom would have made the fortune of every fly-owner and inn-keeper within a radius of twenty miles. In Clare, however, people are used to cliffs, and do not, apparently, think much of them, its visitors preferring Lisdoonvarna, where there are no cliffs, but several brand-new hotels, and springs said to be excellent for lumbago, and where you can have the height of good eating, and drinking too, if your tastes incline that way. Three hundred feet below the ends of their toes the gulls were sitting by myriads—grey feathers upon grey rock — not to be distinguished,

save by a very practised eye. Higher up, where the
rocks were more friable, puffins squatted in colonies,
each before a hole which he had scraped for himself.
Lower, the outlying rocks and skerries were black or
brown with cormorants, stretching lean necks, and
gazing ravenously upon the water, green as their
own eyes. Beneath all these again the dark heaving
surface was mottled and traversed in every direction
by moving reticulations of white, broad in some
places as the sails of a man-of-war, attenuated in
others until they were no thicker than the thinnest
of thin threads, rising and falling, sweeping rhyth-
mically hither and thither, under the impulse from
below. The wet rocks took the sun's rays upon their
glittering sides ; the spray rose in the air like the
dust of a submarine explosion, and fell again with a
thud that was like the fall of many fortresses, drain-
ing away through their twenty thousand mouths, and
streaming back to sea, to be promptly caught and
sent back upon the same errand again and again, and
over and over again.

Familiar as it was to both of them, neither of
the two men was wholly indifferent to the scene.
Hurrish drew a long breath, and his eyes grew dim
and misty. Maurice's, on the other hand, brightened,
and his hands clenched, as the warm west wind sent
its strong elixir through his veins, and breathed encouraging promises into his ears,—promises big with
coming realisation. It seemed to. him as if whole
fleets of good things were being floated in from the
West—the Land of Promise—fleets of which " shmart
young fellars " like himself would be the captains, as
by nature and reason they ought to be, able to turn

all opposing old fogies overboard, or string them up
to the yard-arms if need were. He was an orator
by nature as well as by calculation, and he felt that
this wind inspired him. What a tide of eloquence,
what illustrations, what denunciations, what gor-
geously decorated hopes and anticipations, flooded his
brains and rose to his lips as he stood drinking in that
warm west wind — very breath of Celtic eloquence!
If he had had a crowd about him at that moment,
he thought excitedly, begad, how he *could* have
spoken! how he could have thundered against the
"enemy"; what "argiments" he could have used—
arguments, it need hardly be said, addressed exclusively to the imagination,—so much larger and more
interesting a field to work upon than any dull plod-
ding faculties which demand that the arguments addressed to *them* should be proved, or, at any rate,
provable. It really seemed a wicked waste of a
magnificent opportunity.

Hurrish's thoughts had meanwhile got diverted to
less heroic and more concrete objects. A little to
the left of where they were standing, a narrow zigzag
path led down to a small saleen—*anglicè*, little creek
—famous for the supply of seaweed which collected
there after every storm. A woman was coming up
this path with a "kish" of oar-weeds and bladder-
wracks upon her shoulders, which she had been
collecting below. The last bit of the ascent was very
steep, and the poor creature was evidently nearly
worn out. Her face, bathed in perspiration, was expressive of a perfect agony of exhaustion. With a
sudden ejaculation, Hurrish ran down to meet her,
and, bidding her turn round, took the kish off her

back, and carried it in his hands to the top of the
cliff. Even for his strength it was a considerable load.

"That was Marty O'Kelly's wife over from Tullalogue," he said, when the poor woman, with many
thanks, had again taken up her load and trudged
away. "You wudn't think it to luk at her, but siven
year since she was as purty an' nate a gurl as ye'd
wish to see—not a spryer at a jig nor a riddier at a
wake in Clare! 'Tis a crool hard life on the women
hereabouts, an' no mistake, God help thim!" he
added, pityingly.

Maurice merely nodded. His thoughts were otherwise engaged, and he did not care to have them
diverted to such uninteresting details as these.

"I'll be oncommon glad when you're married t'
Alley an' took her away wid yer," Hurrish went on.
"She's too dilicate an' purty for this work entoirely.
Tis thim sort gives in first, and gits bated an' ould.
'Twud jist break the heart in me, so 't wud, if I seen
poor little Alley lookin' all nohow and draggledy like
that a one"—pointing to the retreating figure of Mrs
Marty O'Kelly, of whom only a very short red petti-
coat, two lean brown heels, and a mountain of wet
seaweed, was visible.

For several reasons Maurice Brady felt aggrieved
by this speech. For one thing, it jarred unpleasantly
with that high tide of sentiment upon which he had
been floating so buoyantly, and seemed to drag him
back to the mud and shallows of unilluminated everyday life. It brought back, too, the recollection of that
start and look of dismay with which Alley had
greeted his proposal of transplantation, and the double
irritation found vent in his reply.

"You seem in a tremendous great hurry to get rid
of Alley this afternoon, whatever the reason is!" he
said irritably. "I'm sure, if I saw my way to taking
her away at once, I'd do it, and be delighted. '*Tis*
hard, I suppose, on a man feeding and lodging a girl
that's no blood kin of his own, and so, I'll be bound,
Alley feels too; but, please God, 'twon't be for long
now."

Hurrish's broad face reddened with sudden anger.
"Is it wantin' to be *rid* of her ye think I am?" he
said, in a tone of sterner displeasure than the good-
natured fellow had often been known to show before.
"Ye niver made a greater mistake in all yer life if ye
think *that*. 'Twud be like a man wantin' to throw
away a little juwl that had come and pinned itself
to his breast—he'd need be a born fool, or hav the
divil's own black heart, 'ud do sich a thing. An' ye
talk of her aitin'! Poor Alley! 'twudn't make the
difference of a full-growed chicken an' a pullet all
she'd ate wan way or t'other in the day, God hilp
her! 'Tis her own swate self I'm thinkin' of, that
niver complains, but wark, wark from marnin' to
noight, an' allays a smoile for ivery wan! T'ull be
loike pullin' the very heart out ov me brist to let her
go; but sure, a man wud be no betherer nor a baste
that 'ud think ov himsel' and not of a swate crather
that's no more fit for harsh tratement nor the flowers,
nor to be mixed up wid common folks 't all!"

Maurice Brady felt a momentary twinge of discomfort, almost shame—a most unusual sensation.
He was even visited by a passing suspicion that
Hurrish's view of the matter might be the higher,
on the whole, of the two. He shook it off, however,

by saying to himself that Hurrish was so stupid and
narrow-minded, he always took you to mean something entirely different from what you really did,—
it was sheer waste of time talking to him. Of course,
he must have Alley's interest more at heart than any
one else. Wasn't he going to marry her—bring her
up to his own level—make a "lady" of her ? What
stronger proof of affection could any man give than
that ?

The two men parted soon after this,—Maurice retracing his steps along the top of the cliff, skirting
the heights of Moher, where the Hag's Head rose
dark and threateningly against the sky, then rounding the grass slopes of Liscanor Bay, past Lehinch,
to the greener and more commonplace stretch of country where Miltown-Malbay stands. Several times, in
the course of his walk, Hurrish's words recurred to
his mind, and each time with a fresh sense of annoyance. Hurrish ! it really was too absurd ! The idea
of a fellow like that affecting to have finer feelings
and a tenderer regard for Alley than himself ! The
idea was simply intolerable !

It was so intolerable that it was fortunately easy
to prove that it was impossible, and before he had
reached his destination Maurice had quite got over
his temporary self-annoyance, and, as a consequence,
had almost forgiven Hurrish. He was not a bad
creature in his way, he admitted, and had a very
proper appreciation for those above him ; but when
he came to talk of anything beyond his cows and
potatoes—really it *was* laughable. He wondered
now at himself for having listened with so much
patience.

On going into his lodgings he found a couple of
friends waiting for him, who at once began eagerly
talking about a report that had come down from
Dublin as to the chance of an election then pending.
Maurice was regarded as quite the "coming man" in
the political circles of Miltown-Malbay and Lehinch.
His gift of speaking gave him that sort of direct influence which—common as that gift is—it never fails to
procure amongst his countrymen, who, like the Athen-
ians of old, live mainly by their ears.   He was brimful,
too, of all the socialism of the day, knew all the latest
catch-words, and was a *doctrinaire* of quite the most
advanced type.   Though he had declined—chiefly
from prudential notions—to join any of the secret
societies established in the neighbourhood, he was
upon friendly terms with most of their wire-pullers
—more courted, in fact, than if he had actually committed himself.   To a young man with not much to
lose and a great deal to hope for, a state of social
ferment, of "veiled" rebellion, is undoubtedly a highly
commendable state of affairs.   To the old, the timid,
the owners of the perishable goods of this world, it
may be a source of bitter trouble, anxiety, and consuming terror, but certainly not to him.   Maurice
perceived this fully, and had often reflected that the
revolutionary elements afloat in the country made it
—despite some self-evident drawbacks—a much more
promising field for a "shmart fellar" who knew what
was what, and had thoroughly realised his own good
points, than a more settled and less fluctuating social
condition would probably have been.   In this sense, and
to this extent, he was unquestionably and unreservedly
patriotic.

CHAPTER IX.

AN UGLY NEIGHBOUR.

Meanwhile the position of affairs between Hurrish and the elder Brady was growing daily worse and worse. The rate at which hatred increases and develops, under favourable circumstances, has apparently never yet been scientifically ascertained; it increases, at any rate, not arithmetically, but geometrically, like the germ in the yeast, or the aphis on a rose-bush, which was one yesterday and is a million millions to-day. Take an originally brutalised one-idea'd nature, without a restraining influence of any sort —even the jail and the hangman—and plant in that nature the seeds of a hatred, the object of which it is continually being brought into contact with, and the result will startle even those who believe themselves experts in the darker capabilities of our poor humanity. Mat Brady's hatred of Hurrish dated from years back: he could hardly perhaps himself have said how or why it began, but everything that had happened since had gone to foster it.

That this result was not a little helped on by the raw whisky in which he habitually soaked himself needs no telling. Acting upon an originally amiable foundation, drink excites chiefly to maudlin sentimentality, rarely to violence. Acting upon a brutal foundation, it arouses the blackest of animal passions, which grow and grow until the drunkard himself becomes the mere slave of them, and differs little, if at all, from the homicidal madman. To injure Hur-

rish in some way, to have him in his grip, to wreak
his vengeance upon him, was his one thought night
and day; he lived upon it, ate, slept, breathed, and
grew drunk upon it. In this direction his ordinarily
sluggish nature was even spurred to activity, tortures
unknown to Ojibeway Indians, or the familiars of the
Inquisition, flattering his dreams and exciting his
waking thoughts—tortures which he had inflicted, or
was about shortly to inflict, upon the unconscious
Hurrish. That these imaginings would long ago have
been turned to reality is unquestionable, but for one
deterring fact. Mat Brady—sot though he was—
was enormously strong, capable of fighting any two
other natives of Tubbamina. Hurrish O'Brien, however, was stronger still, and could easily have thrashed
two Mat Bradys—had, indeed, already administered
condign chastisement on more than one occasion,—as,
for instance, when that amiable person had waylaid
poor little Alley Sheehan, and frightened her half out
of her innocent life, from sheer spite of her protector.
Then indeed Hurrish's wrath had not been slack, nor
his hand slow to smite !

Even the neighbourhood of Tubbamina—not a cen-
sorious region as regards violent crimes—was scandalised by Mat Brady's excesses. He had not atoned
either for his failings in this direction by any marked
virtue in another. His ill-temper and brutish mis-
anthropy had kept him from sharing the predominant
excitements and dangerous councils of his neighbours.
He was not a member of any secret society—nay,
was even suspected of having been more than once
tampered with by the enemy, though of this there
was no actual proof.

What more perhaps than anything else infuriated
him with Hurrish, was the indifference with which,
as a general rule, that good-natured individual regarded
his proceedings.   Toleration is not at all an Irish
characteristic, and is perhaps the mental attitude
which an Irishman of the baser sort least endures or
forgives in an antagonist.   Abuse him, curse him—
he answers you with curses readier and more fluent
than your own, then goes his way, and forgets the
matter.   Pass over his attack in pity or contempt,
and he will bear you a grudge to the last hour of
your life.

His determination to take the vacant Maloney
farm had originated wholly in the desire to come to
close quarters with his enemy,—hate of this burning
kind, like love itself, not easily brooking distance from
its object.   That farm " marched " with Hurrish's ;
and the opportunities which a possessor of it would
enjoy for harming and generally annoying that hated
individual, filled his soul with spasms of ferocious
delight.   That he already occupied more ground than
he was capable of working, and that the farm—even
at the low rent at which it was offered—would be a
loss rather than a gain to him, was nothing.   Such
trifling considerations were not even weighed in the
balance.   Mat Brady would have parted with every
shilling he possessed in the world, and have brought
himself to the workhouse or the emigrant-ship, if by
that means he could only at last have wreaked his
rage upon Hurrish.

They were not safe times for a man—no matter
with how purely private a motive—to take a farm
from which another had been evicted.   No popu-

larity, no previous reputation for virtue or patriotism, would have made it a safe proceeding, and Brady had neither popularity nor virtuous reputation to intercede upon his behalf. The very day after he had formally taken possession, and had had his cattle driven into their new pasture, an enormous skull and cross-bones were found rudely daubed in black and white upon the wall which divided his old and new farm; and stepping out of his cabin-door early the following morning, he had all but stumbled into a sinister-looking trench, dug in the night across the path, and almost touching the threshold. It was as significant as the unstrung bow-string of the Chinese emperor, and not less likely to be followed by serious consequences.

With the one-idea'dness of your thorough-going hater, Brady set down both these demonstrations solely to Hurrish's account. Hurrish hated him; Hurrish would do anything to spite him; Hurrish, he was convinced, would kill him if he could; the only chance of preventing him from doing so, was by himself first killing Hurrish,—the whole question, to his mind, narrowed itself to that.

Like every Irishman of his class—whether Coercion Acts are in force or whether they are not—he had an old gun hidden away in the thatch of his cabin. This gun he now took down, and occupied his leisure moments in cleaning, scouring, and oiling it, and preparing bullets out of stray bits of old lead laid by with some such purpose. He even took the trouble of carrying it one afternoon under his coat to the top of Lug-na-Culliagh, the conical-shaped hill in which the valley ended, and there, safely

shrouded by the loneliness, practising at a patch of
lichen on a rock, so that, when the occasion arose,
his hand might be safe and his revenge sure.

All this he was able to do with the more ease that
he was quite alone in the cabin—his ferocious temper
rendering it impossible for any one else to inhabit it
with him, even had he desired such company. His
brother was away at Miltown-Malbay; the two men
whom he employed upon the farm had cabins of their
own; even the beggars, who find gratuitous food and
lodging at every cabin they pass, hurried silently past
Mat Brady's door, so effectively had his brutal reputation shielded him from demands which no poverty,
however abject, is held in Ireland to be any excuse
from exercising.

When his day's work was over, he got into the
habit of every evening betaking himself to that group
of ruined oratories which, as the reader will remember, lay upon the verge of the two farms, and there,
coiled up in one of the cells built for the purposes
of devotion, with his loaded gun held between his
knees, he would spend long hours watching, waiting,
on the mere chance of some accident bringing his
hated enemy within his reach.

More than once he fell asleep at his post, and
awoke in the grey of the morning, cramped, miserable,
a prey to all the horrors of the habitual drunkard
who, for some purpose, abstains for a while from the
familiar demon. Even then, however, hate triumphed,
and seizing his gun, he would crawl out of his refuge
into the nipping night air, and stride backwards and
forwards over the rocks, his eyes sweeping to and fro
in the darkness, hungry, as the eyes of a wild beast

are hungry, when it fails to secure its prey. Twice he went down and watched the O'Briens' cabin all night, crouched in the shelter of the little " bohereen " that ran at the back of it. No opportunity, however, arose ; Hurrish never appeared, and he was obliged, when daylight came, to withdraw, cold, cramped, wretched, and fuller of hatred than ever, to the shelter of his own cabin.

While he was occupying himself in this cheerful fashion, his own doom had been decided upon. Several farms had lately been reoccupied in the neighbourhood ; an example, therefore, was badly wanted, and an example, it was decided, was to be made of him. He knew the penalty ; he had chosen to act in opposition to it ; nothing surely could be simpler or more conclusive. Between the judicial sentence and the carrying out of an execution there is apt, however, to be some delay. Brady was an exceedingly awkward individual to meddle with, and there was a general feeling, even amongst the men who clamoured loudest for his punishment, that some one else ought to be the person to carry out the sentence. Why Andy Holohun didn't do it, Peter O'Flanagan, for instance, couldn't possibly imagine. Andy was always talking of his hatred of land-grabbers, and here was a land-grabber ready to his hand, yet he showed no disposition to grapple with him ; while Andy was equally astonished at the un-accountable backwardness of Peter. So scandalous a want of public spirit as was exhibited on that occasion at Tubbamina has rarely, in fact, been paralleled in the history of Ireland !

Maurice, as it happened, had been away from Clare

during this exciting time, having been sent to Limerick
by the shop to which he belonged to select light goods
for the approaching season, and it was not therefore
until his return that he learnt what was on foot.
When he did so, his wrath was great, and was
directed chiefly against Hurrish, whom he held to
be mainly responsible for this fresh outburst of
popular feeling against his brother. If *Hurrish*
would have left him alone, he said to himself, other
people would have done so too. The latter was
engaged a few days later in digging bait in the
Donologue saleen, preparatory to an afternoon's fishing, when, chancing to look up, he saw Maurice
coming towards him over the sands. The young
man looked excited and fierce. His face was paler
than usual, and his red moustache twirled danger-
ously.

"What's this, Hurrish, 'bout you and Mat?" he
began at once, in a tone of violent displeasure.

Hurrish paused in his digging, and stood still
staring at him with unfeigned astonishment.

"I dunno as there's anythink *par*ticular, Morry,"
he said mildly, resting one foot upon the spade while
he leaned his weight upon the other.

"Anything particular! Why, I'm told there's
been a meeting over at Tullalogue at the Harp of
Erin, and a gun bought, and the lots drawn, and all,
and 'tis you as is to do the job on him."

Hurrish opened his eyes. "Is it a *killin'* job ye
mane?" he inquired. "Not batin', nor frightenin',
nor the loikes ov that, but killin' out an' out?"

"Killing? Of course; what would I mean but
killing? Much Mat would care for anything else."

"Then 'tis the biggest lie iver was tould—as big as th' ould Bull Rock out there," Hurrish said, slowly. "Sure I haven't been nigh th' Harp of Irin this month o' Sundays, nor don't mane nayther. That affeer of poor Buggle turned me stomack—so 't did."

Maurice Brady's wrath was brought to a sudden standstill. He had come over from Miltown-Malbay in a towering rage, determined to have it out with Hurrish; no one should meddle with *his* brother with impunity! Now, however, he was puzzled. Hurrish was no liar. His manner, too, was quite inconsistent with the theory of his having made up his mind to avenge his own and the community's wrongs upon the common enemy. It was neither hilarious nor yet morose, the two invariable concomitants of such a resolution.

"'*Tis* true all the same, then, whatever you may say," he answered, doggedly. "It was one as was there that told me all about it."

"An' how *cud* it be true, Morry, avick, whin I tell you 'tis the first word good or bad I've heard of it, an' have no more intintion of shootin' him aither nor ov shootin' me own mother? Not but what he desarves it," he added, parenthetically.

Maurice turned and walked a few steps off, irritably kicking aside as he did so the small round worm-casts which mottled the sand.

"Look you here, Hurrish, and mind now what I'm saying," he said at last, turning round and speaking in that tone of authority which he had latterly begun to assume with his older companion; "I wouldn't have any one think I was forgetful—not obliged, I mean, for anything you did for me when I was a gos—

H

when I was a boy. At the same time, I tell you
plainly, if you or any one else, I don't care who the
devil 'tis "——(he was working himself up into fresh
anger by this time)—"has hand, act or part, in
meddling with *my* brother Mat, sure as God is above
us I'll have his life ! If there's justice in Ireland, or
out of it, I'll hang him !—God, I will. I've taken
an oath to do it, and I'm not one to go a-breakin' *my*
oaths. Sure as we're standin' here, I'll do it, so now
I've given you fair warning. Friend or enemy, it
don't make no matter to me ; I'll have his life. No
one shall have it to say that he killed Maurice
Brady's brother, and that he stood by and put up
with it ; I'd die rayther than have such a thing said."

There was no affectation about this violence. Cool-
headed as he was, there were certain things which
moved him strongly. Mat *as* Mat he cared little
about, but Mat as *his* brother was a sacred object,
and any one who laid hands on it should assuredly
feel the weight of his revenge.

Hurrish drove the spade which he was still holding in his hands into the sand, and left it standing
there. He, too, was considerably excited by the
other's passion. It did not anger him as he would
have been angered by most men's violence ; on the
contrary, he respected the young fellow for taking
his brother's part, sot and irreclaimable savage though
he was. He did not say, as a harsher or more experienced critic might have done, that it was because
Mat Brady was *his* brother—that he belonged to him
—that the young man's egotism was so rampant, that
it extended to anything that touched himself, however little he might care for it personally ; he simply

gave him credit for his spirit, and for his sense of
family obligation—a trait which always wins respect
in Ireland. If at that moment he could have made
Mat Brady's life absolutely safe, for Morry's sake he
would have done so, despite his own quarrel with
that most obnoxious of Calibans. He did not see,
however, that there was any way in which such a
consummation could be accomplished.

"The buoys is terrible sot agin him, there's no
denyin' that, Morry," he said, scratching his head
seriously with an air of reflection. "Though I've
had nought to do wid their meetin's, I've hard talk
'bout the country—plinty. 'Tis an essample they
say 's wanted—lastways, that's what big Moriaty—
him that's back from 'Mericay — says. No good
won't be got for Oireland 't all widout thar's more
essamples. Dades an' not words is what's wantin',
and that's what the Laigue's wantin' too, he says."

"Then he's a d——d fool, and they're all a pack
of d——d blundering savages, that's what they are!"
the young man burst out fiercely. "Mustn't *I* know
what the Laigue—the League—wants better nor
they do?—ignorant beasts! I that am hand and
glove with Mulcahy Donallen, that's own cousin to
Mr Egan, and as safe to be returned for Ballyna-
garaty at the next election as if he was sitting in
it! 'Tis the blunderingest thing ever a set of fools
did, murdering here, and murdering there—and what
for? Nothing but just their own spite and folly and
devilments! Much they think of the Cause, the
bletherin' idiots! If *they* was to be put out of it,—
strung up here in a row, and only the decent *sinsible*
men left,—it would be about the best thing could

happen to the country, and so you may tell them,
with my compliments."

(Maurice's eloquence, it will be observed, had for
the moment entirely got the better of his newly
acquired phraseology. But what eloquence, it may
be asked, is worth a rush that does not do so?)

Hurrish scratched his head again, puzzled, yet
carried away by his companion's rhetoric.

" Well, Morry, ye knows more about it nor I do,
that's sartain," he said, in a tone of conviction; "an'
if the Laigue 'ud only give out the word to have no
more bloodshiddin', nor maimin' ov baists, nor frightenin' ov women, nor nothink ov that sort all over the
country from this day out, there's not a buoy 'ud be
gladderer nor meself, so thar wudn't. An' as to
what ye say 'bout Mat, ye may make yer moind
aisy so far as I'm concarned. Me an' Mat has niver
got on yit, an' we're not loikely for to begin for to
do so now; but as far as his loife goes, 'tis as safe for
me as if he were th' holy Father—God forgive me
for sayin' such a thing! Cum what may, I'll not
forget he's your brother, Morry, me buoy; for there
was ner a one I warmed to yit as I warmed t' you.
An' why not?—you that was loike a chilt ov me
own, in an' out allays, and that cute and cliver wid
yer tongue, 'twas a wunder; didn't I allus say from
the furst ye'd be a gran' man? We mayn't be jist
so thick now," Hurrish added, after a pause devoted
to reminiscence; " 'taint surprisin', so much as ye've
larned, and such a gintleman born as ye look—
speakin' so foine, 'tis a wonder t' hear ye—still for
me yer the same, Morry dear, an' wud be if ye was
the King ov all Oireland! An' as to threatenin' t'

hav me hung, an' the loikes ov that, sure I know 'tis
the last thing ye mane ! 'Taint *that* 'ud be stoppin'
me anyhow, but the thought that 't 'ud be displasin'
to you, an' t' Alley too, since what's yours is hers.
Wudn't I cut off me own head, an' gladly too, 'fore
I'd hurt aither the one or th' tother of ye ? "

Maurice made no immediate reply to this unusual
effort of oratory upon Hurrish's part. His anger
was too fresh to subside readily. He was somewhat
mollified, however, by the other's words. He had
always been proud of his influence over this big, hot-
tempered, warm-hearted fellow, whom everybody in
the neighbourhood was more or less in awe of on
account of his strength, in spite of its being qualified
by his ordinarily easy-going disposition. Latterly, it
is true, there had been more irritation than compla-
cency in his relations towards him—a sort of indul-
gence and forbearance on Hurrish's part, which
grated at times against his pride. He had a feeling
that Hurrish under no conceivable circumstances
could be afraid of him, and Maurice was a man who
liked to feel that he could inspire awe. He was
annoyed too about Alley. Jealousy, under the circumstances, was, he assured himself, out of the question ; still he felt irritated. That look of dismay with
which his plan of transplantation had been received
by her kept constantly recurring, and there were not
wanting other incidents which showed Hurrish's influence to be greater than he considered it ought to
have been. In the end, however, he made up his
mind to accept the latter's assurances—provisionally,
at all events.

" All right, Hurrish, I'll take it as you say," he

said, in a tone of somewhat condescending gracious-
ness. " I know you're fond of me, and, unless you
were led away, you would not wish, I'm sure, to do
anything that was displeasing to me. Shake hands."

They shook hands—Hurrish melted, on his side,
almost to tears by Maurice's goodness. It gave him
the keenest delight to think that all was once more
smooth between them. He had an admiration,
amounting to absolute worship, for the other, which,
when it inspires an older for a younger man, is probably far stronger and more deeply rooted than the
other way. He was in a state of the wildest and
most uproarious satisfaction all that evening, which,
but for his known sobriety, might fairly have given
rise to the most injurious suspicions. Poor Hurrish!
His satisfaction was not long-lived, but, at least, it
was warm and glowing for the time it lasted. While
we are about it, let us, above all else, give thanks for
that veil which hangs between us and our nearest
future. Were it to be lifted—nay, but an inch or
two—how many of us, I wonder, could confidently
confront our pillows this evening ?

CHAPTER X.

HURRISH'S CRIME.

It was the day of the half-yearly fair at Ballyvaughan, the metropolis, in some sort, of the Burren.
Like a good many other metropolises, it is not par-

ticularly conveniently situated as regards that area
of which it is the nucleus. Lying upon the sea-
shore to the extreme north of the region, it suggests,
and is, a fishing much more than an agricultural
centre. The straggling single street sloping directly
down to the harbour consists of some three or perhaps four dozen whitewashed structures, the more
important ones slated, the rest thatched and over-
topped in summer with a gorgeous nodding crown of
wild-flowers—sedums, poppies, snapdragons—town-
gardens of a distinctively Irish pattern !

Hurrish had some calves to dispose of, and had
brought them overnight to Ballyvaughan, their
chance of a good sale being naturally better if not
previously overtired. Feeling uneasy towards evening as to what might be taking place at home with
Mat Brady so close at hand, and himself away, he
left the calves in charge of Lep and a herdsman, and
walked all the way back to his cabin, arriving there
about midnight, and starting again by cock-crow next
morning.

Early as it was, every one was astir to give him
his stirabout, and see him off. Little Katty came
toddling across the floor from the other room, half-
naked, and rosy with sleep, and seized him by the
flap of his coat, as he sat upon a low stool hastily
devouring that satisfying condiment.

" Dada, bring Katty sugey-shtick," she whispered,
rubbing her little rough head, like some small tame
animal, against his sleeve, and looking up in his face
with an insinuating grin.

It was an appeal which Hurrish, even at his
busiest, could never resist. He picked Miss Katty

up on his knee, and gave her a mouthful of the
stirabout, by way perhaps of an instalment.

"Sugey-shtick indade! git out wid ye, yer im-
perint Kitteen," he said, admiringly. "D'ye think
yer dada has nought to do but be goin' round the
town gettin' you sugar-shticks! Be aff this instant
minute,"——he set her down and got up himself,
taking his blackthorn from where it was lounging
at ease against a corner of the wall as he passed.

Katty however was not to be daunted. With a
crow of delight, she trotted after him to the door,
where she again repeated her demand, laying hold
of the formidable blackthorn as she did so to
enforce it.

"Alley, Alley Sheehan! Och, Alley, cum quick!
I'm helt! I'm cotched! sure I won't be able to get
away to Ballyvaughan the day! Kitteen's a
houldin' ov me!——Och, wirrastrue, wirrastrue, what
will I do at all, at all?" he exclaimed, pretending to shake the stick violently, while the child
capered and shrieked with delight at the other
end of it.

Alley ran to the rescue, and picked up Katty, still
capering and shouting, in her arms. Hurrish, however, delayed yet a minute longer to kiss the little
red and brown face thus brought nearer to a level
with his own.

"Maybe I'll be seein' Morry over beyant," he
whispered, with a glance towards his mother, who
was still by the fire. "Have ye ere a bit ov
message for him, Alley 'cushla?"

Alley did not immediately answer. She twisted
the stocking she had been knitting around the

needles, so as to keep their points from Miss
Katty's wriggling pink legs, and looked down.

" I dun know as I have, Hurrish, an' I dun know
as he'd care 'bout wan aither," she said, not coquettishly, but seriously.

Hurrish looked disturbed.

" Blur an' agers, Alley, don't be sayin' sich things !"
he said, in a tone of eager remonstrance.   " Sure the
pore buoy luvs ye as he luvs his own sowl ! he luvs
yer very shady on the rocks, as any wan wid half an
oye can see.   Yer thinkin', I s'pose, he's a bit heady
these toimes—that's what's in yer moind.   But after
all what wonder ?—so much as he's thought ov—
ivery wan in the whole counthry rinning afther him,
an' consultin' wid him !—Sure if he wasn't a troifle
'bove hisself 't wud be *onnatural*.   But he's the good
heart Morry has, an' that's at the bottom ov all.
He's not loike one ov thim darty *bodaghs*, so sit up
whin they get a bit 'bove thimselves that there is no
holdin' thim—loike an ass-cart wid a new sate, that
takes itself for a coach-and-four—that proud, the
spalpeens, they wudn't shtop and spake to the
mother that bore thim !   But Morry's not that sort,
divil a bit.   He's the good heart, an' that's iverything
in this mortial world ! "

Alley sighed.   Hurrish must know best, she
thought, but still —

" The fact is, yer altogether too young an' ignarant,
Alley, to ondershtand the granjeur there is in Moray,
an' that's the truth," Hurrish went on, in a tone of
lofty superiority.   " There is not the aqual of him
in Clare—no, nor in twinty counties round, so there
isn't.   He'll be a gran' man yet, as I've telled ye

offen, jist you wait an' see if he isn't—the top an'
king of thim all! An' thin sure 'tis yourself 'll be
gran' too! Trath, 't 'ill be a wonder if ye spake to
any ov us 't all!"

Alley smiled a little, but rather sadly. "I don't
want wan bit for to be gran'," she said, almost
tearfully.

"Och, Alley asthore, what's cum t'ye 't all? I
know the most of the colleens does be allays changin'
and choppin' ov their moinds, loike the sky, that's
blue wan minute an' rid the nixt, but I thought you
was betherer nor to go on wid sich wark. Don't ye
know roight well that 'tis wicked to be choppin' an'
changin' yer moind wid a man? Is it breakin' his
heart ye want wid sich talk?"

Alley made no reply. She looked up at Hurrish
earnestly for a minute, as if about to speak. Then,
with a sudden blush, she turned away, and appeared
to be absorbed in arranging Miss Katty's disarranged
garment—a somewhat complicated task, one of that
young lady's fat legs having just succeeded in getting
through a considerable aperture in her little red flannel
petticoat.

Satisfied that his exhortation had had its due effect,
Hurrish pursued his way, turning up Gortnacoppin,
alongside of its milky torrent, fed by the violent rain
of the day before. It was a lovely morning. The
sun was still low, and the rocks which overhung the
path flung heavy violet shadows before his feet.
Everything seemed to be either violet or blue,—a
sort of spiritualised blue, such as these desolate limestone regions sometimes show in clear weather. The
wet places, where a slow ooze crept over the rocks,

showed a faintly bluish iridescence, the blue-grey
sheets of rock, the grey-blue sweeps of sky, the blue-
grey sweeps of Atlantic—it was all steeped in light,
penetrated with light, pathetic, solitary, ethereal—a
spiritualised world, fitted, one would say, for anchor-
ites and pious souls " enskyed and sainted," whose
traffic is less with this warm substantial earth of ours
than with the unfamiliar heavens.

Hurrish, his thoughts filled chiefly now with his
calves, tramped on, his shadow flinging itself in exag-
gerated bigness upon the weather-worn surfaces, his
iron-studded shoes awaking sharp echoes upon the
level rocks. Trailing branches of pale pink spiny
rose dangled out of the crevices overhead ; masses of
blood-red crane's-bill dotted the pale grey sheets of
limestone, and the dwarfed bushes of hawthorn which
rose out of the stony dykes were white with blossom.

He had reached the amphitheatre where the oratories stood, and where the stream disappears with a
great rushing, bubbling noise into the bowels of the
earth, when his eye was caught by a large object,
conspicuously white amongst the surrounding greyness, lying close to a reddish granite boulder, raised,
as many of these iceberg-dropped " foreign " boulders
are, upon a foot or stalk of limestone, which, protected
by its cover, has remained intact, while the rock surrounding it has been gradually worn away.

Striding up to the spot, he discovered that the
white object was no other than a sheep,—one of his
own sheep, stark, stiff, and dead, a hideous gash across
its innocent white throat telling out too plainly how
it had come by its end.

Hurrish loved his beasts, not merely for their

mouey value, but with that natural liking of a warm-
hearted man for anything living that he calls his own.
Next to his children, to Maurice Brady, and Alley,
they were, perhaps, the things he cared most for in
the world.   A hot tide of anger rushed through his
veins, and his cheerful, open face grew suddenly red
and corrugated with passion, as he looked fiercely
round in search of the perpetrator of the deed.   As
usual, however, none was to be seen.

He was still standing there looking down at the
dead beast, when he was startled by a slight but significant sound.   The thin clear whistle of a bullet
whizzed past close to his head, and the next second
the bullet itself fell flattened off the granite boulder
beside him, while, at the same moment, the solitary
valley rang with the report of a gun.

Hurrish started upright, and, with an instinct of
self-preservation, ran to the other side of the boulder,
thus putting it between himself and the direction
from which the shot had come.   He was only just
in time !   Another bullet whizzed by, grazing his
shoulder as it did so, striking against the rock, and
again falling deadened at his feet, while again the
report resounded through the silence, dying away only
when it had crossed the watershed, a faint prolonged
echo returning with a hollow boom from the valley
beyond.

Although a minute before the valley had seemed
bare as a man's hand, no idea of supernatural agency
on this occasion occurred to his brain.   Leprehauns
and ghosts are known to throw stones, and even to
upset curaghs, but no one, even in Connaught, has
ever heard of their firing a gun !   The question which

now arose was, how was he to look round the corner
of the boulder without thereby offering a mark to the
enemy who had twice missed him so narrowly ?   A
sudden idea struck him.   Stooping down to where
the boulder was raised, as already explained, upon a
limestone foot or pedestal, in the same way that a
mushroom is raised by its stalk, he peeped through the
worn-away space below, and was thus able to command
the whole of the valley before him.   Straight in front
lay the little group of oratories, the oblique rays of
the rising sun gleaming upon their low grey roofs,
and upon the white cross set as a pious symbol above
the tiny doorway, and, underneath this white cross, in
the very doorway itself of the one nearest to him, he
saw a face—the red, repulsive, baboon-like face of
Mat Brady peering out as an animal's face peers from
its lair, the light catching upon the barrel of a gun
which he held in his hands.

Hurrish's indolent, good-tempered soul was roused
to fury in a moment at this sight.   Mat Brady it
was, then, that had fired at him !   Mat equally of
course that had killed his sheep !   *Mat*, whom he
had spared a dozen times after the most outrageous
provocations !   *Mat*, who, by the unwritten laws of
the neighbourhood, stood condemned to death !   It
was the quarry attacking the hunter—the criminal
assaulting his judge ; the last drop in the long gathering cup of wrath !   All the man's previous provocations rushed through his brain in a single fiery moment, as a flame rushes through a pile of inflammable
materials.   Every other consideration,—his own
desire to avoid quarrels — his recent promise to
Maurice,—everything went for nothing before that

suddenly uprisen fire of vengeance. Clutching the blackthorn in his hand, and utterly heedless of the danger to himself, he rushed from behind his defence, up the hill, over the steep rocks, springing across the fissures, straight upon the little pious hermitage, with its innocent small white cross, and that hideous brutalised face in the middle of its ruined doorway.

The suddenness of the impulse proved his salvation. If Mat Brady had kept calm, now was his opportunity. He had not provided, however, against the emergency. His gun was unloaded, and, being a muzzle-loader, required time to recharge. Unarmed, he was, as he well knew, no match for Hurrish. Panic seized his soul, and he sprang from his lair and turned to flee. To scramble through that narrow doorway, however, took time. Hardly had he got himself free from it, and begun to ascend the stony incline, before Hurrish's step was close at his heels, Hurrish's voice sounded in his ears. Then, like a beast, he turned at bay, and like a beast's was the face which presented itself,—the lowering brow, the huge jaw, the mouth distorted and gnashing with rage and terror ! A hideous sight—to dream of, not to tell—a man in the likeness of a beast, worse than the very ugliest variety with hoofs or claws.

His gun being useless in any other way, he tried to club it : before he had time to do so, however, Hurrish had struck it out of his hands, and the next instant " crash," with one sweeping, annihilating blow, the blackthorn had descended like a sledge-hammer full upon his head,—not on the top, where the thickness of skull would have defied any blow, but a little to one side, full on the temple—that part, owing to

the position of his head, having come uppermost;
and with an oath, strangled in its very utterance, Mat
Brady fell backwards, and lay at full length upon
the ground, his head striking against a rock with a
dull hideous thud as he descended.

Hurrish remained where he was—the blackthorn
ready for action—waiting to see him rise. He would
not strike even Mat Brady when he was *down*. Minute followed minute, however, and still no sign of life.
The echoes awakened by the struggle died slowly
away, as a roughened circle dies upon a still pool.
The uncouth body lay there quietly at his feet like a
log that had been felled for burning. Could he be
shamming death? Why did he not get up? What
was the meaning of it? That the man could be
dead, or even badly hurt, did not at first occur to
him. Death from a single blow of a stick is almost
unknown, particularly in Ireland, where the weapon
is in much repute and constant practice. He was
stunned simply—"knocked silly,"—and would get
up again in another minute. He waited accordingly,
expecting to see the chest begin to heave, the eyes to
open, the hands to clench themselves—waited and
waited. Minute slowly followed minute, but still
Mat Brady neither stirred nor showed any signs of
returning animation.

Puzzled, and rather startled, Hurrish at length
stooped down over the fallen man, took hold of him
by an arm, and lifted him into a sitting position.
His head fell back, however, limply upon one shoulder, the other hand and arm hung down helplessly at
his side, his eyes, partially opened, looked up at the
sky with a hideous distorted expression, but without

any sign of life.   A cold sense of discomfort began to
creep over the other.   He had seen dead men before
—men, too, who had come to their deaths by violent
means,—and he began to have an uneasy suspicion
that this one before him closely resembled them ; an
uneasy recollection, too, that his own arm had come
down with very unmistakable velocity.

Laying Mat Brady down upon the rock, he sped
back to the stream, and returned with his felt hat full
of water, which he dashed into his late adversary's
face, then waited anxiously to see the effect.   There
was no effect at all !   The water poured off the man's
face as it would off a stone : not the twinkle of an
eyelid, not the slightest quivering motion, followed
the experiment.   The sudden collapse of that mass
of animal strength, a few minutes ago so brimful of
life and of vindictive passion, had something terrify-
ing about it.   It was so utterly unexpected, that
there seemed to Hurrish to be something uncanny,
almost supernatural, about it,—like the trick of an
evil goblin.   The unbroken silence of the stony
amphitheatre, too, was appalling.   Had there been
any one to share the situation, it would not have
been nearly so bad.   It was not the mere fact of
Brady being killed, so much as the whole circumstances,—the suddenness, the unaccountableness of
the phenomena,—that quelled him.   He felt daunted,
as if a cold hand had been unexpectedly laid upon
him in the height of his passion.

What was to be done ?   that was the next question.
If Mat Brady was really dead—and it must be owned
that it looked uncomfortably like it,—then his own
safety must be provided for ?   What was he to do ?

Where was he to go? As to giving himself volun-
tarily up to the authorities, and explaining the unin-
tentionalness of the homicide,—*that* idea, needless to
say, did not occur to him for a moment. It would
have been repugnant to every sentiment of his class,
in whose eyes the law is *the* Arch enemy,—the one
thing which it behoves every man, in honour no less
than in self-defence, to avoid having any dealings
with. There was a rule, however, for such cases—
a very well established and habitually followed one.
This rule was, quietly to walk away, and betake yourself to your customary occupations as rapidly as possible, leaving to the next passer-by the duty of finding
the body, raising the hue and cry, and sending, if he
thought fit, for the police.

Hurrish smiled grimly to himself as he thought
of the police. Much good *they* would do! The
strong arm of the law, the first thing that a man so
circumstanced in almost any other country in the
world would have thought of, was the last that
troubled him. He thought of his own people,—
what *they* would say and think. His mind glanced
to his mother, and a sudden intense disgust filled
him, as he thought of her satisfaction; of Alley, and
he caught his breath in a prayer that she, at least,
might never know his share in the deed. Then he
thought of Maurice, and with that thought followed
a rush of grief—of grief so violent that it seemed to
tear its way through the man's whole body. What
would Morry say? What *would* he do? It was
not fear for himself which prompted the thought.
It was the bitterness of feeling that he had been
betrayed into doing the very thing that he had sworn

I

to Morry that for his sake he would never do, or
allow, if possible, any one else to do. When he
remembered the promise given only one short week
before, he felt like dashing his own brains out then
and there against the rocks. Not that he believed
for an instant in any of those threats which the
other had uttered. That Maurice, despite his own
solemn declarations to that effect, would dream of
denouncing him to the Government, was an idea
which did not so much as cross his brain. To one
of his bringing up it would, in fact, have seemed the
one *impossible* thing ; the thing which—no matter
with what excuse, or under what provocation—no
man could do without being branded as a traitor
throughout the remainder of his life. It was entirely
the personal point of view, the personal relations
between their two selves, that made him miserable.
The thought that he and Morry could never be
friends again,—never, never, in all their lives,—
nearly drove him mad. He had no hope either
that he would fail to recognise his handiwork,—
nay, he would almost have preferred that he should
know it. That remorse and bitter accusing self-
reproach which, as regards the dead man, hardly
troubled him at all, he felt acutely,—as acutely as
any man so circumstanced could feel it,—as regards
the dead man's brother. He would have given all
that he possessed, or ever hoped to possess in the
world, to bring Mat Brady back to life again,—not
for his own sake, not the least from any sense of the
innate sinfulness of the deed, not even from any dread
of the possible consequences to himself, but solely and
wholly for the sake of his promise to Morry.

Odd thoughts, you will say, for a homicide !—for one whom the law, could it lay its hands upon him, would unhesitatingly proclaim a murderer ; but they were none the less the first that did occur to him. An anomalous state of affairs begets, no doubt, anomalous ideas, and, as far as remorse went, Hurrish's ideas were pretty much those which would have passed through the brain of any other man in his position, even where provocation had not made his act to some extent excusable—nay, even where there had been no provocation at all.

Meanwhile there was the recognised rule, and to have a prescribed rule to follow is always an immense comfort and repose to the mind. With a calmness which, to those unacquainted with so abnormal a state of affairs, would have seemed incredible, he left the body and walked leisurely down the hill, crossing the dead man's own ground as he did so. He did not even think of breaking into pieces or otherwise destroying the stick with which the deed had been committed. He simply thrust it into the heart of a large furze bush, the first he passed, pulled his coat down, buttoned it over his shirt, which was slightly stained by his own wound, brushed off the mud and dirt which had adhered to him, felt along his neck to make sure that the wound was not of a sufficiently serious character to signify, then— without another glance at the dead man—walked away across the slope, and up the sheep-track lead· ing towards the high-road. Then—remembering that it might be as well not to be seen there at that precise moment, particularly as he would shortly have to pass a police-barrack—he turned to the left,

threading his way between a number of boulders
standing on end one behind the other, crossed the
base of a hill,—its name, to be topographically accurate, was Cashlaundrumlahanah,—keeping its ridged
mass between him and the road.   Then—still keeping away from the main route—he struck off toward
the sea, under a tall, nearly vertical sweep of cliff,
and along a track which would bring him in time,
he knew, to Ballyvaughan.

When within about four miles of his destination,
what with the heat of the sun and his rapid walking,
perhaps, too, a little with the emotions of the morning, he began to grow thirsty, so turned aside at
Gleninagh to have a drink out of the famous well
there.   It was approached by a couple of stone steps,
and covered over with an arch surmounted by a
cross.   Hurrish hastily climbed the steps, and taking
up a vessel, left benevolently for the service of
passers-by, drank long and thirstily.   He was in the
act, having done so, of putting the drinking - cup
down again, when he suddenly perceived, with some
dismay, that it was a skull; another and much
older one, of which this was evidently the successor,
lay a little way off on the ledge, half covered with
green mould.   It was not exactly a pleasant incident, especially to one whose morning's work had
been what Hurrish's had been !   It was a comfort,
however, to reflect there was nothing actually unlucky
about it.   On the contrary, skulls were formerly, and
in some places are still, considered absolutely indispensable to the proper efficaciousness of a holy well.
By the time he reached Ballyvaughan, Hurrish, at
any rate, had nearly forgotten the incident.   The

fair was drawing to an end, so there was no time
to lose, and in the course of ten minutes he found
himself engaged in a brisk chaffer with a gentleman
from Mayo, a large grazier, who wanted to get the
whole of his stock of calves at at least nine shillings
a-head under what their owner considered their
value,—Burren calves fetching, as every one knows,
better prices than those of any other district in
Ireland.

Not merely was he not alarmed, but—save when
he thought of his promise to Morry—Hurrish was
not even particularly disturbed by his morning's
work. He had not, of course, intended to kill Mat
Brady, and in cold blood would never, under any
circumstances, have done so. But this had been far
from cold blood. The man had shot at him deliberately and treacherously from behind shelter, and,
armed only with his trusty blackthorn, he had
rushed upon him, struck down his defences, had
brought the stick down—once—once only—upon
his head. He had not even struck him again.
That first sledge-hammer blow had done the work,
and the man had fallen. To a great degree it was
an accident, for who would ever have believed that
a single blow, however delivered, would have struck
the life out of that great powerful man-mountain?
Hurrish knew nothing, it need hardly be said, about
the mechanism of the human anatomy, but in blind
rage, without calculation or thought at all, he had, as
chance directed, brought his stick down upon the one
spot in that huge mass of strength where life could
have been extinguished by such a blow—as a hunter
by good fortune may chance with his first bullet to

reach the one vulnerable spot in the carcass of some
brute, which would otherwise have gored him to
death. It had been the work of chance,—perhaps
even of Providence,—and as such he accepted it
modestly, without any self-glorification, beyond the
habitual satisfaction he found in his own strength,
but certainly without an iota of that horror, dismay,
and personal remorse which would have filled the
breast of a man less inured to hearing of deeds of
violence. He even forgot it by moments, when the
bargaining grew brisk and exciting ; and although,
when the calves were all sold, and his hands for the
moment unoccupied, it rushed back upon him with
vivid realisation, it was less with a sense of horror
than with a feeling that a new epoch of his life had
been reached, an important turning-point which it
behoved him to guard carefully, so that he might not
be led away by this one act into sharing others where
the justification might be less clear.

Before the reader resolves to be utterly disgusted
with this callousness, and to dismiss Hurrish O'Brien
once and for ever as a monster of brutality, he
must first kindly consent to take the circumstances
of his life a little into consideration. We are all
children of our environment—the good no less than
the bad,—products of that particular group of habits,
customs, traditions, ways of looking at things, stand-
ards of right and wrong, which chance has presented to our still growing and expanding consciousness. Hurrish's history must so far have been very
imperfectly told if it has not been realised that he
was well disposed and kindly above the average ;
pitiful, and disposed to use his strength for good

rather than evil. Yet the fact that he had just been
guilty, no matter with what justification, of another's
death did not—nay, *could* not—present itself to his
mind with any of that sharply-defined horror, that
passion of self-dismay and self-reproach, that it would
have awakened in the mind of many a far less kindly
and, in his way, conscientious man, who had been
unused to hearing violence and bloodshed spoken of
as the natural panacea for all the disagreements
which may happen to arise between man and man.
He would rather it had not happened,—when he
thought of Morry and his promise to him,—very
much rather. But as unfortunately it had happened,
he resolved in his own mind that, as soon as ever he
could with safety to himself, he would pay for masses
to be said for the repose of Mat Brady's soul—feeling that he was certainly acting generously; for had
not Brady been the aggressor? had he not come out
that morning with the express purpose of killing
himself?—an intention which only the merest accident had hindered him from carrying out. Moreover, if the matter had ended the other way, and he,
Hurrish, been the one to have been killed, he felt
perfectly convinced that Mat Brady would never for
a moment have thought of having masses offered up
for the repose of *his* soul !

CHAPTER XI.

ALLEY'S PUNISHMENT.

That horror and self-disgust which he was incapable of feeling for the act itself would probably have been strongly — nay, passionately — aroused, could Hurrish have foreseen the circumstances under which Mat Brady's body was destined to be discovered.

Early the same day, Bridget O'Brien's turkeys had taken it into their heads, as they had often done before, to stray away in a body from the house; and about an hour after the deed had been committed, and when Mat Brady's body was beginning to get rigid and cold on its stony bed, Alley Sheehan was walking leisurely up the Gortnacoppin path, and approaching nearer and nearer to the fatal spot.

Poor little Alley! She was enjoying her stroll in the warm sunshine, and thinking no harm of any one. She had driven the turkeys away from the vicinity of the stream, and they were now innocently engaged in pecking at the small white moths which rose in crowds from the trefoil growing upon the rocks, so that she felt she could safely linger a little out of reach of Bridget's eye. She picked a bunch of white mountain dryas and crimson crane's-bill, and tied them together with a withey, telling herself as she did so that they were for the children. She had so little idea that beauty was a thing admirable in itself, that she would probably have given a denial to any one who had asked her whether she took pleasure in the arrangement of these vividly contrasting colours, set off, as they were, with a big feathery handful of adiantum, growing more luxuriously in those deep-sheltered recesses than in many a carefully tended hothouse.

The day had changed since Hurrish had come up the path, and the holy calm of morning had been suddenly killed by the sound of strife. The pearly light had given way to a broad serenity, rare in that storm-driven region. Not that the sky was cloudless. A great line of snowy cumuli, united at their bases, clear in the upper portion of their summits, was drifting slowly over the open spaces of sea and collecting in white packs upon the horizon. Against this opaque whiteness the three isles of Aran stood out with unusual distinctness; the circular mass of Dun Ængus—greatest and most famous of all surviving raths—showing its grey and broken circle upon the highest point of all.

Alley had too much of the Celtic Eolian-harp temperament not to be influenced by the character of the day and scene. With her it usually took the more direct form of devotion. Her pure, singularly transparent spirit seemed to float away in visions of faith and tenderness, which her very ignorance—if you will superstition—only made the wider and the more embracing. Certain types repeat themselves eternally at all ages of the world, and hers was the type of all those gentle ascetic natures which at every period and under all variations of circumstances have sprung up spontaneously. There had probably been Alley Sheehans here in Burren ages

before this one had been born, for these stony fast-
nesses, with the neighbouring ones of Aran, had for
centuries been the resort of the pure, the pious, the
pitiful, who had succeeded in escaping from that
pandemonium of carnage which year after year, and
century after century, had made the rest of the
island a fit habitation only for some blood-besmeared
rabble of hell.

What she would have done had her lot been cast
in a different communion, it is difficult even to imagine. It was the central heart of that creed—that
mother who is the type of all motherhood—which
drew her and kept her upwards. Her prayers, those
she used on non-official occasions, were an odd med-
ley—half self-invented, and as elementary, therefore,
as the cooings of a wood-pigeon, half made up of,
to her, nearly incomprehensible fragments from the
slowly elaborated ritual of Christendom. She possessed a little tattered 'Key to Heaven,' which, like
the rosary, had belonged to her mother, and which
she took to chapel with her on Sunday. The greater
part of this work was as dark to her as if it had
been written in Latin or Hebrew. Here and there,
however, she managed to pick off a scrap, as a building bird pulls a leaf off a tree. There was the
anthem and litany to our Lady of Loretto, for
instance, which, by dint of much repetition, had
acquired a sort of meaning—not its own meaning,
doubtless, but something that did just as well,
possibly even better. Whenever Alley knelt down
to pray, a bit, from long habit, seemed to spring to
her lips. First, perhaps, a bit of the anthem—
" Despise not thou our prayers, but deliver us from

all dangers, O ever glorious and blessed Virgin ! "
Then the invocation, " Mother most pure, Mother
most chaste, Mother undefiled, Mother most admir-
able—Mary, mother, pray for us ! Seat of wisdom,
Cause of our joy, Mystical Rose, Flower of David,
Gate of Heaven, Morning Star, Health of the weak,
Refuge of Sinners, Comforter of all the afflicted—
Holy Mary mother, pray for us ! "

There was something about all these grand words
which gave little Alley a distinct feeling of pleasurable excitement, for, like most of her countrymen
and countrywomen, she had an ear for the sonorous,
and they were about the nearest thing to poetry she
had ever heard. Her own mental pictures of the
same gracious image were very different, however,—
at once clearer and less definite. They had caught
some of their traits, no doubt, from the prints and
images at Tubbamina chapel, but were mixed up
besides with the sun and the stars, the sea where it
was calm, the flowers in the cracks of the rocks—
a vague brooding image, unformed, yet real enough
too to herself. Sometimes, when she had been
sitting a long time quite alone, this realisation
would grow curiously, nay even startlingly vivid, so
vivid that if a white form had come slowly towards
her over the level rocks, and a face—the face which
every painter has tried to paint—had looked down
gently at her with its eyes of pity, she would have
felt more awe and wonder than actual astonishment.

In trouble especially her instinct was to fly to this
refuge, as a small frightened creature flies instinctively to its sheltering-place. She was very troubled
now about Maurice Brady, and Hurrish's last words

had brought this trouble into a sort of focus. She
had never put it to herself whether she loved Maurice
enough to marry him, for that was not the form which
her reflection took, but she did ask herself what would
become of her if she went on being so dreadfully afraid
of him as she had lately been. When he had informed
her that he intended to make her his wife, she had
simply been pleased without thinking much about it ;
she had been only sixteen at the time, and young
even for that not very advanced age. That was two
years ago, however, and two years had taught her a
good deal. She was not given to introspection—
that, happily, not being one of the vices of the class
to which she belonged ; but none the less she had a
feeling that it would not be well for her and Maurice
to marry. She admired him, wondered at him, was
proud of him, but in her heart of hearts she was aware
that she shrank from his approach. Fear—even in
a minor degree—is, to one of her gentle timorous
nature, the worst probably of sensations, and it was
one that she never could entirely get over with him.
He was so authoritative, so hard, clear, decided in all
his notions. That cold vein of egotism, too, which
was an integral part of his nature, had made itself
more clearly felt in their *tête-à-têtes* than at other
times. The unknown is always invested with a mysterious terrór in minds as naïve as hers, and Maurice's
life, plans, objects, ambitions, and future, were all alike
utterly unrealisable to her imagination. She had a
feeling that in marrying him she embarked upon a
new life, one for which her previous one had by no
means fitted her,—that many things might be required of her that she did not feel able to respond to,

and from which she shrank back as a child shrinks
from an unknown brink. She had no ambition—
not even for fine clothes; she liked what she knew,
and what she felt herself capable of understanding.
This wild Burren—grim as it would have seemed to
most people—had wound itself round her heart, as
the first environment it has known does wind round
a young impressionable nature, especially in one of
her race. The little dells where the grass grew thick
and rich; the wells full of offerings to their respective saints; the rifts into which she could plunge her
hands, and bring them up filled with flowers; the
isles of Aran opposite, where the saints used to live,
and at which she looked in consequence with such
reverence; the wild clearness of the sea, and great
environing arch of sky—Hurrish's kind face, which
seemed a part of it all. If Maurice would only agree
to settle in some small cabin, quite close to Hurrish's,
where she could see him every day, without having
to be ordered about by old Bridget, then indeed, she
thought, she would be quite happy, and not one bit
afraid to marry him at once!

She had reached the point where the valley opened
into an amphitheatre, and the cluster of beehive oratories rose solitary in the hollow, when she all at once
remembered that this part of the valley was now no
longer Mick Maloney's, but Mat Brady's property.
Alley's terror of Mat Brady amounted to monomania.
Never could she forget the day, now more than a year
ago, when, happening by ill-luck to pass close to his
cabin, the great red-headed, half-tipsy Caliban had
suddenly darted out of it and had pursued her over
the rocks. How she had run, and how he had fol-

lowed faster than she could escape, and how he had
caught her, and held her fast, swearing at her for her
terror, and exhaling a portentous smell of rank whisky!
It is true that he did not actually hurt her. He was
not, perhaps, even as brutal at bottom as many an
English, certainly as many a French, yahoo of the
same mental calibre would have been ; but he frightened and sickened the fragile girl with the horror of
his presence, with the sense of her own powerlessness
under the grip of his hand, by his loud voice, and
coarse, grinning, baboon-like face so close to her own.
It was like some delicate domesticated half-humanised
bird or animal in the clutch of a wild ferocious speci-
men of its own species, whose wrath it has evoked
and knows not how to allay. She had trembled like
a leaf, and had implored him with tears to release her,
which he for a long time had refused to do. At last,
however, her tears and terror had had their effect, or
he had not known what else to do, for, with a laugh
of brutal triumph, he had flung her away so violently
as almost to throw her down. Now, as she remembered that dreadful day and her own sensations, she
glanced nervously round, fearing to see the uncouth
figure of the detested Brady. No, thank God, there
was no one in sight, and she breathed more easily.
Poor little gentle Alley !

Her glance was passing away, and in another moment would have reverted to the flowers. But what
—what was that on the ground ?—huddled together
like a heap of seaweed ? At first it seemed to her to
be merely a bundle of clothes,—some man had left
his coat there, probably, while he was at work. It
was too large, however, for that, she perceived on a

second glance. There was a boot, too—why should a man leave his boots behind him? The boot was so twisted and shapeless that it did not occur to her at first that there could be a foot in it. Still, she found herself looking at it with growing feelings of bewilderment and suspicion—that vague sense of something amiss which often precedes the actual certainty.

All at once her blood seemed to stand still, her heart to send great thuds upward to her throat; her knees knocked, her breath failed, and she almost fell to the ground with horror. It was only a *hand* she saw,—a large lividly white hand sticking out of the side of the bundle of clothes,—a hand flung, back downwards, upon the ground, the fingers hanging loose and half hidden in the grass and daisies. Poor Alley's very soul seemed to cleave together and die away with horror at the sight, the innocent grey rock and grasses to turn black and yawn suddenly under her feet, as if an earthquake had passed over Gortnacoppin. With the unwilling fascination of horror she looked and looked again at the horrible object, and now she could see a face—a grey distorted face—which seemed to be gazing up at her with its dull dead eyes. The lower part of this face was hidden by the shoulder against which it had fallen, but the eyes were wide open, and over them hung a mass of red hair—hair surely familiar to her? More than this Alley did not stay to see. The cup of horror was already full and brimming over; to escape was her only thought.

With a shriek—the shriek of a creature in extremest terror—she tore madly down the valley in the direction of the cabin. To get within reach of

some other living human being, to escape from the
dreadful sight of those dead eyes, was her only desire.
It seemed to her terrified imagination as if that form-
less, hideous thing that had been a man, had risen too
from where it had lain, and was following her—nay,
was gaining step by step upon her. On and on she
ran, and always as she ran, there, close behind, she
felt it still, always in the same attitude as before, yet
somehow moving faster than she could, and gaining
rapidly upon her. Every moment she fancied she
might feel its touch upon her shoulder, might see that
face peering into her eyes, those livid hands clutching
hers, those twisted limbs in contact with her own.
She flung out shriek after shriek of horror into the
silent air, startling the larks as they circled in melodious rhythmic curves over her head. On and on
down the silent lifeless valley, over the innumerable
rifts and fissures, scrambling across the boulders, her
feet hurt and bleeding from the stones—still on, on,
on she ran.

How she reached the cabin, how she got the door
open, she never precisely knew. Half crazy with
terror she rushed into the house and up to Bridget,
whom under ordinary circumstances she was too much
afraid of even to approach, caught at her dress and
flung herself, like a criminal escaping from justice, at
her feet, hiding her face in the folds of her red flannel
petticoat.

The old woman's astonishment at first literally de-
prived her of the power of speech and movement.
The next it turned to anger.

" Quit yer holt this minite, ye cutty ! How dar
you be clutchin' at me like that ? Is it shleep-walkin'

ye are, ye flag-hopper ?   Quit yer holt, or begorra I'll
lay yer flat wid me pokar, so I will ! "

But these angry words, which usually she would
have shrunk from, had no effect at all upon the girl's
mortal terror.   She would rather have been beaten,
rather have been killed by a living and breathing
woman, than be left alone to that dread which was
clutching at her very soul, and paralysing the vital
actions of her whole body.

Twice she opened her mouth to speak, and each
time her parched tongue refused' utterance.   At last
she got the words out.

" Thar's a man—kilt—dead ! " she stammered.

Bridget's face changed.   A gleam of wild satisfaction came into her eyes.   She caught the girl in
her turn by the arm, and peered curiously into her
face.

" A man kilt ?   What sort of a man is it, acushla ?
Till me quick, gurl ! " she said, eagerly.

Then, as Alley's paralysed tongue remained dumb
—" Is it Mat Brady ?   Whist, chilt, don't be dashed ;
sure what is there to scar ye ?   A man kilt !—trath,
an' if that's all, 'tis scared enough an' more nor
euough you'll be before you're much older, glory be
to God ! "

They went back together to the field.   Great as
Alley's terror was of the place, she was more afraid
still of remaining behind.   Who could tell whether
the thing might not leap on her from behind the
door, or fall headlong down the chimney, and lie
there, staring up at her with those horrible livid eyes
which would never, never close again.

No one had been in the field since she left.   The

K

turkeys were still pecking at the moths, which rose
out of the clefts of the rock. The bunch of ferns
and flowers still lay precisely where she had thrown
it down in her frenzied flight; the grey overhanging
rocks were gay with sedums and crane's-bill; the larks
were circling overhead, pouring down a rippling vol-
ume of clear star-like notes. Spring, even in the
Burren, was revelling in a thousand dainty fancies.
And there before them on the ground, amidst all this
free, pure, beautiful upspringing nature, lay, horribly
twisted and deformed, that miserable heap of clay
which that morning had been a man.

Bridget walked straight up to the corpse, and stood
looking down at it, wild gleams of triumph irradiating
her witch-like face and black gleaming eyes.

" 'Tis there ye're, are ye ? " she muttered jeeringly.
" Shtill an' cauld, an' qui't enough *now*, Mat Brady !
D'ye know who's standin' over yer ? D'ye know
that Hurrish O'Brien's mother's lukin' down at ye ?
Ach, an' 'tis th' ugly corpse ye make ! I wudn't
have the layin' out of yer for saxpence, so I wouldn't,
ye baste ! A gun ! " she muttered, looking down at
the weapon, which still lay where it had been thrown
upon the ground. " But 'twas na gun dun *that*"—
looking at the corpse and the dark brown mark of the
wound on the temple,—" na, na, na gun, but a shtick.
An' a good man, too, 'twas hild that shtick, so 'twas.
Hurrish ? Na, na, 'twasn't Hurrish. Hurrish is too
saft. Hurrish 'ud do most anything raytlier nor he'd
kill a man. Maybe 't 'ul be 'bout," she went on muttering to herself, as she peered eagerly around amongst
the stunted hawthorns and low bushes of furze, which
sprouted out of the clefts of the rocks.

Suddenly she gave a scream and a pounce, pulled a stick out of the tuft of furze, waved it frantically in the air, then, with the shriek of a maniac, fell plump down upon her knees on the ground.

"'Twas! 'twas! 'twas himsel' dun it!—himsel' alone an', no other! Glory be to God and the saints this day! Me shame's wiped out! Hurrish, darlint, yer old mither's shame's wiped out! 'Tis crying for joy she is this minute! Oh, me darlint son! me boy! An' I that thought he was too chicken-hearted for to kill a man! I wronged you, Hurrish, darlint! Core of my soul! where is he, that I may bliss him? Where is he at all, that I may get at him an' bliss him for this day's work? Hurrish! Hurrish, alannah!"

She had quite forgotten Alley in her excitement. Her withered face was alive with hate and love; her eyes blazed like live coals in the wrinkled setting. The girl, however, had understood, and her cheeks turned from white to red: for the second time that day she clutched her old tyrant by the arm, almost shaking her in her anger.

"How dar' you say 'twas Hurrish dun it?" she exclaimed. "Hurrish wudn't ha' touched him! How *dar'* you say Hurrish killed him? Yer a wicked woman, so ye ar,—a bad wicked woman! an' I'll tell Hurrish meself on yer, so I will. *You* might ha' dun it, but Hurrish wouldn't,—he wouldn't hurt a fly. For shame to ye sayin' sich a thing! An' if I were strang enough, I'd bate ye for it, so I wud!"

It was a vulture flown at by a ring-dove! For a moment the old woman was petrified and almost cowed with astonishment. The next she sprang up,

seized the girl by the shoulder, and shook her as if
she meant literally to shake her to death, then brandished the stick violently before her eyes.

" D'ye see that, ye little fool ? D'ye see that, ye
imperent cutty ?   An' iv 'twasn't for Hurrish hisself,
I'd lay ye cold thar too for yer imperence—be my
soul ! yis.   To dar tell me I didn't know me own
son's shtick.   Luk at that, an' say agen 'twasn't
Hurrish dun it—God presarve him for it this day
an' ivermore, Amen !   An' if ye dar say word to
livin 'soul, 'twill be the last ye spake on this arth,
so mind that !   'Tis cauld and shtiff loike that ye'll
be, ye insilint cutty !   Staalin' into other folk's
houses, aitin' their mate an' drink, and takin' away
their good names ! "

But Alley hardly heard the end of this exhortation. The sight of Hurrish's stick—that familiar
stick, which little Katty had played with so innocently only that very morning—overcame her as no
words could have done.   Horror struck home to her ;
horror, and a sickening paralysing chill, which seemed
to petrify her whole body.   This time she uttered no
cry, only a low gasping sob, and turning, ran back
the way she had come, leaving the old woman alone
with the dead man.

When she got near the cabin she paused abruptly.
There was no home for her there—no home ever
again anywhere in all this weary world.   Hurrish
had done this thing—kind Hurrish, whom she loved
so much.   *He* had done it ; had beaten this man to
death—perhaps when he was drunk—murdered him,
and left him there, dead or dying, upon the rocks.
The horror of it was too great, too impossible, for her

to contain. She threw her shawl over her head and
ran wildly on, heedless of where she was going,—
ran, ran, ran, as a creature runs after it has received
its death-blow.

CHAPTER XII.

"HOW CUD HE BE THERE, AN' HE DEAD?"

It seemed indeed to Alley as if the end of the
world had come. Father Peter had been preaching
about it only a few Sundays before, saying it was
near, and now, perhaps, it had arrived. To a loving
heart sudden loss of faith in a being that it has loved
is a catastrophe which needs no external one, no loud
sounding crack of doom, to make more terrible. The
idea crossed her mind of running off to Galway to
the convent where her sister was, and asking to be
taken in there. She was afraid, however. She would
have to go to Ballyvaughan, and there take the steamer
across the bay—a journey more fraught with terror
to her untravelled imagination than any pilgrimage
to Rome or Jerusalem to one of another bringing up.
She simply ran and ran and ran, heedless of where she
was going, till she found herself upon the shore, at the
top of the rocks, which were here not of any great
height. She did not even pause here, but clambering
down, heedless of the sharp-pointed peaks, studded
at their lower part with acorn barnacles, hid herself
in a sort of cleft or shallow cave just within reach of

high-water mark. If she could only stay there for
ever, she thought, wildly—remain there till she died
—never see old Bridget again—better still, never see
Hurrish—never see any one belonging to her old life !
She did not think of Maurice Brady at all. She was
too confused and miserable. Had she done so, however, it would only have been an added pang, for was
not the man that had been killed Maurice's brother ?

The cave was narrow and tapering, covered with
an immense, nearly horizontal, block, which spanned
it like the capstone of a cromlech. It was nearly
quite shut in at the back, but at one point a little
ray of light threaded its way through the rocks,
throwing a pale yellowish illumination upon the floor
below. To poor Alley this yellow light seemed like
an eye peeping in at her, and she cowed down anew
to avoid its gaze.

The tide was low, but had turned, and was creeping steadily up, its voice rising from time to time in
a long choking sob. Every now and then, too, over
the furrowed expanse of rock, a tall single shooting
column of white spray would rise, towering like some
great tropical blossom—an aloe or agave—into existence, and then dying suddenly down again immediately.

The sob of the waves, the hollow chuckling noises,
the great white shining expanse of sea—all so familiar
that no thought of alarm had ever mingled with them
before—filled poor Alley to-day with unaccountable
terror. The thud underneath, caught by an echo,
sounded like blows struck upon the roof of the slab
under which she was crouching. She thought it
must be some one moving above there, and shivered

and crouched yet more closely down, heedless of the
masses of dripping seaweeds and slimy red sponges
which spouted at her out of a hundred gaping orifices.
It was all strange, all new, all terrible to-day, as the
most familiar scenes become when seen for the first
time under the light of some blighting calamity.
Terror was in her very soul—terror of everything
and of everybody.   What point had she to turn to ?
where could she look for help ?   Even God, the
saints,—the blessed Virgin herself,—seemed to have
changed their aspect.   Hurrish—the one earthly
being to whom she had hitherto clung—kind Hurrish,
good Hurrish, who had taken her to live with him,
who had been father and brother both to her,—
Hurrish—impossible yet hideous realisation—Hurrish
had done this.   Hurrish was a murderer !   She
pressed her hands tightly over her ears, as if the very
air was full of the horrible sound.

She had remained there crouched among the rocks
for nearly an hour, stunned and hardly conscious of
the lapse of time, when she heard the sound of some
one approaching.   Several times before she had
fancied she had heard steps, but it had turned out to
be only her own imagination.   This time, however,
it really was some one coming along the strip of
shingle which lay between her and the sea.   First a
shadow upon the rock before her—the shadow of an
elongated hat ; then a larger and vaguer mass ; then
a crunching noise sounding above the hollow roar of
the sea, and a figure in a suit of brown tweed appeared
in sight.

Alley, who had shrunk back into the cave expecting to see a stranger, gave a faint involuntary cry at

sight of this figure, which caused it to stop and look up, and their eyes met.   It was Maurice Brady.

He too stared open-eyed with astonishment.   Of all places it would never have occurred to him to meet Alley here upon these lonely rocks, so far from home.

"Alley !" he exclaimed, wonderingly.   "Why, Alley, whatever brings you here ?   Is anything gone wrong ?   You look scared somehow and white.   Has that old beast Bridget been beating you again ?   I wonder that you'd stop with such an old scawl-crow. I wouldn't, if 'twas me !"

But Alley, instead of answering, only stood still staring at him, white and stiffened with terror, like a little statue of Fear, at the mouth of the cave.   Her hair had fallen loose, and hung in a dishevelled mass upon her shoulders ; her poor little naked feet, cut with the stones she had run so wildly over, were stained here and there with thin trickles of blood ; her whole attitude was expressive of only one thing—terror—as she fixed her great eyes upon the young man without speaking.

"What brought ye 't all ?" she stammered at last.

Maurice gave a little laugh, rather an embarrassed one.   "Well, now, 'twas a mighty queer thing that brought me, and that's the truth, Alley.   The queerest thing ever happened to me yet, so it was !"

He waited, expecting her to express surprise or interest, but Alley said nothing.   She simply stood and looked at him, all her remaining consciousness bound up in the resolution not to tell, not to tell, not to tell.   That was her only thought.

"Sit down upon this bit of rock, and don't look so

silly and scared : you make me feel quite queer, so you do," the young man went on, indicating a recess where she was to seat herself.

Alley obeyed. She was in such a state of mental and physical collapse, that she would have yielded to any suggestion. She sat mechanically down upon the piece of rock in front of the cave, and Maurice seated himself beside her.

"Now, mind, Alley, before I tell you anything, you must give me your word not to repeat a word to any one," he began, authoritatively. "I don't know what mightn't happen if you did. They might put it into the papers, perhaps, with my name and all! Troth, if they did, I'd run away, and never come back at all, but go and settle maybe in America."

He waited to allow this dreadful picture of his own probable expatriation to sink into Alley's mind before proceeding any further. As she said nothing, however, but simply stared blankly at the sea, he concluded that she was still thinking about whatever it was that had upset her, and that he had better tell his story first, and exact a promise about keeping it a secret afterwards.

"The curious thing is that it should have been *me* that it happened to, for if there's one thing I've always set my face against, it's the rubbish fellars go on with about ghosts, and fetches, and suchlike old-fashioned talk. Now, if it had been a fellar like Hurrish seen what I saw this morning, he'd have been screaming ghosts and goblins all over the country !"

In spite of this assertion, a physiognomist would have perceived that the young man was not quite so calm as he would have appeared. Instead of its

usual self-sustained air, his face wore rather an un-
settled and excited expression, and he glanced from
time to time over his shoulder, with a slight air of
suspiciousness.

Alley, however, noticed nothing.   Her mind was
enveloped in a mist—a mist that obscured all lesser
objects — sometimes closing up entirely, sometimes
opening a little way to reveal hideous visions, but
never entirely disappearing.

"Well, Alley, mind now what I say about not
a word of this to any one.   I'd some writing to do
this morning, so I got up early—not having to be at
the shop till nine—and went down to the sea, thinking I'd do it better upon the shore, for the room
I have is small, and there's another young fellar
in it besides myself.   Well, I got a nice comfortable
place, much as it might be here, only instead of rocks
it's all sand there, stretching along the sea for miles.
I was busy with my writing, for when a man writes
for the newspapers he has to be very particular, and
I happened to look up for a moment, thinking of
a word I couldn't remember.   There was a sort of
a gap in front of me, something like Gortnacoppin,
only smaller, and, in the middle of the gap—are you
minding what I'm saying, Alley?—in the middle of
the gap who should be standing there but Mat, looking as usual, only a bit queer, as if he'd been drinking,
and his eyes wide open, and a black mark on his
head, just there, to the left of—I say, don't be clutching at me like that, Alley; sure I'm not going to run
away—listen now!   I jumped up, and 'Well, Mat,
what are ye doing here?' says I, and went over
towards him; but when I come to the place the devil

a sign of him was in it at all. So I thought maybe
he'd dodged behind one of the hillocks, not wanting
me to know he was there, and I went round, but no,
not a sign of him there either ; so I climbed up
another big hillock there was, where I could see all
round me and into the hollows, but not a sign of any
one 'cept some sheep, and a little boy minding them ;
so I run up to him, and asked, did he see a man
pass ? and he said, No, ne'er a one had passed 't all
that mornin', only myself—and he between me and
the road, you mind ! So when I heard that, I
gathered up my papers like a shot, and back with me
to the shop, and made them give me leave for the
day, and off I come to see what took Mat there, or if
it was himself at all. For it's the queerest thing ever
I knew, and somehow I can't get it out of my head."

Poor Alley ! Before one terror had begun to subside another had sprung up and taken its place !
Her attention, which at first had wandered, had
gradually grown more and more concentrated upon
the narrative, and long before it had ended she was
trembling from head to foot. Her previous expression of blank despair had changed for one of active
absorbing terror. Her teeth chattered ; her eyes were
set like the eyes of a sleep-walker.

" My God, how cud he be there, an' he dead ? " fell
almost unconsciously from her quivering lips.

Maurice Brady started and stared—started and
stared again. He had told her his story chiefly from
an impelling desire to tell it to some one, no matter
who—to get the thing, as it were, outside himself—
certainly not with any idea that she could throw
light upon the mystery. At this startling corrobora-

tion, however, panic seized him. Could it mean—
could there be anything *in* it? Was it, could it be
meant as a warning? Fear shot suddenly through
his blood, like a stream of icy water. Alley's pallor,
which he had been too self-absorbed at first to notice
much, rushed back vividly upon his mind. *Did* she
know something? *Had* she seen anything? If so—

" What's that yer saying 't all, Alley ? " he exclaimed, springing to his feet and speaking in a tone
of authority. " What d'ye mean by Mat being dead?
How should he be dead, when he was as alive as
meself three days ago? Speak up 't once if yer don't
want me to think that ye're raving out and out," he
added, stooping and seizing her by the shoulder, as if
to arouse her.

Poor Alley turned her large terrified eyes upon
him. What had she done? What had she said?

" Oh, Morry dear, don't mind me! Sure, 'tis dis-
traight I am, I dun know what I'm sayin' 't all! " she
cried, clasping her hands piteously.

But Maurice's suspicions were too thoroughly
aroused to be allayed now.

" You *must* have meant something, Alley! " he
answered violently. " Has anything happened?
Speak up—d'ye hear me? " he added, giving a slight
shake to the shoulder which he still held. " Do what
I tell you this instant : arn't I going to be yer husband? Do you dar disobey me? If ye don't tell me,
begorra I'll take yer back to Hurrish, and see what *he*
has to say. If I don't have it out of you, I'll have
it out of him. And, by God! if I find——"

But poor little Alley had reached the point where
endurance could go no further. The concentrated

anguish of the last two hours, and now Maurice's
sudden unkindness, were too much for her. She fell
back half fainting upon the rock, and lay there white
as a little ghost.

The young man's anger was too vehement, however, for him to experience any sudden revulsion
towards tenderness. He was fond of her, in his way,
very fond ; nevertheless his feelings at that moment
were less those of pity than of anger at her incon-
venient feebleness — anger at being balked in his
desire to plunge into the heart of his mystery, which
was fast driving him mad with anger and excitement.
He was not particularly tender by nature, and his
love, strong as it was, was for the moment too
entirely in abeyance to anger for him to care very
much whether Alley suffered or not. His strongest
desire now was to get away. What was the use of
staying with a girl who only cried and fainted ? If
anything really had happened, the only way to satisfy
himself was to go and see. As soon, therefore, as he
saw that she was beginning to revive, and that a faint
colour was returning to her cheeks, he left her where
she was, saying that he would be back soon, and
started as fast as he could across the level platforms
of rock, past Hurrish's cabin, and up the hill in the
direction of his brother's cabin, which took him, as a
matter of course, straight through the Gortnacoppin
valley.

By the time he reached the rocky amphitheatre
which had been the scene of that morning's tragedy,
it was no longer deserted. A small crowd, chiefly of
ragged boys and girls with a few women, had gathered
upon the ridge, and were peering down curiously at

the dead man. Two policemen, armed with their
guns, stood posted as sentinels on either side of the
body ; a party of four more, in front of whom walked
Mr Sub-inspector Higgins, were coming down the
path, their black official figures sharply defined
against the pale-grey luminous background.

Until that moment Maurice had hardly known
what he feared. Now he stood still, appalled by the
sight before him—appalled by the sudden realisation
of his worst fears. That that dark heap beside which
the policemen stood was his brother Mat's body, he
had not an atom of doubt. He put up his hands to
his head, and staggered back against a rock, white,
and sickened with horror.

His mind was not idle, however. Alley had known
of this ! That point was beyond a doubt. If she
had known about it, who then could have committed
the crime but Hurrish ?—Hurrish, who had sworn so
lately that for his sake nothing would ever tempt
him to lay a finger upon Mat—Hurrish, who pretended to be so devoted to him ! The certainty
seemed to burn itself into his very brain. All the
particles of evidence rose up one by one before him,
and each seemed to strengthen and confirm that
belief. Who would Alley be so anxious to screen
as Hurrish ? Who so likely to meet Mat here at the
juncture of the two farms ? Clearly Hurrish. Hurrish had done it ; everything pointed to it. All at
once the desire for revenge—hot, insatiable, all-
devouring—rose and rose in his breast, until everything else became submerged under its torrent. Had
he not sworn—sworn to Hurrish himself—that if any
one laid a finger upon Mat, he should pay for it ?

And now—by God! if justice was to be had, he
should pay for it!

The second party of policemen had by this time
made their way down the hill, and had joined the
group below. He could hear the inspector's clear-
cut voice issuing orders to his men. Suddenly he
started forward, and hurried down the slope, pushing
through the crowd—an inquisitive and excited rather
than overawed one—until he, too, stood beside the
corpse, which still lay upon its back, just as it had
fallen when the breath of life had left it. His first
impulse was to put his hand above his brother's
heart; the next to try and lift his hand. It was
already cold, and as stiff as if carved in wood.

The inspector was beginning to put the usual
inquiries—who had last seen the man alive? had
any sound of the struggle been heard? Suddenly
Maurice started to his feet with an impetuous gesture.

"Don't be wasting your time asking no questions!" he exclaimed imperiously. "Go down to
that house there and arrest the man what's done it,
that's what you've got to do. This is my brother,
Matthew Brady, lying here murdered, and the man
that's murdered him is—Hurrish O'Brien!"

There was a start, a sudden "sensation" amongst
all present. Even the policemen—most of whom
had been a long time in the district—were taken by
surprise, for there was no better known, or on the
whole better liked, name than Hurrish's.

Mr Higgins alone was impassive. To him all
these strange names sounded precisely alike.

"Who do you say?—Hurrish—H-u-r—— How

do you spell it ? " he inquired, taking a note-book
out of his pocket and beginning to enter the name in
it with a stylographic pen.

Maurice disdaining to answer, the necessary information was supplied by one of the policemen, who
at the same time whispered something into his superior's ear.

" Yes, yes ; of course. What are your reasons for
believing this man to be the criminal ? " he inquired,
turning sharply to Maurice : Mr Higgins never hesitated on duty.

A whirl of conflicting ideas rushed through the
young man's brain at the question. If possible he
would screen Alley, he hastily resolved. Her name
should not be dragged into it if he could help it.

" I've reasons enough, and more than enough," he
said, sullenly. " 'Tis he that's done it. There's no
more doubt about it than that the sun's in the sky.
Every one knows that he and my brother are enemies
—have been these years past."

Mr Higgins was rather perplexed. Over-readiness
to proclaim the name of the guilty man had not
hitherto formed part of his experiences of agrarian
outrages ! He was a zealous officer, however,—one,
too, to whom opportunities for distinguishing himself
had hitherto been rather wanting,—and he was not
disposed therefore to allow the present occasion to
slip from his grasp. Unfortunately there was a
hitch. The local resident magistrate, to whom under
ordinary circumstances application would have been
made for a warrant of arrest, happened to be away,
having been summoned to attend a trial in Limerick,
and in his absence the nearest unpaid magistrate was

Mr O'Brien of Donore. Now Mr Higgins would have given a good deal not to have been obliged to present himself before that gentleman so soon after that last parting of theirs, the memory of which still rankled unpleasantly. Duty, however, was duty, and he was not the man to allow personal considerations to stand in the way of it. Desiring the policemen in attendance to remain where they were, and on no account to allow any one to approach the body until he returned, he accordingly reascended the side of the glen, followed only by a single policeman, and regained the road where he had left his horse.

Arrived at the top of the pass, he turned by a natural instinct to look back at the scene which he had just quitted. The sides of the valley were so steep that the groups below seemed to be almost vertically underneath. Fresh figures were descending the rocks on the other side,—three men and two women, the madder-red petticoats of the latter forming bright moving spots of colour upon the wilderness of grey. Below stood the policemen, conspicuous by their blackness, gathered together in a compact formal-looking group. And, erect beside the dead man, his arms crossed upon his chest, his pale handsome face set like a mask, stood Maurice Brady—an image of vengeance waiting for its victim.

L

CHAPTER XIII.

IN GORTNACOPPIN VALLEY.

Mr O'Brien was standing beside the lake, with his
eyes fixed upon the surface. The poor man had been
busy all day at different points of the estate, and had
brought away a tolerably severe heartache from each.
There were some labourers at that very moment employed in clearing out a ditch not far off, whom he
visited punctiliously from time to time. He was his
own steward as well as his own agent, maintaining,
not unreasonably, that a property which could hardly
pay its own expenses could still more forcibly not
afford to be encumbered with a burden of annuitants.
It was a gallant resolution, but it had been a bitter
one to carry out, and the source too of some of his
worst unpopularity. Labourers! Who that knows
Ireland but has a responsive groan to offer upon the
altar of that topic? Poor Mr O'Brien had expended
many groans, but they had not been very fruitful
ones. To obtain a fair day's work in return for a
fair day's wage, was a feat which he had set all his
pride and all his powers of will to accomplish. He
had argued, pleaded, bribed, had done everything that
man could do to procure that end. Needless to say,
he had been beaten at every point. He had given
up the contest now. He employed fewer men than
formerly, but those few had as comfortable and satisfactory a time as any set of "labourers" within the
four seas. Whereas, formerly, he had been rather

given to surprising offenders,—pouncing upon them at unexpected moments, and from unlooked-for points, —now, on the contrary, he was careful to make known his approach by loud coughs and other unmistakable signals. He was rewarded by invariably finding a magnificent display of industry whenever he approached—every man plunging his spade into the soil with a sort of desperation, as if a bet of a thousand pounds, at least, depended upon his individual industry.

At the sound of hoofs clattering up the avenue he looked round with an air of surprise, and a frown came to his forehead when he perceived his visitor.

Mr Higgins, however, gave him no time to speak. He dashed at once into the thick of the subject.

" I am sorry to be obliged to—ar—trouble you, Mr O'Brien," he said, reining in his horse beside him, and speaking in a tone of formality. " But I have come upon a matter of—*business*,"—the emphasis upon the last word was very emphatic.

Mr O'Brien bowed, and stood waiting to hear what the business was.

" There has been, I—ar—regret to say, an atrocious crime, a—ar—murder, perpetrated within my district, and—Mr Cavanagh being at Limerick—I am obliged to come to you as the nearest magistrate for a warrant for the arrest of the—ar—criminal."

Another murder ! Mr O'Brien fell back a step or two, and gazed upon his informant with a face of horror. " Who is it ? " he said, hoarsely.

" A man of the name of Brady—a tenant, I believe, of your own."

There was a discernible note of triumph, for Mr

Higgins had not forgotten their last conversation. Mr
O'Brien, however, only heard the fact itself.

" Good God ! " he said, below his breath ; and then
" Good God ! " again.   " The man is dead, you say ? "

" Stone dead.   I left the body where it was found,
and expect to find the coroner there upon my return.
The place is a—ar—valley about two miles from
here."

Mr O'Brien turned away.   The indifferent officialism of the other's tone jarred upon him.   " Good
God !   Good God ! " he repeated over and over inwardly.   He had begun to lull himself into a sort of
half belief that matters were really at last beginning
to mend, and here now was a fresh crime, and at his
very door.   He forgot that the other man was waiting—forgot everything but the fact itself.   It had
been a common enough occurrence for him to have
got " used," perhaps, as people say, to it, but who
ever really succeeds in getting " used " to such incidents ?   His horror was not quite impersonal either.
It was *he* who had put this man Brady into that farm
for the occupying of which he had doubtless met his
death.   Against advice too he had done it.   Hurrish's
words, " There'll be bad wark—the divil's *own* bad
wark ! " came back vividly to his mind.   The devil's
own work, indeed !   Was the country given over
then to devils ?   Were they all in a league together ?
Was there never, *never* to be an end of these horrors
which blackened the very name of Irishman ?

" What did you say about wanting a warrant
against some one,—who is it ? " he inquired, turning
eagerly to Mr Higgins, whose face expressed his ill-
restrained impatience.

" A man called—ar—O'Brien,—Hurrish O'Brien."

The other man also called O'Brien fell back, and stared at the inspector with an air of stupefaction. "Nonsense!" he exclaimed at last, indignantly. " Hurrish O'Brien! Nonsense! Impossible!"

Mr Higgins stiffened his chin. " It is the man's own brother who has given the evidence," he said.

" What man's brother?"

" The murdered man's."

" 'Tis a lie then, whoever says it! Why, I've known Hurrish O'Brien ever since he was that high. He would be as incapable of killing a man in cold blood as I should myself!"

Mr Higgins shrugged his shoulders. " Let us hope it—ar—is so," he said. " In the meanwhile the evidence seems to me to be of a—ar—very serious character. May I trouble you to sign this warrant. You will see that it is ready filled up. Allow me to offer you a stilo."

Mr O'Brien took no notice of the stilo. " I tell you, I totally disbelieve in Hurrish O'Brien having anything to say to it," he said angrily.

Mr Higgins smiled serenely.

" *Totally* disbelieve in it, do you hear?" the other repeated.

Mr Higgins smiled again. " You will scarcely decline to sign the warrant upon that account, I—ar— presume?" he said significantly.

It was the wrong note to strike. This insistent officialism was exactly calculated to set Mr O'Brien's pride bristling at once.

" On the contrary, that is precisely what I *do* decline to do," he said curtly. " If upon further exam-

ination the man is found to be guilty,—which I totally
disbelieve,—there will be plenty of time to arrest him
then. If not—as I am convinced will turn out to be
the case—the Government will be spared another
blunder brought upon it by the zeal of its officials. I
decline to sign a warrant for the committal of a man
whom I believe to be as innocent as myself."

Mr Higgins was genuinely incapable of answering.
New as he was to this work, he was an official to the
backbone, and that any one would refuse an official
demand was an idea which had never entered into his
imagination.

"You—ar—decline !" he exclaimed, in a tone of
stupefaction.

"Emphatically. I wish you good morning, Mr
Higgins ; you will excuse me,—my men are wait-
ing for me in the next field,"—and away walked Mr
O'Brien across the grass.

To describe Mr Higgins's feelings as he rode back
with the still unsigned warrant in his pocket, would
be beyond my powers. The refusal was in his eyes
rather a grosser violation of law, if anything, than the
murder itself. Refuse to sign a warrant ! Refuse to
support the authority of the constabulary ! The man
must be *mad*. There could be no other explanation !
It is true that it was not necessary, in strict law, to
obtain a magistrate's warrant before arresting a supposed criminal,—the constabulary being perfectly free
to do so without one. They did it in that case, however, at their own risk, and there had not been wanting cases lately where such an excess of zeal had
been rewarded with anything but comfortable consequences. On the whole, therefore, he decided, though

against his will, to delay taking any further steps until Mr Cavanagh's return from Limerick, which was fortunately expected that very evening. But if this fellow O'Brien took the opportunity of escaping in the meanwhile? Mr Higgins's feeling was that in that case his namesake ought to be tried, and if necessary hanged, in his place!

By the time he got back a much larger crowd had collected in the amphitheatre,—the news of the deed having spread with the rapidity with which such news seems invariably endowed. It had awakened some excitement and more curiosity, so that gradually every one belonging to Tubbamina, with the exception of those away at Ballyvaughan for the fair, had gathered around the spot. To none did the news come with more startling surprise than to the very men who, as will be remembered, had undertaken that duty themselves, but had been prevented by a succession of such accidents as will occur even in the best regulated societies. Andy Holohun was at first disposed to give the credit of the achievement to Peter O'Flanagan, and Peter O'Flanagan to Andy Holohun. When, upon further inquiries, passed rapidly from mouth to mouth and ear to ear, it turned out that neither of these heroes could claim the credit, the perplexity and excitement deepened perceptibly. As for Hurrish O'Brien, no one at first even thought of him. He had put up with Mat Brady's provocations so long, that his patience had become a sort of local proverb; and although at the drawing of lots it had been arranged that the lot should fall upon him, it had been more a sort of support to other backsliders, than from the slightest expectation that he would really

undertake the office. When, therefore, it became
known that Maurice Brady had actually denounced
him, and had demanded that a warrant should be
taken out against him, a thrill of genuine excitement
ran through the whole assembly. Every one liked
Hurrish; every one was aware of the sum of in-
debtedness which Maurice Brady owed to him.
Murder is a trifle, but ingratitude of this sort is a
crime which strikes with the fullest possible effect
upon an Irish imagination.

Long before the coroner had arrived, measures had
been taken to warn Hurrish. A boy had been secretly
despatched to Ballyvaughan, to let him know what
was on foot, so that if he decided to escape he could
do so, or at any rate could keep out of the way until
after the coroner had sat. When that important
official at last appeared upon the scene, there was
a general slipping away on the part of all the men
present, none of whom particularly desired being
called upon to serve on the jury. It was not, therefore, without some difficulty and considerable delay
that the necessary dozen demanded by the law were
secured, and marched down the hill under the charge
of an escort of police.

A wilder, more essentially law-defying dozen were
rarely perhaps gathered together at the command of
the law. Some of the men looked scared ; others
fierce and excited ; others again sullen and indifferent ; while some, including the two recreants Andy
Holohun and Peter O'Flanagan, were evidently rather
pleased and tickled by the whole proceeding. Not a
few of the jurymen were in absolute rags,—tatterdemalion loafers at the corners of the street, and hangers-

on upon the charity of others. Several were very
old men, wearing the knee-breeches and tail-coats of a
generation ago, amongst whom was our old acquaintance Phil Rooney, who had been attracted like others
to the scene, and been promptly pounced upon as .a
" dacent " man, less likely than others to give a verdict in direct opposition to the evidence. No intelligence or educational qualification, however, is required
in a jury of this kind. Indeed poor Thady-na-Taggart
was one of the original dozen, and only escaped by
taking to his heels, and starting across the rocks at
a pace which the official who had secured him did
not see his way to imitating.

When all were collected, they were marched down
to take up their places at the bottom of the amphitheatre, where the coroner, Mr Higgins, and Maurice
Brady were already assembled, — the constabulary,
who had by this time been recruited by others from
a more distant barracks, keeping order, and preventing the crowd from pressing too closely upon the
group around the body.

A strange scene truly !—characteristic of people,
country, times ! On one side the dozen unwilling
ministers of the law—whole-coated or ragged-coated,
as the case might be ; on the other the coroner, a
stout little man in a suit of rusty black, with a pock-
marked, dim-complexioned face, imperceptible nose,
and air of vulgar importance. Beside him Mr Higgins, stiff and thick-set, stolid English officialism
stamped upon every line of his heavy-featured, commonplace face. A little way off, in marked contrast
to these two, Maurice Brady, tall, slight, and erect,
his arms crossed upon his chest, his pale handsome

face and resolute disdainful air giving him rather
the aspect of some political prisoner — an Emmet
or a Wolfe Tone—at the bar of his country's enemies.   Behind, and as a background to these, the
wild helter-skelter crowd of idlers and lookers-on—
women with blue cloaks, bare feet, ragged red petticoats ; old hags, bewrinkled and hideous ; half-naked
boys, who skipped about, active as goats, amongst
the rocks, and were with difficulty restrained by the
police.   Every now and then some fresh figures
would appear over the edge of the basin, hurrying
eagerly down to the scene below.   After its long
ages of idleness and vacancy, the amphitheatre had
at last vindicated its existence.   It was a theatre indeed to-day ! a theatre brimming over with eager
spectators.   Ledge above ledge, rock over rock, the
rows of wild, excited faces rose one above the other
—the sun streaming in sleepy oblique bands over
the whole, a few astonished sheep or goats showing
their white, impassive faces here and there amongst
the crowd.

After a little delay the examination began.   Maurice Brady was the first witness.

Questioned by the coroner.   " The deceased is your
brother ? "

" Yes."

" When did you see him last alive ? "

" Four days since."

" He was then in his ordinary health? "

" Yes."

" Have you reason to think that your brother was
upon bad terms with any one ? "

" I have."

" With whom ? "

" With Hurrish O'Brien."

At this answer, given in a clear distinct tone, a sudden murmur ran through the crowd,—a low buzz of anger, indignation, contempt. A thrill of excitement passed through Maurice Brady. It was the first note of popular displeasure he had ever heard! It nerved him for the moment, however, rather than daunted. " Fools ! did they suppose he cared a ha'porth about *their* opinions ? " he thought contemptuously.

The examination continued. Was it in consequence of his brother having taken the farm from which the Maloneys had been evicted that he and O'Brien had quarrelled ?

To this, rather to the surprise of some of the hearers, the witness answered " No."

Questioned further whether he had ever received any warnings that his brother was in danger ? Answered, " Yes." " Was the person he was in danger from Hurrish O'Brien ? " Answered, " Yes." Questioned who had given him that information ? Answered—nothing.

His examination was then suspended while the other witnesses were called. The first was one of the constabulary, who deposed to having been told by a boy who was passing the barracks that a body was lying in the valley below. That he and another constable thereupon came to the place, and found the body lying as it was at present. The boy, he said, had run off, and had not been seen since, but they would no doubt be able to lay hands on him if he was required. He also deposed to finding the gun,

which he produced, both barrels of which were
empty.

The next witness was the dispensary doctor, who
had partially examined the body previous to the
arrival of the coroner. The deceased had, in his
opinion, he said, died from the effects of the blow
visible upon the temple. There was no gunshot
wound, or other wound or concussion of any kind, so
far as he had ascertained, with the exception of a
slight injury to the back of the head. The blow
upon the temple must have been given by a very
heavy weapon, probably a hammer or a loaded stick.
Death in all probability had resulted directly from
effusion of blood to the brain : he should be able,
however, he said, to form a more decided opinion on
this point after the regular *post-mortem* examination.
His evidence ended by his stating that so violent and
so instantaneously fatal a blow could only, in his
opinion, have been inflicted by an unusually powerful
man.

This was practically all the evidence. There was
not much delay either about the verdict : accidental
death was evidently impracticable, even to the ingenuity of an Irish jury. No man, by any stretch of
activity, stupidity, or ingenuity, could have given that
blow on the head to himself. There was only one
other alternative, therefore. The twelve men unani-
mously brought in an open verdict—murder against
some person or persons unknown.

As soon as this business was finished, and the
embodied majesty of the law had broken itself up
again into its individual insignificance, four of the
constabulary advanced, lifted the body of the unfor-

tunate Brady from the ground, laid it upon a hurdle, kept at the barracks for such purposes, and, taking each a corner, bore it away uphill at a brisk walk.

The crowd fell back on all sides as it advanced through their midst. Some of the women crossed themselves, and the elder men removed their hats. The rest, including those who had just been serving on the jury, stood looking on with an air of sullen indifference. When, however, Maurice Brady followed, this indifference changed. Symptoms of anger broke out. No actual menaces were uttered, but all eyes, even those of the women, fixed themselves upon him with an expression of sudden repulsion. He was only half aware of this himself, however, as he avoided looking any one fully in the face, his chief desire being to get away from them all as quickly as possible, and to be alone.

It was a long hard climb for the four bearers, and they were obliged several times to put the hurdle down in order to rest. A couple of men who had followed at a little distance were called to once and offered money if they would assist in the carriage, but they peremptorily declined, and turned away immediately down a side-path. When the top of the ridge was at last reached, the narrow, hemmed-in world of rocks in which they had been all this while enclosed, changed suddenly to a wide-reaching world of sea, and land, and sky, green on the side of South Clare, grey where the terraced hills of Burren stretched for miles. Tubbamina lay immediately below them, a melancholy cluster of whitewashed cabins, surrounding a squat and sordid-looking chapel; beyond lay the beautiful widely open mouth of the bay of Gal-

way, with the long low line of coast reaching from
that town to Greatman's Bay ; and far, far away, over
the shimmering waters of the bay, and over all the
low-lying country between, the saw-edged outline of
the Twelve Pins of Bennabeola rose, one behind the
other, softened, made mystical, spiritualised, against a
clear blue, milky-looking sky.

Land and water were so mingled, one might almost
say interpenetrated, in the picture, that it was hard
to say where the one began and the other ended.
The stern, forbidding rocks beyond Blackhead were
bathed in soft caressing sunlight, as the sea broke in
green volumes along their base. At one point the
water could be seen glittering far inland in a number
of tiny lakes, linked together and melted into one by
distance. At another, small rocks and islets—illauns,
carricks, and carrickeens—bedotted the edges of the
coast, where two or three brown-sailed hookers were
slowly creeping along, every sail set to catch the
capricious breeze. Due west the three isles of Aran
streamed across the mouth of the bay,—the two great
cyclopean forts of Dun Ængus, and its brother Dun
Conchobhair, even at this distance the most conspicuous features in their low, flat, tabular outline.

The descent upon the other side to that lower col
or ridge upon which the Bradys' cabin stood was
another change again. They had to pass along a
narrow lane, sunk deep in the rocks, through breaks
in which small square fields, covered with stones,
became visible. Here and there were a few scant
patches of potatoes and oats, all neglected and deep
in weeds. A quantity of sea-gulls were collected in
screaming excitement at one spot. Crows stalked

to and fro over the grass with an air of protectorship, and some large red and white cows looked up with an air of mild-eyed interest and wonder as the gloomy little procession passed them by. To them, no doubt, as to others, it was quite a cheerful and pleasing break in the uninteresting monotony of their lives.

CHAPTER XIV.

MAURICE'S NIGHT THOUGHTS.

At last they reached the cabin. It was unspeakably miserable,—several sizes larger than Hurrish's, but naked, bald, and dreary beyond words. Not a tree— not even the all-prevailing hawthorn; not a flower; not an attempt or a pretence of a garden; not a paling—nothing to relieve the stark and stony air of desolation. The walls had once been whitewashed, but the big stones had long ago reasserted themselves in all directions over the surface. What remained of the whitewash was all smeared and streaked with long green and yellow weather-stains, giving it an indescribably dank, bilious, and soddened aspect. A large cow-house flanked it on one side, and a pig-sty on the other; but these symptoms of prosperity were if anything rather more filthy, rickety, and tumble-down than the original building. To Maurice this ancestral abode of his had always been a source of unspeakable discomfort, the more so that his brother was a well-to-do man, with plenty of live-stock, and even a considerable sum of money laid away in bank. To-day he hardly heeded it, however. The external aspect of things had ceased, for the time being, to produce any particular impression one way or other upon his mind.

They laid the unfortunate Mat upon his own bed, which was in the inner room. Then the policemen came out, and stood waiting. Maurice, with that ineffaceable instinct of hospitality which survives all vicissitudes, looked about for whisky, but could find none. There were three or four empty barrels lying about, and a whole mountain of empty bottles at one corner. The furniture was originally of a better quality seemingly than at Hurrish's house, but broken for the most part almost to splinters, as if habitually used as missiles. The fire, too, had gone out, and though the afternoon was warm, the black dismal fireplace struck a sense of chilling desolation. It seemed as if Death had seated itself in bodily presence upon the hearth.

Maurice looked round for some means of relighting it. There was no turf to be seen, however, so he went outside to the stack, which was close to the cow-house. At the door he encountered one of the two men who worked for his brother,—a big, ragged, hulking fellow, who stood staring about, his mouth half open, in idle vacancy. This man he ordered, in his usual tone of unquestionable authority, to go and fetch some turf, and make the fire up at once. The fellow waited until he had done speaking, then, suddenly turning upon him, cursed him with a hideous oath, and asked him whether he supposed that he was going to demean himself by doing anything for

a —— informer ? turned on his heel, and so walked
away.

Maurice Brady stood still as if a thunderbolt from
heaven had fallen upon him.   An informer !   The
word seemed to echo and vibrate with brazen tongues
and trumpets all about the place !   The constables,
finding probably that no refreshments were forthcoming after their long climb, came out, and one of
them told Maurice in passing that they would be on
the road by turns all that night, in case of any disturbance.

He made no answer.   He was incapable of speaking.   " An informer ! "   That was all he heard,
knew, thought of.   He, Maurice Brady, an *informer!*
When they had gone, he stumbled back into the house,
and sat down upon the first stool he met with, his
head ringing with the word, a whirling noise like the
rumble of machinery sounding continually in his ears.

If any one of a higher calibre even had said it, he
could have borne it better.   But a fellow like Lanty
Bradigan !   a hind, a savage, a cutter of turf and
drawer of water !   a wretched ignorant creature, whom
he had always swept into the very dust with his
contempt !   It stung him to the very pith and
marrow of his bones, through his pride, through his
self-respect, through everything.   It seemed a fore-
taste, too, of other scornings and hissings which he
was likely to encounter, as if fierce contemptuous
fingers were being pointed at him in all directions.
" An informer ! "   Word summing up everything
that to an Irishman of his type is expressive of
ignominy !   Heavens and earth !   he, Maurice Brady,
to be branded as an informer !

M

How long he sat there he could not afterwards
have told. Suddenly he came to himself with a
start, and looked round. There was not a living creature there besides himself,—not a cat even, or a dog.
In front the black hearth stared at him with its
sickly air of conscious desolation. It had begun to
grow dark, too, and the corners of the room were
already deep in shadow. The door of the inner one
was partially opened, and he could see a corner of
the bed and a bit of the blanket. He averted his
eyes from it in quick horror—a horror which seemed to
rise like some sort of foul exhalation from the ground.
All the scenes of that long day rushed back upon
him suddenly. He felt glued to his seat by a creeping terror, which rose and rose, until it seemed to
clutch at his throat with icy hands. All his life he
had prided himself upon his exceptional freedom
from superstition of all sorts, but the events of the
day had been against him. He had the blood of
endless generations of Connaught peasants in his
veins, and he found himself battling in vain against
the rising demon.

The whole house was like a grave ! His blood
congealed, and a cold thrill of terror seemed to shoot
along his spine. Alone with a corpse ! He remembered his mother lying dead there in that very room:
he had been only a boy at the time, still he recalled
it vividly. How white and thin she had looked,
poor woman, worn out with much trouble and many
tears. Suddenly a fresh terror seized him. What
if she should come back to-night to look down at
this step-son who had used her so brutally ! His
teeth chattered at the thought. A sense of other

presences —intangible, invisible, terrible—filled his brain with horror, and he rose with a violent effort from his stool, resolved to escape. Nothing should induce him, he determined, to remain there a minute longer.

As he approached the door a sudden loud rap came to the other side of it. He started violently, and hesitated, then went forward after a moment and opened it.

It was no very formidable invasion! Only a couple of poor old crones, who had come up from the village, according to custom, to do the last offices for the dead man, and to offer, if his brother wished it, to spend the night in the house. The two old creatures' hideous, mumbling, bewrinkled faces were as beautiful to Maurice at that moment as if they had been a pair of white-winged seraphs. Telling them to do whatever they chose, and to get whatever they wanted, he hastily gave them a handful of silver, took an ulster belonging to him over his arm, and, leaving the house, ran down the road with an elastic sense of escape.

It was not until he had got outside that he remembered that he had literally nowhere else to go. To return to Miltown-Malbay at that hour of the evening was impossible. There was not a house in the neighbourhood which would have consented to take him in, and had there been even, his pride would have forbidden his stooping to ask for a shelter which might have been refused. Happily the night was fine ; he could sleep anywhere,—in a cave, under a bush, in a hollow—no matter where. Suddenly he remembered a place where he had often

lain out as a boy. He would go there, he resolved,
and, so resolving, climbed over the nearest wall, and
betook himself along a sort of cornice or ledge which
extended for some distance above the line of small
fields in the direction of the sea.

After about half an hour's walking he came to the
place, a small pocket or hollow in the side of the
ridge. It had once probably been a little lake or
"corrie," but was now empty, the subterranean stream
which formerly fed it having got diverted elsewhere.
It was quite dry, and on the upper side a low but
dense fringe of dwarf hawthorn bushes sheltered it ef-
fectually against the wind, so that even in very cold
weather a man might lie here and be, comparatively
speaking, warm. Maurice spread out his ulster upon
the bottom of the hollow, threw himself upon it,
pulling a piece over his legs, and lay down, pillowing
his head on his hands.

The small patches of cultivated ground were by
this time all behind, and only the rock-covered side
of the landscape visible from where he lay. Far as
he could see the grey stony waves of the Burren
extended. He could see the thin jagged line of rocks
which marked the opening to the Gortnacoppin valley,
but the eye passed over it almost without a break.
A few clouds had gathered, and all round the western
horizon a heavy flouncing of solemn-looking purple
rose above the sea. Higher up the sky was clear
and almost colourless, everything seeming to be united
in one clear uniform wash of grey. It was extraordinarily desolate. In the direction in which he
was looking, not a house, not a moving speck, not
a living thing of any sort or kind, was to be seen.

You might have imagined that no foot had ever trodden the earth, no sod ever been turned, no sower ever gone forth with his hands full of the grain of the coming years. Trackless, untamable, solitary, the wide hungry-looking country sloped away to the grey, solitary, all-devouring sea.

Under ordinary circumstances Maurice Brady would hardly have noticed whether it was desolate or not. He was not particularly sensitive to external impressions, having too much to think of generally to care what sort of a landscape he was looking at. Neither did he in the least mind being alone—as a rule preferred it—so few of the people he knew were worth being with. To-day, however, it began after a while to make an impression upon him. He wished that he could see something moving, if it were only a sheep or a cow. The cold vacant face of solitude impressed him here as the sense of unknown and unseen companionship had impressed him in the house, only in a different way. He felt chilled, nervous, forlorn, as if he had just been driven away from all human companionship—an outcast and an alien from all his kind.

The experience is probably not exceptional. Loneliness is only one word, but it covers a perfect multiplicity of sensations. Days, weeks, months of a man s own society may slide by without his often being even aware of them—without the faintest sense of loneliness coming near him. At another time a few hours is sufficient to create a feeling of alienation which seems to brand the very soul, and to carry it to the uttermost brink of despair, madness—death.

He tried to shake it off by dwelling upon other

things—upon the future. But what future had he
now? he asked himself bitterly. A single day, a
few hours, had sufficed to bring about the ruin of all
his prospects, all his hopes. He remembered how he
used to lie here as a boy looking out at this same
naked world of crags, pining like a young hawk in a
cage for the time when he would be a man, when he
would take his place in the world; planning how he
would distinguish himself,—he was not very sure
how, it is true, but certainly be universally praised
and admired. It was almost inevitable that this train
of thought should bring with it the thought of
Hurrish O'Brien—Hurrish who, of all his surroundings, had alone encouraged him in these visions. He
could see his face—the good-natured mouth half open
with admiration and wonder; the eyes——   No, he
would not see it,—he resolved he would *not*. He
sprang up hastily, and, leaving his ulster behind him,
mounted a few hundred steps above the corrie, and
sat down again upon the ridge, turning his face in
the opposite direction.

Here the most prominent object was the Donore
woods and lake which lay immediately below. The
dusk was fast blurring all minor details, but he could
see the outline of the lake, and the grey mass of the
house with some white steps in front. A few lights
shone in the upper part of the house, but the bottom
was all dark and blank. He sat here a long while
with his elbows upon his knees, not thinking definitely, but glooming dismally over everything. He
hardly thought of Mat now. The nearer and more
personal trouble was wearing away the other, as a
stronger acid eats out a weaker one. His own

balked ambition, his own blighted prospects, gnawed
at his heart, and seemed to rise up before him like
a bodily presence, and to reproach him with their
changed aspects. He shivered with discomfort and
bitter angry self-dissatisfaction. Then a wind arose
and made it chilly upon the ridge, so that he shivered again with cold, and after a while returned to
the corrie, wrapped himself in his ulster, shut his
eyes resolutely, and soon afterwards fell asleep.

He dreamed wild confused dreams—dreams of
struggling and fighting, guns firing, men falling over
cliffs, Mat and Hurrish fighting and struggling together, but always, somehow, Mat attacking Hurrish
and trying to kill him, never the other way. Then
he dreamed that he was in a boat alone, he did not
know where, but the motion was very strange,—not
like that of a boat, more as if he were being carried
along over rough ground. All at once he was struggling in the water, only it was not water at all, but
sand, like the sands at Miltown-Malbay,—great yellow
waves of sand blown by the wind, passing one over
the other, and engulfing him horribly in their depths.
Again and again he tried to escape, but the more he
tried the more they swept down upon him, and rolled
him over and over, and filled his mouth, and his ears,
and his nostrils, and he sank down deeper and deeper,
and there was a noise as of mill-wheels, and it was
all dark and horrible, and like a grave. Then he
dreamt that he saw a coracle coming with a bright
white light fastened in the middle of it, and in the
coracle sat his mother and Hurrish and Alley. And
Alley screamed when she saw him, and hid her face ;
and his mother screamed too, and told him to be

gone. But Hurrish jumped into the sand and tried
to pull him out, but the sand held him fast, and he
could not get loose; it was like pitch,—as fast as he
got free in one place he was seized in another. And
all at once he perceived that it was not sand at all,
but people,—men and women, hundreds and thousands of them,—all clamouring, and roaring, and
making hideous faces at him. And they all shrieked
with one accord that he was " an informer! an informer !" and that he must be torn in pieces. And
Hurrish tried to pull him away, but failed. And
some of the people had dog's faces, and others had
helmets like the policemen ; but most of them seemed
dead, and had their eyes shut, and white bands under
their chins. Then suddenly Alley took up the light
and held it close to the crowd, so that he could see
them all distinctly. And the light seemed to make
the people melt as if they had been made of wax,
and they fell back little by little, and lay in heaps,
one on top of another, until at last he saw that they
were not people at all, but seaweed. Then Hurrish
took him up in his arms and put him into the boat,
and they rowed away together up the Gortnacoppin
valley until they came to the cabin where old Bridget
was standing stirring the pot, and when she saw him
she shrieked, and took up the boiling pot in her hand
and ran at him, and tried to fling it over him ; and
he struggled, and they both fell together upon the
floor, and the boiling water rolled everywhere and
spread about like a new sea. And with that he
awoke and found himself upon his back in the corrie,
a newly-risen moon shining full upon his face, and
all the stony country around swimming in a silver

mist, which almost hid the Atlantic. And he shivered and gathered the ulster closely about him, for the air was very chill, and soon afterwards fell asleep again, and this time dreamed pleasanter things—of his boyhood, of Hurrish's admiration, of the great things he himself was to do when he grew up to be a man. But when he awoke the second time, and found that it was daylight, one of the first things he did was to wonder whether Mr Cavanagh, the resident magistrate, had yet returned from Limerick.

CHAPTER XV.

ALLEY'S NIGHT THOUGHTS.

Alley Sheehan came to herself very gradually after Maurice had left her. For some time she lay upon the same spot, hardly knowing what had happened, or why she was there at all. The act of fainting was so unfamiliar, that it seemed like a sort of death —as if she had passed out of the world, and then come back to it again. Little by little as she recovered, all the dreadful weight of gloom came floating slowly back across her poor little soul, as black thunder-clouds float back across some tiny pool or brook. She was too utterly worn out, however, to try and think it all out now—she who in the course of her short simple life had never hardly had to think before. After a while, therefore, she gathered herself up from the ground and began wearily retracing her

steps, turning instinctively towards what she called
her home, and crawling over the rocks with the
languid, trailing step of one suddenly overtaken with
old age.

She was met at the door by Bridget, who hailed
upon her a furious volley of abuse and execrations,
which would probably have proceeded to yet more
violent extremities but that the old woman was too
excited by the day's events to be able to turn her
thoughts for more than a minute in any other direction.   She moved about the cabin with an air of
savage exultation, waving her hands and crashing
them down with triumph upon every object they
encountered.   "At last!" her expression seemed to
say.   "At last, ye gods—at last!"   So visibly ex-
ultant was she, that it was probably just as well for
Hurrish that the police did not come at once to the
cabin in search of him, or even those professional
dullards might have succeeded for once in extracting
something from her in her present excitement.

Alley kept out of the way as well as the narrow
dimensions of the cabin would admit of, too weary
and sick at heart even to feel any alarm.   Happily,
when night came, Bridget roughly ordered her to un-
dress at once and go to bed.   The old woman was in
a state of constantly increasing and now almost con-
vulsive excitement.   The boys had come in, and had
repeated what had happened at the inquest, of which
they had formed part of the irregular audience.   Hurrish had not yet returned from Ballyvaughan,—indeed
his mother did not know whether he intended to do
so, or to try and escape at once.   She was proud,
and pleased, and excited, and horribly frightened all

at once; above all, she was suspicious, and Alley
Sheehan was the chief object of her suspicions. She
had always regarded the girl as an interloper—an
eater of other people's bread,—an intruder where she
was not wanted and had no business to be; and now
in addition she began to suspect her of being a spy,
a traitor. The scene beside the dead man's body
that morning had suggested to her violent and utterly
unreasoning old wits that Alley would be capable
of betraying Hurrish—selling him to the "polis"!
With this idea in her mind she never allowed the
poor child out of her sight, following her about all
the afternoon with angry bloodshot glances, as she
moved to and fro about her various household duties,
trying as usual to bring a little order into the crowded
and chronic disorders of the scene. Fortunately for
herself, Alley knew nothing of these suspicions. And
when she had given the boys their supper, washed
out the black pot and left it with a supply of water
ready to Bridget's hand, she crawled thankfully into
the heap of rags and straw, covered with a blanket,
which she and little Katty shared in the inner room;
and there, gathering the child up closely first into her
arms for comfort and sustainment, worn out with the
events of the day, she sobbed herself to sleep.

When she awoke it was still deep night, but a moon
had risen, and was sending a thin, straggling, zigzag
ray of light through the window set in the stone
wall immediately above her bed. It was not often
that the moonlight was able to come in there, for the
window was so small that it was only at one particular angle that it could hit off the tiny square,
barely six inches either way—a square, alas! care-

fully puttied in on all sides, and utterly useless
therefore for the much-needed purpose of ventilation.

Alley lay for a while looking at the silver ray, as
it partially lit up the narrow, dusty interior—the
bed where the two boys slept, the corner where a
number of chickens were reposing upon a bar of
wood stuck into the wall for their convenience, the
fly-blown prints which constituted the only approach
to adornment. Then moving carefully so as not to
awaken little Katty, who lay curled in a pink ball
with her two fat thumbs in her mouth, she got upon
her knees and lifted herself up until she could peep
through the window— putting her face necessarily
close to the solid, greenish glass for that purpose.

After the narrow obscurity of the dim interior,
there was something startling in the luminousness of
that stony world which met her view without. Under
the wide wash of moonlight every stone showed
visibly, each dashed in in white, as if a slight shower
of snow had lately fallen. The deep rifts which
crossed the platforms in every direction looked black
and sharp, as if ruled in ink upon that snowy surface. Some big nightbird—probably an owl—flew
by with a sudden whirring of its wings. The wide
arch of sky was bare of cloud right down to the
very horizon, a few stars pulsating faintly far in the
dreamy West. Alley shivered, and felt frightened at
that immensity. It seemed to confront her sternly
and threateningly, as if to demand her secret, and
she turned hurriedly back to the small room and its
overflowing occupants, with a sense of relief and
human companionship.

The door into the outer room was open, and the

moon had by this time found its way in there too.
Her eye mechanically followed the white guiding
finger, as it traversed the thick darkness, heavy with
human breath, and the lingering smoke from the big
chimney. It lit upon the top of a bed—the only
one in the establishment deserving of the name—
brought there, as she knew well, by her aunt, Mary
Sheehan, upon her marriage. A black curly head
lay upon the pillow of this bed, and the white guiding finger, which had just travelled to the spot, rested
full upon the features of Hurrish, as he lay with one
arm outside the blanket, which heaved slowly up
and down, under the rhythmic rise and fall of his
broad chest.

Alley had been used to seeing Hurrish there ever
since, as a child of nine years old, she had first come
to the cabin. As to there being any impropriety or
indecorum in such close neighbourhood, such an idea
had never even distantly crossed her imagination.
She was pure as only a girl brought up in such a
state of utterly savage innocence could be pure—
pure, that is, to the point of barely realising the
existence of impurity. Now, however, she started
up, and gazed at him with widely-distended eyes, as
if she had seen him there for the first time. It
brought back all the terrors of the day before with
such horrible, such appalling vividness. She seemed
to live over again the moment when she had first
discovered the dead man, and that still worse moment
when old Bridget had flourished the blackthorn stick
in her face, and had told her, with fiendish glee, that
Hurrish was the murderer! Was it true? Was he,
could he be, that dreadful thing? Would he be

sleeping there so peacefully—as peacefully as his
own little Katty curled up in the bed beside her—if
he had really killed Mat Brady ?   A murderer she
felt sure would look very differently,— more like the
ugly yellow Judas in the picture which hung over
the dresser—angry, scowling, dark,—not good and
kind like Hurrish, whose face looked pleased and
friendly even in his sleep.

Like every girl of her class and country, Alley
was perfectly well used to hearing murder talked of,
and talked of, too, without any special reprobation.
She had heard such talk going on around her all her
life, though the deeds described were naturally rarely
called by so offensive a name.   In all these cases,
however, there had been a certain vagueness about
the actual perpetrator.   It was " justice," the " society,"
the " brotherhood "; and the " society " has in Ireland
long since come to occupy in popular imagination the
place of a despised and derided executive.   Even so
Alley had often shuddered at the ideas which the
talk had called up.   Sensitive natures, however accustomed to horrible images, rarely accept them in their
entirety.   They start aside and cry, " Not that ! not
that ! "   They invent some other and less terrible
explanation to account for what they hear.   Even a
Roman girl, accustomed from babyhood to hearing of
the delights of the amphitheatre, must now and then
have turned sick with horror, one would think, when
first some time - honoured piece of barbarity was
enacted before her eyes,—must have implored, with
streaming eyes, that this or that particular victim
might be allowed to escape.   Alley, poor little trembling soul, was no Roman maiden, and the harsh

realities of her lot pressed with cruel severity upon
her gentle timorous spirit. She remained there for
some time kneeling upon the bed, suffering as only
such a spirit can suffer when brought for the first
time face to face with those hideous and, alas! not
imaginary phantoms—Death, Suffering, Crime. At
last, with a sort of despair, she got up, crossed the
room, took down her rosary from the nail where
it hung, got back into bed again, crossed herself,
and began to pray.

She prayed for Hurrish, for Maurice, for herself—
that she might be good, that she might not be so
frightened, that she might be delivered from evil.
As the beads slipped one by one through her fingers,
her lips mechanically repeated the prayers given to
be recited with them. Her thoughts, however, out-
flew the words. There was a native tide of adoration, a flow of innocent love in her spiritual nature
which seemed to supply the place of that intellect
which she certainly did not possess, and which gave
her strength in the midst of her fears. Kneeling
there upon her miserable bed, her face uplifted, her
wide innocent eyes fixed upon the small square of
light overhead, she might have suggested the image
of some pure and sainted soul, come from its serene
abode to visit some dark and loathsome tomb. Her
slight girlish figure, denuded of the uncouth clothes
which she wore in the daytime, and half bathed in
the stream of white light, looked vaporous and unreal.
She was hardly herself conscious of her body, hardly
conscious of her fatigue—even the terrors of the day
before seemed to melt away in the glow of her
thoughts. It was as if she were caught up by some

power external to herself—caught as in a mother's
arms. That was her own feeling. Often when she
prayed it did actually seem to her as if a mother's
arms were around her. Was there not, in fact,
a mother always near — a kind, tender, pitying
mother ? a mother whom no amount of weakness
or faultiness could weary or alienate ?

At last she began to pray for Mat Brady. The
very thought of his name frightened her at first. She
seemed to see the scene again as she had seen it that
morning—the stony glen, the singing larks, the dead
man hideously twisted upon the ground, his blank
eyes fixed upon the sky, his hands lying loose amongst
the grass and flowers. The shock and terror returned,
and a horror filled the air. As she went on, however,
she gathered strength, and these terrors little by little
passed away. There was a particular prayer to be
used for the dead which she tried to remember. She
could not do so, however, so had to fall back upon
her own artless words instead. Her innocent spirit
followed the dull, brutish, crime-encumbered one, as
it fled into the darkness and the mystery. As she
prayed, this darkness seemed gradually to melt, and a
vague sense of light, of pity, and of opening doors, to
take its place. Then the light itself grew vaguer.
There was a sensation of hovering and floating, and
sounds like birds chirping, and the buzzing of bees.
Then these all melted together into a great silence
and poor little Alley was once more asleep.

When she awoke again it was broad daylight.
The boys were up and running about, half-dressed,
and lively as crickets, and old Bridget's harsh screaming voice was heard calling to her from the other

room to get up at once for a lazy hussy, and bring the child in.

She got up, feeling as if she had been beaten, and could hardly summon energy to collect and put on her own and little Katty's clothes. Washing was a ceremony for which—well-to-do, comparatively speaking, as the O'Briens were—there was, alas! remarkably slight provision.

When she got into the outer room Hurrish was sitting by the fire, lighting his pipe with a sod of " live " turf held between his finger and thumb; Lep —his lustrous brown eyes fixed upon his master— sitting erect beside him. She noticed that Hurrish did not turn round as he generally did and greet them with a laugh and a joking word; and although little Katty ran up to him at once, and caught him round the leg with her fat pinching fingers, he allowed her to do so without lifting her to his knee, or making any response to her baby prattle. Bridget, too, had lost her air of exultation, and stalked about the kitchen sullenly, only opening her lips to give utterance to some word of reprobation, usually addressed to Alley herself. The boys were the only people, in fact, who behaved as usual, and watched the pot and the manipulations of their grandmother's iron spoon with their customary air of eager, puppy-like expectation.

Twice while she was helping Bridget to prepare the stirabout a man came to the door, said a word to Hurrish, and then ran away again. He sat stolidly on by the fire, however, his pipe in his mouth, his eyes fixed upon the smouldering sods of turf. Suddenly a sound of panting was heard outside—" pant, pant, pant "—like a dog hard pressed that nears his

N

shelter. The door was flung open, and poor Thady-na-Taggart the "natural" rushed in. He stood stock-still for a moment on the threshold; his lank hair, blown wildly about by the wind, hung loosely over his white vacant face; his lack-lustre eyes—dazzled from the daylight—roamed round evidently in search of some one. At last he distinguished Hurrish, and rushing up to him, clutched him by the arms, urging him vehemently, though silently, to get up and come away with him. Lep barked and sprang angrily at the new-comer, then, as if ashamed, wagged his tail, and licked Thady's hand. Thady, however, took no notice; all his thoughts evidently were concentrated upon Hurrish. He first tried to pull him off his stool; that failing, put his arms bodily round him, as if to induce him to stand up. Then—Hurrish still declining to yield, and his weight being too great for him to pull him up by main force—he began frantically pulling off his own clothes, and hastily thrusting the first he got loose over Hurrish's head, evidently with the intention of dressing him up in them.

What wild idea of exchange of identity passed through the poor creature's bewildered brain Heaven alone knows! But that it was touching in its devotion, the idea was laughable to the last degree. Hurrish was considerably over six feet high, and broad in proportion; the idiot almost a dwarf, his ragged clothes, rain-shrunk and sun-discoloured, would barely have covered a third of the other man's body. At first Hurrish simply stared, failing to realise the meaning of the manœuvre. When he did so, a smile of sudden pity came into his face, and he caught hold

of poor Thady's hands to hinder the process being
carried further, which in another minute would have
left him standing stark naked upon the floor.

" Thire, thire, Thady! Sure I ondershtand what
ye're manin' *now*," he said, soothingly. " Don't be
shtripping of yersel' no more, for sure the clothes
wudn't cover th' half ov me. Be aisy, Thady dear ;
you'll see me safe again, sure an' sartin, whativer
happens ! "

Apparently the words failed to make any entrance
into the idiot's mind, for he remained, his clothes half
off, staring blankly, with an expression of piteous disappointment. The boys, who at first had remained
apart, now drew near, and stood gaping at him, as at
some strange wild animal they saw for the first time.
Suddenly Thady opened his mouth to the widest possible extent, and burst into loud lamentations, the
first sounds he had uttered since his entrance. Hurrish endeavoured to soothe him. Alley, too, drew
near, with an impulse of pity. But the idiot would
have none of their consolation. Gathering the remainder of his rags, and leaving the one that he had
tried to force upon Hurrish still lying upon the floor,
he ran towards the door, the tears streaming down his
poor face and making long light channels upon his
cheeks, flew out of the cabin, his bare feet sounding
for a minute—patter, patter, patter—upon the flags,
and then ceasing suddenly.

There was a general pause — the boys staring
blankly at one another and at their father, as if to
ask the meaning of what had happened. Finding,
however, that he took no notice, and quietly continued smoking, the paramount interest of breakfast

soon resumed its dominion over their minds. The
stirabout was boiling, and all the party were sitting
silently waiting for it to be ready, when there came
a new, and this time a more formidable interruption.
A sudden startling rat-tat-tat sounded on the half-
opened door. Instinctively Alley, who was nearest,
ran to see who was there, but fell back the next
minute with a loud cry of dismay. It seemed to her
as if the whole world had suddenly become filled
with policemen! Two were in the actual doorway,
and three more a little way off in the bohereen below!

CHAPTER XVI.

THE ROAD TO JAIL.

Mr Cavanagh, the "resident" magistrate (so called
because the only one of the magistrates *not* a per-
manent resident), had returned from Limerick the
previous evening, and had been at once interviewed
by Mr Higgins. Upon the evidence laid before
him, he, to that gentleman's keen satisfaction, not
only issued a warrant for Hurrish's arrest, but expressed himself in high terms of reprobation as to
Mr O'Brien's unaccountable conduct in having hesitated to do so. Within as short a time, therefore, as
was possible after his arrest, our hero found himself
upon a car, with one well-armed policeman beside
him, and two more upon the other side, bound for
the assize town of Ennis, there to be lodged in jail

to take his trial for murder—bail in a case of such
gravity being, as a matter of course, refused.

He was not particularly alarmed for his own
safety, and was able, therefore, to take the proceedings with a considerable amount of equanimity.
He had had plenty of time to escape had he wished
to do so, but had deliberately made up his mind
against that course. Had he done so, beggary, pure
and simple, would have stared his mother, the children, and Alley in the face. He had little or no
money laid by, and as none of those left could have
taken on the farm, of which he had only a yearly
tenancy, within a very short time they would have
had nothing to look to but the workhouse.

Over and above this, the mere fact of leaving
Ireland—for life, as, under the circumstances, it must
have been—would have been little less objectionable
to him than death itself. He had never felt the
faintest beckoning towards that delectable Land of
Promise which lay upon the other side of the Atlantic. Had he not in his youth had the farm to
look forward to, and had been forced to emigrate, his
one thought day and night would have been to put
together a sufficient sum of money and return to
Ireland by the next ship. The only other alternative—that of remaining in the country *without* giving
himself up—though a safe proceeding enough, is a
remarkably uncomfortable one. Hurrish had seen
others who had tried it, and knew its miseries.
A week of such shuffling, skulking, shivering, night-
wandering existence, would have driven him, he
knew, into giving himself up to the police as a
preferable alternative.

Going to jail—though a distinction, of course, in
itself—was not, it is true, the precise form of distinction which he would have chosen ; but then how
few *are* entirely free to choose their own laurels ?
As to the danger of his incurring the further distinction of being hung, that was an idea to which he
hardly gave a thought. He knew the situation well
enough to feel pretty sure that the danger incurred
in that direction was of the slightest. As for what
an Englishman would probably have considered the
safest thing to do — pleading manslaughter or un-
avoidable homicide, and disclosing the whole circumstances as they really occurred — that, save under
seal of confession to his priest, was an idea which
would never for an instant have visited his imagination. In his eyes—probably in those of his legal
adviser also—it would have seemed an act of simple
and reprehensible self-destruction.

The road from Tubbamina to Ennis is about as
desolate a one as is to be found in the whole west of
Ireland, which, it must be owned, is saying a good
deal. Once the rocky hills of the Burren were left
behind, the car entered upon a wide, grey-green, un-
dulating tract, treeless, featureless, almost houseless,
one low green or brown hill rising after another in
endless succession as far as the eye could see. What
cultivation there existed was of the most rudimentary
type conceivable. Small weedy-looking fields, divided
from the road and from one another by dry walls of
the lace-work variety, in some places by green dykes,
with a fringe of willow or osmunda. Flakes of snow-
white bog-cotton waved over dreary patches of swamp,
and the dark heads of the reed-mace crowded hollows

from which turf had been cut and carted away. The houses, few and far between, were for the most part sunk below the level of the road. At one place three or four women were grubbing languidly at a sickly-looking plot of potatoes; at another two men were thatching, who turned and watched the car sullenly till it was out of sight. Then a mile or more without a creature save a stray cow on the roadside, or a sleepily-moving ass-cart. Suddenly they rattled round a sharp corner, and found themselves in the middle of a closely crowded cluster of houses, where the people all ran eagerly to the doors to see them go by, and the women spat, shrieked, and shook their fists passionately at the policemen. Another smaller but more prosperous-looking hamlet was passed, where a smart, newly-built chapel flaunted its cut-stone masonry and twirling weathercock, and a sinister old castle looked blackly down from a windy green hill hard by. Just after leaving this village, in the middle of a particularly lonely bit of road, a wild-looking young fellow—a total stranger to Hurrish—sprang actively over a wall as they were passing, bounded up to the car, though they were going at a smart pace at the time, and asked him in rapid Irish whether he wanted a rescue. The three constables simultaneously pointed their guns at him, and told him to remain there at his peril. The young fellow, however, took no notice, but ran lightly on, his brimless felt hat falling back from his black curly head, his sunburnt face and wild hawk eyes fixed exclusively upon the prisoner: evidently he was good for another ten miles if need were. Hurrish, however, shook his head. It was not a rescue he wanted, but an acquittal, he explained. His unknown friend thereupon slackened speed suddenly, made a clutch at his hand to shake it, missed it, and disappeared immediately over another wall. From his appearance to his vanishing again there were scarcely three minutes.

When they got near to the outskirts of Ennis the car stopped at a police-station, and a short conference took place between the constables in charge and those within. Only one constable remained upon the car, and he appeared to be taking no particular heed of the prisoner. Hurrish, however, waited quietly. He had no idea of escaping. What would have been the use ? It would only have been to begin the whole troublesome business over again. Better remain and see it out as it was.

A delicious brown trout-stream was sweeping under a bridge a little ahead of this point. A heron rose from its bank a few hundred yards lower down, spread its great sail-like wings, and flew away towards the west, its brown legs stretched stiffly out behind it. Hurrish followed it wistfully with his eyes as it grew gradually smaller and smaller, until it was lost to sight in the distance. A sudden yearning, a sudden wild, fierce desire for liberty, swept across him like thirst in a desert. He had hardly realised before that he was a prisoner, but now it seemed as if all at once he knew it. *He* could not turn back as the heron had done; *he* could not get home to his own house and his own people ; he was a caged animal ; a beast with a rope round its leg,— driven against his will as a sheep or a cow is driven to the market. To any one, but especially to so wild

a son of the soil, the first realisation of this fact has
something in it that maddens. He looked suddenly
round, first at the sleepy, vacant country, then up
and down the road, and for a moment a thought of
escape crossed his mind. Only for a moment. The
hopelessness of the attempt rushed back upon him
forcibly. He caught the eye of the constable, too,
looking inquisitively at him across the well of the car.
An impulse of self-respect made him relax the eager-
ness of the gaze, turn his head the other way, and
resume his former air and attitude of indifference.

A minute after the other two constables returned,
and directing the carman to take a detour which
avoided the main street, got again upon the car and
drove rapidly to the jail. Their way lay along a
dirty but tolerably prosperous-looking street, where a
number of peasant women were bargaining for the
gorgeous crimson and magenta shawls and petticoats
hung up in tempting array along the outsides of the
shops. It was market-day, and they were too eager
to finish their purchases, and get back to their don-
key-carts, to take much notice of the prisoner or his
escort. Hurrish gazed at it all with the aching interest a man feels in the last things he beholds before
the doors of a prison close behind him. Ennis, with
its crowded market-place,—the centre of all the other
smaller villages round about—its gorgeous new cathe-
dral ; its statue of the Liberator ; its political pretension ; its air of bustle and importance,—was London, Paris, Vienna, all at once to him, and this glimpse
of fashion and brilliancy was not, even under the
circumstances, without a pleasurable excitement.

He had not much time to enjoy it, however. The

shops ceased ; a line of stone walls, cold, high, and
vacant-looking, took their place : they had arrived at
the door of the jail. The three constables jumped
down and took him by the arms. The door opened,
and he was marched inside. Some one in authority
advanced. Then, after a few minutes' delay, he was
marched down a narrow passage, with iron-clamped
doors on either side ; one of these doors was unlocked,
disclosing a narrow cell about the size of a bathing-
box. Into this he was walked, and the next minute
—almost before he had fairly realised what had happened—the door shut behind him with an emphatic
bang.

He stood still a moment, half stunned, then stumbled over to the bed and sat down. It seemed as if
the concussion of the door had shaken his ideas clean
out of their usual courses. He felt numbed and
stupefied, as if he had suddenly changed his identity
with some one else, and had not got accustomed to
the new one.

He was roused by a peculiar sensation of discomfort. The window of the cell was set in the outer
wall of the prison, and a full blaze of daylight was
pouring through it at that moment. It lit up every
atom of the narrow space, glaring with immaculate
whitewash, which reflected itself in twofold brilliancy
at all the corners, and threw a responsive gleam upon
the magnificently scoured boards. Hurrish felt dazed
and giddy as a fish would have been, suddenly exposed to so brilliant an illumination. An unreasoning hatred for this glaring self-righteous place, into
which he had been pushed, rose to his mind, and it
was with some difficulty that he resisted rushing

against the door and wounding himself in a vain
effort to break through. Next to the whitewash, the
worst offence—alas! poor Hurrish—was the ultra
self-glorifying cleanliness! The ghastly cleanliness
and whiteness together nearly made him sick. Out
of doors he was used, of course, to light, but then no
one out of doors is surrounded by a girdle of dazzling
whiteness, a few feet from the end of his nose. How
he yearned after his own brown weather-beaten cabin,
with its smoke-obscured corners and multitudinous
litter! Was there nothing else he could look at, he
asked himself—*nothing?* If he had to stay staring
at those sickening white walls for the next three
weeks, he should go mad, and that would be very
nearly as bad as being hung!

Suddenly the window itself caught his eye. It
was high up in the wall, but by mounting upon a
chair and pulling himself upwards, he was able, by
sheer muscular effort, to get his nose and eyes over
the ledge, and this he proceeded to do. It was
strongly secured, but to his relief he found that it
looked, not into the courtyard, but into the outer
world. By stretching upwards he could even see a
bit of the street below, and people passing and re-
passing. A black-faced beggar, with grimy professional clothes hanging on by a few alarmingly fragile
ribbons, was leaning against the opposite wall,
stretching out from time to time a mechanical hand
for alms. An old woman, with a basket of apples
before her, was squatting upon the ground, and at
her feet a small fair-haired child, presumably her
grandchild, was amusing itself by picking up fragments of apple-peel, and throwing them into the

gutter. A feeling of unaccountable affection for these strange people filled Hurrish's mind, and the tears sprang into his eyes. The little girl was a pretty little creature, dressed in a single ragged garment, which left her small limbs and neck completely bare ; against the grimy obscurity of the wall beyond, they looked wonderfully fresh and white. Suddenly a car came round the corner, imperiling the feet of the group. Hurrish, with an impulse of alarm, instinctively stretched out his hands as if to protect the child. A young man was seated on the car,—a slight active figure in a well-fitting suit of grey tweed. He was not really at all like Maurice Brady, still there was sufficient suggestion of resemblance to give Hurrish first a feeling of pleasure, to be immediately followed by a sudden bitter start of pain. Maurice Brady ! That was the worst of all,—the only part of the misfortune that had overtaken him which *was* unendurable. He let himself drop from the window, and sat down again upon his pallet, his arms and legs falling despondently together,—a mere nerveless heap of dejected frieze !

When he had been first told that Maurice had denounced him, the intelligence had roused him to a fit of violent indignation—not against Maurice but his informant. He absolutely refused to give any credit whatever to the assertion. When, little by little, the truth of it, however, began to sink into his mind, it had produced a sort of torpor. He could not conceive it,—could not realise it, or get hold of the idea at all. All the time he was standing before the magistrate, all the time he was on the car, his thoughts kept recurring to it, and each time with the

same dull sense of unreality. It was not merely
painful or disagreeable, but it was inconceivable—a
thing past imagination or finding out. If Maurice
had attacked him, shot him, assaulted him in any
way—*that* he could have understood, for a brother,
after all, is a brother; but to denounce him to the
police, to the Government!—" th' *Inglish* Govern-
mint!"—he kept repeating over and over to himself,
as if it was in the very least likely that Maurice
would have denounced him to the Spanish or the
Dutch one!

Three or four hours after he had been in jail a
warder brought him a large piece of bread, and some
broth swimming with grease. He was very hungry,
and ate with a good appetite. He tried to get into
conversation with the man, but he turned away and
shut the door without answering. Hurrish spun out
the eating of his bread as long as he could, but all too
soon it came to an end, and again vacuum stared him
in the face. It seemed as if he had been already
weeks in jail—as if all his previous life had been a
dream, and this the reality. The punishment of
imprisonment no doubt varies enormously, and to so
wild a son of freedom—one to whom wind, rain,
storm, all varieties of weather were welcome, but who
had never yet spent an entire day in the house in
his life—the misery must indeed have pretty nearly
attained its maximum.

After a while he clambered up to the window
again and resumed his gaze. It was his only link
with the outer world, and as such he clung to it.
Night came on, but still he remained. The figures
below had by that time become mere phantoms,—

still they were human phantoms, and moving ones.
By the light of the one lamp at the corner, he saw a
sooty object in coat and hat pass an equally sooty one
in petticoats and a shawl; then both looked back,
mutual recognitions ensued, and they stood a while
conversing amicably. A beggar was meanwhile bawl-
ing out a song, walking leisurely up and down the
middle of the street, with his mouth wide open.
Hurrish caught a stray word now and then—"The
mas-a-cree-in va-ga-bonds" . . . "me dar-lint Paa-
a-ady Wh-a-ck." Suddenly a turnkey entered behind and roughly desired him to get down and go to
bed. The lights were going to be put out. He got
down, and, pulling off some of his clothes, threw himself upon the pallet. It was as hard as a brick floor,
but that made very little difference, and within half
an hour he was sound asleep,—and so his first day's
experience of Ennis jail came to an end.

CHAPTER XVII.

MR THOMOND O'BRIEN UPON THE REQUIREMENTS
OF IRELAND.

Amongst the many touches of unconscious humour
with which all life and history abounds, few perhaps
are odder than the minuteness—the inconceivable
minuteness—of the points upon which a man's good
or bad reputation turns with his contemporaries.
Ever since he had been settled at Donore, Major

Pierce O'Brien had done, or had at any rate tried to do, everything he could think of for the welfare and advantage of its people, and had been rewarded with suspicion, hatred, and ill-will, ending with repeated threats of death. All of a sudden, by the merest piece of chance, for declining to do what he ought no doubt in strictness to have done, and thereby setting himself in momentary opposition to the established powers, he suddenly, and at a bound, sprang from the blackest depths of unpopularity to the very summit of popular admiration !

Within a dozen hours of the "outrage," and simultaneously with the news of it, all over Ireland had flown the news of his refusal to sign the warrant for Hurrish's arrest,—news which was received, commented upon, praised, or condemned according to the politics of the hearer. In the course of an excited and somewhat incoherent article, that advanced organ ' The Wolfhound' had rejoiced next morning to learn that the once glorious and patriotic name of O'Brien was again to be seen upon the blood-stained banner of the people, and had commended him, in involved but evidently complimentary terms, upon the courage with which he had set the Government and its brutal hirelings at defiance. The consequence of all this, joined to the popular feeling in favour of Hurrish, had suddenly—as if with the finger of a magician— lifted the ban that had so long hung over Donore, and flung it for the time being to the winds. In every cabin upon the property, and at every wake, fair, and local meeting of any sort, this performance of the "mhaster's" was the theme of universal commendation, which amongst his own particular retainers rose for the moment to a pitch of absolute enthusiasm.

To no human being did this sudden and most undeserved rush of popularity come with more complete astonishment than to the recipient of it. In refusing to sign the warrant for Hurrish's arrest, Mr O'Brien had been actuated by no sympathy, assuredly, with the blood-stained banner of the people, but simply by a prosaic disbelief in his guilt, combined, it must be owned, with a small and very private grudge against that self-satisfied official Mr Sub-inspector Higgins. He was no more of a Nationalist, or a Liberal even, than he had ever been. As for opposing the Government, and throwing himself upon the popular side, such an idea—despite his small private admiration for that shilly-shallying abstraction — had never, it need hardly be said, dawned upon his imagination. He scoffed openly at the manifestations of this change of popular opinion whenever they came under his notice, but though he scoffed, it must be owned that in his heart of hearts he was rather pleased than otherwise. Can you, after all, blame him ? What friendly-minded man, who has been condemned for years to a winter of black looks, averted eyes, and all the hundred and one petty proofs of inveterate dislike, can avoid a certain thrill of pleasure when suddenly brows clear, hats are doffed, and faces beam with delight at his approach. The temptation to sue for an ephemeral popularity is greater perhaps in Ireland than in any other country in the world, for the reason that in none is the reward so spontaneous. The proverbial smiles and frowns of her climate are not more start-

ling in their transitions than are the often equally
unaccountable ones of her sons. Certainly that Mr
O'Brien, and all the tenants on the estate, and all the
other cottars and small people round about, should be
of one mind upon any subject, and that subject a
murder, was a sufficiently surprising fact to be
worth recording !   There were differences, it is true.
Whereas he genuinely believed Hurrish to have had
nothing at all to do with the matter, they as genuinely
believed him to have done it deliberately, and ap-
plauded him heartily in consequence.   The difference
you will say is considerable, but practically it came
to much the same thing in the end.

It happened that the week after these events had
occurred, Mr O'Brien's solitude was broken in upon
by the advent of a nephew, one Thomond O'Brien—
a name that awakens stirring memories in Clare.
This Thomond was a son of his youngest brother, and
had been wont to spend his holidays under his uncle's
roof; indeed Pierce O'Brien, having only daughters,
had come to regard the lad in the light of a son.
And a very masterful son he had proved, his holiday
having invariably been the signal for a sort of pandemonium and wild licence let loose upon Donore.   He
had danced jigs with the maid-servants ; made bonfires on all the hills around ; visited every wake,
faction-fight, and wedding he could hear of in the
neighbourhood ;   wasted everybody's time ;   made
everybody run hither and thither to do his errands,
and been universally adored — as no O'Brien since
'48 probably had been adored.

He was only eighteen now, and five years in her
Majesty's navy had not entirely subdued the native

O

humours of his blood.   He descended upon Donore
and its inhabitants as upon a conquered country,
which he proceeded at once to parcel out as seemed
good in his sight.   As he drove along on the car
from the station, his small, sharp, brown eyes gazed
around him right and left with the conquering glance
of a Napoleon.   To him it was all still the " kingdom " of the O'Briens.

   To any one who only skims the merest surface of
things, there is no lack of " divarsion," happily, still
extant in Ireland.   The fun, it is true, is on the
surface, the bitterness, discord, misery down at the
roots, in a distracted present and an unforgotten past.
Poor Pierce O'Brien knew this uglier side of the
shield only too well.   The weight of it had eaten
into his heart, and into the very marrow of his bones.
He was not so ossified in gloom, however, as to refuse
to hail the diversion with a feeling of satisfaction.
As for young Thomond, he simply and honestly dis-
believed in the gloomier side of things altogether.
As for his uncle Pierce having ever been in peril of
his life—that he dismissed as utterly incredible and
monstrous !—a fiction of " the Government " and the
police.   They were always getting up some cock-and-
bull stories or other ; they had nothing else, poor
devils, in his opinion, to do !

   He had not been half-a-dozen hours in the place
before everything was turned inside out, and put
upon a new footing.   He got out the boat, which
had long slumbered, half full of water, in its moss-
grown boat-house, and had it cleaned and baled.
One man was despatched for a mop, another for a
landing-net, a third had to go and dig bait, a fourth

was sent flying to Tubbamina for more fishing-line. Young Thomond had inherited a considerable smack of the old Thomond's ways, and had remarkably clear views on the subject of getting himself obeyed, and obeyed sure enough he was. There was more work done and more activity displayed in that one morning at Donore than there had been for months, nay, years past; but then everybody had something to do that was not precisely his own business, and that in Ireland is an enormous incentive to industry.

Pierce O'Brien stood looking on, lifting his eyebrows, mocking at the boy, but pleased the while. Young Thomond was not by any means pleased. He complained that everything had got into a shameful state of disorganisation during his absence.

" I say, what on earth have they been doing to the trout ? " he inquired, indignantly. " That Pat O'Gorman says there's hardly any in the lake now, and they used to be as thick as peas."

" Poached," his uncle responded, laconically.

" Poached ! I'd poach them ! Why don't you catch half-a-dozen, and run them in ? "

" In where ? "

" Into jail ; or give them a right good hiding. That's what I'd do if I were you."

" They are very much more likely to give me a hiding," Mr O'Brien replied mildly.

Half an hour later—

" I say, those fellows of yours are the greatest lot of muffs I ever saw in my life. They're not worth twopence the whole box and dice of them. Can't we shunt them, and get some one else ? What's become of that big fellow, Hurrish O'Brien, who used to fish

with us ?   Send off for him.   He's worth a dozen of
these butter-fingers.   He used to be a nailer, I remember, at night-lines."

"Unfortunately he has been what you call 'run
in.'"

"Hurrish run in ?   Good Lord! what for ?   Not
for poaching ?"

"Worse than poaching."

"*Worse!*   What's worse than poaching ?"

"Murder."

Young Thomond's jaw dropped, and he nearly let
the line he was reeling fall on to the grass.

"Murder!   Look here, I say, uncle, don't chaff a
fellow," he said, indignantly.

"I'm not chaffing, unfortunately."

"Why, do you mean to say——   Pooh! it's pre-
posterous.   Why, he used to be the decentest fellow
we had."

"So he is still."

"Then why do you say he's murdered some one ?"

"*I* don't say it.   On the contrary, I don't believe it."

"Who does then ?"

"The Government."

"The *Government!*   What business, I should like
to know, has the Government to interfere with *our*
people ?   Who do they say he's murdered ?"

"A man called Mat Brady."

"I remember.   Big ugly brute, with a jaw like a
hippopotamus, and a coxy brother.   I don't expect
he's any loss, anyhow."

"Perhaps not.   Still you see brutes—at least when
they happen to have only two legs—can't be killed
with impunity, can they ?"

Young Thomond shook his head, declining to commit himself to any decision. It was his fixed opinion that his uncle's laxity in his dealings with his "people" was at the bottom of half what was amiss on the property. If Irish country gentlemen —those of the old stock particularly—would only put their feet down resolutely, encourage the decent fellows, drive all the agitators into the sea, and bid the English Government mind its own affairs and leave the management of Ireland to *them*, everything, in that clear-sighted young gentleman's opinion, would go as it ought to do.

The dinner-bell rang, and he was obliged to suspend his operations, and allow his exhausted assistants to retire, worn out by the unusual labours of the day, to their respective homes. At dinner his uncle gave him an outline of the events of the past week, not without some satisfaction in finding an auditor to whom to recount his version of the points at issue between himself and Sub-inspector Higgins. Young Thomond more than accepted that view, and would willingly have gone off there and then to do battle with the miserable official who had dared to come between the O'Brien and his own. Who should decide whether they were guilty or not except their own landlord ? His five years in her Majesty's navy notwithstanding, the young gentleman possessed, it will be observed, a cargo of ideas of a truly distressingly antiquated description. He was a survival, a forgotten fragment, a small leaf from the fallen tree of the past. " Our people," " our ways," " our land," " our country," were words never out of his mouth. That an O'Brien should be the

father and protector of his people, and that they in
return should yield him a loyalty which stopped
short at nothing, even death, seemed to him the most
commonplace of self - evident propositions.   Where
precisely the boy had acquired these very defunct
ideas of his it would be difficult to say.   Absence,
no doubt, had a good deal to say to them, and had
fed a stream which flowed naturally in his blood.
He had been travelling backwards while the country
and the world had been travelling forwards.   Those
five years too during which he had been away had been
five very momentous ones, it must be remembered.

For the next few days he was too busy getting
everything to his liking at Donore, and issuing his
orders, to have time for any longer excursion ; but
the third day after his arrival he set off by himself
to Gortnacoppin to inspect the scene of the outrage,
not without a private belief that his observation
would probably be equal to alighting upon some
clue, which the police and " Government " between
them had hitherto failed to discover.

Leaving the edge of the lake, he clambered up the
ridge which rose immediately above it, and got upon
that narrow stony pathway which, as the reader may
remember, ran past the Bradys' house until it joined
the high-road, from which point you diverged a little
lower down into the Gortnacoppin valley.   It was
all part of the Donore property, and our young friend
looked round him, therefore, with all the gravity of a
responsible guardian, innocent of a certain redoubtable
Land Bill, which was at that very moment hovering
in the air, and upon the point of descending.

He paused a moment before the Bradys' house,

and shook his head with an air of reprobation. He
did not remember for the moment who it belonged
to, but its aspect of filth and desolation scandalised
him.   A little further down, on a small eminence to
the left of the road, he noticed a young man sitting
by himself, whose appearance rather perplexed him.
He was not a gentleman, certainly, and yet, still more
forcibly, he was not a frieze-coated " tinint," and anything between these two alternatives was foreign to
his previous experiences at Donore.   When he got
as close as the path ran to the spot, he perceived that
it was no other than that " coxy brother " of the man
whom Hurrish O'Brien was accused of murdering, and
whose farm, he now remembered, covered this part of
the hill.   This did not seem to him to be any reason
for not stopping and speaking.   He had always been
in the habit of speaking to every one connected with
the estate, and, without actually formulating that
opinion, had always concluded, in a general way,
that his notice could never be anything but gratify-
ing to the recipient of it.

" Hullo !   How d'ye do ? " he called out, stopping
short and nodding his head in a friendly fashion.
" You're Maurice Brady, aren't you ?   Didn't recognise you at first.   You hadn't grown a moustache
when I sailed, and that changes a fellow so.   Every
one is changed about here, I think, except some of the
old chaps—they don't alter much."

He had got over the fence while he was speaking,
and advanced, holding out his hand with the utmost
affability.   Maurice Brady, however, drew back as
precipitately as if a sociable rattlesnake or cobra had
been presented at him.   It was impossible for him to

have encountered any one more intensely irritating to
him in his present frame of mind than this complacent little sailor, who looked as if the world at large,
and Donore in particular, was a sort of holiday kingdom, specially laid out for his entertainment; who
had that air too of unconscious patronage which, of
all varieties of the human manner, was to Maurice
Brady the most insufferable upon earth. Even at
the shop he had always, whenever it was possible,
avoided having any intercourse with men of his own
age—those, that is, who stood upon a higher social
platform than his own. Ladies he did not so much
mind. His self-confidence had its effect upon them ;
besides, a shopman is always naturally, and as it
were officially, the superior of his female customers.
He told himself that the reason of this dislike was on
account of his deep-laid democratic convictions: it
was unendurable to him to see a fellow-creature who
appeared to think himself better than another. In
reality, however, it was rather that he was conscious
of his democratic convictions not being quite so deep
as they ought to have been. The will was there, but
the power, unfortunately, was wanting. No Irishman
—no Irishman born of peasant parents at any rate
—is ever genuinely and at heart a democrat. The
whole theory is exotic—never has been, and never
will be, otherwise. Maurice Brady had done his
utmost to assimilate it, but had failed, and the struggle told upon his manner. Instead of that mixture
of easy courtesy and self-respect which becomes a
polite citizen and an equal, it had alternations from
suppressed servility to open surliness, and of this he
was too intelligent not to be himself aware.

Young Thomond, though a little surprised at his manner, merely thought that he was taken by surprise, and awkward in consequence. Very likely he was shy—fellows were apt to be shy when they were spoken to by their betters. That any man in young Brady's position could fail to be gratified by being noticed by one in his—Thomond O'Brien's—was an idea which would have required a great many convincing proofs to impress upon his mind.

"I say, what an awful thing that was about your brother," he began again in a tone of eager cordiality. "It's perfectly scandalous to think of fellows being murdered like that in broad daylight, and not a soul found to give evidence about it. Of course, though, *you* don't believe this ridiculous story the Government have got hold of against Hurrish O'Brien? Why, he is the *last* man that would have done such a thing! My uncle has the highest opinion of him possible, and so have *I.*"

He waited a moment, but as the other still said nothing, went on again. "I remember his bringing you over with him once to Donore when you were a little bit of a chap. He was always the decentest fellow out and out about the place, and the best tenant too. I'd rather have him than a whole cargo of the rest!" Another pause, and then: "Look here, I say, you *don't* believe this rubbish of his having anything to say to it, do you?" he added sharply, irritated by the other's persistent silence.

Maurice's brows had been growing darker and darker.

"I'm not going for to say whether I do or I don't," he said sullenly. "If you want to find out

about it, you'll have to wait till the 'sizes. You'll
hear enough of it then, or you can read about it in
the newspapers. If Hurrish O'Brien is innocent,
he'll be able to prove it fast enough; and if he's
guilty, it don't make much matter what other people
think about him, only what the jury think."

Young Thomond's open boyish face darkened
sensibly, and he drew his short little sailorly figure
up to its full height. He was quick to catch a
hostile note; and that the fellow meant, as he put
it to himself, to " give cheek," there could be very
little doubt.

" My uncle and I are *certain* he had nothing to
say to it," he said in his lordliest tone and air.

" Oh, you *are*, are you ? Then that settles the
matter, *of* course ! " Maurice Brady replied with a
bitter sneer.

The blood flew to young O'Brien's cheek, and he
made half a step forward. Another minute and his
fists would have been in the other's face. Maurice
watched him with a sullen gleam of satisfaction.
Nothing could have pleased him better or done him
more good at that moment than to have had a hand-
to-hand tussle with this complacent young sprig of
landlordism. He felt a savage delight in the mere
thought of having him by the throat and pounding
that patronising face of his into a jelly. For a
moment the two antagonists measured one another
with their eyes. Maurice was by several years the
elder, and a good four inches the taller. On the
other hand, young O'Brien was a mass of muscle,
strong as a bull-dog, and active as a cat—a fighter,
too, by birth, instinct, and profession, which Maurice

was not. Had the struggle come on, a good judge
would certainly have laid the betting upon the
smaller man. Happily for the interests of peace,
young Thomond's pride was at least as strong as
his pugnacity. What, come to fisticuffs with the
brother of a " tinint " ! condescend to a scuffle by
the roadside ! He, an O'Brien of Donore ! He
clenched his hands tight, and rammed them down
to the very bottom of his pockets as a preservation
against temptation ; looked the other in the face
exactly between the two eyes ; turned upon his
heels, stalked back to the fence, clambering over
it with as much dignity as was consistent with his
haste, and marched rapidly away down the road—
his head in the air, his shoulders squared, his foolish
young face red as a turkey-cock's with suppressed
passion.

He quite forgot in his excitement his intention of
visiting Gortnacoppin, upon which he was steadily
turning his back ; forgot everything but the fact that
he—a gentleman—an officer in her Majesty's navy—
an O'Brien of Donore—had been insulted, deliberately
" cheeked " upon his own lands by a common fellow,
a tenant on the estate. Once he halted with a
sudden impulse of turning back, and showing the
fellow which was the better man. His blood was
up, and thirsty for the fray. He would willingly
have given five years' pay at that moment to have
been free to gratify the impulse. He drove it back
again resolutely, however, and marched on. No, he
would not, he would *not*. If it had been a stranger,
—a man with whom he had no connection,—he
would have allowed himself the gratification in an

instant.   But a " tinint," a fellow " off the estate,"—
no, a thousand times no; pride, honour, everything
forbade it.   To abstain was gall and wormwood, but
to yield would have been a thousand times worse.
A gentleman had to pay, after all, for being a gentleman.   No man, he reflected, could expect to be
born an O'Brien of Donore for nothing !

CHAPTER XVIII.

MAURICE TRIUMPHS OVER ALL HIS ENEMIES.

Maurice Brady looked after his retreating figure with
a fierce scowl upon his handsome face.   " Got rid of
you pretty easily, me fine fellar," he said aloud.   " You
didn't take much to put you off fighting ! no stomach
for it, had you, me young cock ? "   He knew very
well that it was not the case,—that pride, not want
of pluck, was what had hindered the other from facing him.   But even so, and though there was no one
by to hear him, it did him good to say it.

Matters had been growing worse and worse since
the day of his brother's death.   The storm of indignation which his denouncement of Hurrish had cre-
ated, far from subsiding, was growing louder and louder
every day.   Even at the funeral—which, despite the
elder Brady's unpopularity, had been largely attended
—not a soul had spoken to him.   He had been tabooed,
sent to Coventry—" boycotted," in short.   He had
returned the following day to Miltown-Malbay, but

his position there was, as he soon discovered, if possible worse, in so far that it brought him more forcibly into contact with others. So intolerable was it,
that a few days afterwards he gave notice to the master
of the shop, and left hastily. The sudden revulsion
from popularity to contempt and execration was
horrible to him. The very men who had admired,
followed, imitated him, were now the loudest in denouncing him. The whole of that anti-English, anti-
legal machinery which he had so often gloried in,
which he counted so fully on making use of for his
own ends, was turned against him. He was in direct
opposition to the whole popular sentiment of the
country. An informer! What more was there to
be said?

There was something bewildering to a man like
Maurice Brady in the suddenness of this downfall.
He had been sailing along so successfully; so buoyantly confident of the future; so absolutely secure of
his own powers. And now! The rapidity of the
fall made him feel literally sick. He could have torn
his hair, gnashed his teeth, and rolled over and over
on the ground from sheer bitterness of rage and disappointment. He was done for! That was the long
and short of it. Everything was at an end. His
career wrecked,—finished before it had fairly begun.
Not in Clare alone, but from one end of Ireland to
the other, his name was the signal, he knew, for contempt and execration. Never would any Irish con-
stituency open its doors to receive him; never would
his voice be heard in the halls of Westminster, or
anywhere nearer home either; never would a single
one of those visions of success and triumph, upon

which he had floated so securely, now come true !
Even his life as an obscure individual would, he foresaw, be made intolerable. As soon as the trial was
over, he would have, in all probability, to leave the
country. Nay, the voice of execration would pursue
him, he knew well, from one end of the world to the
other. Wherever an Irishman was to be found—no
mean area nowadays—there he should find an enemy.
Was ever such cursed spite ? Did ever so damnable
a fate befall a brilliant and spirited young man
before ?

He could not turn back either, even had he wished
to do so. He had given his evidence, and, whether
he liked it or not, at the next assizes of Ennis he
must assuredly appear. He was not at all sure that
he *did* wish it. Anger against Hurrish was fast becoming, not merely a secondary, but a primary motive. His imagination—so vivid in everything that
concerned himself—ran perpetually forward to all
the ignominy that he had still to endure, and backward to Hurrish as the direct cause of it all. He
ground his teeth with a vindictive fury that was fast
effacing all earlier reminiscences of gratitude and kindliness. They should see,—those fools who turned
their backs upon him—that insolent young spark
who had just left him,—they should see, he thought,
whether their pet could get out of his scrape as easily
as they imagined. If there was justice—his favourite formula—in Ireland or out of it, Hurrish O'Brien,
he swore, should have the benefit of it.

He had been sitting there chewing the cud of his
anger for about half an hour after young Thomond
had left him, when another figure appeared in sight,

coming down that little frequented path,—a stout roundabout figure in a suit of black broadcloth, with a high hat of surpassing shininess—a shininess so surpassing, that it seemed to reflect the sunlight like a crow's back or a newly polished pair of shoes. It was Father Denahy, the parish priest of Tubbamina.

Maurice half rose with an impulse to escape. A second impulse made him seat himself again. Father Denahy, as every one knew, had the eye of a hawk for a recusant parishioner. Better stay where he was than have the ignominy of being pursued, as pursue him he knew very well his reverence would, if he wanted him. In three minutes more the priest was on a level with him, and had made a halt in the middle of the pathway, exactly as young O'Brien had done. He was a big heavy-jawed man, with cheeks somewhat upon the pattern of those of a cod-fish. At the first glance he looked exactly like all the rest of his order, who to an outsider seem often as difficult to know apart as the individuals of a flight of crows. Closer observation, however, disclosed a peculiar kindliness, a sort of exuding benevolence in the big loose-lipped mouth, and small, round, keen-looking eyes. He had a warm heart, a sharp temper, and a Johnsonian capability for hatred. He kept the last two for his political enemies, but his kindliness was all given to his flock.

"And is that you, Maurice Brady, sittin' there, and your parish priest standing opposite to you?" he began, in an irregularly pitched Kerry brogue, and a tone of surprised remonstrance.

Maurice rose sullenly. He would have given a great deal to be able to turn on his heel and walk

indifferently off; but thus openly to insult his
" clargy " was more than at present he could venture
upon.

" I've been wanting this week past to have some
words with you," Father Denahy went on in a more
placable tone, " so I'm glad to see you where we are
to our two selves. 'Tis a long time since you were
at confession, Maurice Brady," he added with sudden
sharpness.

To this the other made no reply. If he had
spoken at all, it would have been to inform the
priest that he had no intention of ever going to
confession again. Confession ! He knew better than
to be taken in by *that* stale trick !

" Will I expect you to-morrow ? 'Tis the day, you
know."

Still no answer.

Father Denahy waited a minute. His anger was
rising, for there was an unmistakable air of contempt
about the young man's manner. He was too wise,
however, to press that particular point further. He
knew the character of each of his parishioners in-
timately, and was aware that Maurice Brady was
a very awkward fish to tackle, much more likely to
break away altogether than to yield to any pastoral
angling, however dexterous. After a minute, therefore, he began again with a fresh cast.

" This has been a black week for you, me son," he
said gravely—" a black week for others too. Those
poor O'Briens ! I've been round to their house just
now, and 'tis a sad sight ! To think of Hurrish
O'Brien in Ennis jail !—Hurrish that was the credit
of the parish—never a day short in his dues, and

the best of sons and fathers,—a good father to you, too, Maurice Brady, when you wanted one badly," he added significantly.

He watched narrowly, to see if there were any indications of yielding, but there was not an atom. Maurice's pale handsome face was like a stone mask, and his eyes had a cold light in them that was not encouraging.

His reverence tried another fly.

" I was speaking to Alley Sheehan. Poor innicent young creature ! 'tis a sad sorrow to be laid on her, and she so young. I used to think wan of these days you and she, Maurice, would have been coming and asking me to give the Church's blessing on you both. Maybe, though, I was wrong ? "

Again he paused and watched narrowly. He knew as well as the young man himself did, that he and Alley had been engaged to be married. It was better, however, if possible, to surprise an admission than to take it for granted.

This time Maurice was less indifferent. He was thinking rapidly. He was as anxious to marry Alley as ever, and if forced to leave Ireland, as seemed inevitable, his wish was to take her with him. He had enough money to be able to make a fresh start in some new place ; and to leave her behind, to hear of her marrying some other fellow, was simply intolerable to him. That if he called upon her to come, she would do so at once, he had not a doubt ; but in that case it would certainly be necessary for them to call in Father Denahy's assistance, as nothing, he knew, would have induced her to wait to be married till they were in America, or wherever he might

P

finally decide to go. These thoughts produced at
once a corresponding effect upon his manner.

"You're right there, Father Denahy," he said in a
tone of suitable respect. "Alley Sheehan and me
have understood one another this good while back,
and please goodness, we'll be asking your reverence
to make man and wife of us some of these fine days,
and before very long too, most like."

Father Denahy's small eyes gleamed. His last
hook had struck home.

"So soon as you've done helping to hang Hurrish
O'Brien, is it ? " he inquired mildly.

Maurice started. Even to himself the words had
a hideous sound. He rallied quickly, however.

" 'Tis himself that's doing that, not me," he said
angrily. " Do you think I'd let my brother Mat be
killed, and the man that did it go free ? If you do,
you must think me the meanest-spirited beast that
crawls upon the face of th' earth ! "

" I think you've about the blackest and the hardest
heart between this and Cork, Maurice Brady ; and
that, if you wish to know, is what I think," the
priest retorted as sharply. " I don't believe there's
another—least, I hope an' pray to God there's not—
would have thought ov doing what you've done.
Denouncing him that's given you meat and sup, and
-been better nor a father to you ! Giving him up to
those that care no more, for the most part, than the
crows do, whether a man's innocent or not, so they can
clap him in prison. Why, a *haythen* wouldn't do such
a thing—not a black haythen—so he wouldn't."

The attack was vigorous, and might have been
effective if brought to bear upon another man, but it

was mistaken as directed against Maurice Brady.
He was one to whom opposition only supplies a
stimulating prick of excitement.   Whatever he might
feel alone—face to face at once with the future and
the past—in the presence of an opponent he became
hard and fixed as a rock.   A priest's opinion, too,
was the very last that would have moved him.
Like most advanced Irishmen of his day, it was a
distinctive "note" with him to abjure all priestly
authority, and utterly to deride the presumption of
one of that order pretending to interfere in politics
or anything else — strictly sacerdotal matters, of
course, excepted.   His naturally supercilious face
took a cold repellent air, and he eyed the worthy
priest with a smile that was not, however, unaccom-
panied by considerable inward rage.

"Sure don't we know your reverence is alway
mightily partial to Hurrish O'Brien ? " he said,
with a sneer he no longer attempted to conceal.
" 'Tisn't every man puts his clergy before everything
else nowadays ; nor 'tisn't every one would let his
own kith and kin starve or eat dirt, so they had the
fat of the land.   Many's the fine chicken and turkey
that will find its way to other quarters than it does if
Hurrish O'Brien was once out of it for good and all."

Father Denahy's broad ruddy face grew purple,
and the veins in his forehead swelled with the effort
to repress his rage.   He had too much self-respect,
however, to descend to the level of a scolding match,
or to remain measuring swords with an antagonist
who not merely had no respect for his cloth, but
actually made it a ground for reproach.

" Hearken to me, Maurice Brady, and mind what

I'm saying to you, for these are the last words of
mine maybe you'll hear," he said emphatically.   " I
denounce you! I throw you off! I've done with
you for good and all, for better or worse, from this
day forth and for evermore! Never say you were
raised in my parish, for I wouldn't have no one
think it. I wouldn't have any one suppose I'd
ought to do with such a black-hearted miscreant—
false to his Church and his friends, and everything
he ought for to vinerate. From this day out, you're
to me as if you were dead or had never been born;
and so good-day, and the Lord have mercy on you,
Mister Maurice Brady!"

And with a gesture of renouncement of his two
uplifted hands, that was not without a certain sturdy
dignity, Father Denahy stalked away down the road,
leaving Maurice, for the second time that afternoon,
victor upon the field.

If he had been disposed to espouse Hurrish's cause
before, it is only admitting he was human to say
that the worthy priest was about ten thousand times
more disposed to espouse it now.   From a merely
parochial matter, it had all at once sprung into a
personal one—to ensure an acquittal being an object
for which he felt prepared to strain every nerve.
Probably in his heart of hearts he did believe him to
have been guilty; but he also, with perfect honesty,
believed that a greater injury would be done by his
being condemned than by his being acquitted.   Hurrish—some slight peccadillos apart—had always been
a credit to the parish—a good son, husband, father,
neighbour, Catholic.   For such a one to be hung, or
thrust into that sink of iniquity, an English prison,

would, in Father Denahy's eyes, have been a disaster
of the first magnitude—an injury at once to public
morals and to the man's own soul. He was a warm-
hearted man, and—despite Maurice Brady's sneer—
by no means a particularly grasping one,—a pecca-
dillo which the circumstances of their lot is apt, it
must be owned, to engender in his cloth. He hated
England, it is true, and the English Government, and
the English connection, and everything that even remotely pertained to it, with a deadly hatred, which no
benefits, let them be never so accumulated, could in
any degree have modified, and which he had proved
upon a dozen platforms; but that was perhaps his only
serious failing.

Yet what had this same detested England done to
him, after all, some impatient reader will perhaps ex-
claim, that such a sentiment—intelligible enough once
—should be preserved, like a fossil scorpion or other
bottled venom, to the misery and undoing of two
countries? That, I reply with the shrug of the exponent, is an excellent, nay, an unanswerable argument,
dear sir, in logic, but no argument at all, unfortunately, to a deep-seated, to all appearances an ineradicable, sense of injury, which has its seat, not in the
brains at all, but in the blood. Hate, once engen-
dered there—kept alive from generation to generation
—becomes engrained, like gout or any other heredit-
ary disease; and the physician who will undertake to
cure it has yet, it is to be feared, to be born. When
he is, the Irish problem will *begin* to be solved.

Maurice Brady, left alone meanwhile victorious
upon his hillock, was not at first without a few
slightly uncomfortable sensations. A priest's curse

(and Father Denahy's parting words, if not quite
amounting to that, had certainly gone some way in
that direction) could hardly fail to excite the imagination of one who, let his private emancipation be ever
so complete, was still a Catholic, and the son of
Catholic peasants. He shook off the feeling, however, with no very great difficulty. After all, what
could Father Denahy *do ?*—that was the question ;
and he was materialist enough not to trouble his head
very greatly about any other.

Before many minutes had passed, he had left off
thinking about that side of the matter, and had turned
to thinking of another—of Alley Sheehan,—that subject having been brought into prominence by the
priest's words. He had always, as we know, taken
his engagement to that modest little maiden with a
very leisurely and lordly ease—nay, had wondered at
himself not unfrequently for having ever entertained
such an idea at all. It was a case of Cophetua and
the beggar-maid—a condescension only to be accounted for by that accident of beauty which had raised
one whom he would never otherwise have looked at
into a thing to be desired—an object which even the
lordliest male could hardly pass over without desiring
to appropriate. Possibly the fact of this slighting
habit of regarding her had, by a not uncommon
nemesis, caused her image to strike deeper into his
breast than it would otherwise have done. At any
rate, in the first heat of his fury against Hurrish, he
had told himself emphatically that everything was
now at an end between them. It would be intolerable to him to be married to one who, though no real
blood relationship connected them, would still hourly

.

and momently remind him of his brother's murderer. A little experience, however, proved that it was easier for him to make up his mind to cast her off than actually to do so. Though of a distinctly amorous turn by nature, he had somehow never had a genuine love affair, save with this poor little Alley. Others whom he might have been disposed to court were out of his reach ; while the ordinary bouncing damsels of his own class—such, for instance, as Sal Connor—were unmistakably not to his taste. Alley's very simplicity, humility, and deep-rooted piety were perhaps all the more seductive from their utter unlikeness to anything in himself ; at any rate, he found his thoughts of late recurring to her with a frequency that was almost humiliating. Every fresh slight he received, every fresh proof that his boasted power over his contemporaries was gone for ever, sent his thoughts flying with greater vehemence in her direction. He longed, as he had never longed before, to find himself beside her—to be soothed by her gentle voice, to look into the mild light of her great grey eyes. In the first maddening smart of newly wounded egotism some such tender, unexacting affection — a soft tone to soothe, a pair of admiring eyes in which he still stands as the chief of heroes—is to a man of Maurice Brady's temperament not merely a want, but an absolute craving necessity.

Since the day he had left her half fainting upon the rocks, they had hardly seen anything of one another. Once when he had joined her for a few minutes on coming out of mass, it had seemed to him that she shrank away—probably, he told himself, from fear of a quarrel arising between him and

some of the O'Brien faction. He, too, had a keen
dislike to anything of the sort, and this had prevented him going to see her at the cabin. Now, however,
he resolved that he must do so. Apart from his own
imperious need of her, it was absolutely necessary
that they should have a serious talk before the trial
came on. His first intention of shielding her had
given way by this time to a realisation of the absolute
necessity of her appearing as a witness. No summons
had as yet, he believed, been issued, but he was aware
that one would have to be. His own evidence, in
fact, depended largely upon being supported by hers,
and it would be essential, therefore, to prepare her
mind for this necessity.

Not without an effort—for his memory was naturally a tenacious one—he had succeeded in placing
his brother's fate, and his own duty as the avenger
of that fate, in the very front of his consciousness,
and of fixing all his thoughts upon it. It was the
only plank of self-respect which he had now to cling
to, and to secure such a plank was, to a man of his
type, an absolute necessity. The very price he had
paid for it decided that. To take a step which ruins
your whole life, brands you in every one's eyes as a
heartless traitor, leaves you the mark for every kind
of insult and reprobation, and after all fails—recoils
with annihilating effect upon yourself, but hurts absolutely nobody else! Could anything be conceived
more utterly unendurable to a man to whom power
in some form or other had always been the one possession which his soul imperiously craved—the vision
of his whole life ? He resolved that he would at once
seek out Alley, explain the whole matter to her, and

impress upon her the absolute necessity of being
guided, not by any of the O'Brien lot, but exclusively
by *his* judgment and directions. Then, when he had
made this perfectly clear to her, and had received her
promises, he would reassure her with regard to any
of those fears which she might naturally have entertained as to his deserting her. Poor little Alley!
Poor, soft, gentle, dependent creature! How happy
it would make her to know that all was still right
between them! that whatever else happened, she
would always have a protector—a kind, generous,
affectionate protector—in him! To be able to gratify
one's own strongest wishes, and at the same time to
perform a truly generous and magnanimous action,—
surely this is the very climax of satisfaction!

CHAPTER XIX.

TEAMPULL A PHOILL.

There was a spot, not a quarter of a mile from Hurrish's cabin, which was a favourite resort of Alley's,
and near enough, fortunately, for her to be able to
escape there and return almost without her tyrant
perceiving her absence. It was a tiny valley, deep in
the rich grass of the Burren, sunk like an open shaft
in the middle of the rocks ; and in the centre of this
small enclosure rose, grey amongst the greenness, the
remains of no less than five chapels and monastic
buildings, ruined and roofless, but, with the persist-

ence of their wonderful masonry, resisting century
after century all the efforts of rain and wind storm
to subjugate and utterly make an end of them.

Though later by some centuries than the barely
human wigwam-like oratories of Gortnacoppin, their
origin and the date of the original settlement of their
monkish architects seem to be equally lost in the
mists of the Atlantic. All that is known is that a
certain St Mhic Duagh, after whom the oldest of
them is called, lived here, and that the date of the
newest and largest — known as Teampull a Phoill
—is believed by experts to be about the middle of
the tenth century. A small stream runs down the
middle of this tiny valley—a gay, dancing, rippling
thread of water, clear as crystal — glad too, apparently, of the sunshine and the freedom, but, like all
other Burren streams and rivers, rushing back again
underground, as if startled, with a wild hurry-scurry
of excited bubbles, a few hundred yards lower down.

Coming upon it unexpectedly, there is something
singularly winning in the aspect of this little grassy
retreat — stolen, as it were, from the surrounding
savagery. Ruined as its buildings are, there yet
lingers a distinctively human look about the whole
—an air of expectancy and invitation—which somehow thrills the heart. The stream, the well, the
bright yellow lichens of the walls, the broken cross
which stood at the entrance of the "ahaliah" or
sacred enclosure, the well-worn door-steps trodden
into a curve, where century after century the naked
or sandal-shod feet of the monks trooped to their
daily portion of prayers, — the whole scene has a
completeness, a look of habitation, that speaks of long

usage. There is none of that cold and repellent
grimness which generally hangs over such husks and
shells of discarded habitations. Masses of honey-
suckle and dog-roses hang from the crevices of the
rocks ; the floor of the valley is blue in spring-time
with small dainty-flowered harebells, or white with
tiny bed-straws. Huge flowering-leeks—a legacy,
it is said, of the monks—stand crowded into a sheltered corner; and in the actual doorway of the
largest church an ash seed — fallen Heaven knows
how or from where!—has taken root between the
top of the jamb and the next stone to it, sprung into
a tree—the largest possibly in the Burren—and,
summer after summer, waves its feathery festoons
in youthful verdant triumph over its time-worn protector.

Alley loved this little glen with a sort of personal
love. The sternness of those interminable platforms
of rock above pained her eyes, the wide-reaching
panorama chilled her spirit, but this little enclosed
spot, speaking of peace, faith, long continuance, filled
her mind with images of a tender and homely tranquillity.

One morning, a few weeks after Hurrish had been
committed to prison, and not very long before the
time fixed for the trial, she had finished her work
early, and had betaken herself here as usual, carrying
her knitting with her. It was one of those sunless,
rainless, vacant-looking days, very characteristic of
these western solitudes. Further inland it would
probably have been hot; but here, upon the very
brim of the Atlantic, the air was alive, though there
was very little of it—hardly enough to stir the grass,

or the leaves of the great tree-mallows which rose in
a towering cluster out of the nettles by the little well.
It was wonderfully dreamy in that narrow flowery
nook in the middle of the desolate Burren.   All
the bees that ever visited that unprofitable hunting-
ground seemed to have collected about the masses of
yellow trefoil which linked the grass and rocks ; a
pair of water-wagtails were flirting upon the brink
of the stream ; a flight of fieldfares kept precipitating
themselves like schoolboys, now to one side, now
to the other, of the glen ; and overhead the wild
remote cry of a passing sea-gull fell from time to
time upon the ear.

Alley was feeling tired, and glad to get away from
the harsh, raucous voice of her old tyrant—glad to
rest in the warm soft air, so comforting and so
kindly.   She sat quietly for some time upon the
edge of the well, with her knitting in her hand,
looking down into the water.   Though called a well,
it was in reality a spring, bubbling freshly out of the
ground, and enclosed with a low wall consisting of
single blocks of stone laid side by side without mortar.   A collection of queer-looking objects lay at the
bottom, which, upon closer inspection, were seen to
be fishing-hooks, buttons, bits of tape, needles and
pins, and similar articles, thrown in from time to
time as votive-offerings.   Alley looked down at them
meditatively, wondering who the different ones had
belonged to, and what their owners had wished to get
in return for them.   The fish-hooks no doubt were
for St Mac Dara, the chief Connaught patron of
fishermen, to whose chapel upon the Oilian Mac
Dara opposite all passing sails were bound to lower

twice, on pain of speedy shipwreck. The buttons
and tapes had nearly melted away, and the needles
and pins had become so rusty that they might easily
have been mistaken for small twigs or straws. It
looked, Alley thought, as if the saint upon whom
they had been bestowed had not found any use for
them.

Sounds travel far in stony and vacant regions like
the Burren, where there are no houses, trees, or fences
to break it. Alley had not sat very long upon the
edge of her well before a sound reached her, — a
sound of footsteps, first in the distance, then drawing
nearer, and evidently coming directly towards her.
There was no path to the glen, and so completely
was it out of the ordinary track that except when,
under some special impulse of devotion, a woman
came and threw a pin or button into the well—an
event which rarely happened—she had the place to
herself. Who could it be ? she wondered. A man
evidently, by the tread. Her thoughts flew instinctively to Hurrish, and then stopped short with a
sudden pang. Whoever else it was, poor Hurrish,
alas ! it certainly could not be.

She was not long kept in doubt. Another minute
and Maurice Brady's head appeared on the ridge
above, near where a gap left between the rock and
the wall of one of the chapels led into the glen. He
came down the narrow passage with a slow, deliberate
step, reached the cross which stood in the centre of
the little valley, and stood there, his arms crossed in
his favourite Emmet attitude upon his chest, looking
down at her without speaking, while she, on her side,
looked up, startled, wondering what he was going to

say. Had anything fresh happened? Why had he
come there to look for her, she wondered?

Certainly a magnificent actor, no less than a magnificent demagogue, was lost in Maurice Brady! He
had all the dramatic instincts, the realisation of the
value of " pose," the ready alternatives from appeal
to denunciation, from denunciation to appeal, the
cold, quick, dominating eye, necessary for the his-
trionic side of the latter part. His present intention
was to overawe, and even, if necessary, a little alarm
Alley, in order the better to impress upon her the
absolute necessity of obeying his directions, and
abiding by his judgment in contradistinction to that
of any of the O'Briens. Then—when he had firmly
established this in her mind—he would reward her
by suddenly relaxing into greater tenderness, a warmer
show of affection than he had ever exhibited before.
He had an intense need, as we have seen, of finding
some one over whom he could still rule—with whom
his influence was still paramount,—a soft, tender
yielding some one, who would soothe his smarting
egotism, repay his lordly kindness with a woman's
tenderness—above all, admire and love him. It was
impossible for him to suppose that Alley had ceased
to do so—ceased to look with pride to the thought
of being his wife. What he conceived was that she
had been teased, threatened perhaps, into promising
to do everything in her power to screen Hurrish,
should she be called upon as a witness. And this
he felt that it behoved him to put a stop to at once
—firmly, emphatically.

" It's a long while since I've seen you, Alley dear,"
he began, gently.

" Yis, indade, Maurice."

" This has been a bad time for us all, Alley ! "

" 'T has indade, Maurice."

Then there was a little pause before he began again.

" I'm sorry to have to let you stop on there "—pointing his finger in the direction of Hurrish's house. " And if I could have taken you out of it, you should have been took before this ; but, please goodness, you'll not be in it long now."

He had planned this speech beforehand, as the most effective method he could conceive of proving to her that she would be expected to give up all future connection or intimacy with the O'Briens. Alley, however, merely opened her great eyes wonderingly.

" An' why wudn't I shtop in it, Maurice ? Sure where ilse have I iver shtopped ? " she inquired, simply.

It was not a particularly easy question to answer, seeing that there was nowhere else for her to go to, and that she certainly never had " shtopped " anywhere else. It irritated Maurice into quitting his calm tone for a more authoritative one.

" You can't *wish* to stop in the house of a man that's done what Hurrish has, surely, Alley ? " he said, energetically. Then, as she still showed no symptoms at all of agreement, " Is it in the house of a *murderer ?* " he added, harshly.

Alley winced, and quivered from head to foot. The bolt went straight home, and shot its cruel dart through and through her delicate sensitive frame. They were terrible words for her to hear—they were

cruel ones too, and, to her thinking, wicked ones,
angering almost as much as they frightened her.
All the more for their very cruelty—nay, for their
very truthfulness—she gathered her powers to resist
them. A tinge of pink colour came into her cheeks,
and her soft eyes looked up steadily at him.

"I'd shtop in Hurrish's house, let him hav dun
what he wud," she said, resolutely.

Maurice started and stared open - mouthed and
speechless. Such overt rebellion was the more
astonishing from being so utterly unexpected. That
every one else in the neighbourhood was fiercely op-
posed to the part he had taken against Hurrish, he
was aware ; but that *Alley* should also have espoused
that side of the quarrel, had not even occurred to him.
She was *his* property, not Hurrish's : what he did,
she must think right ; what he thought, she must
think also ; were they not all but man and wife ?
The case evidently called for severity.

He came a step nearer, and fixed his eyes upon her
with an air of authority. She must be made to understand what she was risking by her rebellion.

"Attind to me, Alley, and mind what I'm saying,
for I always keep to my word," he said, in a tone of
impressive displeasure. "What I say I won't go
back of again,—no, not for all the begging and the
praying in the world. So sure as you stop in that
there man's house one minute longer nor I give you
leave, so sure everything will be at an end between
you and me for good and all. I'd throw you off
same as I would an old shoe, if you was to dare
disobey me. You're not to listen to any one else
at all, only to me. You're not to obey any one at

all, only me. You're to remember that you're to be
my wife, and that if you ain't obedient, everything
will be at an end between us, out and out. Mind
that, for I always mean what I say, and more, too."

He expected an instant change. Tears, promises
of absolute obedience, entreaties that if he would
only forgive her, she would obey him in everything,
—their courtship had been largely made up of that
sort of thing. Nothing of the sort came, however.
Alley stood still, trembling, it is true, and clenching
her two hands tightly together, but when she spoke
her voice was firm enough.

" Thin, maybe indade, Maurice, 't 'ud be bether so,"
she said softly.

He sprang back as if she had flung something at
him. His expression changed. The air of calmness
and authority fell off like a badly-fitting dress, and
the natural passion of an undisciplined and under-
civilised man came to the front. She defied him,
did she ? This girl, this puny creature, whom he
had drifted into loving, he hardly knew how. She
joined the rest of them—the curs ! the cowards !
who had turned against him,—she threw him off,
she *dared* to do so ! He stood and glared at her as
a wild beast glares before it springs.

In Maurice Brady's despite, Alley, as it happened,
was looking especially lovely that day. The innocent wild-flower face, with its great pathetic eyes,
had that glow and soft transcendent flush which it
seemed often, like the clouds, to catch from something external to itself—something which filled and
irradiated it. Standing before him, with her two
bare feet upon the grass, her soft face upraised in

Q

piteous entreaty to his furious one—the misty gleams
of sunlight falling upon her dark uncovered head,—
poor red-petticoated Alley was a poet's dream, the
very picture of an ideal purity and innocence con-
fronted with dark and unknown dangers.   Now
Maurice, for his misfortune, was intensely susceptible.   He had that keen relish for feminine
loveliness which seems, for some reason, to be but
rarely bestowed upon his class.   He ground his teeth
savagely at the thought of her escaping him.   Never
before had he so realised her beauty ; never before
had he realised how strongly his mind was set upon
that beauty being his,—his very own,—his chattel,
—his private personal property, like his dog or his
cow.   A hot furious jealousy of Hurrish—one which,
despite their relationship, had often secretly smoul-
dered before,—sprang up suddenly, as if at a touch,
to full maturity.   She loved him—he felt sure of
it.   She mightn't know it, probably did *not* know it,
but it was the fact all the same.   As long as their
interests had gone together, she had been true to
himself ; now that they were severed she flung him
off, without a word or a qualm.   In a nature like
Maurice Brady's, jealousy for a long time, perhaps
for ever, may be kept at bay.   Pride, an innate
certainty of the superiority of his own claims to
those of any other claimant whatsoever, prevents
his succumbing to it.   Let this supreme certainty,
however, once be broken down, and the same pride
which would have kept the idea of rivals far from
his thoughts becomes a lash to drive him to distrac-
tion, a barb in the side of his anger.   It was so now.
His love, which had hitherto been a placid possession

enough,—a sort of small side rill, flowing half disre-
garded beside other and more serious currents,—
suddenly became a consuming torrent, taken up into
the main channel of those others, and outswelling
them all.   Rage, jealousy, desire,—three fierce devouring wolves,—all bore down upon him at once.
He could have caught Alley to his arms, in her own
despite, and strained her to his breast in jealous
revenge and passion rather than love.   He did not
do so, however.   The "cake of custom" is strong,
happily, even over a man who considers himself to
be superior to it; and purity is still, thank heaven,
the distinctive note of the Irish peasant in such
relations.   Though custom and instinct restrained
him in this particular, to be brutal in another way
came unfortunately only too easily and too naturally
to him.

He came close to her, his dark eyes gleaming
savagely out of a face distorted with passion.

" D' you know what I've a mind to do, and what
I'd do if I did what was right, Alley Sheehan ? " he
said, with the slow deliberation of concentrated fury.
" I'd kill you this minute as you stand there, and
leave you dead upon that grass at my feet.   Why
shouldn't I ?   What's to hinder me ?   You arn't *fit*
to live.   D'ye hear what I say—not *fit* to live.
You're a wicked girl—a bad, heartless, wicked girl !
A girl who goes back of her word isn't fit to live.
Arn't you all one and the same thing as my wife,
and a wife that turns against her husband is a
disgrace to the earth, and will go to hell when she
dies !   Ask your priest else."

He paused a minute to gather breath, and then

went on, this time apostrophising rather than directly
addressing her.

"A girl that no one else would ha' looked at ! A
girl without a shoe to her foot, or a penny to her
fortun', or larning, or manners, or a thing ! A girl
that was nothing nor a drudge ; living on charity—
and what charity ?—bits, and scraps, and dirty ends
of things, that nobody else, not the pigs, would touch,
and batings with that ! And I that was ready to
make her me wife, and a *lady*, and give her the best
of eating, and drinking, and clothes, and everything.
And what do I get ? Nothing but ingratitude—
black, wicked, heartless, grovelling ingratitude." (The
last adjective was not perhaps precisely what he
meant, but, like other orators, his stock of that com-
modity had its limits.)   "She'd rather stick by
Hurrish O'Brien, that's kept her in rags and misery,
than be learned by me, and do as I bid her ! If
such a one doesn't deserve killing, there never was
one in this wide world did yet.   But "—and he put
his face nearer to her, and ground the syllables slowly
out one by one—" But I'll *not* kill you, Alley Sheehan,
and I'll tell ye why.   If I did, you couldn't bear
witness against Hurrish O'Brien, and 'tis that you'll
have to do next Tuesday three weeks.   It's you'll be
called first of all, and 'tis on *your* evidence they'll
hang him—d'ye hear me ? *hang* him.   'Taint no good
your thinking you'll get him off with lying either, for
that will only make them harder on him nor ever.
If you'd been true to me, I'd have saved you all I
could, and maybe not have told what you said to
me down by the rocks yonder ; but now I'll go straight
to Ennis, and tell them that's there every word of it

—how you told me that Mat was dead, before any
one else knew. And they'll know the reason why.
That it was because you *knew* Hurrish had done it;
and 'tis my belief you *seen* him do it, for you was
always bitterest of all against Mat, that might have
his faults, poor fellar, like another, but wasn't a
murderer anyway, like Hurrish O'Brien!"

Poor Alley! She had sunk upon the grass, her
lips apart, her face ghastly white and almost devoid
of expression, as, with the stupefaction of utter misery,
she gazed blankly at her tormentor. Maurice felt no
pity, however. His own rhetoric had quickened and
intensified the sense of his own wrongs, as the way
of such rhetoric is. He felt *glad* she suffered—glad
that her punishment had already begun. It was all
true, every word that he had said to her. She *had*
vowed to be his wife, and she had gone back of her
word; and Hurrish *had* killed his brother, and it was
his duty and his right to avenge him. He looked at
her for a minute longer, then turned and walked
deliberately away toward the narrow passage leading
out of the glen.

Suddenly Alley's lips moved, and a sound came
from them,—a single word repeated over and over
again. "Maurice!" "Maurice!" "Maurice!" she
cried, like one under the torture.

Involuntarily he paused, and looked back. A misty
gleam was streaming through the narrow doorway of
the little Teampull a Phoill, shining upon the golden
lichen of its roofless walls—upon the tall gable ends,
upon the well with its wall, and the tiny rippling
stream. There was an indescribable look of appeal
about the whole scene—that wistful yearning expres-

sion which such ascetic scenes sometimes assume—as
it were a cry from man to God, from God to man, an
appeal for peace, hope, mercy, for a tenderer and kind-
lier humanity. Alley kneeling there—her white face
upraised in piteous entreaty—seemed to echo and
intensify this appeal; the appeal which, at all ages of
the world, and from innumerable lips, has gone forth
wherever man—the erring, the feeble, the ignorant—
affects to judge and to condemn his brother man.

"Maurice, for God's sake! For the sake ov th'
holy crass beside ye, and the blissed Vargin that's
over us all — be marciful!" she cried. "Sure ye
wudn't do it, you couldn't, you'd niver have the
heart? Is it Hurrish? Hurrish that was allays so
good to you an' to me, an' to ivery wan that come
nigh him. Think of thim poor little childer, Maurice!
Wud ye lave them widout a dada to put bread in
their mouths? And for *me* to be the wan to spake
against him! to sware away his pricious life! whin
ye know I'd rayther rin into the say fust an' be
drownded—God forgiv me for sayin' such a thing!
Till me ye didn't mane it, Maurice! Till me you
wudn't go for to do such a thing! Sure, I know
you've the good heart if ye'd only let yerself hear it
spake. Don't we want to be gettin' marcy all of us,
an' how 'ul we iver hope to get it if we don't show
none fust?"

He had stood still, riveted, in spite of himself, by
her look and words. They did not soften him, however; on the contrary, they made his desire for revenge burn deeper. She had turned against him!
This soft, supplicating creature, who looked so gentle
and yielding—whom he had regarded, and regarded

still, as his own—his thing, his creature, his property! It was because of *Hurrish's* danger, and for
Hurrish's sake, that she was imploring him, not for
any other reason. The last drop of venom seemed
infused into the bitter current of his soul.

"I'll *not* have marcy," he said sullenly. "D'ye
think I'm going to let him kill my brother and get
off without anything ?—go off and kill some one else
most like! I hope to God he will be hanged, and
I'd go any distance, if it was to the very end of this
world, to see it done, so I would!"

Alley's eyes widened slowly with horror. Then
the very extremity seemed to give her courage, for
she got up from her knees and stood erect, trembling, but facing him.

"Then I'll not ask ye again, Maurice Brady," she
said. "An' 'tis yersel' 'ul be the worse for it an'
not Hurrish, for I don't believe God 'ul iver let him
be killed, for *He's* merciful if you're not, an' He
knows that Hurrish is not a bad man, whativer he
may do when the timper's on him. An' I'm not
afear'd for all ye say, for there's One I've put me
trust on, that 'ul bring him out of this, spite ov the
worst you can do."

She was not thinking of any earthly assistance,
but he thought that she knew, as he himself in fact
did know, that the chance of Hurrish being really
condemned was, under the circumstances, a very remote one ; and this, and the reproach of her words together, put the apex to his fury.

"He may get off at Ennis, then, for there's liars
and vagabonds everywhere," he almost screamed ;
" but if he does, he'll not get off from *me*, and so you

may tell him : I'll hunt him down same as I would
a mad dog : He needn't hope to escape me—not if
he were to go and hide himself under the sea itself!"
He was still standing beside the cross, and, with
that strongly dramatic instinct that ran through his
whole nature, he now turned deliberately towards it.
" Sure as God made me, and sees me now, and seen
him kill my brother Mat, so sure I swear, if he gets
off at Ennis court-house, I'll do for him yet! Night
or day, early or late, sooner or. later, by God's help
or the devil's help, *some* way or other, I'll do for him !
There, I've *shworn* it !" and he struck his hand down
violently upon the broken top of the cross.

CHAPTER XX.

IN THE COURT-HOUSE AT ENNIS.

All day long in the crowded court-house, in the
dust, and the heat, and the glare. Faces everywhere.
Cold, decorous, indifferent faces ; faces framed in wigs ;
polite faces surmounted with well-brushed hair ; faces
rising serene above black broadcloth and white spot-
less linen. Behind and on either side faces, too,
more faces, nothing but faces. Wild, unkempt, excited, perspiring faces, packed close as cattle in a
cattle-truck. A few familiar ones here and there.
Old Phil Rooney, looking odd and unnatural in his
loose grey hair, without the inevitable battered high
hat. Father Denahy, close at hand, broad, friendly,

and genial, a very sustaining point in the confusion. Hurrish, a long way off, pale and strange-looking, with a policeman on either side. Bridget, excited but awed, with a huge black shawl over her tousled hair. These were some of Alley Sheehan's experiences of Ennis court-house on the day of the trial of Horatius O'Brien for the murder of Matthew Brady.

She had been put into the witness-box about one o'clock. Bridget, half mad with excitement, had flown at her like a vulture a little while before, and had hissed directions into her ears. She was to do this, not to do that; she was to say this, not to say the other. Alley, however, hardly heeded. She was very tired, and dazed with the crowd and unaccustomed surrounding, but she was wonderfully calm. The scene with Maurice had left upon her mind a sort of exaltation—a sense of inward support. Seen by herself, detached from the crowd around, her sweet young face, with its peculiarly nun-like look of innocence and purity, produced an immediate effect, and a slight murmur of admiration made itself heard.

She was asked how she had known that Matthew Brady was dead before any one else had done so, and had been made to describe coming upon his dead body in the glen, and running back to the cabin to tell Bridget. Then there was a few minutes' pause, and she began to wonder whether it could be all over. Every pair of eyes in the whole building was fixed upon her. For her own part, however, she saw no one distinctly—it was all a mist and a confusion. Then the counsel for the prosecution arose—a stout, burly man, the native humorousness of whose expression was only partially modified by a sense of his own importance.

" Now, my good girl, listen to me, and be very careful what you say. Who did you see in Gort-nacoppin valley that morning besides the dead man ? "

" Ne'r a one 't all, plaze, sor."

" Ne'r a one 't all ? Now be careful. Think ! On your oath, did you not see Hurrish O'Brien ? "

" 'Dade no, sor ; I never seen a sight ov him."

" Where did you see him last that morning ? "

" At the dure."

" What *dure ?* "

" Th' house dure."

" What did he say to you ? "

" Said he was goin' to Ballyvaughan, sor."

" Anything else ? "

A blush flew over Alley's soft cheek, leaving it as pale as before.

" Said somewhat 'bout Maurice Brady," she murmured.

The last words were so low that no one in the court heard them except the counsel for the prosecution, who was nearest, and he only the last one.

" Said something about Brady, did he ? Come now, my good girl, what was it ? " he said, with an air of elation.

Alley did not blush again ; she hesitated and looked unhappy.

" Come, come, my good girl,—no prevarication. Tell us what it was."

" Said he had a good hart, sor," she murmured.

The counsel's jaw dropped, and a laugh, beginning

amongst those in front, and spreading quickly to the crowd behind, ran round the whole court.

"*Said he had a good heart ?* " he repeated, in a tone of mystification. " Nonsense, my good girl ; don't be wasting the time of the court like that. He couldn't have said anything of the sort."

" He did indade, sor." Alley's great eyes were lifted for a moment to her interrogator's face, and their expression of limpid truthfulness it was difficult to gainsay.

" Nonsense, I tell you ! Impossible ! Why, we know that they were always enemies."

" Is it he an' Maurice ? Sure Hurrish and Maurice was allays frinds, sor, allays—lastways till now," she added, with a sigh.

" Oh, Maurice ! It was *Maurice* Brady he said had the good heart ? "

" Yes, sor—Maurice."

" Oh, pooh, we're not here to make any inquiries about Maurice Brady's heart ! Go on, and tell the court what else Hurrish O'Brien said to you that morning."

" Nothin' more, sor."

" Which way did he go when he left you ? "

" Straight on over the racks, sor."

" Would that way take him through the Gortna-coppin valley ? "

Alley hesitated again, trembled, cast a wild despairing look around for help, then, as no help was forthcoming, murmured piteously, " Yis, sor."

" Very well. Now, that second time when you came back with Bridget O'Brien, what happened then ? "

This was really the perilous point. Fortunately
for Hurrish, nothing at all had transpired about the
stick. It had been sought for, but not until the next
day, when it had been found in its usual place in the
corner of the cabin, where old Bridget's instinct had
told her to replace it. Any of the men who had
seen him at Ballyvaughan could, of course, have
sworn that he had been without it there; but then
no one, equally of course, had chosen to do so.

Alley trembled. She, too, knew the peril well
enough. She had not yet seen Maurice Brady, but
she felt instinctively that his eyes were upon her as
she spoke. Had she been subjected to a sufficiently
severe cross-examination, it is almost certain that her
innate truthfulness would have betrayed her, and that
she would have revealed something. As it was, she
had only to repeat what she had already said—
namely, that she was frightened and afraid to look
again at the dead man, and so ran away and hid herself amongst the rocks by the sea.

There were a few more questions, but nothing further of any consequence was elicited, and she was
allowed to leave the witness-box and return to her
former place.

Father Denahy received her, spoke encouragingly,
and found a place for her beside himself in a corner
where she was a little screened from the pressure of
the crowd.

She hardly heard what Bridget, who was the next
witness, said, though, from the shouts of laughter
that ran round the court, it was evident that the old
woman was affording that entertainment so dear to
the hearts of *habitués* at Irish trials. Suddenly she

saw that Maurice Brady was in the witness-box, and
lifted her head in terror, and tried to listen. She
could not, however, distinguish very much. He looked
excited and eager, and spoke rapidly with an air of
authority and importance. Then another gentleman
in a wig—not the one that had questioned her—got
up, and it seemed to her that Maurice was annoyed
by the questions he asked, for she could see his face
flush and his brow darken angrily. A sullen murmur
greeted him as he, too, stepped from the witness-box,
but this demonstration was speedily put down. Then
more witnesses, one after the other, appeared, popping
up like puppets in a puppet-show, though whether
they were speaking for Hurrish or against him Alley
could not make out. She was very tired, worn out
by the long drive in the early grey of the morning,
and the long day in the hot and crowded court-house;
worn out, too, by all that she had gone through
beforehand. Her head nodded wearily, and at last
fell back against the chair. Father Denahy had had
to leave her, in order to go and give his evidence in
favour of Hurrish's general character, which was also
confirmed by Major O'Brien and by young Thomond,
who had insisted upon being allowed to get into the
witness-box. Of this Alley, however, heard little or
nothing. She was not sleepy, but she had reached
that point of weariness when everything becomes
dream-like. It was perhaps only a horrible dream,
she thought, that Hurrish was being tried for murder.
His face she saw distinctly; all the rest was blurred,
misty, undistinguishable.

At last the witnesses ceased popping up, and then
one of the wigged gentlemen rose and began to speak

—" Buzz, buzz, buzz, buzz," his voice went on for
hours—days as it seemed to Alley. At length, however, it came to an end, but immediately afterwards
another got up and began a fresh " Buzz, buzz, buzz,"
all over again. At last this, too, ceased, and then
there followed a long delay. She had been given a
piece of bread, which she broke a bit off mechanically
from time to time and put into her mouth. The
court-house had now to a great extent become empty.
The gentlemen with wigs had nearly all gone. Hurrish, too, had been taken away by the two policemen,
and there was a great vacant place in front of her
where the crowd had lately been. The jury were
deliberating.

Alley did not leave. She remained where she was,
for Father Denahy had decided that it was best so.
The comparative coolness revived her, and she looked
up at the window in front of her. Through the dirt
and manifold cobwebs she could see a little bit of
pale blue sky and a bird flying by. It seemed strange
somehow that there should be birds and sky still outside. It made her think of Teampull a Phoill, and
she tried to say a prayer, but could not for the life
of her remember any. Bridget, wrapped in her big
shawl, was rocking herself to and fro on a bench,
muttering what sounded like curses between her teeth.
Alley looked at her, and would have liked to say
something to comfort her if possible, but was afraid
—she looked so appallingly fierce and forbidding.

She was aroused by a fresh bustle around her,—a
fresh tramp of hasty feet pouring into the court-house.
The gentlemen in wigs were all coming hurrying in
again. The judge had taken his place ; Hurrish was

being hastily replaced in the dock.   All eyes were
fixed upon the door by which the jury were about to
return.

At last it opened, and the twelve appeared.   The
foreman stepped forward.   He opened his mouth to
speak—a cough !   Opened it again—a second cough.
What a moment for a man to be affected with a catching in his breath !   Opened it a third time ; and this
time a word came out—" Innocent."

It was caught up by a hundred voices—hoarse,
shrill, guttural, declamatory.   A buzzing as of ten
million imprisoned bees and wasps, suddenly escaping
from a bag, filled the building.   Every frieze-coated
man in or near the court-house shouted it at the top
of his voice to his neighbour ; every arm was waving
exeitedly ; every coat-sleeve bursting at the shoulder
—all Irish coats seem to have a tendency to give way
at the arm-holes ; every one struggling madly to get
out into the open air at once.   Alley was helped to
her feet by Father Denahy, who took her by the arm
and almost carried her through the crowd, warding off
any excited elbows which otherwise might have hurt
her.   Old Bridget was just in front, making her way
by the aid of her own redoubtable fists and elbows.
They were outside now, in the open air, so cold
after the close and suffocating air of the court-
house.   Another minute and Hurrish himself appeared, escorted by a couple of constabulary.

At sight of him a roar, as of a whole drove of mad
bulls suddenly broken loose, rose and mounted sky-
ward.   The entire crowd seemed to be convulsed.
Big, broad-shouldered fellows were sobbing like infants, thumping one another violently for pure joy,

cursing, shrieking, blaspheming—they did not in the
least know why, but presumably for happiness.   Old
Bridget flung up her two wrinkled hands to heaven.
Her attitude, however, was certainly not one of gratitude.   She clenched her fists and shook them passionately, as if in triumph, at the sky, uttering shriek upon
shriek as she did so, shrill and piercing as the whistle
of an express train.

Alley was too scared and bewildered to join in
all this excitement.   She realised that Hurrish was
safe, and so far was thankful, but she could not
catch the contagion.   He himself kept calm, too,
amongst the commotion.   The weight of the prison
was perhaps on him still.   He shook one or two of
the hundred hands held out to him and thanked
their owners, but looked around at the same time
as if for a way of escape—" There, there, boys ! aisy.
Arrah, God bless yis all ! aisy !"—his voice was
heard from time to time above the tumult in a tone
of expostulation.

The car which had brought them from Tubbamina
was waiting in the market-place, but it was impossible to get to it.   A rush was made by the crowd
to seize Hurrish and chair him round the town—an
honour which he only succeeded by main force in
evading.   In every direction hands were held up
and hats waved.   People who had never seen him
in their lives before, and would not have cared two
straws if he had been comfortably hanged and done
for, were apparently convulsed with joy, pouring out
countless blessings upon his head, and in the same
breath cursing the Government and the " polis."

All at once, and in the very height of the excitement, there came a new diversion—a fresh commotion. Alley did not know why all the people suddenly turned and ran back towards the court-house, or why faces that a minute before had been wet with emotion, suddenly grew hard and hideous with ferocity. Hurrish knew, however. Maurice Brady had waited some time behind to allow the tumult to subside, but was now coming out of the court-house, and there was a general rush to get at him.

He ran back, and, with the aid of Father Denahy and one or two others whom they persuaded, rather unwillingly, to help, got between the crowd and their object, so as to try if possible to turn this new tide of popular excitement. Old Bridget was amongst the first that rushed back,—not with this object, however,—her gleaming teeth and outstretched hands keen and hungry for revenge. Alley for the moment was left alone in the street. In front she saw a dense sea of people—shoving, pushing, screaming, elbowing; striking out madly with sticks, and fists, and feet. Wild, hardly, as it seemed to her, human faces, seen sideways, with cheeks expanded and mouths protruding; hands held up, clutched, brandished above the sea of heads; lumps of mud sent flying through the air, hissings, "booings"—a favourite weapon just then of offence—shrieks of women trodden on—the very houses seemed to her to rock and tremble with the tumult! Presently the crowd began to retreat backwards towards her. Alarmed, she retreated before them, and so they proceeded downhill towards the market-place. Suddenly, through a narrow lane opened through the

R

people, she saw Hurrish and Father Denahy waving
their arms and expostulating, and above — upon a
flight of steps raised half-a-dozen feet over the rest
—she saw Maurice Brady, white as a sheet, but
looking down, with arms disdainfully crossed, at the
bristling array of sticks and fists shaken menacingly
in his direction.   Then a squad of constabulary
pushed their way rapidly through the crowd, shoving the people right and left, and rapping the more
troublesome over the head or knuckles.   The gap
widened ; a flying tangle of men, women, and children came streaming down towards Alley.   Frightened, she turned and ran before it, not knowing what
to do or where she was going.   Happily the market-
place was wide enough to disperse the crowd, and
she was able presently to find refuge in a small
grocery shop, the proprietor of which allowed her to
shelter herself, and here a quarter of an hour later
she was found by Hurrish and Father Denahy, who
came hurrying down in search of her.

Even now they were obliged to wait, as old
Bridget was still missing.   Father Denahy offered to
go in search of her, leaving Hurrish with Alley.
There was another half-hour's delay, and then the
two appeared.   Whatever antagonist the old woman
had found to exercise her energies upon, it was evident that for once she had had her fill of fighting.
Her hair was hanging .about her in ragged wisps ;
one side of her face showed a long black bruise ; one
of her sleeves had been torn away, leaving the bony,
stick-like arms bare.   More serious dilapidation still,
she had lost her black shawl, the hoarded treasure of
years.   She did not seem to heed it, however.   Her

eyes shone with the gleeful triumph of the victor, and she reeled along the road as if she were drunk, though, as a matter of fact, she had tasted nothing.

They mounted the car, Hurrish and Alley on one side, old Bridget and the priest on the other. The affray between the people and the police had already almost effaced the previous excitement about Hurrish, so that they were able to get away without difficulty, and almost without notice. Just as they were leaving Ennis, old Phil Rooney ran up. He had come all the way to the trial in a donkey-cart, and was going back the same way, and did not expect to reach his own cabin till early the next morning. He was breathless with haste, and with the buffeting which he had encountered in the street, but his wrinkled old face beamed as he wrung Hurrish's hand, flourished his stick in the air, cut a wonderful caper in the dust—he had been a noted jig-dancer in his day—then ran back and clambered into his donkey-cart, settling himself again amongst the straw, his legs stretched out luxuriously before him, the poor patient beast setting off immediately, as if aware that it had twenty weary miles of up and down hill to traverse before it reached its mouldy straw.

It was with a sense of intense thankfulness that Alley found herself away from all the people, out in the open country amongst the dull green fields and monotonous lace-work walls. As they were passing the trout-stream close to the town, Hurrish lifted his head and looked eagerly away to the west, where the Burren hills were faintly discernible in grey unevenness against a pale saffron-coloured glow. Then he inflated his lungs suddenly with a breath which seemed visibly to expand his frieze coat, and almost lift him bodily off the car !

Hardly a word was exchanged on the drive. At first Father Denahy's voice was heard in pastoral rebuke to the belligerent Bridget. Finding, probably, that he was only wasting breath upon that unprofitable subject, he soon subsided into silence. Once, when they were passing a chapel, Hurrish, who had instinctively lifted his hand to his hat, turned with a sudden impulse to his companion.

" Ye said a bit ov a pray-er for me now and again, Alley, did ye ? " he inquired in a whisper.

" I did, Hurrish."

" I thought maybe y' had."

Then they relapsed into fresh silence.

After the sun had set clouds gathered thickly, and before they had done a third of the distance, the rain descended in a torrent, sending the dust flying before it in grey scuds along the road. Father Denahy unfurled a huge brown alpaca umbrella, and held it over himself and his companion. Hurrish looked at Alley with an expression of disquietude.

" What'll ye do 't all ? Sure ye'll be drownded," he said, anxiously.

" Arrah, I'll do well ! " She had nothing at all over her head, and only a thin old woollen shawl above her cotton bodice.

He took off his own greatcoat and put it cloak-fashion around her, keeping the flaps for himself. When they had got within about eight miles of Tubbamina, a miserable heap of small wet arms and legs were discovered upon the roadside, which presently unrolling itself, turned into the two small boys, Clancy

and Andy, who had run out all this way so as to be
the first to hear the result of the trial.   They were
promptly picked up and put upon the well of the car,
an elevation from which Andy soon slid down, and
settled himself into a small pulpy bundle between
his father and Alley.   She let him wriggle till he had
established himself comfortably against her shoulder,
then spread out a piece of the capacious frieze coat
and held it round him, so that he, too, might have a
share of its shelter ; and so, rolled in a bundle together,
they proceeded.

When she next peeped out of her own private corner of the pent-house, Alley's heart gave a sudden
bound.   Though it was nearly pitch-dark, she could
distinguish the wet grey limestone of the Burren.
She could see the flat tombstone-like platforms stretching in all directions, with huge boulders rising here
and there like headstones.   Her eye followed de-
lightedly the crooked contortions of a fissure, as it
sprawled its ugly length through the rocks, like some
fragment of sea-shore, which, not content with keeping its proper place, had stretched inland over the
entire country.   To a stranger, nothing could possibly
have been more grimly unattractive ; to Alley it was
home, peace, shelter.   No more repellent to her imagination than the native uncouthness of some kind
familiar face it has known from babyhood is repellent
to the imagination of a little child.

CHAPTER XXI.

The next day was Sunday. When Alley got up,
nearly an hour later than usual, and went to the
door, the rain had vanished in a pale blue mist. The
sun was shining brilliantly. The great flagged surfaces shone steel-blue with reflection ; the little pools
of water upon their indented hollows were of a ruffled
lapis-lazuli. Across the valley the chapel bell at
Tubbamina was ringing for matins, and the sound
came faintly to her ear. The sea was smooth, or
seemed at this distance to be so. Three " pookhauns," their small red-brown sails set to the fullest
possible extent, drifted leisurely past the headland ;
the grotesque prow of a coracle, lifted high out of the
water, showing black as ink against the luminous
satin-like surface.

Hurrish and the two boys had gone off to fish, but
old Bridget still lay fast asleep in her private lair,
the sound of her sonorous snoring filling the cabin.
Alley half dressed little Katty, and, leaving her in
the inner room, went into the kitchen to see about
preparing for breakfast. Hurrish had lit the fire, and
put the pot on to boil, before going out. Accordingly,
she went to the sack of oatmeal, filled a quart can
with it, stirred it into the water, then returned and
repeated the operation, singing softly to herself as she
did so.

Bridget, whose snores had been growing more and

more apoplectic, awoke suddenly with a final snort, and sat up and gazed round her, with the lowering air of some carnivorous animal unexpectedly awakened. Then, fetching down a comb from some obscure recess, she made a clutch at a bundle of clothes, and began making her toilette where she was, her skinny arms, bare to the shoulder, moving backwards and forwards actively as she did so.

Alley's singing had stopped instantly. Her terror of her tormentor was chronic, and never ceased entirely : she always had a feeling that Bridget might suddenly launch some unexpected missile at her—an incident not by any means, indeed, of unfrequent occurrence. Little Katty—her small garments still in a state of wild disorganisation—ran in from the other room and up to her, turning round to have some strings and buttons arranged. Alley knelt down on the floor to do so, thus bringing her face on a level with the child's. She was about to get up, her task finished, when Miss Katty—not a young lady generally prodigal of caresses—flung herself suddenly upon her, hanging on her neck like a round ripe plum, and rubbing her little warm red cheeks, as a kitten does, up and down the girl's pale satiny ones.

Old Bridget, with a scowl, lifted her vulture-like face, and glared savagely at the pair. She was about to growl out something, when the doorway darkened and Hurrish appeared, the two small boys trotting briskly in his wake.

Breakfast that morning was quite a festivity ! Hurrish had a string of fishes in his hands, which he proceeded to clean and prepare for broiling, tak-

ing down at the same time a large piece of bacon
which hung over the chimney, and giving it to Alley
to cut into slices for frying. She did so, and when
the meal was ready waited upon them all, feeding
Katty with a spoon, and settling a dispute between
Clancy and Andy as to which was entitled to the
last slice of bacon. Hurrish insisted, however, upon
her sitting down and eating, heaping up a goodly
portion upon her plate, and standing sentry over her
until it was finished. By the time breakfast was
over and the plates washed, it was time to begin to
get ready for chapel. Bridget peremptorily declined
going, probably on account of the increasing blackness of one side of her face, the result of her martial
efforts the day before. To Hurrish, as well as Alley,
this decision was a relief. His mother's ferocious
satisfaction in his escape from the clutches of the
law did not gratify him, somehow, as much as might
have been expected. It was so evident that her joy
lay in believing him to have been really guilty of
the worst, and to have escaped merely by dint of
much vigorous equivocation, and by favour of a
patriotic jury—not a view of the matter the pleasantest, perhaps, for him to contemplate.

With that reticence which is not incompatible
with the most primitive degree of openness, he
shrank from speaking upon the subject to her, and
still more so to Alley. That the latter should have
been mixed up in it at all, gave him indeed the
keenest pain, the period of her cross-examination
having been worse to him than all the rest of the
ordeal put together. What the girl's private view
of his guilt was, he could not of course tell, but sus-

pected that she had come to realise the matter pretty nearly as it really stood, and therefore rested in that belief. To himself the whole subject was full of quite unfamiliar pain, and with the indestructible light-heartedness of his race and type, he made haste therefore to throw it as far behind him as possible. The hardest thing thus to fling away and get rid of was the remembrance of Maurice Brady's share. Even this, however, after a while, he succeeded in doing. Either Maurice had felt it his duty, in some inexplicable way, to do what he had done, or he had been led away by temper, and for both alternatives Hurrish could feel a brotherly sympathy. They had now each something to forgive the other—there was a satisfaction in remembering that—and he cherished a hope that some day the two offences might, as it were, balance one another, and all be again as it had been before.

The scene at Tubbamina, as he came down to the chapel, with Alley and the two boys beside him, was in the style of his reception outside the court-house the day before;—the numbers, that is to say, were smaller, but the enthusiasm even greater. Sal Connor—whom it is to be hoped the reader has not forgotten—was one of the first to rush forward and pour out tears and exultations over his escape. Despite a succession of other swains who in the interim had laid siege to her hand—despite even his own hardened ingratitude—Hurrish still retained the foremost place in that unresenting damsel's affections. She had been one of the most furious against Maurice Brady,—indeed it was well for him that they had not chanced to meet, otherwise he would have

stood a considerable chance of having to defend himself against her own maidenly hands. She had a
new suitor now in attendance—a young gentleman
from Limerick, engaged in the bacon trade—but it
was evident to all intelligent beholders that it only
wanted a word from Hurrish for that youth's chances
to vanish utterly. A man just out of jail ! Other
merits apart, what patriotic maiden's heart could hope
to withstand so irresistible a plea ?

It was a long, long day of absolute idleness—*free*
idleness !—delicious combination of words ! Hurrish
took Lep, and went off to the saleen, throwing himself down upon the sands there in an ecstasy which
he would have been ashamed perhaps to exhibit before any more critical audience. Lep was sympathetic, however, and paid no particular attention,
beyond wagging his tail and snapping sleepily at the
flies. He had exhausted himself in enthusiasm the
night before, and felt perhaps that it behoved him to
regain a soberer and a less expansive deportment.

There was something luminous—almost, as it were,
Biblical—about the scene to-day. The grey limestone hills, warm and faintly iridescent under the
hot kisses of the afternoon sun, might have reminded
a traveller of those other limestone hills, more mem-
orable, for all their aridity, than the most favoured
tracts of other lands. Hurrish naturally did not
think of this, but a suffused sense of wellbeing filled
his soul, and by an association of ideas he looked
across the sea to that point—a little south of the
Aran isles—where the last well-authenticated sight
of the O'Brasil is said to have been obtained. It was
a position better laid down in the mental charts of

the neighbourhood than half the genuine islands and
sandbanks.   Hurrish himself was troubled with no
doubts at all as to its existence.   To have been so
would have been to show himself, in fact, no better
than an atheist, seeing that, as lately as the time of
Phil Rooney's grandfather, a young man, blown out
to sea during a squall, had landed there, and been
sumptuously entertained for three days by the inhabitants, who feasted him upon such rich viands as
only the Blessed eat, and imparted to him, on leaving, many valuable secrets—" by which means," says
a contemporary chronicler, " some seven or eight
years after, he began to practise both chirurgery and
phisick, and so continues ever since to practise, tho'
he never studyed nor practised either all his life before, as we that knew him from a boy can averr."

It was not till the shadows, thrown backward from
the sea, were beginning to grow long and straggling,
that he got up and began to retrace his steps, Lep
following close at heels, as if in dread of his again
disappearing mysteriously into space.   When they
had got within a quarter of a mile of home, Alley
was discovered sitting upon the rocks, with little
Katty beside her ; Clancy and Andy tumbling about
together, like a pair of young bears ; the poor old
donkey, who took Bridget to market and Hurrish's
fish to Lisdoonvarna, also rolling comfortably upon a
bit of green turf hard by, its four well-worn legs high
in air, like some unusually dilapidated variety of bed-
posts.

Alley was trying to teach the child to repeat her
" Hails," whereas Miss Katty much preferred pluck-
ing the young leaves of sorrel which sprouted out of

the clefts of the rocks, and nibbling them with her
small front teeth, making wry faces expressive of delighted disgust at their tartness as she did so.   Hurrish stopped and sat down beside them, Lep moving
a little way off, with rather a supercilious air.   The
colour rose to Alley's cheeks, as it had done each
time the last two days Hurrish had come near her.
It was the pleasure of seeing him free and safe again,
she told herself; what else, in fact, could it have
been ?   Certainly the character of *his* affection for
her had sustained no change !   The bare idea of
being fond of her, in any other sense from that in
which he was also " fond " of his own three-year-old
Katty, had never dawned upon him, nor would probably have dawned upon him had they lived for a
hundred years together.   It would have been wrong,
but, apart from that, it was not a direction in which
his thoughts strayed, or had any temptation to stray.
Why, he would have asked, should they do so ?

Why indeed ?   There seems no answer one way
or other, save the perhaps rather feeble and unsatis-
factory one of national peculiarities.   Despite his
susceptibleness in other directions, it really did seem
as if Hurrish, like so many of his type, hardly knew
whether a woman was handsome or the reverse.   To
be strong and active, to have a " clane skin,"—
these he recognised as important points, but beyond
these his perceptions rarely strayed.   He had never
dreamt of being " in love " with his own poor Molly
Sheehan, though they had been the happiest of
couples, and he had mourned her loss with a passion
which would have left many a susceptible gentleman
far behind.   Perhaps it is as well.   If that delusive

Will-of-the-wisp, which makes wise men foolish and sober ones mad, were to exercise an equal ascendancy over such pieces of touch-paper as our friend Hurrish, —if he and such as he were to be as excitable in this direction as they are in some others—politics, to wit, —surely not all the rain that ever fell upon Ireland would keep that unlucky island from being in a state of perpetual conflagration !

It was a happy moment, but it came to an end only too soon. The evening was closing in, the sun sinking like a red-hot cannon-ball into the grey, cool breast of the Atlantic. After a while, therefore, they got up, and proceeded homewards, Hurrish and Alley abreast, each holding a fat hand of Miss Katty's in theirs ; then Lep, sniffing the air, and passing the still recumbent donkey with an air of superiority ; the boys—scuffling and running after one another— bringing up the rear. The western sky was clear, and almost colourless, but upon the other side, beyond the intervening Burren hills, it was a mass of finely graduated colour. A multitude of arrowy flames, like the *disjecta* of some aerial volcano, were shooting their fiery points, one after the other, in a continuous flight across the zenith. They had attracted apparently even old Bridget's attention, for she was standing at the cabin door as the others approached, and looking up at the sky, an expression of fierce exultation lighting up her wrinkled face, which seemed to be inspired by some more exciting idea than the mere contemplation of its beauty. " Red as the divil ! red as the divil ! " they heard her mutter to herself, as her eyes followed the blazing masses.

Hurrish nudged Alley's elbow. " 'Tis the gran'

fightin' she got yisterday she's thinkin' ov," he said, with a wink.

Alley tried to smile, but she felt a sudden shock, and her innocent pleasure fell dead. The old woman's look and manner frightened her. More, it gave her a vague sense of impending trouble — a sense of something about to happen of which others knew, though she did not. The serenity which, half an hour before, had fallen upon her like a benediction, vanished, and a cold fear took its place. She thought of Maurice Brady, and of his words and looks that dreadful day at Teampull a Phoill. Did he, could he have meant what he said· then ? she wondered, or was it only a cruel threat,—a way he had taken of punishing her ? She had never found courage to repeat his words, chiefly from a childish feeling that the mere fact of doing so might somehow tend to bring them to pass. She thought of them constantly, however, and always with fresh fear, always with a vivid recollection of his look and manner, which made it difficult to dismiss them as mere idle threats. They lay like a dead weight upon her mind—a weight which every sudden movement caused to press and hurt intolerably. Thus, though Hurrish was safe and out of prison again, the future was not by any means wholly free from clouds.

CHAPTER XXII.

A FLASH IN THE DARK.

Two months had gone by since the day of the trial. Other and equally exciting scenes had occurred in the interval, so that it was no longer a matter of much interest even on the spot. It was a bad moment, in a bad year. Though the long nights had not yet come, there was a dangerous spirit abroad. The harvest had in many parts been bad, and a considerable harvest of another sort had been reaped from its failure. All over Ireland there had been scattered crimes, and rumours of coming outbreaks. In lonely cabins, far from roads, far from the possibility of help of any kind, frightened women were lying awake at night, trembling to see the ill-protected door fly open, and blackened faces appear to drag away son, husband, father, to ill-usage, perhaps to death. On the hills around horns were sounding at the dead hours. The cries of tortured animals — not less audible, perhaps, for being inarticulate—had again and again risen for vengeance to the sky. The whole country was in one of its periodic fits of excitement, terror, revolt. Vague expectations were everywhere afloat, dreadful or hopeful according to the anticipations of the individual. In the more reckless and desperate spirits, a wild belief in the speedy oncoming of some glorious pandemonium. when the torch and carnage would stalk over the country ; in the more passive, a vague unquenchable

expectation of a millennium which would make them
rich, happy, prosperous, as by a miracle. In more
practical heads, an eager political ferment,—a feeling
that old things had passed away, and all things had
become new. Brave men were nervous; sober men
excited; every one uneasy, uncomfortable, restless.
Nowhere stability; nowhere confidence; everywhere
a feeling that ordinary routine was henceforward set
aside. Of what use, it was asked, to slave one's self
when one might at any moment become rich without
doing so ?   Still more forcibly, who but a fool would
"dishtroy" himself working to pay . the rent, when
all the world knew that henceforth no rents would
have to be paid at all ?

Clare has always claimed a prominent position in
times of disturbance, and it was not behind its old
fame on this occasion. Several barns had been
burned, several obnoxious individuals waylaid and
chastised, and there were warnings of more vigorous
doings still. In no other part of Ireland had Cap-
tain Moonlight appeared in greater force or with more
absolute impunity. An impalpable reign of terror—
invisible, but none the less real—lay upon every one,
and every man looked distrustfully at his neighbour.

Mr O'Brien had his full share of these troubles.
No rent had been paid, of course; but that was merely a preliminary. Threatening letters had again
begun to form an ordinary item of the morning's
post-bag. The momentary popularity which he had
won by his defence of Hurrish had flickered and
died. That, it was felt, was after all only an isolated
case, whereas his misdeeds were perennial and unin-
termittent: he asked for rent; he professed his de-

termination to have it; he declared that he could not exist without it. Brave indeed would be the man that defended him!

Young Thomond was still at Donore, and was the hardest to convince that anything was seriously amiss with the state of the country. One evening, however, even his confidence got rather a shock. He had been pooh-poohing the alarms of the newspapers, declaring the Government and its myrmidons to be at the bottom of half the crimes reported. When night came, and his uncle had retired to bed, the whim took him to go for a midnight walk. It was a beautiful evening, warm and soft, with a moon sleeping peacefully over the sea, the whole world seemingly at peace and at rest. He turned away from the Burren, across the wider fields of the southern part of the property. As he was sauntering along, not far from the edge of a lane, his hands in his pockets, and his thoughts nowhere in particular, his attention was arrested by a mutter of tongues proceeding apparently from the ground below him. Startled, he approached, and stepping quietly up to the edge of a bank which skirted the lane, peeped cautiously over. Four men were crouched together under the opposite bank, which rose steeply above their heads. Two were lying at full length, the others squatting,—all with weapons—they might have been sticks, or they might have been blunderbusses—in their hands. Young Thomond held his breath, for he was aware that he had stumbled upon perilous ground, and that an incautious breath now would probably be his last. Presently up rushed a big sinister-looking man, exceedingly ragged, two wild bloodshot eyes

S

looking out under the tattered remnants of an old felt hat. The men in the ditch sprang up to hear what he had to say. Thomond listened too, but was unable to catch anything. The ragged man never ceased speaking, but he was hardly articulate, the gurgling syllables dying away half uttered in his throat, and never getting any higher. After a while all five crept stealthily away along the bottom of the ditch, their weapons protruding like stiff tails under their coats. Master O'Brien waited till they had all gone, and then went home considerably sobered, and was observed to be much less loud about the pacific proclivities of the county Clare for some days afterwards.

Alone amongst the Donore tenants, Hurrish still maintained friendly relations with Mr O'Brien. This, which under other circumstances would have been a source of no slight peril to himself, was in his case allowed. There was a feeling that he had done his part, and might be allowed to rest upon his laurels— a theory which, it may be said, entirely chimed in with his own views.

Of Maurice Brady nothing had been heard for some time. There was a rumour afloat that he had been engaged in more than one local misdeed—by way, perhaps, of wiping out the recollection of his late falling away from the popular ideal—but no proof of the fact had been forthcoming.

Meanwhile, in the Burren at any rate, the potato harvest promised to be excellent, and the corn— where there was any—had ripened as it had not ripened for years. It had been extraordinarily still for nearly a week, the whole coast seeming to be wrapped in deep dreamless sleep. The sea heaved, but its surface was hardly broken, the great rollers flinging themselves down as if exhausted when they reached the shore, and passing away immediately into stillness. The very gulls and kittiwakes seemed to have temporarily changed their character, and floated inertly about, like so many farmyard ducks, upon the surface. The smoke of passing steamers trailed behind in a long-drawn lazy column. Now and then a catspaw would pass over the bay, beginning at the furthermost point of Iar Connaught, turning the pale satiny greyness of the surface into a deeper tint, and then vanishing suddenly. Down at the rock-pools, however, which were protected against such incursions, the very stillness of death prevailed, the particles of water seeming to be literally glued together. Through this oily tenacious surface the inquiring claw of some predatory crab, prowling amongst the seaweed, might have been seen now and then to rise, gesticulating excitedly, like the hand of some one in the act of drowning, or those supplicating hands seen by Dante above the lake of pitch; then the broken surface would settle together again, and all would be stillness. On the fifth day, however, this unnatural calm gave way. Noises sounded in the air. Dark masses of cloud rolled over the sky, and vivid weather-galls— green, violet, and orange—appeared in two or three directions. It was plain to every one who knew anything that dirty weather was coming.

Hurrish had left his coracle as usual on the small crescent-shaped strip of sand at the end of his own saleen. It was safe enough there in ordinary occasions, but in very big storms the whole of this space

was covered with foaming monsters, rolling in through
the narrow mouth, and rushing with fury against the
cliff. The tide, however, was out now, so that there
would be time enough for him to see about it before
it returned. In the meantime, as the day drew in,
and the suspicious symptoms increased, every effort
was being made to save the little crop of oats, which
had been begun to be cut the day before in the
small triangular field nearest to the cabin. The
whole family were out together, — the two boys,
Alley, and old Bridget collecting the bundles, while
Hurrish, and another man got in to help, laboured
away with their sickles. They were all intent upon
their work, when a sudden exclamation from one of
the boys caused them to look up. A solid-looking
wall of lead - coloured cloud, with a thin, wicked-
looking splinter of white light where the base touched
the water, was stalking steadily in towards them over
the face of the sea. Two of the Aran isles were
already caught and swallowed up, while the third
was just beginning to be engulfed in the maw of
the monster. The Connemara mountains, which had
been extraordinarily clear all that morning, had
wholly disappeared, and the dark mass was now
laying hold of the nearer headlands — Roundstone
with its ragged retinue of islands, and the nearer
Cashla : clearly before another ten minutes were past
it would be upon them. They could see distinctly
the jet - black layers of rain streaking the dun-
coloured mass, a looser outlier of cloud sweeping
away south like an advanced guard,—the sails of
two or three " pookhauns," which had been all but
becalmed an hour before, standing out like small

triangles of burnished gold against this sinister background.

The whole party loaded themselves to their utmost possible powers, and hurried to the cabin with their burdens—Hurrish and the other man speedily returning and setting to work desperately to cut down the corner of upstanding oats that still remained. By the time the rest were back, the storm, though still at bay, was creeping nearer and nearer. It was intensely hot. The perspiration poured down every face. The sun, shooting suddenly from behind a pair of round-backed clouds, blazed furiously as if excited upon the little field in its iron setting of rocks, then suddenly vanished, and was seen no more, and a hollow roll of thunder followed in a slow prolonged rumbling from the west.

By dint of desperate labour they got the work accomplished, though before the last arm-load was in, the rain had begun—huge single drops falling with a dull thud upon the dried-up surfaces of the rocks, and raising a round white puff of dust at every descent. It had got very dark, too, though it was not yet sunset.

Having packed the oats into a compact heap in the outhouse, Hurrish pulled on an old tarpaulin cape, kept for such occasions, tied his hat tightly round his head with a piece of string, and set off for the saleen. The moment he had gone, old Bridget called Alley and ordered her peremptorily to go and drive in the milch cow, which was tethered some distance away. She obeyed, though the rain was now coming faster, and she had no tarpaulin to put on—only her poor little thin woollen shawl, which ten

minutes sufficed to drench. She had reached the
place—a small green square shut in on all sides by
low lace-work walls—when the long-delayed storm
suddenly burst in all its strength. The darkness
grew to blackness. The cloud-bank had touched the
shore, and straightway the sea itself—everything, in
fact, except the immediate foreground — vanished.
Great sweeping gusts of wind bore down upon her,
roaring into her ears, like so many angry messages
delivered through speaking - trumpets, ceasing suddenly, and then followed the next minute by another
and a yet more reverberating roar.

Scared by the suddenness of the onslaught, Alley
looked round for some possible refuge. Where she
was there was not an atom, not enough to protect a
bird or a rabbit. Lower down, however, a ledge of
rock, projecting a little way outwards, offered a partial pent-roof. She ran towards it, and crouching
amongst the dense growth of loose-strifes and rag-
weeds which had sprung up in the shelter, pressed
herself close as possible to the rock, so as to gain
all the shelter she could.

She was not long left in peace ! The wind, which
had hitherto been due west, suddenly veered to the
north, and the rain, instead of falling nearly horizon-
tally as it had hitherto done, took a long oblique
drift. It drifted into her shelter, soaked the flowers,
blew further and further in, till there was now no
more protection than in the open field. Every spot
seemed to be flooded in an instant ; pools stood out
on the bare ridges, and a small torrent began to run
along the hollow left at the base of the rock. What
was she to do ? If Hurrish had been at home, she

would have run back to the cabin.   Alone she dared
not face Bridget without the cow, and to attempt to
lead it through such a storm was evidently impossible.

Suddenly she bethought her of Teampull a Phoill,
which was only a little way off down the hill.   She
had never been there since the dreadful day of her
interview with Maurice Brady.   All her pleasure in
its beauty and seclusion, all her sense of its peculiar
sanctity, had been utterly destroyed and swept away
by that terrible day.   The image of Maurice Brady
—his hand upraised to strike the broken cross—was
the only one she now associated with it.   The very
sight of it was pain to her, and she had several times
made a considerable circuit in order to avoid passing
it.   Some shelter, however, she felt she must have,
and there seemed to be no choice except to go there,
or to return to the cabin, alternatives both about
equally unwelcome.

It was not a moment to hesitate.   The long slant-
ing drifts had already saturated the front of her dress,
and her cheeks were as wet as if she had been crying.
A fresh gust sweeping roughly along the rocky channel decided her.   She sprang up, scampered along
the top of the ridge which had offered her such sorry
hospitality, skirting the field where the cow, despite
the storm, was still placidly grazing ; ran down a
long decline of rocks—the rain rushing after her and
pouring in a small torrent between her feet—round
another barricade of rocks, the last, and down the
little narrow pathway which only just found room to
squeeze itself through the defile, till she came to a
standstill, panting, in the first of the ruined buildings,
said to have been originally the refectory of the con-

vent, a corner of which still retained a fragment of
its original roof, consisting of small flat pieces of
stone overlapping one beyond the other, and supported
by the two end walls.

It was nearly quite dark here, for the storm had
made havoc of the remaining daylight.   Alley, however, knew her way as well as if it had been her own
house, and could tell precisely the position of each of
the stones, which lay in tumbled heaps over the
ground.   She found a dry spot at the very end, the
farthest from the entrance, and sat down on a sort of
ridge, tucking her feet under her, and shivering; the
wind rushing in after her, and tearing round and
round the little enclosure; the rain spreading out
like a grey lattice-work over the edge of the fragment
of roof, the stones of which projected in an irregular
tooth-like outline one before the other over her head.

She hoped that it would leave off soon, and that
she would be able then to return and fetch home the
cow, which even Bridget could hardly expect her to
bring through such a tempest.   There was no symptom, however, of any cessation.   The darkness deepened, but the rain only seemed to be growing heavier,
and the wind to be steadily rising.   Now and then a
jagged flash of lightning lit up the gloomy little scene,
finding its way to every corner of the ruin, playing
bo-peep in and out of the black window-sockets, and
making a luminous background to the tall gable-end,
which rose in a peak over the doorway opposite.

Alley was not afraid, however, for the scene was
too familiar, and even the lightning could not make
it seem strange or formidable.   She gathered her
poor little cold body as comfortably as she could into

a corner, laid her head against the wall, and waited
patiently until she could effect her escape.

She had been there perhaps half an hour, when a
sound reached her that did, however, alarm her—a
sound of some one moving about in the space outside.
She sat up, then went a few steps forward, and peered
eagerly into the darkness. She could see nothing,
however, for the two walls on this side made the
obscurity absolutely complete. She returned, therefore, to her former place, and remained there still as
death, her heart beating, her eyes growing round with
terror. Some one certainly *was* there, a man apparently, for she could hear his boots striking against
the stones. Steps too were approaching, not hurrying
wildly into shelter though, as might have been expected on such a night, but groping their way slowly
and cautiously. She could hear them coming round
the outside of the building where she was, and presently they paused, and a figure stopped short at the
doorway opposite.

It was densely overgrown with ivy, which hung
so low that a man would have had to stoop considerably in order to enter. Alley could distinctly perceive a dark outline against the greyness, but too
vaguely to distinguish any traits. The unknown is
always the terrible, and she held her breath, hoping,
praying, that whoever he was, he might not come in.
He did not do so, but passed on after a moment
towards the west building, which was that of Teampull a Phoill. There was a small window in her
wall upon this side, and peeping through it, she could
now distinctly see the figure of a man, and see, moreover, that he was holding something in his hands

which he seemed to be trying to shelter from the
rain. More than this she could not distinguish.

Another moment, and he would have been out of
sight. She could see the black silhouetted outline
making its way over the soaked grass, and getting
gradually merged in the more comprehensive blackness of the ruin. At that instant, as fate would have
it, another flash of lightning,—the most vivid there
had yet been,—flung its melodramatic illumination
over the whole scene. It gleamed upon the little
ruin, throwing its low cyclopean walls, black hollows,
and tall gable-ends into full relief. It shone upon
the wet grass, swept flat with the beating of the rain;
upon the well with its low wall; upon the encompassing rocks; upon the stream flowing in a thick
brown torrent down the middle of the little valley.
It lit up the figure upon the point of retreating into
the church, and as it did so, threw a momentary but
unhesitating illumination right into Alley Sheehan's
soul. The man skulking there before her was Maurice Brady, and the thing which he was sheltering
under his arm was a gun!

CHAPTER XXIII.

THE WRONG SALEEN.

A stifled cry broke from her lips. She silenced
it instantly, however. Her strongest, most instinctive
impulse, was to avoid drawing Maurice Brady's atten-

tion to herself—not to let him know that she was there, and that she had seen him. But what had brought him? she asked herself in terror; what was he doing there? Above all, what was the meaning of that gun?

A sort of wave seemed to roll over her brain, and then to roll back again, and a flash, vivid as the flash of lightning, to carry conviction to her mind. It meant danger to Hurrish—that and nothing else was what it meant. Maurice Brady had sworn to kill him—sworn it upon that very spot where they were standing—and now he was going to do it. The conviction rose clear as a revelation, and with it a corresponding determination to save Hurrish. She did not say to herself that duty required her to do so, but her whole heart flew out to him in agonised terror and in horror against the other. To get to Hurrish—only to get to him—to get him, if possible, into some place where he would be safe, and then to give notice to the police; to have Maurice seized, put somewhere, locked up—no matter how or where—so that he could not injure Hurrish;—these were the thoughts which flew, not coherently, but as it were panoramically, through her brain.

How to get away without being heard was the first question. She no longer thought of the rain— hardly knew, in fact, whether it rained or not. To get to Hurrish was her one thought, her one instinct. Cautiously she got up, and cautiously crept round the wall of the little refectory, feeling her way along its stones to the entrance. Fortunately, with her bare feet, she could move almost unheard; the wind, too, favoured her, and prevented any slight noise from

being audible. She crept down to the doorway and
peeped out. The fear of such another tell-tale flash
as had unveiled Maurice Brady's presence was strong
before her mind, and made her keep close under
cover. She could see the confused dark mass of the
church opposite. His figure she could no longer, of
course, see, as he had gone inside. There was a
window, though, in the wall, which told her that it
would not be safe to attempt to escape upon that
side. Were she to do so, and his eye to turn to
the window at the moment she was passing, the
chances were, she felt, that he would catch sight of
her.

That being so, the only alternative lay between
getting out of the small window in the wall farthest
from Teampull a Phoill, or else clambering over a
piece of the same wall which had got broken down,
and part of which lay on the ground in a pile of
stones. She chose the latter, for the window was
exceedingly small—so small that she feared that it
might be impossible for her to get through it, at any
rate without making a noise. There was a long slope
of heaped-up stones upon either side, and a small
piece of still solid wall rising out of the centre of
this heap, the upper part being utterly destroyed.
Feeling her way first cautiously with her hands, she
mounted upon the wet pile, her bare feet giving her
a firmer foothold than she would otherwise have had.
Fortunately the stones had fallen years before, so
that weeds had begun to bind them together. Even
so, it was a difficult operation, particularly in the
darkness, and against the tremendous hurly-burly of
wind and rain which assailed her the instant she got

her head above the breach. The first time she tried
to clamber up the solid piece of wall, her foot slipped
upon the slimy stones, and she fell, hurting herself
considerably. She mounted again, however, immediately, and this time, by a great effort, managed to
get her chest over the edge of the wall; then, to
bring her knees on a level with it. A minute after
she was standing upon the top.

As she did so, another, though this time a fainter
flash lit up the glen, and, to her terror, she saw that
the window in her own ruin exactly faced the one in
the ruin opposite, so that had Maurice Brady happened to be looking out, her outline would have
been distinctly visible. In alarm she crouched down
and waited while the dazzling flash faded, and the
rapidly succeeding rumble of thunder also died away,
and was lost in the distance. In the momentary
lull that followed, she could feel her heart beating
like a frightened rabbit's, expecting every moment to
hear Maurice's voice, or his steps upon the stones
below. After a while, however, as everything remained perfectly quiet, she concluded that she had
not been seen, so prepared to get down upon the
other side. The drop was very much deeper here—
so deep that she could not catch a glimpse from
where she was of the bottom. It might have been
ten feet or it might have been ten thousand, for anything she could see.

A fresh terror seized her, and she half made up
her mind to go back. The thought of Hurrish
nerved her, however, and facing towards the wall,
she resolutely leaned her chest and shoulders upon it,
and let her feet drop out into the vacancy, stretching

them lower and lower in hopes of touching the stones
below.   In vain.   There was nothing except the
wall itself, and in that not a single chink into which
she could hook her feet : the old monks' work was
too good, and still after all these years presented an
almost absolutely unbroken surface to the elements.
What she would have done had she been left to
herself it is difficult to say, but at that moment the
wind took the matter into its own rough hands.   A
compact gust,—the most violent that had yet come,
—came tearing down the glen, whisking everything
portable away before it, and shaking the very stones
themselves in their sockets.   It tore away poor little
Alley's feeble grasp from the top of the wall to which
she had been clinging, causing her to fall helplessly
on to the stones below, which, giving way under her
feet, rolled away with her to the very bottom.

She lay for some moments upon the ground,
stunned, and believing herself to be mortally injured.
The sudden violence of the gust, and her own fall,
made it seem more like some deliberate personal
attack than the mere unheeding brutality of the
storm.   After a while, however, she gathered herself
slowly up, the tears pouring from her eyes from pain.
She was dreadfully bruised, and her poor little feet
were badly cut by the stones, but there was nothing
actually broken.   A strong man falling in that way,
and from such a height, would probably have received much more serious injuries, but she was so
light that she had escaped comparatively easily.

As soon as she had realised that she was only
scratched and bruised, her courage began to come
back.   Though she could not help crying with the

pain of her bruises, she struggled to her feet, and, forgetting the poor little shawl which had been torn from her by the gust, staggered up the track which she was close to now, and which led out of the glen on to the level rocks above.

She had to sit down again here under the shelter of a loose boulder to recover herself, for the force of the gale was so terrific, that she was afraid of being again knocked down. Her task was not yet quarter accomplished. Hurrish was still at the saleen. In order to see him, it would be necessary, therefore, for her to make her way across the rocks and down the cliff—a task which might well scare any one in the dark, and in the midst of such a storm as was then raging.

Like a good many other apparently feeble people, Alley, however, possessed a wonderful amount of passive courage. Pain and discomfort, too, were no strangers to her,—an amount of either which would have utterly deterred and paralysed one of a tenderer rearing, hardly counting at all. There was no time to lose, either. If she was to warn Hurrish, she must do it at once. She must get him to come back with her to the cabin. Otherwise, the worst might happen before he received any warning at all.

Suddenly she fancied that she heard a sound in the glen behind her. Perhaps Maurice Brady might be following her—might get to Hurrish before she did! That thought gave her courage, and leaving the shelter of the boulder, she struck boldly out across the naked rocks in the direction of the sea.

The wind was simply terrific; there was no other word for it! It seemed to meet her like a solid

wall, driving everything before it as with a mighty
besom. Over the naked, slightly inclined surfaces—
flat to the eye—the water raced as over the beds of
a mountain torrent, driven in sheets by the wind.
They felt like ice under her naked feet, those cold,
rain-washed rocks, sculptured along the edges in long
narrow grooves and channels, like the half-melted
edges of crevasses. Here and there compact masses
of hawthorn, welded together by many a previous
tempest, presented their dwarf strength successfully
to the blast. Everything else was blown flat, or
swept bodily away. A number of sheep and lambs,
huddled close together for protection under the edge
of a lace-work wall, were bleating piteously, and could
evidently barely keep their footing.

Alley faced it bravely,—her head down nearly to
her chest ; the solid sheets of wind-driven rain falling
upon her bare head and neck, as if shot there through
some directing shoot. The wind seemed to meet her
with determined animosity, as though it knew of her
errand, and was resolved to prevent her from carrying
it out. The blind monster set itself against her puny
girlish strength with the brute determination of a
bully. It seemed as if the gusts were no longer
intermittent but continuous. She began to grow ill
with the pain of her bruises, with the fatigue of the
battle, with the eternal roar and whistle in her ears,
with the sense of opposing ferocity, with the dreadful
loneliness of this solitary unaided tussle. Through
it all, however, the thought of Hurrish drove her on.
It was like a burning fire in her breast, and kept
everything else at bay.

Long ago she was soaked to the skin, and had her

skirt been of cotton, like her bodice, she could hardly
have continued the struggle. Happily it was solid
as a frieze coat, or a Highlander's kilt; and though,
wet as it was, it pressed heavily round her waist, its
weight prevented it from flapping. Her worst enemy
was her own hair, which had got loose, and at every
fresh gust struck her across the face with a blow
which smarted like whipcord.

At last she reached the brink, made clear by the
sudden rise of ground, and by the jagged broken
edges of the rocks. She could see a slight yellowish
lighting around the horizon, and could feel, rather
than see, the great watery immensity below. But
where was the path? Where was the saleen?
Where were Hurrish and the boat? It was all a
mist and a void, indistinguishable as waves, or surf,
or rain, or sea, or sky, or shore—a wild hideous
chaos—as it were a gigantic yawn, in which the
very earth itself seemed in the act of being bodily
swallowed up.

Creeping cautiously along, almost upon her hands
and knees, feeling her way round every rock, blown
back continually by the wind, and almost stunned by
the roar, she followed the edge, searching everywhere
for the path. After nearly an hour thus spent, she,
to her intense joy, hit upon it, and began to descend.
It seemed very blind, and more impeded with rocks
than she had thought; but this, in the confusion of the
tumult, seemed only natural. Arrived at the bottom,
she peered anxiously round her in the darkness. It
was impossible to see more than a few yards at a
time, so after a while she began to call out, at first
feebly, fearing others might hear, then louder and

T

louder, as despair began to gain upon her. There
was not the faintest response! Only the roar of the
wind; only the sough of the rain, joined now by the
louder and more battering noises of the waves as they
flung themselves in fury against the rocks, exploring
fiercely every corner of the space in front. She could
distinguish their white teeth at the edge of the sand,
and the long, sinuous, snake-like curves running towards her, like some sort of sea-dragons or slimy
primeval monsters, thirsting to devour. Otherwise
everything was as dark, or nearly as dark, as in a
room of which the shutters are closed. Suddenly,
groping about the sand, she stumbled over a rock
sticking up in the middle—a peculiarly shaped rock,
with two pinnacles like church steeples, divided by a
gaping fissure. It seemed unfamiliar, somehow. She
could not remember any rock like that in Hurrish's
saleen. A terrible thought struck her, and she looked
agonisingly round, and up at the cliff over her head.
Peering intently into the darkness, she was able to
make out the square top of something like a tower
defined against the sky, with a lower, heavier mass
below. The dreadful truth burst upon her in all its
reality. It was *not* Hurrish's saleen, but another!
In the confusion of her search she must have wandered farther than she had known, and made her way
down another track, which she remembered to have
once descended before, and which led from an old and
now uninhabited castle belonging to the Macmorroughs.
It was all over then! She would never be in time to
warn him! Her struggles, her suffering were all for
nothing! The disappointment, the blank despair,
coming at the end of all her previous fatigues, struck

down upon the feeble remains of her strength like a crowbar. And, with a cry, lost in the roar and shriek of the storm, poor Alley sank upon the ground, utterly incapable of moving another step.

————

CHAPTER XXIV.

HURRISH SEES THE DEATH SPER'RT.

Meanwhile Hurrish had had his hands full. When he first reached the saleen the tide was still going out, and the sea had not even begun to rise, the smooth rollers, deflected by the outjutting horns of the bay, reaching the sand in the most innocent of waves, the long rhythmic sweep racing round and round the little bay, carrying their low white crests in a sort of skating curve along the sand, and rushing in mere playful exuberance over the low weed-covered rocks amongst which ît ended.

It seemed folly not to try and get the boat round to Tubbamina, where, whatever storm might come, it would be safe. Accordingly, Hurrish pulled it down to the brink, pushed it into the water, waded after, sprang in, took to his oars and rowed rapidly out through the narrow horseshoe-shaped opening.

He had just got beyond the rocks when the storm broke. In an instant he was in the thick of it. The darkness descended like a pillar of cloud; the rain flew at his face, as a cat flies, with all its claws outstretched. The water began to bubble and boil.

Multitudes of cross currents — the confused uncer-
tainty of the frightened crowd before it had settled
itself in one direction—making the coracle curvet
and prance like a skittish horse.   Still Hurrish
pulled steadily on.   To a stranger few boats are
more alarming than a coracle.   The slightest sea
sets it tossing like a bubble.   Down it goes into the
very depths of the hollows, rocking the next like a
cork upon the very brim of the ridges ; sea-sickness
itself, if you are addicted to so lamentable an infir-
mity, gives way to sheer panic.   Once accustomed
to its ways, however, this very buoyancy gives confidence.   It will ride like a duck over a sea that
would swamp a more pretentious craft as readily as
it would a stable bucket.   Hurrish, of course, had
absolute confidence in his own boat, and as far as
the danger of a capsize went, would have taken it
out in any gale.

So far, however, the storm had only been prelud-
ing, and had plenty of arrows still in reserve.   That
sudden change to the north-west, which had driven
Alley from her refuge under the ledge of rocks,
caught Hurrish in mid-sea, and in the very teeth.
If he had had a sail he would infallibly have been
capsized.   Even as it was, the coracle seemed for a
moment to buzz like a top, then, like a checked top,
to come to a complete standstill.   He set his strength
to the oar, and toiled at it like a galley-slave, the
bull-voiced monster roaring threats the while into his
ears, and buffeting him actively over the head.   It
was a regular hand-to-hand duel.   Whenever he
gained a few yards, fresh succour seemed to come
pouring in to his adversaries, and bearing down upon

him.   He was one, and they were a host, with other
hosts, too, behind that host.   Still it seemed to himself that he was gaining; Tubbamina was certainly
nearer than it had been ten minutes before.   Suddenly, as ill luck—worse luck even than he knew of
—would have it, there came a defection upon his
own side.   Above the roar and the hurly-burly he
heard, or rather felt, another sound, a small one, but
worse than all the rest put together.   The oars were
old, and, though carefully spliced and mended, were
not equal to being the point of resistance between
two such combatants.   There was a faint crack, and
looking down, he saw that one of them had given
way at the splicing, a little above where it rested upon
the rowlocks.   With breathing-time he could have
made it good, but in the teeth of such a gale it was
obviously impossible.

Reluctantly he was obliged to let the coracle go
about—a victory which the wind celebrated with a
fresh roar, catching it broadside on, and sending a
bucket or two of water to the bottom.   It seemed
hardly a minute before they were back again at the
mouth of the saleen, but the entrance was a tougher
job.   One of the safest of boats in the open sea, a
coracle is one of the riskiest nearing rocks, a touch
which would do another no harm sufficing to carry
death through its canvas sides.   To any one looking
on from the shore, it would probably have seemed an
impossibility to get it in without impaling it upon
one or other of the two points, outstretched like crabs'
claws to catch it.   Here, however, Hurrish's strength
told.   Shifting the disabled oar to windward, he
brought his whole strength to bear upon the other,

resisting the onslaught of the wind and sea, which
would have driven it on the rocks, and steering
straight for the centre of the open.   Another minute
and he was inside, and in calm water.

The tide was still a long way out, so that there
would be a good many hours before the sea would be
at the top of the saleen.   He resolved accordingly to
tie the boat up, get a few hours' sleep, and be back
again at the saleen at early dawn.   It was a heavy
job getting it emptied and dragged over the sand.
With an ordinary boat of the same size it would
have been impossible, but a coracle, amongst its other
merits, is astonishingly light.   Having got it as high
as he could, and secured it additionally with a rope
round the usual rock, he left it lying there, climbed
the pathway, part of which was by this time washed
away by the deluge, and set his face joyfully for
home.

His night's adventures were not, however, ended!
Half-way between the shore and the house, happening
to glance a little to the left, he perceived, to his unspeakable dismay, a white object moving slowly along
a little ahead of him, but apparently in the same
direction.   Sometimes it would stop short, then, after
a few minutes' pause, move slowly on again as before.
It was not a sheep, for it was too high from the
ground.   It was not a man, for it was too white,
and, what was more appalling still, the upper portion
of the figure alone was visible, the rest being either
lost to sight amongst the rocks, or, more probably,
non-existent.   Hurrish, as we know, was saturated
to the very bone and to the very marrow of his
bones with superstition, and that the object before

him was anything but a Banshee, Clurigan, or
"sper'rt" of some sort, did not occur to him for a
moment. The perspiration broke out in great beads
upon his face, and he stopped short, shaking from
head to foot, his knees knocking against one another,
his strength, which a few minutes ago had been proof
against the worst that the sea and the storm could do,
utterly failing against this new ordeal.

But that it was uttering no sound, he would have
felt absolutely certain that it was the "Death sper'rt,"
commonly seen, he knew, by people about to die.
His own great-uncle had seen one—so his mother
had often told him—walking along, sobbing, and
tearing its hair, and he, as every one knew, had been
hanged for shooting a Galway gentleman within the
year. Hurrish was not more afraid of dying than
another man, but the bare idea of receiving a
"warnin'" made the flesh creep upon his bones, and
his hair stand on end with horror. He would rather
any day have faced a thousand substantial dangers
than one such bodiless one. Meanwhile, the white
figure was slowly preceding him, moving apparently
directly towards the cabin, from which a candle,
placed in one of the windows, was throwing a ghostly
tremulous gleam over the rocks. Had it been going
in any other direction, Hurrish would have fled igno-
miniously ; but going in this direction, there was nowhere else unfortunately for him to fly to. Alarm
for the others began, too, to prevail ; so after a minute he slowly followed, shaking like a leaf, his teeth
chattering in his head, ready at any moment to turn
and flee should the sper'rt show any disposition to
approach him.

Suddenly it wavered, fell forward, and the next
minute, to his increasing horror, it began to cry
and moan, sobbing convulsively to itself—curiously
human-like sobs they were—and writhing about on
the ground like a creature in pain. There could be
no further doubt *now*. It was the " Death sper'rt."
He was a doomed man. God help Alley, and his
mother, and the pore little childer ! what 'ud they do
without him, 't all, 't all ? he wondered dismally.

He remained aloof, his eyes starting out of his
head, his blood seeming to turn to water in his veins,
so terrified was he. Terror itself, however, at last
lent him a sort of courage—the courage to escape ;
and he began cautiously making the circuit of the
thing sitting there, sobbing and moaning upon the
ground. If he could only once get to the other side
he could make a rush for the house, and bolt and bar
the door against it. Then, at least, he would no
longer see it, and that would be always something.
He had nearly executed this ingenious manœuvre,
when all at once the sper'rt seemed to perceive him,
for it stretched its arms towards him, uttering, as it
did so, a wild appealing cry.

It was all that was wanting to complete his agony !
Too terrified now to fly, too terrified to move, he remained glued to the ground, shaking from head to
foot, while the figure, finding apparently that he did
not stir, began to move slowly towards him, half sobbing, and holding its hands out piteously the while.

With a hoarse cry he flung himself upon his knees
before it.

" For the luv ov God ! for the sake of the holy
blissed Vargin, keep back wid ye ! " he stammered,

his tongue cleaving to his mouth from sheer terror.
" God 'tween us an' harm, what are you, 't all ! "

" Hurrish ! Hurrish ! "

" Me God, it knows me name ! For the tindher
marcy of heaven keep away wid you ! Don't spake
to me ! Be near us an' purtect us all good this
night ! "

" Hurrish ! Hurrish ! why don't you come ? Hurrish, it's Alley ! Don't you know Alley ? "

" Alley ! " He did not venture even now to approach ; and it was not until she had called to him
twice again, that his terror began to some degree to
give way to conviction.

" The Lord ov grace ! Y'aint goin' for to till me
'tis you, Alley Sheehan, out in the black dead o'
night ? " he said, with a sort of slow incredulity.

" Yis, Hurrish, 'tis me. Won't ye come to me ?
I've hurted me foot, and can't shtir."

She was white enough, poor little Alley, for any
ghost ! white, and torn, and wet, and wearied to death.
Trembling and hardly able yet to shake off his terrors,
Hurrish approached ; and it was not until he was
able in the dim light to perceive her face close to his
own, that he began at last to believe in the reality of
her presence.

" Mother ov marcies, so 'tis you, Alley darlint,
sure an' sartin ! " he exclaimed at last.   " Divil sweep
me for a gomeral if I didn't take ye for a sper'rt.
Will I carry ye home ?   Sure, I see y' haven't the
fut undher ye 't all ! "

He lifted her up, without waiting for an answer,
and began carrying her hurriedly towards the light.
Suddenly, as the reality of her existence pressed more

and more fully upon him, he burst into a loud laugh,
which rang noisily out into the darkness.

"Be the piper that played before Moses, 'tis the
born fule I am, sure and sartin !" he exclaimed.
"Jewel macree, but you guv me the nice fright intoirely this night ! May I never ate bread, if I didn't
think 'twas the Death sper'rt cum to tell me me grave
was dug ! Wait till the boys larn Hurrish O'Brien
was frighted down on to his two bended knees by
little Alley Sheehan. Begorra, I'll never hear the ind
of it till I die, so I won't !" and he laughed again
and again boisterously.

Alley did not echo the laugh. She was too worn
out even to speak. She let herself be carried passively along, thankful to feel herself at last safe and
on the way home. As they approached the cabin,
however, and the light began to stream more strongly
upon them, she began to bethink her of the necessity
of telling him what she had seen while they were still
alone.

"Hurrish, I've a word to say to ye," she said.
"'Twas to luk for you I went out this night, only I
missed the way and got into the wrong saleen ; an'
indade, an' indade I thought I'd niver git home agin,
but have to lie there till mornin'." She paused a
moment to recover breath. "Hurrish, I seen Maurice
Brady," she said, solemnly.

Hurrish, however, did not seem to see anything
alarming in the information.

"Did ye so, Alley ? Thin I haven't hard sound
or token ov him this long while back. I thought
'twas maybe to 'Merikee he'd gone," he said,
placidly.

" No, he was there.   An'—an', Hurrish,—'tind to
me, Hurrish,—he had a gun wid him ! "

Still Hurrish declined to be alarmed.

" 'Tis the fule he is to carry one, thin," he said.
" The polis 'll be takin' it from him, sure as eggs is
mate, and what good will it be to him thin ?   Only a
waste ov good money."

Alley began to lose patience.   She was utterly
worn out, and this difficulty of making herself understood seemed a sort of climax to her troubles.

" Sure, Hurrish, ye don't ondershtand me 't all, 't
all," she said, fretfully.   " Don't I tell you 'twas for
to warn *yersel'* I went down to the saleen.   'Tis *you*
he's carryin' it for, an' no one ilse.   God forgiv' him !
'Tis yersel' he's manin' for to shoot." `

" Is't shoot`me ?   Och now, Alley dear, 'tis dramin'
ye are, sure and sartin.   What the mortial man would
he be wantin' to shoot me for ? " he replied, in tones
of genuine astonishment.

" He does mane it, thin.   He tould me so hisself."

" Told ye hisself !   Gorra ! if that don't bate
Banagher !   Where did he go for to tell ye sich a
thing ? "

" Down at th' ould abbey."

" Is it to-night ? "

" No, not to-night ; 'fore iver the trial cum on.   He
bade me tell you he'd do it."

" Ye never did, thin."

" I know.   I'd ought, but somehow I—*durstn't.*"

Hurrish scratched his head.   They had now reached
the cabin, and he had set Alley down, so that he had
his hand free for that essential part of the operation
of thinking.   The conclusion he arrived at was that

she was too "bothered" and "flustered" to-night to
be able to know clearly what she meant. Very
likely she had "dramed" the whole thing ; that, at
any rate, seemed the readiest explanation. Having
just recovered from one terror, he was not in the
least disposed to entertain another one. He addressed
himself accordingly to the task of soothing her.

"Well now, Alley dear, sure you'll tell me all
'bout it in the mornin'," he said, coaxingly. "Don't
ye say no more 'bout guns nor nothink to-night, only
into yer bed wid ye, where ye had ought to ha' been
hours ago. Drink the laste sup of whisky, an' get
straight in, an' cover yourself up warm wid anything
ye've got. Take me big coat—'tis dry, for I left it
't home. Be aff this instant minute, an' God bless
you, an' ye'll tell me all about the gun and the rist
of it in the mornin'."

These various directions were of necessity whispered, for old Bridget had fallen asleep, and lay snoring in her own corner, and it was a point of considerable importance to both of them not to awaken her.
Alley was too exhausted to make any further struggle.
Weariness had reached a point where a sort of collapse
seemed to set in. She declined the whisky, but went
into her own room passively without another word.
Her last thought, as she wearily pulled off her wet
clothes and prepared to lie down beside little warm
unconscious Katty, was that Hurrish was safe to-night,
and the door shut and bolted. Nothing, thank God,
could possibly happen to him between this and to-
morrow morning !

CHAPTER XXV.

UPON THE VERY BRINK.

She was still sleeping the heavy sleep of utter
weariness when Hurrish got up and looked out of the
little window of the outside room, which faced east.
It was dark night still in the cabin. The cocks and
hens slept profoundly on their perches. Old Bridget's
snores made a deep bass accompaniment to the lighter
music proceeding from the noses of the two small
boys cuddled snugly in their own private corner.
Away to the east, however, a faint greenish light was
rising. The wind had lowered, but still beat in angry
puffs against the house, shaking it irritably, as if to
ascertain whether its strength was really impaired or
not, then racing off with a scampering noise as of a
frightened crowd across the rocks. Having pulled
on his clothes—unpleasantly wet still from the night
before—Hurrish carefully opened the door, glancing
back as he did so for fear of disturbing the others.
Lep, who had been watching these proceedings with
keen eyes, sprang up at this juncture, and ran to him,
curling himself into a comma, and entreating with all
a dog's irresistible eloquence to be allowed to go too.
Hurrish hesitated ; then, remembering that if the sea
allowed of it, he should have to take out the boat, he
ordered him in a whisper to go back and lie down
again.

The dog obeyed, but unwillingly, giving a low
whimper of dissatisfaction, which followed his master

piteously as he left the cabin. As soon as he had
got outside, the rain flew at his face with recovered
spite. The whole scene, as far as he could see it,
was swathed in fog which seemed to envelop the
darkness, which in turn swathed its edges and hid
its extent. Hurrish looked up at what ought by this
time to have been the sky with a grimace of disgust ;
then, first sitting down for a moment on the low wall
to pull on his boots, which he held in his hands, he
set out at a quick pace for the saleen.

The coracle was still safe, but the sea had risen
enormously during the night, and was beating through
the narrow entrance in huge, green curls, which shot
their spray high into the air through the fog. Half
an hour more, and they would be sweeping against the
rocks at the end.

To attempt to row out through such a sea would
have been simple insanity. Upon the other hand, to
bring the coracle farther in than it was was impossible, for at this point the cliff rose in a succession of
perfectly. perpendicular steps, the result of the horizontal stratification of the limestone, quarried inces-
santly away as it was from below by the sea. In
the upper part these steps were partially sheeted with
loose scale-like fragments, upon which larger stones—
fallen from the matrix above—lay about in loose heaps.
The only thing, therefore, to be done was to fix the
boat as firmly as possible, so that the waves, when
they did reach it, should be unable to dislodge it.
Accordingly Hurrish began hastily shovelling in sand
with an old shovel which he kept for digging bait in
a cleft. The tide, however, was rising fast—so fast
that he felt that the time would be too short to com-

plete the operation.   As soon, therefore, as there was
enough sand to protect the bottom of the boat, he began
hastily throwing in pieces of rock, all that he could
lay hands on.   There were not very many about,
the steps rising, as has been said, straight out of
the sands ; so, having collected all that there were,
he mounted the path in order to get at those
above.

He was warm now with his work.   There was a
pleasure, too, in baffling the enemy, and, between the
two sensations, his broad genial face shone with a
glow which ought to have gone some way towards dis-
persing the fog.   He had been up twice, and the second
time he fancied that he heard a movement in the fog
above his head, something that sounded like the stealthy
approach of footsteps.   Surprised by such a sound, at
such an hour, he shouted to know who was there.
There was no answer, however.   The silence was complete, tomb-like.   Concluding, therefore, that he was
mistaken, he hurried to pick up a big block which lay
at his feet, and turned to descend.   He was in the
act of doing so, when again, and this time unmistakably, he heard the sound, and turning, quick as
thought, looked up into the misty vault.   For an
instant—only for an instant—there was the outline
of a head ; the outline of a gun ; then a flash, and
the next moment a stinging, numbing, indescribable
pain right through the middle of his chest caused
him to drop the stone which he had in his hands,
and with a wild cry, in which pain, indignation,
and bitter unspeakable astonishment all seemed to
mingle, he dropped down upon the ledge where
he was standing, while a sound of footsteps, first

nearer, then further, further, further, sounded overhead, finally dying away in the far-off solitary
distance. The murderer had effected his escape.

And Hurrish ! For a while he lay there like one
stunned ; knowing what had happened to him, and
yet refusing to know it ; fighting fiercely against the
consciousness. He was dreaming ! he was perhaps
drunk ! the fairies had bewitched him ! Anything
and everything seemed possible—nay, probable—save
what had actually happened. That alone was the
utterly and the absolutely *impossible !*

And yet through it all he knew—knew as a matter
of absolute certainty—that he had "got his death."
It was all over. He was as much done for as though
he already lay in Tubbamina churchyard, under the
sod which was always so full of camomile flowers.
That good stanch frame of his, which, under ordinary
circumstances, might have defied the slow decades of
another fifty years, that number of hours would probably suffice for it now. The sea underneath was
hardly nearer to him than that other and larger sea
upon whose waters we must all one day float. Oddly
enough, the idea passed through his own mind, though
in another form, and he turned his head slightly so
as to look in the direction where the O'Brasil lay.
The action brought on a sudden rush of blood, accompanied by a pain, the agony of which seemed to
tear through every nerve, sinew, and artery in his
body, finally settling in a dull concentrated ache in
the centre of his breast. He groaned aloud, writhing
in anguish on his narrow perch, and tearing aside
coat and shirt, looked down at the small round hole
through the dark lips of which the blood was ebbing

fast and furiously. It *was* true then! It was *no* dream. He was hit—hit to death!

At first the look was one of mere animal agony, the joint heritage of all of us poor vertebrated brutes. After a while, however, another expression came into it—a sort of mute agonised wonder; a piteous appeal to the rulers of the mysterious, the unexplainable. It was hardly anger, for he was too puzzled, too benumbed, moreover, by fast growing weakness for that. It was rather a deep abounding sense of the mysteriousness of the thing. To believe yourself in a natural world, to find yourself in an unnatural one, to take up a fruit and to find a stone, to stretch out a hand to a friend and to receive back a dagger in your heart, faintly describes the sort of vortex of mystery into which his soul was plunged, and in which his brain seemed to swim with perplexity no less than with pain. It was so overwhelming that it seemed to do away with all thoughts of vengeance— almost with the last ineradicable clinging to life. With the sort of desperation which comes to a man sometimes in the worst crises of his fate, he simply lay down again upon his perch, and rested his head against the rock. If help came, it came; if not, it didn't! Help himself he couldn't. The slightest movement only precipitated the end. God was good, and might help him yet. So he reasoned, in fatalism quite as much as in piety.

As he lay there his brain was visited with odd fancies. Weakness painted certain things with a curious vividness. His fancy wandered away to the cabin, and to little Katty—his own black-eyed little Katty—curled up at that moment like a small tor-

U

toise-shell kitten in her basket, little guessing what
was happening to her poor old daddy ! He thought
of Alley too, but less vividly. He could not direct
his thoughts, but was at the mercy of what came
uppermost. Everything swam and melted, and ran
confusedly one into another. He fancied by moments
that he was lying, not on the rocks at all, but in a
little hollow scooped out of the sands a few miles
further down the coast. It was dedicated to un-
baptised babies whom the Church refuses to let lie
in consecrated soil, but whose memory the pious
feeling of the country cherishes with a peculiar
tenderness. In this graveyard there was one grave,
as it happened, which was not the grave of an infant.
It was the grave of an unknown man, who had been
washed ashore close to the spot, and been allowed to
find an asylum in it. Hurrish had often stopped as
he was passing to look at the grave and its nameless
headstone,—to wonder, with a passing wonder, who
the unknown man had been, and whether any one
had been left to mourn his loss. Now, with the
incoherency of weakness, he felt as if he himself
were that unknown man, tossed there alone, without
a friend or a pitying eye to see him die.

Hark ! something was stirring ! There were steps
over his head. An odd shuffling noise. Was it a
man or only an animal—a sheep perhaps strayed too
near the bank ? With a last resource of strength he
lifted his head and shouted. Such a poor shout ! the
very ghost and wraith of his former ones. Then
waited. There was no answer ; shouted again, and
still no answer. Then feebly, doubtingly, half-
hesitatingly he uttered a word—only one word—

" Morry !" This time there *was* an answer, and over
the edge immediately above him a face gazed down,
the frightened face and wild vacant eyes—not of
Maurice Brady, but of Thady-na-Taggart !

Hurrish saw it and beckoned. It was his last
conscious act. Slight as was the movement, it was
followed by a fresh and more violent rush of blood
from the wound in his breast, and he fell back upon
the rock fainting, unconscious.

When he came to himself he was again alone, but
the bleeding had temporarily ceased. Something had
been done. He could feel that a bandage or piece
of rag of some sort had been applied. He called
twice feebly, but there was no answer. The daylight was everywhere now. A new day had come ;
a new life ! The clouds were still thick overhead,
but the fog had all but wasted away. In every
direction the daylight was shining upon grey rocks
and upon a wild and storm-troubled world of waters.
Everywhere over the wide face of the sea the wind
was speeding home ships that longed for the sight of
land. All along the whole edge of the Atlantic
waves were rushing up with thunder on to shores,
sandy or rocky as the case might be. Away, everywhere over the face of the country, under roofs large
and small, high pitched and low pitched, people were
sleeping, or waking to think of another day. Children were laughing in their beds ; women beginning
to bustle about ; strong men rejoicing in their
strength ; and upon one bare ledge under the pitiless
sky a strong man was fast growing weaker than an
infant as the blood flowed from his veins to bedew
the indifferent rocks. Was no one coming, then ?

no one? no one? he wondered. Must he lie there
till he died ?   What had become of Thady ? of
Alley ? of every one ?   Did none of them know or
care that he was dying there—alone ?

He was consumed now with thirst, that awful
thirst which adds the last horror to battle-fields.
His tongue seemed to cleave to his mouth, and to be
dry and hard as a piece of wood.   The vast watery
immensity beneath mocked him with its multitudinous
rippling waves.   He saw his own coracle below him,
and the sight cut to the quick with a sudden start
of pain.   The first feeling of stupefaction, almost of
resignation, had quite passed away now.   The horrible restlessness of exhaustion was upon him, and he
writhed in torment upon his narrow perch.   His eyes,
travelling in mute despair over the immense arch in
front, rested upon the gulls as they dipped and soared
—very perfection of ideal freedom—with a dull
misery which almost amounted to hate.   What had
he ever done ? what had his sin been, he asked himself, bitterly, that he should have been allowed to be
shot like a dog, and then left to die a dog's death ?
It was only a minute since he was in his own little
cabin, waking, safe and strong and happy.   A minute ?
nay, but a year.   Had he, in fact, ever been so ?   Was
it not a dream and a delusion that he had ever been
that man, who was safe and strong and happy ?   Had
he not rather been lying here always—a miserable
creature, a worm, with a man's capacity for suffering ?
A creature so ludicrously weak that he could barely
clutch at the tuft of daisies springing at his side—a
pitiful thing, writhing and wriggling and making a
moan, but so feeble that it did not disturb the very

gulls over his head—flung out like a barrow-load of
rubbish upon a ledge to die.

Poor Hurrish ! he was a martyr, too, after a fashion,
though he knew it not. A martyr to a not very
glorious cause, one that was certainly not very much
worth dying for. A martyr to a long and an ugly
past—a past in which he, not having been born, had
at least no share of the blame. He was dying because
Hate of the Law is the birthright and the dearest
possession of every native son of Ireland. He was
dying because, for many a weary year, that country
had been as ill-governed a morsel of earth as was to
be found under the wide-seeing eye of God. The old
long-repented sin of the stronger country was the
culprit, as surely as if it had pointed the gun at his
breast. Is that ridiculous ? Perhaps so, and yet it
is true too, as many ridiculous things *are* true.

Another, and perhaps an equally ridiculous, fact
was, that it was only now that indignation against
his assailant was really beginning to find place in his
breast. Not even now, for shooting him—that, though
inexplicable, was comparatively venial—but for deserting him—leaving him there on that naked ledge
to die alone. If he would come back even *now*, be
with him, stay beside him, let him have the comfort
of seeing his face, any human face, and not only this
big, dreadful, empty immensity, he felt that he could
freely forgive him all the rest.

How long had he lain there ? Sometimes he fancied that he had fallen over the ledge, and was tossing
about in the waves below, up and down, to and fro.
The sun shone upon the waves, but it did not seem
to warm him. He was a cork, he was a bubble, he

was a coracle. The fancies followed one another so
fast, that there was no time to recognise them before
they were gone again. At last he was aroused by
something that was not a fancy—something soft, yet
rough, moving backwards and forwards wetly over his
face. He opened his eyes, and opened them into a
mass of tangled fur. It was Lep — poor, honest,
faithful Lep—whining and looking piteously at his
master, and evidently perfectly aware of his cruel
plight. Thady was there too, his white face red with
running, the perspiration pouring from it in great
drops. They were not alone; others were following.
Two men, fishermen from Tubbamina, who came up
with frightened faces and loud ejaculations of dismay.
There was no time for ejaculations, however—no time
either to tell even how Thady had made them understand. The first thing was to get Hurrish home, and
for this it would be necessary, they decided, to get
more help and a door.

There was another inevitable delay. The nearest
cabin was his own, so that it was there they went.
How the news had been told there was no one to tell,
but in a shorter time than would have seemed possible there came a flying sound of footsteps nearer
and nearer. A pause; a low cry of anguish, as of a
soul taking flight, and Alley Sheehan was upon her
knees beside him, her white despairing face close to
his; her great grey eyes strained and dry, with the
tension of an agony too great for tears or words.
Close behind her, like shadow upon light, followed
old Bridget, mad with fury and athirst for revenge.
Seizing the girl, she thrust her aside with a curse,
telling her to keep back, and not be allays meddlin';

then flung herself almost upon her son, at the im-
minent risk of pushing him off his precarious resting-
place.

Mechanically Alley obeyed and drew back. Is
there any passion, I wonder, any human need so
great that it will not give way to habit, if only that
habit has been continuous enough, more especially if
it has its root in fear ?   Hurrish had caught sight of
her face, however, its look of desperate misery striking him through all his languor, and he beckoned to
her to come back, Bridget sullenly making way for
her to do so.

"Don't ye take on so, allanah," he whispered
soothingly. "Sure 'twas to be, or it wudn't ha'
been.   Anyhow, ye did all ye cud, an' no one on
this mortial arth cud do more."

She made no answer.   She was turned to stone.
The worst had come, and what did anything else
matter ?   Let Maurice Brady come and kill her too.
She would only thank him, she felt.

The men had now come back with the door, and
were about to lift Hurrish on to it.   Just before
they did so, however, a new idea seemed to strike
him, for he beckoned her over to him again.

"You see 'twas the Death sper'rt, Alley, I seen
after all !" he said, a faint gleam of humour struggling for a moment across the paleness of his face.

CHAPTER XXVI.

SOME PRECURSORS OF THE MILLENNIUM.

The effect upon Tubbamina of the news of Hurrish's disaster was of the nature of a galvanic shock! —an electric current of horror, grief, dismay, fury, which seemed to rush through all its inhabitants alike. There was not a man, woman, or child who did not feel as if a personal injury had been done them; a valuable piece of property removed; a serious breach made in his or her future comfort. Who first put the general instinct into words it would be difficult to say, but within a very short time of the arrival of the news, every one, as if by inspiration, had struck upon the same name as that of the culprit. There was no question either about concealing *this* murder, or protecting its perpetrator. On the contrary, every one was athirst for vengeance, and eager to bring the offender to justice.

That distinguished upholder of the law, Mr Andy Holohun — prominent member of the Republican brotherhood, and reputed assistant at at least half-a-dozen violent outrages—was the first to suggest calling in the aid of the "polis." No sooner said than done. Three or four men—Mr Holohun himself at their head—ran off straight to the barracks, and laid the case before the sergeant in command; then turned back to concoct further plans. A party of men started off to Ballyvaughan, to intercept him if he attempted to cross in the steamer to Galway. An-

other ran up the Gortnacoppin ridge to see if by
chance he might be lurking in the cabin there.   All
the powers of that underground government which,
as most people are aware, is not without power in
Ireland, were brought to bear upon the matter.   The
very women felt it to be absolutely incumbent upon
them, as good citizens, to suspend all household operations, in order to sit together on the doorsteps and
volubly curse the culprit !   Never had so spontaneous an abhorrence of crime, never so magnificent a
thirst after abstract justice, been exhibited before by
an Irish village !

While this excitement was going on at Tubbamina
a different scene was proceeding at the cabin, to
which Hurrish had meantime been carefully conveyed, and laid there upon his own bed.   Poor Mary
O'Brien's bed ! the one she had brought there with
such pride, and purchased with her own hard-earned
money.   She had died on it, and now Hurrish's turn
had come.   Is there any stranger symbol more significant of all the mingled woof and warp, good and
evil, joy, sorrow, hope, agony, of our perplexing life,
than that same homely and indispensable piece of
furniture ?

In spite of the superior interest of the search,
which had retained a good many of the neighbours,
there were not wanting scores of excited and vehemently sympathetic visitors to the cabin.   The women arrived sobbing, and continued to wail and cry
aloud all the time they remained, standing in a crowd
around the bed, and suggesting every variety of con-
tradictory remedy.   Happily they were at last dis-
persed by the dispensary doctor, who insisted that

the patient should be left in peace, announcing, at
the same time, with bluff outspokenness, that the
case was, in his opinion, a hopeless one from the
beginning. The bullet was not able to be extracted,
though he put poor Hurrish to considerable pain in
his efforts to reach it. He was not a particularly
skilful practitioner, though an excellent man and an
admirable judge of pigs,—a talent which naturally
caused him to be much respected in the vicinity.

After he had left, a few of the sympathisers, whom
he had expelled, stole back under different pleas, and
amongst these Sal Connor. The poor girl's grief was
most genuine, though the manner she took of showing it might have been less exuberant with advantage. The instant she came into the cabin she
threw herself flat down upon the floor, throwing her
overskirt over her head, flinging her two hands into
the air, rocking herself vigorously to and fro, and uttering shriek after shriek, half stifled, it is true, by the
stoutness of the material, but still sufficiently piercing to be decidedly painful to any sensitive tym-
panum.

Hurrish, disturbed by the clamour, lifted his head
from the pillow, and looked with a sort of mute
appeal at Alley, who thereupon stooped down, and
put her arm round the girl's neck.

" Sal, darlint, you wudn't be breakin' his heart,
wud ye ? " she said, coaxingly. " Sure the doctor
left strict ward he wasn't on no 'count to be disturbed. Prayin' is all we can do. Cum outside
wid me, an' I'll tell ye all the doctor said."

Sal Connor allowed herself, rather sullenly, to be
half lifted up and led outside the cabin. Once there,

however, she again broke out into fresh and more
piercing screams of distress, not unmingled now with
displeasure at her ejection.

"'Tis all very foine for you, Alley Sheehan! Half
a nun as y'ar, an' carin' for no man yit, as ivery wan
knows, no more nor the birds in th' air! But I tell
ye I *lov'd* him, I *lov'd* him! Oh, my God! my God!
Ochone! ochone! ochone! to think of him lyin' there,
murdered and kilt before me eyes, lukin' so white,
an' spakin' so wake! What 'ul I do, at all, at all?
'Tis broke me heart is, to think ov it! The toimes
an' toimes I moight ha' married, an' niver wud luk
at one of thim wid thinkin' ov Hurrish O'Brien!
There's Mr Moriaty—him as keeps th' 'Shamrock
of Irin'—if he's axed me wance, he's axed me foive
times, an' wudn't be sich a born loir hisself as to go
denoyin' ov it! Ochone! ochone! ochone! Oh my
God, what 'ul I do, 't all? Sure me heart's broke in
two! me heart's broke in two!"

Alley could only reiterate her soothing words,
which, after a while, appeared to succeed, for Sal's
wrath turned to expostulation.

"Arrah, let me back, an' I'll be shtill as a mouse,
and niver say the word, only sit and watch him
brathin'! Och, Alley Sheehan, Alley Sheehan, if
ye'd the list taste of a woman's heart in yer brist
this blissed day, an' knew what lovin' a man was
loike, sure ye wouldn't go for to deny me!"

To this compromise the other consented, and they
went back to the cabin together. Poor Sal, however, had apparently over-estimated her own powers
of composure. She sat down quietly enough for
about ten minutes, after which she began to sob and

then to howl; finally, with a terrific explosion, half
stifled subterraneally in her petticoats, she got up
and ran out of the house, her cries growing fainter
and fainter until they died away in the distance.

After this the cabin really lapsed into something
like tranquillity. Hurrish seemed to have sunk into
a doze, for he lay with his eyes closed and his lips
parted. Old Bridget's furious lamentations and denunciations had by this time died away, and she
appeared to have sunk into a sort of coma. Seated
on her stool by the fire, the big iron ladle in her
hand, she seemed to be muttering spells into the pot,
rather than occupying herself with cooking. All the
nursing and carrying out of the doctor's directions
fell exclusively to Alley's share, whom Bridget now
no longer interfered with, looking on with a sort of
sullen indifference, as much as to say that since all
hope was at an end, it did not much matter what
happened, or *who* looked after him !

The children, much against their will, had been
taken away by a neighbour, but had been promised
by Alley to be allowed to return later. The only
other person left was poor Thady-na-Taggart, whom
it would have been impossible indeed to remove
short of main force, so determined had he shown
himself to stay. No one could accuse him, however,
of making a noise ! He sat on the floor, crouched
close to the wall, like a sick dog, his eyes fixed
immovably upon the bed. The poor fellow looked
years older than he had done the day before. His
innocent, witless face had a more serious and responsible expression than usual, and his cheeks were
crumpled into a number of fine wrinkles, like a

badly-folded piece of linen.   Lep, equally immovable, and in almost identically the same attitude, lay beside him.

Hark! A distant noise; sounding strange and incongruous in the melancholy stillness of the little interior. A monotonous "tramp, tramp, tramp, tramp," approaching over the flat rocks. Another sound, too, a dull, continuous roar,—not at all, however, like the roar of the sea, — growing louder; broken with whoops, with cries as of derision, with shouts and shrieks of rage and satisfaction.   Tramp, tramp, tramp, tramp! on they came, a body of men stepping together, evidently with the steady uniformity of men drilled to walk in step.   Behind,—like dead leaves at the heels of a storm,—a shuffling, scuffling noise of feet. The cries, whoops, groans grew nearer and nearer, though also less distinct as if intentionally muffled.   Now and then, however, an irrepressible groan filled the air, followed by a prolonged hissing noise as of a crowd of geese driven along a road.

Bridget looked up from her pot with an angry, half-idiotic stare; Hurrish, too, seemed to catch the sound, for he turned his head so as to face the half-opened door.   Nearer and nearer came the steps— now close at hand. A muttering, buzzing, excited sound upon the rocks outside; a rush forward; then a sudden lull, like waves driven backwards—a sound of many voices whispering eagerly together.   Then the door, already ajar, was pushed wide open, and four policemen entered, two by two, and in their midst, with handcuffs on his wrists—hatless, be-spattered from head to foot with the mud and filth that had been liberally flung at him ever since his capture; his lip cut and bleeding, from a stone that had accompanied the softer, if more opprobrious, missiles; his clothes torn, and hanging about him in ribbons,—came Maurice Brady.

Every one was still as death for an instant. Then, as if the sight had broken violently through her lethargy, old Bridget sprang forward, iron ladle in hand.

With one swing of her sinewy old arms, she had pushed the policemen aside, and was standing face to face with the prisoner. The next she had clutched him by the front of his coat, and was shaking him to and fro, as a tigress shakes a man before proceeding to devour him.

" Giv him t' me! Giv him t' me! Giv him t' me!" she screamed. " Giv me up the massacreen miscray-int, till I tear him in pieces 'fore yis all! 'Tis goin' the way ov yer bruder y'ar, ye scum! Yis, y'ar, ye black-haarted bliggard! The blast of Heaven be an ye, and Hell's bells 'tind yer berryin', ye murderin' sweep of th' arth! Luk at him! Luk at him that's lyin' on that bed!—him that was betterer nor a father to ye! yis, an' a mother too, ye onnatural naggur! Hangin's too good for ye; an' if I had ye 'lone, ruin to me sowl, but I'd tear yer flesh to gr-ass wid me two ould hands, an' shmash yer skull agin the vargin arth—so I wud, ye murderin' thief ov the warld!"

It was not without some difficulty, and by the exercise of a considerable amount of physical force, that the constables in charge succeeded in rescuing their prisoner from the hands of his exasperated assailant, who assuredly would have carried out her

threats had she been free to do so; and, handcuffed
as he was, Maurice Brady was of course absolutely
powerless to defend himself.   To his credit be it
said, he retained as much composure as a man under
so remarkably uncomfortable an ordeal well could.
A dull flush passed over his face, and his eyes
gleamed angrily; nevertheless he faced his furious
old assailant with a smile of tolerably successful
indifference.

Suddenly all started, and turned towards the bed.
Hurrish's voice was heard speaking.   At first it had
been lost in the tumult; no sooner, however, was it
perceived, than a deathlike silence succeeded to the
clamour of tongues.   Old Bridget relaxed her hold
on the prisoner; her shrieks sank, and she turned
eagerly towards her son.   It was not to her, however, but to the constable in charge, that Hurrish
was speaking.

"What's the gantleman bin doin' 't all, sargint?"
he inquired, in a tone of mild curiosity.

The constable—a big stupid-looking man, with a
large moustache, and a pair of goggling, greenish
eyes—stared blankly.

"Isn't *he* the man that done for you?   Sure I
arristed him as such," he said, with a spasm of
official rage, half stifled by his official collar.

"Is it Mr Brady?"   Hurrish smiled pityingly.
"Arrah, sargint, I wonders at you,—I do indade!
Whoiver put sich a fule's notion into yer head?
'Tis a thrick they've bin played on ye, whoiver
dun it!"

The sergeant's face was an edifying study!   He
stared first at Hurrish, lying upon the bed, his white

face all the whiter for its dark tangled beard and
hair; then at old Bridget; then at the prisoner, as
if in hopes of extracting the truth from him. The
latter's face, it must be owned, did not particularly
bear out the other's assertion. His lips twitched,
and his hands, with all his efforts to control them,
shook visibly under the handcuffs.

" An' who dun it 't all ? " burst simultaneously,
not from one, but a dozen pairs of lips,—the crowd,
which at first had considerately stayed outside, having
at this juncture pushed in, man after man, till the
cabin was nearly filled.

Hurrish put his hand up to his head as if to assist
his memory.

" 'Twas some parties in a boat, I'm thinkin', but I
can't call to moind essactly," he said, feebly. " I was
cumin' alang the thrack, an' I turned t'wards th' say,
an' all 'tonc't I got the crack in me brist, an' that's
all I know, but I seen a little boat soon afther cumin'
round foreninst the Glassen rock—a wheesy little
dotteen of a thing, nigh well as shmall as me fist, so
'twas," he added, thoughtfully.

There was a general silence. Not a single being
in the cabin, of course, believed a word that he had
been listening to. Not one either but felt a pang of
dismay and disgust at the thought that the murderer
would, after all, escape. So deeply engrained, however, in Ireland, is the instinct under no circumstances to betray a criminal, that the very men who
had dragged Maurice triumphantly out of his hiding-
place, and had accompanied him thus far, with the
amiable intention of hearing that he was safe to be
hanged, felt that Hurrish's conduct was only natural,

and moreover, that, under similar circumstances, they would have done precisely the same themselves.

Oddly enough, the person who felt least inclined to let the matter rest where it was, was gentle, tender-hearted Alley. A flush of anger rose to her cheek, and she stepped impetuously forward, and opened her mouth as if to speak. Then suddenly changing her mind, she turned away, and sat silently down in a corner. Happily for Maurice Brady, it had never occurred to anybody to dream of her as a possible witness.

A sort of sudden gloom, a dull feeling of disappointment, fell upon the entire party, as upon an audience that has been promised some exciting drama which fails at the last minute to come off. The men, one by one, began to file out, leaving only the policemen and prisoner in the cabin. Even Bridget fell back, and sat down, with her former air of lethargy, beside the fire. Hurrish was the first to speak.

" I'd loike, if it's not displazing to yis, to have a word or two wid Mr Brady," he said, looking round, first at the policemen, then at his mother and Alley. " If ye'll lave us to our two selves for a while, I'd be 'bliged."

Sullenly, like one under an irresistible spell, old Bridget went out. Alley followed, avoiding looking at Maurice as she passed him. The policemen, too, moved away, the sergeant stopping as he did so to unlock the prisoner's handcuffs. They did not intend letting him out of reach entirely, in case of any fresh evidence turning up ; but to keep him in cus-tody, and to take him before a magistrate without more evidence than they had at present, was obviously impracticable.

X

The men who had accompanied them from Tubbamina were still outside, standing about together in
groups, and gloomily exchanging suggestions and con-
dolences.   It was a moment of universal brotherhood,—wolves and sheep-dogs meeting and conversing on a sort of common ground.   As far as the good
wishes of the company present went, there were
enough and to spare, every man being perfectly ready
to swear a solemn oath that Maurice Brady, and no
one else, was the criminal.   But, alas! none of them
had seen, or could even pretend they had seen, the
deed done.   Of what use, therefore, all their zeal or
all their excellent intentions, when the victim and
only witness absolutely declined to prosecute ?   As a
proof of good feeling and unanimity, however, it was
certainly edifying in the extreme.   Indeed, to see
Andy Holohun go up to the big constable, and com-
pare notes with him in a low tone of sympathy and
confidential intercourse, was a beautiful sight, calculated to make any one believe in the speedy oncoming of a universal millennium !

CHAPTER XXVII.

FACE TO FACE.

And so, and for the last time upon earth, Hurrish
O'Brien and Maurice Brady were alone together face
to face !   What thoughts passed through their minds,
what ineffaceable memories rose up before them both,

it is easier to imagine than to put into commonplace words. Their new position towards one another was so new, so appalling, so impossible ; their old one so familiar, so kindly, so, as it were, inevitable,—that to Hurrish, at any rate, it seemed only natural to revert to it, and let the rest be. He waited a while, expecting Maurice to be the first to speak. Then, as he did not do so, but remained sullenly aloof, keeping as near as he could to the door, and apparently resolved not to approach, or if possible look at him, he began himself.

" What I axed ye to shtop an'—spake to me for —Morry, me buoy," he said, speaking slowly, and evidently with difficulty, " was to tell you 'bout— Mat. I thought I'd be aisier somehow if ye knew how 't was at the last. I wudn't loike for to go an' for you—'t think—I dun—what ye—thought I— dun."

Maurice Brady started, and his face changed. A hideous, an altogether intolerable thought, rushed through his brain, as the words fell slowly from the other's lips,—a thought so dreadful that it seemed to sear him from head to heel like a red-hot iron, and to leave him racked and shaking with agony. His stoicism, his pride, his bitter furious sense of humiliation, all were swept for the moment out of sight, almost out of existence, by this new shock. Did Hurrish mean—was he going to say that it was a *mistake ?*—that he had *not* murdered Mat ? Was he going to swear *that* to him on his deathbed ? A sudden sickening horror of his own action—a horror which up till now had hardly touched him, even lightly—fell upon him suddenly, consumingly, like a

bolt. Little by little he had been pushed on by the
thirst for revenge, by the unendurable sting of his
own altered position, which he owed, he told himself,
exclusively to Hurrish. Like many another before
him, he had goaded, deafened, blinded himself into a
belief in the necessity of the crime—had told himself
that it was not, in fact, a crime at all, but merely the
acquitting of a necessary debt;—that honour, revenge, justice—nay, the very peace of his brother's
soul—demanded that he should do it, seeing that the
law declined to take the matter into its own hands,
as it ought to have done. He was not a murderer,
therefore, but only an avenger. Suddenly, as at the
touch of some dividing and disentangling rod, these
arguments fled away,—burst, as a bubble bursts,
leaving him there face to face with the real facts. He
saw himself as he was—a murderer!—a foul, brutal,
cold-blooded murderer. And the murderer of whom?
Of his own best friend; of the man who, as old
Bridget had truly said, had been a father to him
when he needed one; had given him a home when
his own was no home to him; had believed in him
when nobody else believed; had made his young ambitions *his* ambitions; above all, had loved him as it
is given to few men to be loved even by their own
fathers. And, in return for all this, what had he, on
his part, done? God of justice and of mercy!—he
had murdered him!

Though slow, the retribution was complete. If
ever the hideousness of a man's crime overtook him
in this mortal life, it overtook Maurice Brady at that
moment. He had not even—like the vast majority
of criminals—that brutal dulness which blunts and

deadens the edges of self-consciousness, making remorse less an inward agony than a mere outward
dread of consequences. His own hard, revengeful
hands had forged the spear, and now his own quick
brains drove it home—home to the very hilt. Like
one gone for ever out of this life, out of hope, out of
the possibility of repentance, face to face through all
eternity with the unending, the ineffaceable, the un-
atonable, he writhed in anguish, turning his eyes to
the bed and to his victim, as such a lost soul might
be expected in its extremity to turn towards its ac-
cuser.

"Hurrish!—my God, Hurrish!—speak to me!"
he said, in a voice so changed that few would have
recognised it. "If you've any mercy or pity left,
don't tell me you didn't kill him! God! if you do,
I'll dash my head against that wall, and die before
you yet!"

That this was no idle threat, no mere rhetorical
flourish, his bloodshot eyes and changed and haggard
face showed plainly. Remorse, flung suddenly like a
burning coal into the lake of the soul, produces tortures the agony of which might well drive a much
less sensitive man than Maurice Brady to try the last
throw of all with destiny, and exchange the worst he
knew for what of worse there might be yet to know.

Hurrish probably saw this, for, quite forgetting his
wound, he sprang up in the bed, and stretched his
hands out as if to arrest him.

"Morry! Morry! Arrah, be aisy, Morry! I kilt
him!—I kilt him!" he exclaimed, vehemently.

"Thank God for that, anyhow!"

The reaction, the relief, fairly overcame him, and,

with a groan, Maurice Brady sank suddenly down on
his knees, and hid his face in his hands, at the very
feet of his brother's murderer.

For some minutes they remained thus, and there
was silence between them. Hurrish lay back and
pressed his hand to his chest, looking down at the
figure beside him. Was Maurice praying ? Probably
he would have found it difficult to say what he was
doing. His brain was in a whirl. Perplexity, anger,
passionate despair, grief, plucked in a fierce beaked
crowd at his breast, and almost drove him mad.

After a while Hurrish began to speak again—
slowly, but with a sort of dogged resolution of getting
through at any cost with what he had to say.

" Yis—I kilt him, Morry—I don't denoy it, why
wud I,—now ?   But I didn't—mane it—not that
way, any way.   I was—cumin' 'long the thrack, an'
he shot at me—from behind ov th' ould hermitige
place, an' I was mad—an' made for him.   He run,
an' I—afther—an' whin I cum up I hot him—wan
on th' head—only wan—an' he fell loike a shtone.
An' whin I waited for him to git up agin' he—niver
—did 't all.   An' afther a bit I walked away—an'—
sure ye know the rist."

Yes, Maurice did know the rest. He had no
doubt either that what Hurrish told him was the
literal truth, the precise way in which the thing had
occurred.   It had been all a fatality from beginuing
to end — a black hideous sorrow and crime-laden
fatality.   Further than this he could not think.   A
weight lay upon his head, so that he could not even
look up.   He dreaded above all other things having
to see Hurrish's face again—that ghastly face, upon

which fast-coming death had so plainly written its
signet. He saw it only too plainly without looking,
—felt, indeed, that he should continue to see it
always—through all his life, wherever he might be,
whatever he might do, perhaps through all eternity,
if there *was* any eternity. He could not move his
lips to ask forgiveness. The misery, the whole fatality,
seemed to him to press to the full as hardly upon
himself as upon his victim ;—more, seeing that he
had to live, whereas Hurrish had only to die ! Maurice did not ordinarily undervalue the advantages of
living, but he was in a state in which all ordinary
feelings ceased, and death seemed an easier thing to
face than his present misery. In the end it was
Hurrish, therefore, who began again to speak.

" I know you'd just take the two oyes—out ov yer
head, if 't wud undo—what ye dun—Morry, dear, so
ye needn't—be tellin' me," he said slowly, subduing
as far as possible, for the other's sake, all signs of
suffering. " Loife's a har'rd job t' us all, an' no
doubt ye felt—druv ; so no more—'bout it. I'm
thinkin' maybe you'd be bether—out ov this—you'd
be bether a dale in Amerikee. You'll have no comfort or intertainmint here 't all, I'm 'feard ; stead ov
which, there—so shmart an' cliver as y'ar ! Tratḥ,
'tis the Prisidint they'll be makin' ye in no toime ! "

Maurice did not respond to the kindly little jest,
though the words struck a chord to which his own
mind inwardly responded. At present he could not
look forward, however, prone as he was to that exercise — could see nothing beyond the fast coming
moment, when that door would shut behind him, and
Hurrish O'Brien would be left alone to die—to die

by his hand. If punishment had fallen upon him,
he would probably have braved it out—might very
likely have grown indifferent even to the moral side
of what he had done; but as it was, the shame and
humiliation of such utter, such absolute forgiveness,
bowed him down to the very dust.

At last he lifted his head and showed a ghastly
face, as ghastly as the dying man's own, and so they
remained for a long minute looking deep into one
another's eyes.

At length, in a choked voice, Maurice found words.
" Hurrish, I was mad! God knows I was mad!
I wish I'd been dead and buried a hundred thousand
times over before ever I fired that cursed shot!
Speak to me, Hurrish! say you'll forgive me," he
stammered.

Hurrish's great gaunt face lit up with a wonderful
tenderness.

" Is it forgiv ye, me pore buoy," he said passionately. " An' sure wudn't I forgive ye, an' wilcome,
if 'twas twist as much ? "

How much more it could have been he did not
stop to think; neither, in truth, did Maurice. He
had risen and stood there, a haggard man, utterly
unlike himself,—an image of despair, driven forth
like a new Cain from before the face of his victim.
He must go. Yet how *could* he go ? There was
nothing he could do—no possible atonement that he
could make ! He must simply walk away, and leave
Hurrish there alone—to *die !* Suddenly he turned,
and frantically—like one under some fierce constraint,
driven forcibly against his will—he staggered blindly
towards the door. Arrived there, he paused irre-

sistibly, and looked back—at the cabin, the familiar
hearth, the brown walls, the crazy furniture, the
broken tawdry bits of crockery, the pots and flyblown
- prints—all the poor, homely, untidy little interior.
Then he glanced at the bed, and at that wonderful
look of pity and forgiveness upon Hurrish's dying
face—a look which seemed to flood the whole dreary,
sordid poverty of the scene as with the light of
another world. The next instant he had turned—
he was gone! The cabin, Hurrish, everything had
passed away for ever from his sight, and he was face
to face with the cold open daylight, with the wide
pitiless arch of sky, which seemed to be flashing its
clearness into his very soul, to be proclaiming his sin
to the four winds, and inviting all creation to look
down upon the traitor, the murderer, going out with
the brand of Cain stamped for ever and for ever upon
his brow.

The little ridge was almost bare. The men, fortunately perhaps for him, had got tired of waiting,
and were gone away. There was no one left except
Alley Sheehan, who, seated upon the low wall with
her rosary in her hands, kept her eyes fixed immovably upon the door, only waiting for him to come
out, that she might return and take up her place
beside Hurrish's bedside again.

When he thus appeared—driven violently, as it
were, by some irresistible force from within—she instantly averted her eyes, with a rapid involuntary
movement of horror, so as to avoid seeing him.
Then, when he had moved a little way off, her gaze
quietly reverted to the door, and she seemed to be
unconscious of any other presence.

He paused, and looked at her as she sat there;
moved a step, and paused again. Should he, must
he go, and make no effort to speak to her ? have *no*
last word at all ! He could not, poor wretch. He
loved her still !

" Alley ! " he said, imploringly.

She gave a sudden start, but did not otherwise
move.

" Alley ! " he said again, and now in a tone of
despairing entreaty.

This time no notice except a slight shiver. Alley
was absolutely impassive—her eyes fixed immovably
upon the door, her face like the face of a statue.
She held her beads in her hands, and was slowly
passing them through her fingers, but even her lips
hardly moved.

He stood still gazing at her. The iron was eating
into his soul as it had not done yet. Shame, bitter,
bitter humiliation, a crushing sense of utter powerlessness, were devouring him. He dared not approach her — dared not challenge her attention
further than he had done. The little, humble,
insignificant girl he had condescended. to, had become a terrible power. She condemned him, and
she scorned him. Whether she knew for certain what he had done or not, he could not of
course know, but her look was enough. *Hurrish*
might forgive him, but there was no forgiveness
here.

So he remained standing and she sitting, and
neither of them spoke again. At last, with a groan,
Maurice Brady turned away, and, striking slowly
across the ridge, turned to the left, and clambered

down the bank into the bohereen, which ran, it will be remembered, considerably below the general level of the ground. The next minute it was as if the earth had opened bodily and swallowed him up!

CHAPTER XXVIII.

" FOR I ALLAYS SAID HE'D BE A GRAN' MAN."

When he had gone, and the sound of his footsteps had quite died away for the last time, Alley opened the cabin door and went in. Hurrish was lying back white and exhausted, but he opened his eyes as she entered, and turned them on her.

" He's gone, Alley ? "

" Yis, he's gone."

" Did ye spake to him, 'cushla ? The poor buoy's very repintint."

Alley made no answer.

" All's at an ind 'tween you an' him, I'm afeard ? " Hurrish went on regretfully.

A sort of spasm crossed the girl's pale face. Her usually gentle, resigned expression left it utterly. An odd, wild, savage look, quite unlike any of her own—a survival, perhaps, from some fierce ancestor or ancestress—took its place.

" I hate him ! " she said, in a low choked voice. " I wish he war dead ! I cud kill him mysel' ! "

Hurrish looked quite startled. " Och, Alley, Alley, dear, don't be sayin' such things ! " he said. " God

be good! sure, we must all die! Alley, it frights me
t' hear ye!"

She made no answer, but turned away, and began
busying herself about some arrangements for his
comfort. Presently old Bridget came back, and
made straight for the fireplace, looking round as
she did so at the bed and its occupant, as if puzzled
as to its meaning. Thady-na-Taggart, who had run
away when the crowd had invaded the cabin, now
also stole back, with his usual slipshod, noiseless step,
and went and crouched down in his former place,
Lep making room for him and settling down again
beside him with an air of satisfaction.

After this Hurrish lay for some time quite still
and silent, his hand pressed to his chest, his face
drawn and white. Presently, hearing a little movement near him, he lifted his head, and saw the three
children—the two boys and Katty—who had been
allowed to come back on promise of good behaviour,
standing together in a small frightened group, a little
way from the bed, the six round eyes fixed simultaneously in awed consternation upon his own face.

He lifted his head and beckoned to them. Katty,
however, instantly shrank away and hid her face.
That strange man lying upon the bed, her daddy!
her startled black eyes and angry pouting mouth
seemed to say—No, no! She knew better than *that*!
She clutched at the rosary, which had been con-
fided to her as a pledge for good behaviour, and held
it across her face as a sort of defence, peeping at him
suspiciously between the beads.

Hurrish's face lit up with its old familiar smile, or
rather the ghost of it.

"Won't Kitteen giv pore dada *wan* kiss?—pore
dada that's goin' away an' lavin' her!" he said coaxingly. "Trath, an' 'tis th' pore dada, sure enough,
he's been to you, my dotey," he added, tenderly.

Convinced apparently by his voice, Katty approached a step nearer, her little face still puckered
into a pout of suspicion. Alley lifted her, so that he
could kiss her without having to stoop, and the soft
round face, with its parted rose-bud lips, and the
white haggard one, so piteously gaunt and drawn
already, met in a long kiss.

"Ye'll kape her—wid ye—allays. An'—make her
a gud gurl—like yersel', Alley?" he said, brokenly.

She bent her head over the child, the determination not to disturb him making the tears spring
agonisingly to her eyes.

The two boys came forward, one after the other.
Clancy had his stout brown fists in his eyes, and his
two red cheeks under them showed long blistered
streaks where the tears had stained them. Andy's
blue eyes were wide and tearful too, but it was evident that he hardly realised what had taken place
more than Katty did. He had on an old coat of his
father's cut down to suit him, which gave him the
quaintest grotesque likeness to Hurrish. Lep, feeling
evidently that his turn too had come, ran over with
a whine to the bed, and, resting his forepaws upon
it, looked up into his master's face. Hurrish patted
him and said a word, and, with another whine, the
dog ran back to the idiot, nestling close to his side
and looking appealingly up into his face, evidently
for sympathy.

There was a sound from the chimney-corner, not

loud, not much louder than a whisper, but so hoarse
and unnatural as to startle the little group around
the bed.

"Dyin' an' lavin' me, Hurrish, me son! Dyin' an'
lavin' me!" old Bridget muttered, rocking herself to
and fro with a sort of dreamy misery. "Me beautiful buoy that they're all jealousin'. Judy O'Malley
—an'—Deb. An' to be kilt by a Fagan chilt—that
I bad him niver go nigh—dorty little spalpeens, not
fit to be whitenin' the flure afther him. An' to think
of their darin' to throw shtones at me beautiful buoy,
that cud ha' kilt the whole ov thim—aisy—only
they got him unbeknownst wid his back turned!
But I'll be aven wid thim yit! I'll—I'll——" Her
voice died suddenly away in harsh confused murmurs.

Hurrish glanced at Alley. "'Tis *stravagin'* she is,
poor sowl," he whispered. "She's thinkin' ov wan
toime I was hit wid a shtone whin I was a gossoon,
an' loike to die. I doubt but 't 'ul go hard wid
her!" he added, glancing pitifully over at the gaunt
form, rocking itself to and fro, and the harsh vulture-
like face, so haggard and piteous in its ragged setting
of iron-grey hair.

Alley made a movement, as if she would have
gone forward to the old woman; then she suddenly
stopped short, overtaken by her habitual terrors.
Almost at the same minute Father Denahy entered.
He had seen the dispensary doctor, so knew what his
opinion was. After a few minutes, therefore, he
hurried away to prepare for the last offices of the
Church, his good-natured prosaic face touching in its
unaffected grief.

By the time he had returned, and this ceremony

was over, and the doctor too had been back, and had
done all that was possible for the wounded man's
comfort, it was night, and dark again. Candles had
been lit,—a magnificent wax pair, long stored for
such a purpose—which, stuck, one into an old twisted
iron sconce, the other into a whisky-bottle, lit up the
little room as it had probably never in its existence
been lit before.

Alley stood beside the bed as she had sat or stood
ever since Hurrish had been brought home, and
watched, and watched, as if her very eyes had grown
to his face. It seemed to her that her own life too
was going away with his, drop by drop, minute by
minute, until now there was hardly anything left.
As the night went on, the wind sank, until the
silence outside was complete. Thady-na-Taggart and
Lep still lay together in a confused heap upon the
floor. The children had long ago sobbed themselves
to sleep,—even old Bridget had sunk into a heavy
stupefied slumber, with her head against the wall.
Alley's thoughts were full of strangeness. Sometimes it seemed to her as if it was all a dream:
sometimes, that they were floating down one of those
strange underground rivers, which disappear so often
in the Burren under caverns—floating, floating slowly along, Hurrish and she together. About three
o'clock in the morning, the door behind her opened
softly, and Father Denahy came in, and advanced to
the other side of the bed, making a sign to her as he
did so to take no notice. Hurrish had grown very
restless latterly, and kept tossing to and fro, flinging
the blankets off, throwing his arms in the air, and
talking rapidly to himself in a low excited whisper.

" Hurry thin, captin, hurry up ! " they heard him
mutter.   " Thar they are, as I telled ye, behint of
the big rock !   Arrah, aisy—aisy an' you'll have 'em.
Who-ooo !   Be glory ! but yer th' gran' shot ! "

Alley went noiselessly forward and straightened
the blanket, bending over him to do so.   Suddenly
his eyes, which had been half closed, opened widely,
and he looked her full in the face.

" Is't thar y'ar shtill ? " he whispered, tenderly.
" Kiss me thin, alanah, for 'tis the best wife iver pore
man had in this warld ye've been to me, Molly
darlint ! "

The poor girl's white face crimsoned agonisingly,
and she drew back as if frightened.   The priest,
however, made her an imperative sign to do as she
was told, and accordingly she bent her head down to
the bed again.   In the interval Hurrish seemed to
have forgotten his request, for he lay looking blankly
up at the ceiling.   Alley was about to lift her head
again ; then, with a sudden irresistible impulse, she
stooped, and kissed him passionately upon the forehead.   Then she drew back so as to be out of range
of the candles, and sat down suddenly upon a low
stool.

An hour passed, and still they remained there,—
Hurrish tossing upon the bed, the other two watching him silently.   Now and then Alley would give
him some water, or settle the blankets and coverlet.
The stillness was absolute, save an occasional long-
drawn sound from old Bridget, the gentler breathing
of the children from the inner room, a sigh or whispered word from the sick man himself, and now and
then the far-off broken mutter of the sea.   Thady-na-

Taggart had awakened, and drawn himself noiselessly up from the ground, squatting like a toad, or some strange Japanese image, with his knees upon a level with his chin, his wild vacant eyes fixed, as a picture's eyes fix themselves, upon Hurrish's face. The daylight was beginning to struggle in through the small green panes of glass, making the candles look faint and wan. The sick man's life appeared to be rapidly slipping away,—so rapidly that it seemed to both the watchers that he was nearly gone. Suddenly he opened his eyes, and looked round the room with an air of surprise.

"Whar's Morry?" he asked, in a voice which sounded almost as strong as ever.

There was no answer—neither Alley nor Father Denahy knowing in the least what to say. He did not seem to require any, however.

"Auch, an' why wud he shtop?" he went on in a minute, with a sort of self-reproach. "Wid all he's —to do, an' all ov thim—wantin' an' clamorin' for him 't onct? Ye'll tell him I was—axin'—for him, —but that I knew he'd ha' cum—if he cud. An' ye'll guv him—me blessin'—pore Hurrish O'Brien's blessin',—an'—tell him I—was proud for to think ov him,—cum to what he is,—riz up here—jist a bit of a gossoon at me knee,—that nobody else—thought nothink ov. But 'tis only what—I espected, —for I—allays—said—he'd—be a—Gran'—man!"

He fell back, breathed a few short gasping breaths, and everything was over.

Father Denahy went forward after a minute's pause and closed the sightless eyes; then, kneeling down beside the bed, recited a few prayers. He

Y

expected to hear another voice join in at the re-
sponses, but there was none, till poor Thady, springing suddenly to his feet with a cry like a dog giving
tongue, broke in with some sort of strange inarticulate
idiot's Latin of his own.   When the priest, getting
up, looked around in some surprise for Alley, he saw
that she had fallen a little way from him, and was
lying in a dead faint, with her face against the floor.

CONCLUSION.

Is there anything more to add ?   A few words,
perhaps.   Maurice Brady got off to America, where
for some time he led a rather uncomfortable life
amongst his compatriots, who persisted, rightly or
wrongly, in looking askance at him, and regarding
him as a traitor to the national cause, and the
assassin of his own best friend.   In the end this
unamiability proved an advantage to him, however,
rather than otherwise, since, instead of wasting his
energies and talents exclusively upon the comparatively barren field of politics, it caused him to carry
them into the more fertile one of business.   He had
a small sum of money to start with, the remains of
what his brother had had in bank, and this, under
his shrewd and intelligent management, became the
prolific parent of what promises in time to be a
large fortune.   He made his way, shortly after arriving in America, to San Francisco,—drawn there,
perhaps, on account of its being the farthest attain-

able point from the shores of Ireland,—got a place
in a large dry-goods store, where his talents and
smartness were speedily appreciated ; and so well
did he prosper, that within the last two years he
has set up a similar one on his own account at
Sacramento, which, according to the report of a
wandering compatriot, is fast drawing to itself the
chief fashionable patronage of that important place.
He is also said to be married, or about to be married,
to the daughter of one of its wealthier citizens, but
this last item lacks, it must be avowed, absolute
confirmation.

Of our other acquaintances nothing equally brilliant
is, I fear, to be recorded. Mr O'Brien is still at
Donore ; still carrying on a hopeless struggle with
fate ; still hoping against hope for some fresh turn
in the hitherto inextricable dead-lock ; still perpetually appealed to by Mrs O'Brien to leave the whole
wretched thing in the hands of an agent, and to join
her and her daughters at Brighton.   Young Thomond
has been appointed to a new ship, and when last I
heard of him, was cruising about somewhere in the
Antipodes.   He is as authoritative as ever about
Ireland, never failing to demonstrate convincingly
to any one who will listen to him, the only method
by which, in his experienced opinion, to cut the
gordian knot in which its affairs have been so long,
and are still to all appearances so hopelessly en-
tangled.

As for our humbler friends, to them, as to most
of us, the recurrent years have brought a mingled
crop—good and ill, disappointment and satisfaction.
From the day of Hurrish's death, Lep and Thady-

na-Taggart struck up a sort of antique friendship, and have rarely since been seen apart. It has never been quite clear to their numerous friends and admirers which of the two partners is the leader, but between them they manage to lead that comfortable and not undignified existence which, in Ireland, is the lot of those who throw themselves with unbounded confidence upon the benevolence of their neighbours.

Hurrish's memory is not at all forgotten at Tubbamina, where his feats of strength are still boastfully recited, and his triumph over the law and the " polis " constantly spoken of in high terms of commendation and approval. It is not, however, exclusively upon these grounds that his fame rests. Whenever any one for miles round finds the burden —whether of life or of " pittaytees "—too heavy to be borne, Hurrish O'Brien's friendly face and strong willing arms rise as a sort of meteor from the past to mock the woes of the present. Whenever any lady or gentleman is refused the trifle of assistance they request, his name is instantly, and as a rule violently, flung in the teeth of the churlish refuser. " Augh, thin, Hurrish O'Brien, dacent man, iv he were 'live, wudn't ha' lit me be putt out 'pon th' road wet an' hungry this cauld noight ! "—promises, by dint of repetition, to become a local proverb. There is a sort of subtle aroma of kindliness and goodwill which is often stronger than any one single good deed that can be recorded of its possessor, and something of this sort still clings, and promises for a while longer to cling, about his homely memory.

Old Bridget did not long survive him. She continued very rambling and incoherent, and it was never quite clear to those about her whether she knew that her son was dead, or merely imagined him to be absent from home. Sometimes she was violent and difficult to manage, but for the most part she sat silently all day long over the fire upon her creepystool, actively engaged in stirring the pot, and equally assiduously whether there was anything in it or not. One day, while thus engaged, she suddenly fell back, the iron ladle still tenaciously clutched in her hand, was taken up rigid, and never spoke again. After her death—which occurred in the course of the month which followed her seizure—Alley Sheehan joined her sister in the convent in Galway, and, after the usual period of probation, became a nun, and is there at the present time. She is very far from unhappy —in fact, may be described as actually happy. Her gentle soul, too tremulous for a world so full of harsh surprises, finds its repose in the fulfilment of a small and very simple routine of well-defined daily duties, and its happiness in the prayers which her Church so humanely and benevolently allows to be offered up for those who have passed beyond the reach of even the tenderest hands. Little Katty—by a special permission of the mother-superior—was allowed to accompany her, and is at this moment the idol and unspeakable torment of all the sisters, but is not regarded by them as at all likely to add a fresh recruit to their numbers.

As for the two boys, they are rapidly growing up, and Andy is more than ever the "moral" of his father, and promises with years to attain to the same goodly proportions. Perhaps by the time they have come to

years of discretion, Ireland will have entered upon a
new departure, though what precise form that departure will take, and whence its brightest hopes are to
come, it is a little difficult, it must be owned, just
now to discern.   Enough perhaps that there are elements in it which have nothing, fortunately, to say
to politics—of any complexion.   Kindliness, faith,
purity, are good spirits which may steer a boat
through even as rough waters as any that it has
travelled through, and bring it into safe anchorage
at last.   Thus far we may allow ourselves to hope ;
the rest must be left to—" Time, the nurse and
breeder of all good."

THE END.

PRINTED BY WILLIAM BLACKWOOD AND SONS.

BIBLIOLIFE

Old Books Deserve a New Life
www.bibliolife.com

Did you know that you can get most of our titles in our trademark **EasyScript**™ print format? **EasyScript**™ provides readers with a larger than average typeface, for a reading experience that's easier on the eyes.

Did you know that we have an ever-growing collection of books in many languages?

Order online:
www.bibliolife.com/store

Or to exclusively browse our **EasyScript**™ collection:
www.bibliogrande.com

At BiblioLife, we aim to make knowledge more accessible by making thousands of titles available to you – quickly and affordably.

Contact us:
BiblioLife
PO Box 21206
Charleston, SC 29413

Lightning Source UK Ltd.
Milton Keynes UK
177674UK00002B/3/A